He had to show himself, accept the risk and run with it

Bolan broke from cover, angling toward the house. The hired guns responded to the twelve-gauge blast, four soldiers fanning out to meet him. He started firing on the run, and the first guy on his right collapsed as a three-round burst ripped through his chest.

The others opened up in unison, unloading like a mobile firing squad. He met them, coming on, with nowhere to conceal himself, no hope of cover on the open lawn. As momentum took him forward, he milked short bursts from the MP-5.

He had to reach the house this time, search out Delpino and his visitor from overseas. A second failure meant the end of everything. He would not have another chance.

DON PENDLETON'S
MACK BOLAN®

Omega Game

A GOLD EAGLE BOOK FROM
WORLDWIDE®

TORONTO • NEW YORK • LONDON
AMSTERDAM • PARIS • SYDNEY • HAMBURG
STOCKHOLM • ATHENS • TOKYO • MILAN
MADRID • WARSAW • BUDAPEST • AUCKLAND

First edition August 1995

ISBN 0-373-61443-8

Special thanks and acknowledgment to
Mike Newton for his contribution to this work.

OMEGA GAME

Printed in U.S.A.

Power, like a desolating pestilence,
Pollutes whate'er it touches.

—Shelley

Every savage wants the upper hand, at any
cost. These days, with the proliferation of
cheap nuclear weapons, the cost is too high for
society to bear. It's time the balance was
redressed—in blood.

—Mack Bolan

For the American casualties of "friendly fire" in Iraq, April 14, 1994. God keep.

Staff Sgt. Paul Barclay
Spec. Cornelius Anthony Bass
Spec. Jeffrey Colbert
Pfc. Mark Anthony Ellner
Warrant Officer 1st Class John Garrett, Jr.
Warrant Officer 2 Michael Allen Hall
Capt. Patrick McKenna
Warrant Officer Erik Mounsey
Col. Richard A. Mulhern
2nd Lt. Laura Ashley Piper
Mike Robinson (Army mechanic)
Staff Sgt. Ricky Lee Robinson
Barbara Schell (U.S. Dept. of State)
Col. Jerry Thompson

PROLOGUE

Krivoy Rog, Ukraine

The specialist was getting nervous, but he dared not let it show. He knew the drill, and his confidence and expertise inspired the others, kept them going when they had to cope with dangers they could only half imagine. If they had known the truth about the risks involved, most of them would have given back the money they were paid and refused to proceed. A wise man would have bailed out then and there.

For him, however, it was different. He was fully conscious of the risk and took whatever steps he could to minimize potential damage. He was also being paid a vastly different wage than his companions, who were merely thugs, crude stevedores with guns.

Together, he suspected they could pull it off.

The specialist refused to dwell on failure. It was self-defeating, a distraction he couldn't afford. The consequence, once recognized, was not a subject to be constantly examined, worried over like the crow's-feet in the bathroom mirror. If he was afraid, his hands might shake, his thoughts might wander.

He couldn't afford a slipup now, when so much more than precious gold was riding on the line.

They drove east from Vinnitsa, picking up their personnel along the way. An army staff car and two covered trucks, authentic looking to the last details. They should have been, at that, since they were stolen from the military, with nothing altered but the painted numbers that would have betrayed them at a glance. The uniforms were equally authentic, even though the men inside them were civilian to the core.

And guns.

Machine guns, automatic rifles, pistols—all in perfect working order. With a dozen armed men at his back, the specialist was confident that he could bring his mission off. That had to be the operative spirit. Expectation of failure might only guarantee it.

Surveillance on the plant at Krivoy Rog had told him it was lightly guarded. Since it was well removed from any border region, no possible invasion would pose any apparent threat, and the local populace were mostly peasants, ignorant and bound to farms that broke their spirits, made them old before their time. The locals would no more attempt to raid the plant than they would lie down on the railroad tracks before a train. Assuming any of them possessed the courage and the brains required, they still lacked contacts to dispose of the material.

You didn't store uranium at home, with the potatoes, bread and sugar beets.

The specialist had contacts. Actually, they had come to him this time. The job had not been his idea, but he was short on money at the moment and it sounded like a relatively easy score. As for the final destination of his cargo, he had no idea and didn't care.

The world at large wasn't his problem. He was focused on surviving with the maximum of pleasure, day by day. For that he needed money, and he had no qualms about performing certain duties on command, providing that the price was right.

The specialist was carrying a pistol, though he didn't plan on using it. A gun belt finished off his uniform, as much a part of the disguise as the insignia pinned on his collar, making him a colonel. When the killing started, he would try to keep his hands clean and save the pistol for a real emergency, if it was needed in his own defense.

He saw the compound from two miles away, beyond a range of hills, orange lights against the underbelly of the clouds. They were making good time, having no one to challenge them along the way. If a legitimate patrol should intercept them, they would have to fight, but that was most unlikely. Research, planning, payoffs—all combined to clear the way for the assault.

And that was what it came down to, he realized. In other situations he had managed to secure material without a fight, by stealth, but this was not a kid-glove situation. Rather, it required brute force and speed, the better to escape before authorities could close the exit hatch.

The compound was a thousand yards square with barbed-wire fencing, living quarters for the staff and guards, and a broad expanse of asphalt all around the structure housing the reactor. To the north, the cooling tower stood alone, resembling a giant termite mound or perhaps the cone of a volcano thrust up from the earth.

Security aside, the specialist was glad that he hadn't been called upon to find material in the United States. The Russians operated no-frills plants, without the massive steel-lined concrete domes constructed to contain radioactive emissions. Life had been cheap in the old Soviet Union, while building materials had been expensive. The end result was compromise in favor of expediency—which would make it that much easier for him to loot the plant.

They didn't need a great deal of uranium. Specifically, two kilos. It would fit inside the heavy lead-lined carrier resembling a soft-drink cooler that was riding in the truck behind them, flanked by guards. The case was empty at the moment, waiting. As soon as it was filled and sealed, prepared for transport, it would draw no more attention than a normal steamer trunk. In fact, it would be shipped *inside* a steamer trunk from Nikolayev on the morning's tide.

If all went well. Either way the specialist would have no reason for concern. He would be rich or dead; there was no third alternative.

A fatalist by nature, he knew how to play the odds. If anything went wrong, he was prepared to make death swift and certain, skip the lingering effects of radiation poisoning that he had seen up close on more than one occasion.

They were through the foothills now and moving toward the compound proper. On the gate a pair of sentries saw them coming and stepped out to bar the way. One young, the other middle-aged and weary looking. Neither seemed especially alert, but they were armed and trained to use their automatic weapons.

From this point on, the danger passed from theory to reality.

He let his driver do the talking, waiting for the sentries to approach. The printed orders had a nice, official look about them, but they wouldn't fool the officer in charge.

Not that he would ever have a chance to see them.

Closing on his right, the older sentry peered in at the specialist and the men behind him, trying to decide if a salute was called for. He was almost close enough, another step or two—

A hand snaked out behind the specialist, brushed past his shoulder, fingers clamped around a semiautomatic pistol with a silencer attached. The sentry saw it coming, took a quick step backward, but he couldn't save himself. Two bullets drilled his chest before he had a chance to raise his gun or shout a warning to the camp, and he slumped over backward, sprawling in the dust.

The staff car's driver drew his sidearm when he heard the other pistol cough, fired once without aiming, his bullet drilling through the young guard's forehead, blowing off the guard's helmet as he fell. Behind the specialist one of his men stepped down and ran around to open up the gate.

They drove through, leaving the pointman standing watch to cover their retreat. The camp was sleeping, with only one or two technicians on the graveyard shift, the others tucked up in their beds. The hour had been carefully selected in a bid to minimize the bloodshed, but they had two dead already and the specialist knew there would be more.

They drove across the compound past the barracks, mess hall, the command post. They parked outside the service entrance to the looming structure that resembled nothing so much as an antiquated mill or factory. The concrete walls were painted gray, as if to emphasize their drabness. They would no more stop a leak than a building constructed out of cardboard.

Would the stupid bastards never learn?

Chernobyl should have taught them something, but they didn't seem to care. Perhaps, he thought, tonight's work would encourage some improvements to security.

The suits were piled up in the second truck. He pulled one on, secured the hood and breathing apparatus, waited while the soldiers followed his example. Only half of them were suiting up; the other stood guard around the vehicles, prepared to deal with anyone who caused a problem this late in the game.

The door would not be locked, of course. There seemed to be no need, with fences, guards and guns. The specialist allowed one of the soldiers to precede him, carrying a silenced pistol loaded with subsonic hollowpoints. His first concern now was safety rather than stealth. A wild round fired near the reactor could potentially destroy them all.

Inside, fluorescent lights leeched color from the walls and made him blink until his eyes adjusted. One of the technicians chose that moment to appear, emerging from a doorway on the right. He stopped short, gaping at their guns, and was about to ask a question when the pointman raised his pistol, squeezing off a shot that drilled the worker's mask and put him down.

They cleared the doorway into the auxiliary room, past large storage tanks for borated water and radioactive waste, past pumps that served the sump and the emergency core-cooling system. Another door stood waiting for them with Cyrillic characters warning of danger within.

They ignored the message, brushed through and surprised the second technician with his back to the door, making notes on a clipboard as he examined the reactor and read gauges. There was no point in wasting time, and so the pointman shot him in the back, two bullets dropping him, a third round in the head squeezed off to guarantee that he wouldn't get up again.

The Krivoy Rog reactor was a breeder, producing more fissionable material than it consumed. The surplus was retained for future use in a special storage vault immediately on their left, and it was here the specialist would begin to earn his money.

Drills and picks would get them into the vault. He couldn't use explosives in such close proximity to the reactor, but he knew what he was doing, and it only took him seven minutes once he started with the drill. Again he blessed the Russian penchant for economy above the health of personnel. Unless he missed his guess, they would have spent more money to secure the outer fence than the uranium locked up inside.

Once he had cracked the vault, he spent another moment checking out the merchandise. Lead boxes, each about the size of a battery for a compact car. Code numbers. Dates. He chose the "freshest" of the lot, directing his assistants to the proper box. They set the lead-lined carrier between them on the floor, then used special tongs to lift their loot from the shelf and place it carefully inside. The lid was airtight, sealed with clamps and screws.

They had been thirteen minutes on the job, approaching twenty-one since they'd come through the outer gate. In normal circumstances, working on a site like this, they would have showered prior to leaving, but there was no time. Instead, once they were outside, they ditched the bulky decontamination suits and left them lying on the ground. A short jog to the waiting vehicles and in, the motors idling, ready.

They were turning toward the gate, the long road overland to Nikolayev and a freighter waiting at the dock, when an alarm began to sound. The specialist was not sure exactly what went wrong, who spotted them or understood that something was amiss. Perhaps another sentry missed his comrades on the gate or glimpsed their bodies. It made little difference, either way.

The staff car's driver stood on the accelerator with the twin trucks staying close behind him. Speeding toward the gate, they heard the first stray rounds of automatic fire begin to crackle from the sidelines, someone on the far perimeter unloading with an AKS. Responsive fire erupted from the trucks, but it was difficult to tell if they were scoring hits.

A sentry ran in front of them. The driver swerved, firing with his left hand, holding the staff car on a hard collision course. The specialist ducked low as bullets cracked the windshield, came within an inch or two of grazing him, then heard the crunch of impact, felt the vehicle lurch over something in its path.

There was no question of stopping for their man on the gate. He was expendable and knew it going in. He would evade, defend himself as best he could, take steps to guarantee that he wasn't captured alive. If something happened and he couldn't manage to escape, it made no difference. The triggermen could not have named their sponsors if they wanted to. They had been kept deliberately in the dark.

Security.

Five miles beyond the camp, they stopped and ditched the military vehicles. Civilian vehicles were waiting for them: three sedans to carry them away. Nine of the gunners would be taking off from there for parts unknown. They had been paid and would be shadowed for the next two weeks, in case loose lips required a punitive response.

The specialist and three companions would be driving on to Nikolayev, where the freighter would receive him and his cargo. He was getting off at Limnos, when they cleared the Bosporus and Turkish waters. Where the shipment went from there was anybody's guess and none of his concern.

The buyers knew where they could find him if they needed more, and they had seen what he could do. It was a matter of determination, skill and training. Anything was possible for those with ample cash on hand.

And he could always use the cash. Expensive food and pricey women, gambling on the Riviera if he felt the urge. The specialist was nurturing a fondness for the good life, long deferred. He owed it to himself, and no concern for mankind as a whole would keep him from enjoying the rewards of his initiative.

They changed clothes swiftly, piled their uniforms inside the second truck and waited, watching from a distance while the military vehicles were set on fire. The searchers, when they got this far, would have a good time picking through the ashes, seeking clues.

There would be nothing to betray him, and if they managed to track down his mercenary helpers, there would still be nothing. None of his companions knew his name, address or anything of substance that would help authorities discern his whereabouts.

As it was two to one, he thought, there would be no public notice of the raid.

Embarrassment weighed heavily on certain governments, more so on some than others. To appear weak or negligent could be a fatal error, most especially for one of the republics that had risen from the shambles of the former USSR. They would attempt to track him down, of course, but quietly, with no real expectation of recovering the stolen merchandise.

Reprisal was a different problem, but the specialist had faith in his ability to dance between the raindrops. He had managed very nicely for the past few years, and he had not run out of tricks yet.

Still, he would feel a good deal better when he was aboard the freighter, steaming south toward Istanbul. A bit of distance made the difference.

The final two-thirds of his payment would be waiting at the bank in Athens, in the numbered account he had established two weeks earlier. A wire from Switzerland, and who cared where the money came from after all?

The specialist didn't know whom he worked for, and he liked it that way. If he posed no threat to those above him, only served them well, they had no reason to dispose of him. He was a useful tool, and much too valuable to be thrown away.

The road was rough and narrow, but he didn't mind. A few more hours and he would be safely out at sea.

The specialist relaxed and closed his eyes, perchance to dream of golden sun, skin, sand—and coins that trickled through his greedy fingers in an endless stream.

The golden image made him smile.

CHAPTER ONE

There are no crops or cattle raised in Grosse Pointe Farms. The stylish suburb of Detroit may owe its name to settlers from the eighteenth century—French traders and the hardy English stock who came along to drive them out—but their accomplishments are long forgotten. By the early 1900s, well before Detroit emerged as "Motor City" to the nation, Grosse Pointe Farms had grown into an enclave for the filthy rich, complete with mammoth homes, a yacht club and a country club taking up nearly one-third of the suburb's total area.

Some of the rich, of course, were filthier than others.

In Detroit, by 1930, there were two main avenues to wealth. Both involved mass production of consumer products, but the merchandise was very different: cars and alcohol. The cars were legal; booze—since 1918 in Detroit—had been proscribed by state and federal law, together with a constitutional amendment. None of which prevented residents from drinking to their hearts content, a circumstance that led one wag to call Detroit "a city built atop a still."

Rich gangsters moved to Grosse Point Farms and purchased a facsimile of class. They were accepted for the most part, while the money lasted; their relationship in Motown strengthened as the mob took over influential labor unions, cutting sweetheart deals and skimming off the profits, calling strikes or breaking heads when there were problems to resolve.

But that was ancient history.

These days some of the wealthy bandits have moved on to Grosse Pointe Shores, Belle Isle and Lincoln Park, but others have remained. One bandit in particular had cast his shadow over Grosse Pointe Farms since 1989, when he had risen fast and far enough to dominate illegal gambling in Detroit.

Of late he had been branching out. His family didn't know it yet, but someone did.

Mack Bolan entered Grosse Pointe Farms at 12:05 a.m. on Saturday. He crossed Mack Avenue on Gateshead, running into Kirby, eastbound from Detroit. A right on Williams and a left on Cloverly brought Bolan eye to eye with Grosse Point Boulevard. Another right, some winding through the smaller residential streets and he was kissing-close to Lake Shore Drive. A neighborhood of walled estates and massive houses hidden from the street.

Security could work both ways. His target was protected to a point, but walls and trees prevented those inside from seeing out, as well as screening their activities from prying eyes. There might be TV cameras mounted at strategic points along the wall, but he would deal with the defenses one step at a time.

The car he drove was new and large enough to pass without a second glance in Grosse Pointe Farms. No one was watching as he parked it on a side street, well removed from any lights, and shed his outer clothing to reveal a jet black skinsuit underneath. A duffel bag behind the driver's seat gave up his military webbing, side arms, and the MP-5 SD-3 submachine gun. In another moment he was dressed to kill and ready to begin.

Detroit hadn't been on his list of things to do until an urgent message out of Washington alerted him to danger in the making. Mafiosi were involved, but it went far beyond the normal vice, narcotics and extortion rackets.

This was big and deadly, with potential repercussions for the world at large.

The Executioner had been en route to San Diego for a visit with his brother when the word came down, and he was forced to change his plans. There was no way for him to dodge the mission. Not this time.

Detroit was boiling over, and he had to put the lid back on.

Before it was too late.

"YOU LIKE THE STATES so far?" Eddie Delpino asked his guest.

"Is fine," Vincenzo Moro told him, sipping at his wine.

It felt like pulling teeth to make the short Sicilian talk, but they were getting better at it. In another day or two, if Moro hung around that long, they might progress to full-scale conversations.

Concentrate on business, Eddie thought. The money would be great and then some if he pulled it off. No more bullshit finagling around with the Commission in New York to cinch a foreign deal when he had private friends across the water.

Friends with heavy weight, damn right.

"I never been to your part of the world myself," Delpino said. "I mean to, but there's always something in the way, you know? My old man's father came here from Calabria, back in the old days. Got his papers, found a wife and settled down, you know? He brought the business with him, so to speak. It's funny, after all this time, me hooking up with you."

"How funny?" Moro asked.

"Not ha-ha funny," said Delpino, hoping that the runty bastard did not take offense. "I mean it's strange, you know? Like ... what's the word? Ironic, yeah. It's like the world keeps turning, and you wind up where your old man—or his old man—started. Only better, huh?"

Vincenzo Moro shrugged and sipped his wine. He either couldn't follow Eddie's logic or he didn't give a shit. Guy had a solid poker face; you had to give him that. Whatever he was thinking, it stayed right in there behind his beady eyes.

"You got your business done in Canada, I guess?"

"Is done," said Moro, almost smiling for a fraction of a second before he caught himself. "You are prepared to deal?"

"Damn right," Delpino said, immediately worried that he sounded too impetuous. "I mean, we need to work the details out, of course, but we're on track. Hell, yes."

The little greenhorn nodded, seeming satisfied. He finished off his wine and waited while Delpino topped it off again. One thing about the old-world mafiosi, they were raised on homemade wine. Delpino reckoned they could drink all day and never let it show.

"Is good to talk here?" Moro asked.

Delpino thought about it for a moment, figured out that he was asking if the mansion was secure in terms of listening devices.

"If it's not, I'm up the fucking creek," Delpino said. "My people sweep it every morning. Twice a day since we heard you were coming."

"Sweep?"

"For bugs. The little microphones, you know?"

"Bugs, yes."

"We're squeaky-clean right now, I guarantee you that."

It seemed to do the trick, as Moro set his glass aside, leaned forward with his elbows firmly planted on his knees. "Is safe, okay. We have much business to discuss."

THE WALL WAS NOTHING: ten feet high, made out of cinder blocks, an easy scramble. Bolan checked a hundred yards of the perimeter in search of sensor beams or TV cameras and came up empty. They were obviously counting on the wall itself, with Eddie D.'s ferocious reputation, to forestall encroachment by intruders.

Better luck next time.

He poised atop the wall and made a check for dogs, the silent whistle warm between his lips from being tucked inside a pocket of his skinsuit. Whistle, wait. A pause, and then repeating it. Once more, for any stragglers on the far side of the property.

And nothing.

All he had to think about from that point on was men with guns.

He used the shadows like a veteran jungle fighter, which he was. Avoiding open ground whenever possible and moving with deliberate speed when it was not. He estimated the estate at some five acres, nothing you could play golf on, but huge by urban standards.

Nicely wooded, lots of cover as he homed in on the house and its detached four-car garage.

The graveyard shift was out, and Bolan met his first opponent ninety seconds into the approach. Not young exactly, but he had not come to forty yet and never would. The guy was pacing off a circuit through the trees, a 12-gauge pump gun tucked beneath one arm, cigar smoke trailing out behind him as he walked his beat. He never saw death coming for him, and it would have made small difference if he had.

The silent SMG was set for 3-round bursts. He let the sentry approach and took him when he was fifteen feet away.

A flurry of 9 mm parabellum rounds punched through the sentry's chest and dropped him on his face without a whimper. Bolan dragged him under cover of some ferns and left him there, the riot shotgun cradled in his lifeless arms. It seemed unlikely anyone would find the body in the time it took for him to reach the house, but allowing for the unexpected was a combat soldier's stock in trade.

He crept toward the garage that would have housed three inner-city families, keeping it between him and the house. Lights burned in the yard, and he imagined they would be kept on all night for reasons of security. A hundred feet across the open lawn that could become a free-fire zone at any time if he was spotted by the guards.

He needed a diversion, but nothing obvious was at hand.

Another sentry solved it for him, picking just that moment to approach his hiding place. The guy was looking for a place to take a bladder break without returning to the house, his fly unzipped and showing off a pair of gaudy boxer shorts. He had time for no more when Bolan shot him in the chest and dropped him in his tracks.

Bolan left the second gunner where he came to rest, exposed to anyone who passed that way or glanced toward the garage. He circled in the opposite direction, pausing at the southeast corner of the building where he pressed a fist-sized plastic charge against the wall and primed its detonator, made it ready to receive the doomsday signal from a small transmitter on his belt.

He kept on moving, trees and shadows, following the driveway as it curved around the house and angled toward the silent residential street out front. He counted seven cars parked in the driveway. Delpino's special toys—the Rolls, the classic Jag, his Bentley—would be back in the garage.

How many men? At least a dozen, minus two.

A dozen, plus Delpino and his special guest.

He crept in toward the nearest car and used its bulk for cover, waiting. It was still too risky for a run directly toward the house. He had to wait until the sentry was missed or his body sighted.

"Hey, Tommy! Getcher ass down here!" The voice came from the direction of his latest kill.

Away on Bolan's left, two gunners were pounding off toward the garage, one of them talking to a hand-held two-way radio. Bolan scanned the drive in both directions, watching out for late arrivals, spotting no one.

It was now or never. He wasn't about to find a better opportunity.

He rose from cover, breaking toward the house—and met the long-haired shooter coming toward him on a hard collision course, emerging from some bushes on the east side of the house. He had Bolan spotted and hauled out a shiny automatic pistol, lining up the shot.

He almost made it.

Bolan hit him with a 3-round burst from twenty feet and dumped him on his backside, but the guy was firing as he fell, two wasted rounds that angled skyward. Neither of the bullets came within ten yards of Bolan, but the shots were clearly audible.

Bolan cursed and made a fast break for the house, his left hand swooping toward the radio-remote clipped on his belt.

IT WAS Vincenzo Moro's first time in America, though he had traveled to Colombia, Peru and Mexico on previous occasions. Drug deals, all of them, with sweaty little men who scowled to make themselves look dangerous. Most of them were, in fact, but they had trouble meeting Moro's gaze.

The short Sicilian radiated malice like a human generator. Weak men had been known to tremble in his presence; strong men studied every move he made and watched their backs.

Moro's trip to the United States was special, firming up connections for a brand-new project that would make him fabulously wealthy, far beyond his wildest dreams. Of course, he was a rich man now, compared to most of those he knew in Sicily, but there was always room for more gold in his Swiss accounts. The Mafia had served him well for many years, but now he thought the Star would serve him even better.

Delpino's operation in Detroit would be a decent place to start if they could come to terms. He sensed the mafioso's greed, and that was good. Greed made the world go 'round, no matter what romantics had to say on love and other ailments of the heart. Self-interest was the dominating force that motivated every man, woman and child on the planet.

It had been an easy trip from Sicily through France and on to Canada, a border crossing with the help of bogus documents and Delpino's people waiting for him on the other side. There were no problems, and he had expected none. The drive from Windsor through Detroit to Grosse Point Farms had shown him the disparity in how Americans of different income levels lived. Even then, Vincenzo Moro realized, most of the ghetto "brothers" were more affluent than peasants in his native Sicily.

Which told him they had cash to spend on heroin and other luxuries forbidden to them by the white man's hated law.

So much the better for a merchant who had product on his hands.

But first he had to strike a bargain with Delpino. It shouldn't be difficult, Moro thought. The man was hungry, ruthless—and expendable. If he didn't work out, it would be simple to remove him and select a venal underling to take his place. It happened all the time in Moro's business. Nothing new.

They started off with small talk, working up to business. Moro had a taste for wine, and it appeared Delpino had a vintage stock on hand. Moro watched his host and judged him by his mannerisms, on his reputation, what he had to say. The words that issued from a man were often meaningless, but this one had a history of dealing fairly with his partners when those partners dealt from strength. He would, as a matter of course, devour any weaklings in his path. That was expected, and Vincenzo Moro would demand no less from anyone who represented him in business.

They were getting down to cases when the house-man blundered in, his face contorted in alarm, to warn Delpino of a prowler on the grounds. The man was still at large, and he had "capped" one of Delpino's men near the garage.

"Explain, please," Moro urged Delpino when the houseman had departed, "what it means to cap one of your people."

"Oh, that." Delpino forced a crooked smile. "It's no big deal."

Still, he seemed agitated, pacing, working on the smile without conviction. He was just about to speak again when they heard gunfire from the yard. Two pistol shots, some shouting, then a shotgun blast.

"I think," Delpino said, "we oughta go down-stairs."

Moro's host had one hand on the doorknob when a powerful explosion rocked the house and shattered windows facing east.

THE PLASTIC CHARGE was big enough to take out half of the garage and leave the rest in flaming ruins. Sec-ondary detonations went off like giant fireworks as the vehicles inside caught fire, their fuel tanks blowing one-two-three. A couple of Delpino's soldiers had been close enough to feel the heat and then some. Several others scrambled backward from the flames in time to save themselves.

But they were not all taken in by Bolan's diversion. A pair of gunners had him spotted by the time he keyed the C-4 charge, and they were charging after him, one of them squeezing off a shotgun blast that fanned the air above his head with buckshot.

Bolan spun and hit a crouch, his submachine gun locking onto target acquisition, spitting three rounds and another three to meet the latest threat. Downrange, the heavy with the scattergun caught one burst in the abdomen and staggered, soaking up the other as he toppled over on his back.

The second gunner pegged a shot at Bolan, veering to his left and dropping to the grass. The short burst Bolan fired in answer missed his target by a foot or more, and he was dodging backward, moving toward the house, when his assailant lurched upright.

Bolan's next burst hit his target in the chest and spun him like a top with arms outflung, his pistol sailing out of range and lost beneath the nearest car. The dead man landed on his back and lay unmoving, stretched out on the grass.

It was a short jog to the house, but he was running out of time and luck. Before his very eyes a flying squad of soldiers cleared the front door of Delpino's lavish home and clustered on the porch, unloading on the stranger with their automatic weapons like a firing squad. He had no option to advance; it was retreat or die, and he would have to do it soon, before a bullet brought him down.

Behind him on his left, the wrecked garage was burning brightly, several gunners silhouetted by the leaping flames while others fanned out on the lawn, obstructing his retreat. No time for head counts, but the warrior realized that he had underestimated his opponents. Even counting cars and multiplying them by three or four, he would have come up short.

Outnumbered and outgunned, he knew that it was time to flee by any means available.

He ran back toward the line of cars, his shoulders hunched and waiting for the impact of a bullet that would send him sprawling lifeless on the lawn. He made it to a black Mercedes Benz and peered in through the driver's window, seeking keys in the ignition.

Moving on, he listened as the cars began absorbing random hits. A low-slung Jaguar was the next in line. No keys.

It was a washout. He could lose it any second now, no place to hide.

The third car was a Porsche, fire-engine red, and this one had the keys in place. He slid behind the wheel and gave the key a twist, his foot on the accelerator as his adversaries sighted on the brief flash of the dome light. Bolan fired a short burst through his window, no real hope of scoring with the hasty rounds. He stood on the accelerator and released the brake, swung out of line and nosed the sportster toward the gate.

Behind him, in the rearview mirror, Bolan saw Delpino's gunmen scrambling for the other cars, prepared to roll in hot pursuit. His immediate concern, though, was the wrought-iron gate in front of him with soldiers standing fast to bar his way.

Two men in slacks and sweaters, one armed with a shotgun while the other had a blue-steel automatic in his hand. They opened up on Bolan from a range of thirty yards, unloading rounds in rapid fire as he accelerated, ducking down below the dashboard. Buckshot pellets and a pistol bullet cracked the windshield, raining pebbled safety glass across his head and shoulders, ripping into the upholstery of the driver's seat.

The soldier with the 12-gauge saved himself by leaping to the side a heartbeat short of impact. His companion was a trifle slower, maybe more courageous, and he stood his ground, unloading with his automatic till the sleek Porsche mowed him down. A human speed bump, there and gone before the racing sports car hit the gate, plowed through with an unholy grating sound, left paint and trim behind but made the street.

There was a nagging rattle underneath the hood, but Bolan kept the pedal down, turned left on Newberry toward Grosse Pointe Boulevard. Behind him, as he neared the intersection, headlights winked at Bolan from the rearview. One car, followed quickly by another.

Hare and hounds. The hunter had become the prey, and he would need the full extent of his experience and martial skill to keep from winding up in someone's trophy case.

CHAPTER TWO

Years spent getting ready for a thing to happen, Charlie Scigliano told himself, and just when you begin to think it's wasted effort—bam! The frigging roof falls in and buries you alive, unless it kills you outright.

He was supposed to be the houseman, not out running in the streets and playing grab-ass with some wild man who had wasted several of his boys already. Still, security was all-encompassing, and when the capo snapped his fingers, Scigliano jumped. If there was time, he asked "How high?"

Now he was racing through the night with Tom D'Amato at the wheel and three boys jammed into the seat behind him, itching to kill. Five more behind them in the second car, and if they couldn't do the job with ten, it wasn't getting done.

It nagged at Scigliano, leaving soldier dead behind him and the house in disarray, but there was nothing he could do about it at the moment. He had orders, and his capo wanted blood. It would be Scigliano's job to bring the crazy bastard's head back on a platter or start praying for an explanation that would get him off the hook.

It was the first time they had had a rumble at the house. The rare intruders from the past were mostly kids, a young reporter once, too dumb to know the ropes, but there had never been shots fired in Grosse

Pointe Farms, not even when they had a war in progress with the family from St. Louis.

"Close it up, for Christ's sake!" Scigliano snapped.

Muttering a curse, the driver bore down on the accelerator, running west on Newberry toward Grosse Point Boulevard. In front of them the stolen Porsche's brake lights winked for maybe half a second, and the car swung left—or south—onto the boulevard.

The gun in Scigliano's lap was an Uzi, full auto, illegal as hell. If they got stopped for speeding, everybody in the car was going down on weapons charges, at the very least. Not that he would stop for the law, but it would complicate the present situation if he had to shoot it out with uniforms.

The neighbors would be calling 911, of course. No help for that, but Charlie Scigliano wouldn't be there when the black-and-whites arrived, detectives asking questions. By that time, somebody would have cleared the bodies out and maybe doused the flames of the garage. Delpino could explain it as a raid by strangers, tell the cops how no one saw a thing and he had no idea who was responsible. The same old bullshit that had covered mob activity around Detroit for generations.

"Goddammit, Tommy, hurry up! We lose this guy, we're fucked big-time."

"He's got Banducci's Porsche, you know?"

"I don't care if he's got a fuckin' UFO. Get after him!"

They swerved onto the boulevard, southbound, tires screeching out in protest. A backward glance showed Scigliano that the second car was hanging in there. They still weren't close enough to risk a shot, though, even with the early-morning traffic being sparse.

"We need to head him off."

"I gotta catch him first," D'Amato answered.

"Git it done, then."

"Right, I hear you."

Up ahead the Porsche ran through a red light, nearly clipped a bakery delivery van and kept on going. D'Amato maneuvered through the intersection, braking slightly, then accelerated in pursuit. A quick glance at the mirror showed the second car behind them, keeping up the pace.

The houseman cranked his window down, wind rushing in his face and filling up the car with noise. Although they were a block behind the Porsche and gaining, it was still uncertain whether they could overtake the smaller car. But he would chance a shot if they could find an empty stretch of road. D'Amato reduced the gap to half a block or so.

Charlie thumbed the safety off his submachine gun, knuckles blanching as he held the weapon in a death grip. It was two years now since he had pulled the trigger on another man, and that had been a simple hit, no highway chase involved, but Scigliano was a pro and he had confidence in his ability to pull it off.

The capo always got what he was paying for, and this time he had ordered up a stranger's head. No sweat. The stupid fucker brought it on himself. You had to wonder how a guy like that had lived this long.

One thing was for certain: he was running out of time.

The houseman leaned out through his open window, dark eyes narrowed into slits against the rushing wind, and sighted down the Uzi's barrel, aiming at the Porsche above the taillights.

Any second now.

And Charlie Scigliano was surprised to find that he could hardly wait.

THE TRAFFIC FELL AWAY to nothing crossing Edgemere. Bolan checked out his rearview mirror, saw the headlights coming on behind him. Four lanes gave his adversaries good room to maneuver; they were trying hard to box him in, and short of pouring on the speed and watching for another route, there was little he could do about it at the moment. Momentum made it difficult to turn, and that was one more problem he would have to deal with in the next few moments if he wanted to survive.

The shattered window was a hazard, cold wind bringing tears to Bolan's eyes and raising goose bumps on his skin, but he would have to tough it out. At least it wasn't raining, Bolan thought. Small favors, but a soldier on the firing line would take what he could get.

A muzzle-flash came from behind him when the gap had closed to roughly half a block, and Bolan ducked his head instinctively. The shots went wild, but that was simple luck, and Bolan knew he couldn't count on staying lucky as the chase went on. He had to change the odds as soon as possible, and to that end he lifted off the gas a little, left the brake alone, entrusting gravity to slow him down.

The chase cars—still just two of them—were running two abreast. Another muzzle-flash erupted from the vehicle on Bolan's right, immediately followed by a long burst from the second car. He ducked again, heard bullets hammering across the trunk, one round and then another punching through the backseat, losing force before they reached the front. A third round struck the dashboard, somehow brought the radio to life with heavy-metal music screaming from the speakers.

Bolan let it play, ignoring the discordant voices and guitars. He concentrated on his driving, brought the MP-5 SD-3 submachine gun to his lap as the pursuers tried to bracket him. If Bolan let them take him in a cross fire, he was finished, but he saw a chance to alter the equation. If he blew it, it was sudden death, but he had no time to dwell on the alternative now. The Executioner was running on instinct now, with his experience and training in control.

It had to be the chase car on his right, he realized, because it would not be enough for him to nail a gunner, even two or three, if he allowed the vehicle to stay in motion. He would have to tag the driver—nothing else would do—and that meant firing to his right, across the empty passenger's seat.

The Porsche had power windows. As he hit the button on his armrest, more wind whipped at him as the right-hand window opened on its own. He drove left-handed, balancing the submachine gun in his right, and watched the rearview as he made his move.

A small drift to the left so that he blocked the chase car trying to approach him on the driver's side. From their perspective it would seem that he was weaving, maybe losing it and running scared. The car on Bolan's left could either brake or ram him from behind, and he was betting that discretion would prevail.

The other car—a Cadillac Seville—was gaining fast, meanwhile. It came up on his right, a gunner in the backseat pegging shots at Bolan well before he had a target in his sights. So much the better if his enemies used up their ammunition on thin air, but it wouldn't be good enough.

He held a steady sixty miles per hours, waiting for the Cadillac to close up on his right. The submachine gun with its heavy silencer was braced against the windowsill, his arm at full extension, his finger curled around the trigger. Waiting, counting down the heartbeats.

When the moment came, he flicked a glance in the direction of his enemy and saw the driver staring at him, getting ready for a broadside, maybe force him off the road if nothing else worked out. The guy was mouthing curses, giving Bolan hell behind a pane of glass that didn't have the look of being bulletproof.

Contact!

He squeezed the trigger twice, six rounds erupting from the SMG at ten feet from the target. Bolan heard the driver's window shatter, spraying glass into his adversary's face before the bullets finished him and left him slumped across the forward gunner's lap. A dead hand took the Caddy's steering wheel in that direction, veering the car to the right across two empty lanes, and Bolan watched it go before he stamped on the accelerator, winding up the Porche's engine with a rising scream.

He gained another fifty yards before the Caddy jumped the curb and rammed a deli in the middle of the block between McKinley and Verly, smashing the broad plate-glass window and vanishing inside the shop. Alarm bells clamored in the night, the noise immediately swept away by speed.

The second chase car hung on Bolan's tail, unloading short bursts from an automatic weapon, peppering the Porsche with bullets. He had cut the risk in half, but that would be no consolation if a wild round tagged him now and finished it before he had a chance to get away.

He kept on looking for a side street that would serve his purposes and recognized it instantly when it appeared.

One chance to get it right, or he could kiss his ass goodbye.

CHARLIE SCIGLIANO lifted off the Uzi's trigger, smelling gunsmoke as he watched the Caddy swerve and crash. D'Amato was about to brake and check the others out when Scigliano punched him in the shoulder, cursing.

"Never mind, for Christ's sake! We can't help those guys. Stay after him!"

"Fucking bastard!" hissed the driver.

Scigliano couldn't tell if D'Amato had meant the words for him or their intended quarry in the Porsche, and he didn't give a rat's ass at the moment. Either way it was enough to have his driver motivated, doing everything within his power to head the wild man off.

The damn alarm would bring cops running, but he couldn't think about that now. If there was anybody still alive inside the Cadillac, they would be bailing out and running for it, clearing out before the law arrived. As for the dead...well, there was nothing anyone could do for them. The car was traceable, of course, but it was registered to a paper corporation in Royal Oak, where inquiries would reveal it had been stolen overnight.

It was time to wrap it up, get done and get the hell away from there before the blue-suits measured Scigliano and his soldiers for a jail cell.

"Close it up! Come on!"

"I'm trying, dammit!"

"Try shit, Tommy! Get it done!"

"Awright already!"

And the dig paid off. Somehow his driver got another six or seven miles per hour from the Buick's straining engine. You could feel it, pushing bodies back into their seats as he accelerated, headlights fastened on the Porsche.

Scigliano was aware of tears streaking his face, blown back from his eyes to his sideburns and dried by the wind. He made a mental note to keep a pair of goggles in the car from that point on when they were hunting, and the notion almost made him smile.

As if you could predict this kind of shit, for God's sake. Hell on wheels, and there was still a chance that they would lose him somehow, let the crazy bastard slip away.

Scratch that, he thought. It was a useless exercise to borrow grief when he was in the middle of a touchy job. Full concentration was required unless he wanted it to blow up in his face.

"Hey, what that—"

Tommy D'Amato was gaping, pointing as the Porsche stood on its nose and swung hard left into a side street, rubber smoking all the way.

"So where's he going?" someone called out from the back.

"You hear him check with me?" the driver cracked, already braking as he tried to keep up with the Porsche.

"Don't lose him!" Charlie Scigliano shouted, pounding on the dashboard with his fist.

"Just watch me!"

D'Amato was good, but this was something else. The Buick started drifting, slammed into a station wagon parked against the curb. The impact jolted Charlie Scigliano, threw him hard against his door so that he caught the padded armrest in his ribs. It hurt him like a rabbit punch, but that was nothing. D'Amato saved it, got them out of there and back in motion. Never mind the stupid paint job. They could always ditch the car when they were done.

But first they had to finish what they started.

"We got him now," said D'Amato and he was almost cackling with delight.

It took a second more for Scigliano to make out what he was saying, then he recognized the street. It was a residential cul-de-sac, with one way in and out. It didn't matter how fast their target ran if he was running out of road.

The guy could crash and burn or he could make a stand and try to shoot it out. One gun against the five of them, and no more lucky breaks like he had scored with Joe Federici and the Cadillac.

No way in hell.

The Uzi's magazine was running low, and Scigliano yanked it, slipped it in a pocket of his suit coat, snapped a fresh one into place. He would be ready when they came up on the snotty bastard, either way.

And it would be a shame, thought Scigliano, if he crashed and made it easy on himself. Much better, thought the houseman, if he had a chance to cap the guy himself. Go back to Eddie Delpino with that news and get a big, fat "attaboy."

A thing like this, the guy who nailed it down and cleaned things up could even be promoted if the capo's mood was right. Why not? It would be nothing less than he deserved for pulling off a minor miracle.

So pull it off, he thought.

Right now.

And Scigliano leaned back out his window with the Uzi, ready for the driver of the stolen Porsche no matter what went down. It didn't really matter if the guy flamed out or made a stand. Whichever way it played, the houseman meant to nail his target and take credit for the kill.

It wasn't turning out to be so tricky after all.

THE CUL-DE-SAC would not have been his first choice, but the Executioner would take what he could get and try to turn it to his own advantage. There was a trend away from Dead End signs these days, another phase of the politically correct society, but it could well turn out to be exactly that for Bolan if he didn't watch his step.

The street was one long block, perhaps a hundred yards from end to end, designed like a cartoon thermometer, with room to turn around when you ran out of road. With houses close on either side, it was far from ideal as a battleground, but his choices were limited at this point. He could run indefinitely, drag his fight through major streets where other motorists would be exposed to random fire, or he could choose the killing ground himself and make a stand for good or ill.

The cul-de-sac was dark, no street lights, and the warrior killed his headlights as he turned the corner, racing toward the dead end up ahead.

With thirty yards to go, Bolan hit the Porsche's brake and cranked the wheel hard left, putting the sports car through a 180-degree turn on squealing tires. He came to rest facing back in the direction he had come from, waiting. Saw the Buick bearing down upon him as he flicked the high beams on in a bid to spoil the wheel-man's aim.

He bailed out of the Porsche, broke to his left, the MP-5 SD-3 loaded with a fresh clip as he scuttled through the darkness, circling around the dead end of the cul-de-sac and crouching behind a thick juniper hedge. Had any of the gunners in the Buick seen him? He would have to take the chance.

The Buick lurched to a halt twenty feet from the Porsche, doors springing open on both sides as soldiers hit the pavement. He counted five of them before they opened up on the sports car with everything they had, raking it with pistols, automatic weapons and a 12-gauge shotgun.

The fire selector on his SMG still set for 3-round bursts, he framed the nearest gunner in his sights and stroked the trigger, watched the mafioso stagger, going down. If any of his comrades noticed, it was not apparent from their action. The surviving four were still focused on the vehicle he had abandoned moments earlier.

One porch light, then another and another, flared along the cul-de-sac. Some of the neighbors would be telephoning for police right now, and the response wouldn't take long in this exclusive neighborhood. Whatever move he planned to make, he had to make it now.

With that in mind, he broke from cover, moving toward the Buick like a shadow while his enemies were busy shooting up the Porsche. Its headlights had been blinded in the first barrage, and all of the remaining window glass was gone by now, the stylish body pocked and scarred with bullet holes. One of the tires exploded, followed swiftly by another and another, while the fourth somehow remained unscathed, the sportster leaning like a drunken man.

He came up on the blind side of the mafioso with a shotgun in his hands, who was unloading on the Porsche in rapid fire. A 3-round burst from Bolan's submachine gun ripped into the gunner's back, between the shoulder blades, and pitched him forward, sprawling on his face.

This time it was noticed. The soldier close beside his latest target spun in that direction as the shotgun's muzzle rapped against his shin. He blinked, glanced up at Bolan, was about to shout a warning when the Executioner squeezed off another burst from fifteen feet away.

The parabellum manglers stitched a line of holes across his adversary's chest and punched the soldier backward, flattening him against the Buick's fender. Rubber legs refused to hold his weight, and he collapsed into a seated posture, head slumped forward, blind eyes staring at his lap.

And that left two. The driver and a comrade on the far side of the idling Buick still apparently had no idea that they were under fire. It worked that way sometimes in combat. You were focused on a target to the exclusion of all else, and death came up behind you, took you unaware.

It was a short jog to the far side of the car, no more than twenty feet, and Bolan covered it in half a dozen loping strides. He went in firing—never mind the niceties when life and death were riding on the line.

He shot the nearest gunner in the back. The determined soldier refused to fall, tried swiveling to face his enemy and answer with the Uzi in his hands. Too late as a second burst cut him short, but he had strength and will enough to go down firing, bullets peppering the nearby houses as he fell.

The driver recognized his danger now and turned to face his black-clad nemesis. He held his Smith & Wesson automatic in a stiff two-handed grip, but he was shaking, going spastic in the panic of the moment, blowing it. His first shot was a good yard high and wide. The second never came.

A final burst from Bolan's submachine gun slammed the driver backward, sprawling on the pavement, twitching for another moment as his life ran out. Ignoring him, Bolan slid behind the Buick's steering wheel and slammed the door, jammed the gearshift into reverse. The heavy crew wagon lurched over some one's body as he backed out of there. After another 180-degree turnaround, he was running back toward Grosse Pointe Boulevard and away from there while time remained.

He passed the first patrol car two blocks north, returning to the spot where he had left his rental car before the strike against Delpino. Lights and sirens all the way, with two more cars behind it, running thirty seconds late. The last thing Bolan glimpsed before he turned off on a side street was an ambulance lit up like Christmas, speeding toward the mafiosi who had no use for its services.

The probe had blown up in his face, and Bolan knew that he was lucky just to be alive. It didn't feel that way, however, when he thought about the stakes involved and his failure to achieve the goal that he had set himself.

Delpino and his visitor were safe and sound. More to the point, they had been warned of opposition in the neighborhood, a circumstance that might well send them under cover, out of Bolan's reach.

He couldn't let that happen. Not with so much riding on the line.

Whatever risks were called for, Bolan had to make it right, without delay. He had no time to waste.

It wasn't just Detroit and some mob operation hanging in the balance. He was looking at a threat that spanned the globe and threatened countless lives.

This time around he knew that he couldn't afford to drop the ball, in case the whole damn court went up in flames.

CHAPTER THREE

The voice from Bolan's past had reached out for him two days earlier, in a St. Louis suburb. He was westbound, looking forward to a visit with his brother in the neighborhood of San Diego when he stopped to place a phone call from Vandalia, Illinois.

It was supposed to be a routine check in with the man who styled himself these days as Leonard Justice. In the old days, when they met as enemies and learned almost by accident that they were allies in a covert war against the Mafia, the little man from Massachusetts had been known to friend and foe alike as Leo Turrin. They were friends and more, as only men can be who have shared mortal danger time and time again.

Nothing on the open line to tip him off, but Turrin sounded nervous. Could he make it on short notice?

Absolutely.

They arranged the meet for Richmond Heights, off Highway 64. A shopping mall on a weekday, with youngsters skipping school and seniors pacing off the mileage in their pastel jogging suits. He parked outside the JC Penny store and made his way inside, browsed past the windows of a Waldenbooks while waiting for his contact to appear at the Orange Julius stand nearby.

He had the stocky figure spotted from a distance, saw his old friend moving with a kind of casual determination through the press of shoppers, barely glancing left or right. Still, Bolan knew the dark eyes didn't miss a thing. A trained magician would have trouble taking Leo Turrin by surprise.

Another moment and the man from Wonderland was at the juice stand, putting in his order. Bolan waited until his colleague had been served, then met him as he turned away. The one-time undercover mafioso's smile was automatic, nothing feigned about it.

"You made decent time," he said to Bolan.

"I was motivated. What's the trouble?"

"Jesus, where to start? How long since you checked in on the Sicilian families?"

"It's been a while," the Executioner admitted. "Is there something urgent I should know about?"

"I'd say. Are you familiar with the Star?"

"Sounds like a newspaper," said Bolan, smiling.

"Don't I wish. I'd cancel my subscription off the top, but no such luck."

"I'm listening."

"We started hearing things like ten, twelve months ago, but there was nothing we could put a finger on. Reports from Sicily and contacts on the mainland that the Mafia was changing, going through a major shakedown."

"You're surprised? They've had some major prosecutions underway the past few years. Assassinations, terrorism at election time—the so-called little men are getting sick of it." He frowned. "Too bad it took a hundred years for them to get pissed off."

"It's more than that," said Turrin. "This is not just another shakeup—it's a major change, beginning at the top. Word has it that the old-line Mafia is fading out, reorganizing. Everywhere we look, we're coming up with rumors of a brand-new global syndicate."

"The Star?"

"That's what they call themselves. Don't ask me where it came from. Anybody's guess. We've got one analyst at Justice who suggests it may be something geographic, after the locations plotted on a map where leaders of the outfit have their operational headquarters. So far, we've traced links to Sicily and Corsica, Bangkok and Bogotá, Ankara, Paris, Tokyo and Montreal. Aside from mafiosi, we've confirmed involvement by the Chinese Triads, Yakuza, the Union Corse and the Colombian cartels."

"It sounds like heavy weight," said Bolan.

"Dope's not half of it," his friend replied. "The smuggling networks go through realignments all the time, you know? We're ready for it. Same for money laundering. These days it goes beyond cocaine and heroin, hashish, whatever. We've got smuggling of aliens, primarily from Asia to the States, sometimes through the Caribbean and Europe. Christ, this whole thing with the Eastern Bloc and Russia is a can of worms we still don't have a grip on, with the borders open after all this time. They're moving everything from drugs and cash to guns and refugees, you name it."

Bolan frowned. "You didn't call me out to talk about an immigration problem."

"That's right." The man from Justice finished off his beverage and dropped the paper cup into a trash can as they passed. "Right now we're sweating over nukes."

"You'd better spell that out," said Bolan.

"Right. You know about the arms trade out of Russia and the new republics, everything from Tokarev's to RPGs and armored vehicles. They're short on cash these days, and some of them are up for selling anything that's not nailed down. The way things are around the world today, they don't have any problem finding buyers."

That was true, thought Bolan. Terrorists from Northern Ireland to the Middle East and Africa had been dependent on the Soviets for decades, coming with their hands out for a steady stream of weapons, ammunition and explosives, cash and training in guerrilla warfare. When the Berlin Wall came down and the Iron Curtain crumbled, that support was terminated almost overnight. The terrorists were sweating, till they realized that *perestroika* and the new world order might turn out to be a great bonanza for themselves.

Instead of being forced to bargain with the KGB, they saw a new world of alternatives in store. The Russians—some of them, at least—were still prepared to keep on trading with their former covert allies, chasing profits now in place of left-wing ideology. But there were also other sources for the military hardware that terrorists required to stay in business: Kazakhstan, Tajikistan, Bulgaria, the severed parts of Yugoslavia, Czechoslovakia, the Bulkan states.

It was a new day, but it didn't bring peace and harmony for all concerned.

"The nukes," said Bolan, prodding him.

"Okay. You know the Russians have been scaling back their arsenal, along with ours. The various republics have their own stockpiles from the bad old days before the breakup, but they need more cash than warheads at the moment. So it goes."

"You're tracking leakage?" Bolan asked.

"And then some," Turrin answered. "Talking to Bureau, CIA and AEC, we've verified at least five cases in the past year and a half where nuclear material has been reported missing from the former Soviet republics. Small amounts, but how much does it take to build a suitcase bomb?"

"When you say 'missing,' what's the follow-up?"

"Confirmed black-market export for a resale overseas," said Turrin. "Big business, partner. It's a million bucks a kilo at the going rate. The way demand is topping out supply, the price could double in a year or eighteen months, no sweat."

"Who's buying?" Bolan asked.

"You name it. Anybody with a major grudge to settle or an ax to grind. If what we're hearing is correct, most of the money comes from oil right now."

"The Middle East."

"You called it. Everybody and his camel wants an A-bomb, just in case the neighbors get a little rowdy or he feels like smoking Tel Aviv."

"Iraq?"

"For one. The ayatollah wouldn't mind a little something extra in his Christmas stocking, while we're on the subject. Neither would Khaddafi or the Saudis. Ask around Kuwait, you want to see some nervous people, since the last invasion. Syria and Jordan wouldn't mind a little fallout blowing over if it meant the end of Israel. Then, you've got as many terrorists as you can name—Jihad and Hezbollah, the PLO, PFLP and Black September. Go ahead and take a number."

"Sounds grim," the Executioner remarked.

"You've got a gift for understatement, pal. It isn't armageddon yet, but some folks think we're getting there."

"So where do I come in? You're talking global traffic here, it seems to me."

"That's one side of it, but we're looking at a solitary case at the moment."

"I'm listening."

"Last month a raiding party tapped a plant in the Ukrane for something like two kilos of uranium. That's weapons grade we're talking, okay? They went in shooting, took out half a dozen personnel and walked off with the door prize. Nice and clean."

"How many kilotons?"

"According to the formulas I've seen, it's in the neighborhood of forty. Call it double Hiroshima, for comparison. Still small enough to fit inside a suitcase or a steamer trunk, depending how they put their toy together. That's enough to level Washington, New York, L.A., you name it."

Bolan got the picture: metals vaporized within a half mile of ground zero, melting at a mile, wood structures charred at two miles out. Human flesh suffered third-degree burns at two and a half miles, never mind the lethal radiation that would linger for months or years beyond the blast. At four miles from ground zero, vehicles would be picked up and thrown around like Matchbox toys, with dwellings trashed beyond repair.

A little glimpse of Hell on earth.

"You have an angle on the buyer," Bolan said. It didn't come out sounding like a question.

"Maybe," Leo Turrin told him. "First we tried to get a handle on the lift team, but we came up empty. The Ukranians are pretty tight beyond the basics of the incident report, but CIA's been working on it through their local contacts. No one who got close to eyeball the intruders lived to talk about it. They were driving military vehicles and wearing uniforms, with decon suits. The wheels were stolen, torched a few miles out. Nobody saw the back-up transportation, incidentally."

"The buyers," Bolan prodded him.

"Okay. We have good information that the cargo went to Sicily. It's nothing that would stand in court, but we're convinced it's solid. The reformers over there are working closely with the Bureau, Interpol and DEA. They're pointing fingers at a capo named Luigi Calo. Ever heard of him?"

"Is this the guy who works out of Catania?"

Turrin flashed a smile, amazed as always by the warrior's encyclopedic memory. "You got it in one. We used to think he was a mustache pete, involved in heroin, black-market scams, the usual. The past few months we've had to readjust our view."

"What's changed?" asked Bolan.

"Last July, Don Calo took a few days off in Tunis. Interpol was on him, also spotters from the anti-Mafia party in Italy. They caught him meeting with a group of Corsicans. So far, it's nothing new, okay?"

"I'm listening."

"Then, out of nowhere comes a couple guys from Tokyo, confirmed as Yakuza. On top of that, two Palestinians identified as militant defectors from the PLO. Same guys bailed out when Arafat went 'soft' and started talking peace with Tel Aviv."

"You're thinking politics instead of profit?"

"Maybe both," said Leo Turrin. "Figure Calo and his buddies are primarily concerned with fattening their bank accounts. It doesn't stop them doing business with the Cubans or Iranians where dope's concerned. If they can turn the game around and sell to radicals instead of buying from them, it's a bonus. Thing is, what the Arab activists all want is hardware."

"Is there anything connecting Calo with the Star?"

"They don't keep lists of membership, as far as we can tell, but I'm a firm believer in guilt by association. We've got personal meetings and telephone logs, you name it. Calo's got connections everywhere we look. Narcotics, guns, black-market pharmaceuticals, the whole nine yards."

"The nukes?"

"I'm getting there," said Turrin. "Calo has connections with the Russian Mafia, supplying drugs, receiving surplus arms. We've known that for a while. When they began admitting losses from the nuke plants, say two years ago, the Russian mob was suspect number one. They're well connected to the government and military all around. If leaks dry up, they go in with a gun, take what they want."

It was the same old story anywhere the savages had organized to rape and loot society at large. Corruption was endemic, permeating every branch and level of the government. An honest officeholder could be smeared or circumvented—murdered if the need was great enough. The record in Colombia and Sicily spoke for itself.

When all else failed, armed force was still the bottom line.

It was the only language predators could understand.

"So, Don Luigi puts the feelers out for someone with a kilo of uranium to spare," said Bolan.

"Right, or hires a specialist to do the shopping for him on commission. If it comes to smash-and-grab, you pick up mercenaries where you find them. Every nation has its share of triggermen who don't care what they're handling if the price is right.''

They dawdled past a men's store, Leo Turrin checking out the suits. A quick glance back along their path to see if they were being followed. Bolan didn't take it lightly, even in the present circumstances. Vigilance was an insurance policy. It didn't pay to let old habits die.

''We can assume Luigi isn't building a reactor for himself,'' said Bolan.

''Right again. He's got old friends around the Middle East and Asia, from the drug trade, all the way to South America. The drugs and revolutionary politics go hand in hand these days. You can't swing a dead cat in Baghdad or Bogotá without hitting some 'liberation warrior' who lives off the dope trade.''

That was true enough. Unfortunately it left Bolan with a world of suspects.

''Can we thin the herd a little, Leo?''

''I've been working on a name,'' his oldest living friend replied. ''So far, no luck, but we've been picking up a lot of traffic back and forth between Catania and Algiers.''

''That's something, anyway.''

''Not much, I know. We'll try to pin it down.''

Algeria, as both men knew, had been a training ground for radical and revolutionary groups of every stripe for over thirty years. Black Panthers from the States had gone to boot camp there, along with members of Fatah, the IRA, Basque militants, the Red Brigades and Baader-Meinhof gang, the Shining Path, Moluccan separatists—the list went on and on. In a country where Muslim fundamentalists had declared open war on the government, assassinating President Mohammed Boudiaf in 1992, it almost seemed that any armed fanatic had a place, as long as he could pay his rent in cash and keep his nose clean—more or less—on Algerian soil.

"So what's the handle?"

"Close to home, for starters," Turrin responded. "You know a guy in Motor City named Delpino?"

"Edward John," the Executioner replied.

Another grin from Turrin. "Man, I wish you'd teach me how to do that."

"Homework," Bolan told him.

"Right. He's heavy into drugs and prostitution, well connected up in Canada."

"That's Eddie."

"He's also been in touch with Don Luigi, going back six months or so. We've got phone calls—scrambled, but we know where they originate and terminate—along with faxes, cablegrams, a couple visits by subordinates."

"Not family business?" Bolan asked.

"I thought about that, too. Last month Delpino drove to Windsor for a meeting with some Triad representatives. Don Calo had a man in town, same time."

"Drug talk," the Executioner suggested.

"With a drop-in from Jihad? I don't think so. Not *all* drugs, anyway."

"I need to work Delpino, then."

"There's more," said Turrin. "Eddie's looking for a visitor, next day or so. We've got the word confirmed. A stone life-taker from Palermo named Vincenzo Moro."

"That's a new one," Bolan said, unable to retrieve a face or record that would fit the name.

"Hey, wonders never cease," the man from Justice cracked. "He's forty-something, been a shooter for the

Mafia since he was seventeen years old. Did three years on a murder rap back in the early seventies before a dying man confessed and got him off the hook. He used to be a homeboy, but he's jet set all the way the past two years. We've got him pegged from Hong Kong to Toronto, anyplace the bad boys get together. Last month he was hanging out in Moscow, three days that we're sure of.''

"Working for the Star?" asked Bolan.

"That's affirmative," said Turrin.

"And he's on Delpino's guest list?"

"Coming in from Canada tomorrow or the next day," Leo told him. "He's been huddling with the boys up north since Tuesday. Chinese and Italians, talking to a couple of the separatists from Quebec."

It would be too much to suggest, thought Bolan, that the visitor from Sicily was bearing stolen U-235 from the Ukraine. Still, if he meant to close the pipeline down—and that was paramount, from what he had already heard—he would require a starting place. It may as well be Motown and Delpino's guest.

From there he would be playing it by ear, and where it led him would be anybody's guess.

"I'll need some help," he said at last.

"What did you have in mind?"

"Grimaldi."

Turrin smiled. "He's down in Arizona, cleaning up some business on the border. I can have him in St. Louis by tonight."

"I won't be here," said Bolan. "Send him to Chicago. We can run a charter from O'Hare."

"Suits me. What do you need in terms of hardware?" Leo Turrin asked.

"I'm packed," the Executioner replied. "Jack wants to bring some back-up hardware, that's okay with me."

"I'll set it up," said Turrin. "Hey, Sarge, I hate like hell to blow your plans."

"It's no big deal," said Bolan, even though they both knew how he prized the rare times he could spend with brother Johnny, standing down from active duty in the never-ending war. "I'll tack some R & R onto the other end."

"I hope so." Turrin frowned. "Christ, if this was just a drug thing or a standard arms deal, we could let it hang awhile. But nukes, man, it's too much, you know?"

He knew, all right. The threat had been on Bolan's mind—on everybody's mind—for years on end. Scores or hundreds of terrorist groups around the world, each with its own politico-religious grudge to settle, blood debts to collect. The leaders prayed for nukes, a first-strike capability that would allow them to wreak havoc in the heart of London, Belfast, Washington, Johannesburg, Madrid or Moscow. One man with a briefcase or a package ticking in the back seat of his rental car was instantly empowered to turn the whole world upside down.

It was a threat as old as Hiroshima, rendered imminent by the advances in technology. Nowadays you didn't need a bomb the size of a Chevette to get the job done with destructive force and lethal fallout that would linger in the soil for years to come. And short of mounting Geiger counters every thirty feet on urban streets, there seemed to be no way of ruling out that threat.

Unless, perhaps, you nipped it in the bud.

It wasn't hopeless yet, not by any means. The FBI had logged its first nuclear blackmail threat—a bogus call, as it turned out—in 1974. The other threats recorded since that time had also come to nothing, though a couple of the would-be terrorists had contraband uranium on hand. As a result, the Nuclear Emergency Search Team—NEST—had been created. With a yearly budget of fifty million dollars, they were trained—at least in theory—to locate and neutralize weapons ranging from homemade devices to Chinese and soviet warheads.

This time, if Bolan did his job, that expertise would not be needed. If things went well, he could stop the ball in someone else's court and keep it there, but if anything went wrong, he knew the game could blow up in his face.

And when the game was nuclear, a fumble meant the worst kind of disaster.

He picked up Highway 75 northbound, roared onto terraces of Pontiac and turned east to Lake Orion. Forty minutes later, more or less, arriving, he'd...

CHAPTER FOUR

And now the game had started to unravel off the top. Bolan saw a risk of losing it entirely, letting both Delpino and his visitor escape if he didn't intervene to salvage something from the play.

His first step was to ditch the liberated Buick and retrieve his own car, parked within a quarter-mile of the Delpino estate in Grosse Pointe Farms. Police were out in force, but they were focused on Delpino's place, responding to the panic calls evoked by gunfire and explosions. None showed any interest in the Buick or its driver, nor was Bolan noticed as he left the neighborhood in a nondescript four-door sedan.

He knew where he was going, from the backup information Leo Turrin had provided, supplementing Bolan's own encyclopedic knowledge of the mob in Michigan. Delpino had a hideout north of Pontiac on Lake Orion where he sometimes spent long weekends with a girlfriend or retreated when the heat was on around Detroit.

But would he run in that direction now?

It was a gamble, but the Executioner had no alternatives in sight. If he intended to pursue the enemy, he had to go where Eddie Delpino was likely to appear.

And where he found Delpino, he would also find Vincenzo Moro.

He was gunning for the Star.

He picked up Highway 75 northbound, got off on 24 northeast of Pontiac and followed it to Lake Orion. Forty minutes on the road and it was pushing 3:00 a.m. when Bolan found himself in striking range. Still dark, about three hours before the sun came up.

By then, he would be finished with his probe and long gone toward another destination . . . or he would be dead.

Small towns are noisy, but they turn in early. There was no one on the street as Bolan passed through the town of Lake Orion, homing on the lake itself. Trees flanked the two-lane highway leaving town, with houses set back from the road. He passed Delpino's private driveway; nothing distinguished it from any other on the rural route. The warning signs and sentries would be situated toward the back, beyond the line of sight for passing motorists. No point in tipping teenage pranksters off that there was anything worth checking out in the vicinity.

He drove on by and found a gravel access road some distance farther on, turned left and drove for half a mile until he placed himself approximately on a parallel with Delpino's retreat. It would be overland from there, relying on a compass as his guide.

He spent a moment suiting up. Black webbing, the Beretta 93-R underneath his left arm in a shoulder rig, the Desert Eagle .44 Magnum on his hip, spare magazines for both. He chose the MP-5 SD-3 submachine gun once again for its silent capabilities, and draped a bandolier of extra magazines across his chest. An O.D. satchel went across his shoulder.

It was pitch black among the trees, but Bolan was accustomed to the night. The forest felt like home, a place where Bolan knew the way despite the fact that he had never set foot on this ground before. Wind whispered through the trees, and night birds called to one another in the topmost branches. Rodents scuttled clear of Bolan as he made his way along a narrow game trail, watching every step to keep from making noise that would broadcast his presence.

It took him twenty minutes, following the trail for something like a hundred yards, then veering off when it began to turn away from Delpino's estate. Slow going once he left the trail, but he had time.

The long night wasn't over yet.

And Bolan's war against the Star had just begun.

VINCENZO MORO HATED being forced to hide and scurry like a fugitive. He was a proud man with a heavy reputation to protect, and he would not allow himself to be humiliated. Anger dominated his emotions at the moment, with a measure of regret that he had ever come to the United States for meetings with Delpino. Apparently he had stepped into the middle of a shooting war, and if it wasn't resolved in short order to his complete satisfaction, Moro knew that he would have to reconsider doing business with the mafioso from Detroit.

For the moment, Moro found himself in the middle of nowhere, huddled in a strange house, surrounded by guns and trees. He was a prisoner of sorts, and it didn't sit well with him to place his life in someone else's hands.

Especially when those hands were trembling at the outset.

Moro sipped a cup of coffee spiked with liquor, waiting for the glow to spread and his anxiety to fade. They were secure, at least in theory, and removed from the police investigation that would certainly be going on around Delpino's home in Grosse Point Farms. The grim Sicilian still had no idea of who had staged the raid, and he wasn't concerned as long as the disturbance was restricted to Delpino. He could always find himself another representative in the United States.

But first he had to separate himself from Eddie Delpino.

"We are secure here?" Moro asked.

"No doubt about it," said Delpino. "Anybody tries to follow me out here, they're in a world of hurt. I've got the whole place covered, guaranteed."

"In that case—"

Moro's comment, instantly erased from conscious thought, was interrupted by what sounded like a shotgun blast outside the house. Delpino bolted from his chair and spilled a glass of whiskey in the process, charging from his study to confront a pair of soldiers in the outer hall. Moro followed closely on his heels.

"What's happening out there?" the lean American demanded.

One of his defenders shrugged. The other spread his hands and said, "You got me, Boss."

Delpino flushed bright crimson, leaning toward the gunman, shouting in his face. "So haul your ass out there and get some answers, Mickey!"

"Yessir!"

They were off and running, guns in hand while Moro and Delpino watched them go. The Sicilian faced his host, unable to suppress a sneer.

"The basement once again?" he asked.

"Let's see what's happening before we panic, shall we? Somebody gets nervous after what went on in town, and he can crank a round off at a rabbit, okay? It could be nothing.''

Moro slipped the button on his jacket, making access to the Walther automatic pistol in his waistband easier. The more he saw of Eddie Delpino, the less inclined he was to trust this new acquaintance who had corresponded with Don Calo from a distance. If he was called on to defend himself, so be it. He was not afraid to kill, had done it in the past, and would again.

Beginning with Delpino, if it came to that.

''I think it would be best if we continued our discussions at a later date,'' Moro said.

''Hold on a second, will you? This is nothing. We have problems, I can work it out.'' Delpino hesitated, frowning. ''Don Luigi wouldn't want you bailing out like this.''

''The choice is mine,'' Moro told him stonily. ''If I am called on to explain myself, I will defend my choices to Don Calo privately. Now—''

He was interrupted for a second time, not by a single shot this time, but with a volley from the grounds outside. At least two automatic weapons, plus the shotgun and scattered pistol fire.

Delpino had begun to sweat, with blotchy color showing in his cheeks. His hands were shaking visibly before he clenched them into fists, white knuckled.

''Jesus Christ!'' he muttered. ''What the hell?''

Moro had seen enough. He drew the Walther, flicked the safety off and thumbed the hammer back. ''I'm leaving,'' he declared. ''You may decide to stay or come with me. In either case, I need a car and a driver.''

Eddie Delpino was gaping at him, checking out the pistol, dumbstruck. When he found his voice again, he muttered, "Hell, I'm going with you. Follow me."

All hell was breaking loose outside, the sounds of gunfire growing closer as they moved along the hallway, through a kitchen pantry, moving toward an exit on the south. They hadn't entered this way when they reached the house, but Moro had to trust Delpino...to a point.

If it turned out his host was trying to deceive him, Delpino would have a rude surprise in store.

The last one of his life, in fact.

THE GUARDS WERE OUT in force, all packing automatic weapons, sawed-off shotguns, talking back and forth with hand-held radios. Bolan counted four men on the south, immediately opposite his place among the trees. Away to Bolan's left, or west, two more were visible, and voices warned him of at least two more. The east side of the house was also covered, one man standing at the corner, others certainly prepared to back him up. As with the house in Grosse Point Farms, Delpino's garage was a separate structure with a gunner on the broad front door.

There would be no way in without engaging the defensive cordon. Bolan saw that from the start, but he wasn't prepared to charge the hostile guns and sacrifice himself in any kind of futile grandstand play. It would require some stealth and planning, but he had no time to waste. Whatever Bolan meant to do, he had to do it soon.

He worked his way around the house to reach the front, relieved to note that it was not illuminated like the mansion back in Grosse Pointe Farms. Three cars were parked in front—a Lincoln stretch with four-door Chevrolets like bookends, shielding Bolan from the soldiers on the porch as he went down on knees and elbows, creeping from the forest toward the house.

He reached the limo moments later, worked the satchel off his shoulder, opened it without a sound. He took out a plastic charge and detonator slightly larger than a pack of cigarettes. He primed it, reached up toward the forward wheel well, balancing the charge atop the Lincoln's tire.

Still undetected, Bolan moved on to the second Chevrolet in line, repeating the procedure with another plastic charge. Two out of three was all he needed, and he crept back to the shadowed woods, prepared at any moment for a shout or gunshot that would mean he had been spotted by the enemy.

So far, they had missed him in the darkness, maybe concentrating on the driveway or perhaps secure in the belief that they had left their problem in the city. Who would follow them this far, when he had missed the shot in Grosse Pointe Farms?

The Executioner, for one.

He circled to the north, confirmed that guards were watching that side of the house as well, and knew that it was time to make his move. Not rashly, with a hell-for-leather blitz, but in considered style. Set up his targets for the kill.

For that, he had to show himself, accept the risk and run with it. Reverse the odds against him through a mixture of audacity and cunning.

Starting now.

He moved with all deliberate speed toward the detached garage, deciding he would take the solitary gunman first. A prelude to the others, if it went down as he planned.

He came on from the shooter's blind side, leading with the SMG, and nosed around the corner far enough to spot his target from the flank. A low-pitched whistle through his teeth, enough to bring the mafioso's head around.

Before the guy could make out what was happening, the silent SMG spit three rounds from a range of fifteen feet. The parabellum shockers took him down, blood spouting, but his finger clenched around the shotgun's trigger, squeezing off a buckshot charge that bit a chunk out of the whitewashed eaves.

And that was all.

Bolan broke from cover, angling toward the house while Delpino's hired guns responded to the 12-gauge blast. Four soldiers fanned out to meet him, and he started firing on the run, the first guy on his right collapsing as a 3-round burst ripped through his chest.

The others opened up in unison, unloading like a mobile firing squad, no time to aim. He met them with no hope of cover on the open lawn. Momentum took him forward, milking short bursts from the MP-5 SD-3 as he ran.

He had to reach the house this time, search out Delpino and his visitor from overseas. A second failure meant the end of everything. He wouldn't have another chance.

It would be now or never, do or die.

And Bolan knew that it could still go either way.

DELPINO HEARD the rapid-fire explosions coming from the far side of the house, around in front. The cars, for Christ's sake—it had to be, but he and Moro weren't stranded yet. He had more vehicles available, prepared for an emergency no matter what went down.

Moro's pistol was a bit of a surprise. Delpino knew the guy was packing, sure, but Moro's attitude had taken on an air of menace. Not quite threatening—he didn't come right out and say it—but you got the feeling he would leave you in the gutter if he didn't get his way.

What else was new?

Delpino dealt with hard guys every day, and he had always dealt from strength . . . but this was something else. Vincenzo Moro wasn't just some errand boy from Sicily, sent out to close a deal. He had the full weight of the Star behind him, and that went beyond the Mafia, including at least half a dozen other criminal fraternities. They spanned the globe, pulled strings in ways and places that your average capo mafioso barely dreamed of. If the Star was on your case, you might try hiding in Antarctica for all the good that it would do.

"This way."

Somebody was unloading with a ton of automatic fire outside, and Eddie Delpino could only hope it was his soldiers doing most of it. A crazy feeling, being forced to run and hide from trouble in his own backyard where he had always had a sense of being safe and sound.

Things change.

Vincenzo Moro seemed to think it was a local problem, but Delpino couldn't think of anyone who hated him this much and had the wherewithal to make it stick. He had a constant beef with the Colombians, of course, but he had also kicked their asses three times running, and it didn't take a genius to avoid that fourth ass-whipping. Anyway, the boys from Bogotá would never try their hand in Grosse Pointe Farms, much less at Lake Orion. They were concentrated in Detroit and did most of their killing there, among their own.

Who, then?

Once more it didn't take a rocket scientist to figure out the link between these wild attacks and Moro's visit. Eddie Delpino was no believer in coincidence. Shit happens, right, but he had never seen it happen twice within a single night unless someone had planned for it to happen in advance.

All things considered, Moro had a lot of nerve to try to throw his weight around when it was probably his fault that they were under fire to start with. If he got too sassy, there were ways for Delpino to deflate his ego, but they had to clear the latest trap before he tried to show who was in charge.

Survival was the first priority, and he could sweat the other stuff when they were safe. Right now, distractions were enough to get him killed.

Moro followed him until they reached the exit, where Delpino paused and peered out through a smallish window in the door. The gunfire sounded louder now, but there was no one visible from where he stood. A body—one of Delpino's soldiers—was stretched out on the grass near the garage, but that was all.

"Let's go," Delpino said. "We bag a car, we're outa here."

"You drive?" Moro asked.

"Who else?"

The man from Sicily seemed satisfied, but Delpino noticed that he kept his finger on the automatic's trigger all the same. The cautious type, okay. At least he hadn't aimed the gun at his host yet. That would require some kind of action, and Delpino didn't need a wrestling match to complicate things in the middle of a firefight.

He was leading when they left the house, the air cool against his face, and he could hear his own pulse pounding like a bass drum in his ears. The joke would be on him if he collapsed now from a heart attack or some damn thing. Like something from a movie, Jesus.

But his heart kept right on beating as he made his way across the lawn, aware that it had gotten quiet suddenly around the far side of the house. Good news, perhaps, if it was winding down. God knew that he could use a break right now to change his luck.

He glanced back at Moro, saw him hesitate and barked, "Come on, for Christ's sake!"

The man followed, picking up the pace, and Delpino concentrated on his destination. The garage. Ignore his soldier sprawled out on the ground and leaking blood from chest wounds. Screw him if he couldn't keep himself alive. On second thought, Delpino veered off course and grabbed the dead man's shotgun.

Just in case.

He had the broad garage door halfway open when a shout from Moro brought him back around to face the house. He stared past the Sicilian, saw a tall man dressed in black approaching, moving cautiously but making no attempt to hide himself. He had some kind of automatic weapon in his hands, and he was wearing military gear—suspenders, ammo pouches, the whole lot.

Before Delpino had a chance to use the shotgun, Moro stepped into his line of fire and raised his automatic, sighting on the black-clad figure. Easy shot from that range, any way you sliced it.

But the stranger wasn't waiting for Moro. He squeezed off a short burst from his piece before the Sicilian found his mark. Delpino saw his visitor go down, a rag doll folding right before his eyes, and that was it. The Star would have to find a new ambassador.

And Eddie Delpino would have to save himself.

He pumped a shotgun blast in the direction of his adversary, knew that he would miss and didn't care. It gave him time to duck beneath the broad garage door, racing toward the nearest car. A Benz, and he had the keys. A few more minutes and he could haul ass out of there and save himself.

Where were his soldiers, dammit? How many were left if his assailant felt secure to wander around the grounds that way? How many other men in black were waiting for him even now?

Delpino threw himself behind the wheel, the shotgun in his lap, and twisted the ignition key. The motor caught at once and he released the brake, enjoyed the surge of power as he stood on the accelerator. Smashed a brand-new exit through the broad garage door with the sheer weight and momentum of the Benz.

He burst through, almost laughing—right up to the moment when he saw the dark man standing in his path.

SOMETIMES YOU BEAT the odds; it was just that simple. Go in firing from the hip and take your chances, killing anything that moved. That was war distilled to its essence of heroism and brutality, with life or death riding on the twitch of a finger, the path of a bullet.

Any one of the first four gunners could have taken him, but luck was holding fast on Bolan's side. He met them as they came, the MP-5 SD-3 spitting silent rounds that dropped them squirming in their tracks. A bullet stung his biceps, there and gone, a graze that Bolan managed to ignore. He had more pressing business at the moment. He could spare a little blood.

More soldiers found him as he made his way around the east side of the house, proceeding back toward the detached garage. He had to find a way inside, but Bolan had no wish to leave any army at his back when it could trap him in the house.

Reloading on the run, he met his latest adversaries with the same determination, slamming parabellum rounds into the hardmen as they came before him. Gunners stumbling, reeling, going down. Blood and gun smoke, flailing limbs and bullets wasted on the night.

It ended suddenly, no targets left in sight. He kept on moving, reached the backyard as two men broke from the house, jogging off toward the garage. He recognized Delpino, guessed that his companion must be the Sicilian.

Close enough to take them now, but he had more in mind than simply killing these two if he had a chance to grill them first. Advancing as they covered ground, and Eddie Delpino swung to his left, scooped up the shotgun from his fallen sentry's outstretched hand.

The older man glanced back as Bolan crossed the lawn. Delpino was at the broad garage door now and lifting it. The stumpy sidekick turned and froze at the sight of Bolan making his approach. He had a pistol in his hand and raised it, sighting down the slide. Delpino turned to gawk at both of them, the door half-open.

Bolan had no choice. He gave the short Sicilian three rounds from a range of twenty feet, and three more as he fell. No contest as the guy went down, a boneless rag doll stretched out on the grass.

And that left Eddie Delpino.

He vanished underneath the door and pulled it down behind him. Seconds later Bolan heard an engine revving on the inside, hesitated, ready for what had to happen next.

A black Mercedes Benz burst through the door, a storm of shattered lumber raining down, and Bolan saw the juggernaut swing toward him, gaining speed. Delpino's face was behind the windshield mouthing curses as he aimed the car at Bolan like a guided missile.

Bolan thumbed the fire-selector switch from 3-round bursts to automatic, held the submachine gun tight against his hip and fired off half the magazine in one long burst. He racked the Benz's grille and clipped the hood latch, saw the hood fly back, obstructing Delpino's view. The black Mercedes swerved off course as Delpino tried to save it, Bolan rattling off another burst that stitched across the driver's door.

Delpino lost it, swung away, tires losing traction on the grass. The yard was sloping there, a gentle rise, but it was still enough to roll the Benz when Delpino fought the wheel around and tried to make a sudden turn. No violent crash like something from the movies, but it came to rest inverted, back wheels spinning as the engine revved in vain.

Delpino tried to wriggle free, his left arm hanging at a crazy angle. Bolan met him on the lawn and had him covered with the SMG when he looked up and recognized his peril.

"Who the hell are you?" he demanded, sounding scared and weary all at once.

"I'll ask the questions," Bolan said.

"Go screw yourself."

Three silent parabellum rounds reduced his knees to jelly. Eddie Delpino let out a wail that must have carried even in the woods, but there was no one left to hear or help him out.

"Let's take it from the top," said Bolan.

Gasping with the pain, Delpino managed an uncertain nod.

"Your friend back there. That's Moro?"

"Yeah. You know him?"

"He worked for Don Luigi, right?"

"Tha's right."

"One more. I need to hear about the nukes."

Delpino looked confused, not faking it. "What fuckin' nukes is that?"

"Don't make me ask you twice."

"I'm tellin' you, I don't know what you mean!" The pained expression on his face made Delpino seem sincere.

"I guess you're useless, then," said Bolan.

"Wait! I—"

Three more parabellum rounds at point-blank range closed Delpino's mouth forever, leaving Bolan as the sole survivor on the field of battle. And aside from confirmation of Delpino's link to Sicily, the Star, he knew no more than when he'd started.

He would have to work it out the hard way, then.

No problem.

He had gone that route before.

CHAPTER FIVE

"I'm telling you, it just feels weird," said Jack Grimaldi as he settled into his window seat.

"Relax," said Bolan, belting in beside him.

"Do you think they'd let me take her up if I asked nice?" Grimaldi was smiling now in case his friend thought he was serious.

"Enjoy the flight," said Bolan. "You can use that nervous energy when we get on the other side."

Their transport was the Concorde, lifting off from JFK International at 9:15 on Sunday morning under slate gray skies. The supersonic transport would deliver them to Orly Airport in Paris, some three hours and twenty-five minutes after takeoff. That shaved the normal trans-Atlantic flight time by an estimated forty-five percent, and Bolan knew it was the best that they could do.

By traveling commercial, they were forced to leave their hardware on the ground, and Grimaldi was chafing at his unaccustomed status as a passenger instead of manning the controls. Still, it was quicker than arranging for a military flight, and they had weapons waiting for them on the other side. Grimaldi would be picking up a charter plane in Paris, piloting the final leg to Rome himself. For now, though, he was forced to sit and watch while someone else did all the driving.

The SST was nearly full this morning, as it always was. They kept their voices down and spoke in cryptic terms to prevent sharing any private thoughts or information with their fellow passengers and flight attendants. Only when their flight was airborne and the nearest passengers had slipped their earphones on or settled back to doze was Bolan willing to discuss their mission in some semblance of detail.

They had already done most of the necessary talking prior to liftoff. Grimaldi already knew what had gone down at Lake Orion, how the Executioner had come up short on solid information for the next phase of their critical campaign.

They would be flying blind to some extent, but not entirely. Bolan knew his way around in Italy and Sicily. He was conversant with the ways of old-world mafiosi and had faced them on their home turf in the past. He understood the way they thought and dealt with others, holding power through a mixture of coercion and corruption. Seven centuries had passed since overtaxed Sicilian peasants formed the Mafia to wage guerrilla war against a French invading army, and the world had changed. The heroes of a bygone era had been transformed into bandits, pimps and murderers who preyed upon their own, extorting tribute from the very population they professed to serve. Political control had been secured through bribery and terrorism, lasting even to the present day.

But times were changing once again. Within the past five years or so, aggressive prosecution had begun dismantling the "Honored Society's" web of control, snipping one strand at a time until the lethal net began unraveling across the board. A number of the ranking capos were in prison, along with scores or hundreds of their soldiers. There were some in Italy who said the Mafia was dead, and if reports of its demise were sadly premature, at least there was a reason to believe that end was coming soon.

And then there was the Star.

"These guys want all the marbles, eh?" Grimaldi said.

"Seems like," said Bolan. "Anyway, they're in position."

"It's been tried before," the pilot said. "Like mixing axle grease and ice cream. Pricks can't get along for shit."

"They're trying harder these days," Bolan said. "Incentive makes a difference, right? And don't forget the new frontiers."

"You're talking Russia," said Grimaldi.

"For a start. There's also Eastern Europe, parts of Africa and Asia they could never reach before. New markets, new suppliers."

"Maybe new wars now and then?"

"Why not? One thing about the syndicate, whatever name it's using, you can bet it's got the whole spread covered when it comes to politics. Left or right, who cares? You buy friends anywhere you can and squeeze them if they try to go back on their debts."

"I would have thought the Palestinians were too shorthanded and disorganized to be of any value."

"Everybody's useful, one time or another," Bolan said. "Marcello used the KKK for muscle in Louisiana when he didn't want his people leaving tracks. The Medellín cartel's been using paramilitary groups for years. Remember the supreme-court raid in Bogotá?"

"Unfortunately," Grimaldi replied.

"So, there you go. The Arabs don't mind killing, and the militants would sell their mothers for an A-bomb."

"Mama wouldn't bring much on the open market," said Grimaldi.

"Think about their sponsors," Bolan countered. "All that oil. I have a feeling they can meet the asking price."

"You think the Star's promoting World War III?" Grimaldi asked.

He thought about it, shook his head. "They're not promoting anything but private enterprise," said Bolan. "If I had to guess, I'd say they don't much care what happens in the Middle East or where the fallout goes, but they'll expect the Palestinians to blow it somehow. Maybe get themselves arrested. Dealing with a government in power, that's another story. You've got UN sanctions, hearings and debates, all kinds of stalling. Give a bomb to Baghdad and it's fifty-fifty they'll just brag about it, run some kind of heavy bluff."

"Too risky either way," Grimaldi said.

"That's why we're on the job," said Bolan.

"I got that part. So what's the rumble on Luigi?"

"He's the big man on the island at the moment," Bolan answered. "One of only three or four who haven't been indicted. Call it luck, or maybe he's got good connections. Either way, you want to cut a deal in Sicily, it goes across Don Calo's desk before you pocket any change."

"Old-timer?"

"Pushing fifty," Bolan said. "Third-generation Mafia and hard as nails. You heard about the car bomb early on last year? Took out the prosecutor in Marsala."

"Don Luigi's job?"

"Smart money pegs it that way," Bolan answered, "but it never went to court. It's not the first time that a prosecutor facing Calo bought the farm."

"Sounds like a prince."

"The Star thinks so, I gather," Bolan said.

"That's firm?"

"As can be. He's connected everywhere you look, the last two years or so."

"Including Russia?" asked Grimaldi.

"Especially Russia. Interpol has placed a couple of his men—including Moro—on a flight to the Ukraine three weeks before the raid went down at Krivoy Rog."

"I liked it better when the mustache petes were more traditional," Grimaldi said. "You know—some dope, some women, shakedown rackets. Anybody asks me, they should leave the space-age stuff alone."

"That's just the point," said Bolan. "No one asked us, but we get to tell them anyway."

"You think he'll listen?"

"I suppose we'll have to make some noise, get his attention," Bolan replied.

"That sounds familiar," said Grimaldi, stifling a yawn. "Long night. You mind if I try to catch some sleep?"

"Sounds like a plan."

The Executioner leaned back and closed his eyes. He didn't plan to sleep—how could he, with his mind so full of things to plan and carry out?—but in another moment he was drifting, weightless, off beyond the clouds.

In Bolan's dream he chased a hulking shadow figure, racing over barren, rocky ground—or was he running through the darkened streets of an abandoned city? A necropolis? No matter how he poured it on, the figure held its lead, too far away for him to make out any details of the face, except for burning eyes that caught him now and then, a quick glance back across the runner's shoulder.

Bolan's quarry had a satchel in his hand. It had a heavy look about it, but the shadow man paid no attention to it as he ran. It was a natural extension of his arm, as if one fist had swollen five or six times normal size. The runner scrambled over obstacles, ducked under barricades and never set his burden down.

The race seemed to go on forever, and Bolan felt exhaustion dragging at his legs, his muscles burning while his adversary never appeared to tire. A glance around and they were definitely in a city now, but it wasn't deserted any longer. Scattered bystanders were visible if Bolan took the time to search them out in doorways, darkened windows, seated in parked cars. His lungs felt close to bursting, but the only sound he heard, aside from boot heels slapping on the pavement, was a mocking laughter from his quarry up ahead.

Another moment, and his adversary disappeared around a corner. Bolan hesitated, sniffing out a trap, and reached inside his jacket for the heavy automatic that he wore in armpit leather. Cautiously he followed, blinking as the street in front of him exploded in a blaze of neon, headlights, men and women jostling one another on the sidewalks, window shopping, ducking in and out of bars, cafés and theaters.

He recognized Times Square, had seen it frequently enough on screen and in the flesh to know exactly where he was. The shadow man had foxed him this time. Bolan couldn't hope to find him in the crush of bodies, rushing vehicles, horns blasting, music blaring from the bars and strip clubs.

But the dark man raised a hand and waved to Bolan, beckoning. In retrospect, it was amazing that he hadn't seen his quarry instantly. Instead of merely blocking light as bodies do in silhouette, this man gave the appearance of *absorbing* light. He was a black hole in the middle of Times Square, a personal affront to nature with his glowing eyes and mocking smile. He occupied a traffic island in the middle of the square. The heavy satchel stood between his feet.

As Bolan struggled through the crowd to reach him, he could feel the stranger watching, waiting for the proper moment. Bolan reached the curb and saw him stooping, big hands reaching for the satchel. In a flash, he knew it was imperative to stop him now, before he dipped a hand inside.

The heavy automatic leapt into Bolan's hand, spit fire and sudden death. He squeezed off half the magazine, ignoring the pedestrians who scattered from his path, convinced that if he did not stop this stranger now there would be no bystanders left to fret about.

And yet his hasty rounds had no effect. He wasn't missing; that wasn't the problem. Rather, Bolan's target had absorbed the bullets just as he appeared to soak up light and sound, with no apparent ill effects. His crimson eyes were fixed on Bolan, glowing still, and there was no way to prevent his left hand from opening the satchel while his right slid inside and out of sight.

"You lose."

The voice was deep, sepulchral, more a feeling than a sound, like the vibration from a thoughtless neighbor's stereo. Before the Executioner could try another shot, the world bloomed into blinding radiance, a dazzling white that seared his retinas before the shock wave deafened him and pulverized his bones.

No, he wasn't quite deaf. There was a chiming sound, a faint alarm, as if to mock his failure. Too damn late for warnings now, but there it was.

His eyes snapped open, focused on the Fasten Seat Belts sign above his head. A flight attendant moved along the aisle, adjusting seats, reminding passengers to stow their carryons and fold their trays. The pilot's tinny, disembodied voice told Bolan they were making the approach to Orly.

Christ! How long had he been out?

The human body will assert itself, he realized, when the necessities—nutrition, rest—are not forthcoming in sufficient quantities. Exhausted men could sleep through damn near anything, including cannon fire, as Bolan knew from personal experience.

His trans-Atlantic sleep had not been restful, though. The memory of Times Square vaporized was fixed in Bolan's mind, imagination filling in the gaps.

How many dead, if a device of thirty-five or forty kilotons was detonated in New York, Los Angeles or Washington? Say millions, just in the initial blast, and triple it for radiation victims, some of whom would not display their symptoms for a year or more. And what of the survivors who were seemingly unscathed? What of their mutant, deformed children five or ten years down the road?

But he must stop letting his gloomy thoughts rush ahead. There was a world of difference between two kilos of uranium and an effective bomb. Assuming that the sale was made to someone in the Middle East and they were able to construct a functional device, smart money said that it would probably be detonated close to home. In Tel Aviv, for instance. Maybe even Baghdad or Tehran. Perhaps the proud new owner would be satisfied to keep his lethal toy in storage, blustering and threatening a world of self-made enemies—but was that a chance to take, given what was at stake?

Most Arab radicals were pledged to wiping Israel off the map, but U.S. aid to Tel Aviv had long since marked America the status of another major target on the hit list. Americans were constantly at risk wherever Palestinian commandos or Islamic fundamentalists convened to plan their next assault.

He could not automatically dismiss a strike against the States, but the location of ground zero barely registered in Bolan's mind. A blast in Tel Aviv, Jerusalem or Ankara would only be less terrible in terms of raw statistics—dead and wounded, property destroyed. It was impossible to quantify the human suffering involved.

"We're getting there," Grimaldi said, his words breaking into Bolan's reverie.

"Looks like."

"Figure an hour, ninety minutes, we'll be on our way."

The touchdown was immaculate and uneventful. Customs used up forty minutes, mostly waiting, neither one of them with any items to declare. The customs officers were bored and apathetic, checking every sixth or seventh passenger from force of habit, passing Bolan and Grimaldi through without a second glance.

They were unarmed, in any case, no contraband for anyone to find. Grimaldi led him through the concourse, down an escalator to the basement-level office where a small gray man was waiting with their charter contract. There were no signatures required; no cash changed hands. The details had been put to bed by Hal Brognola, stateside, with some marginal assistance from the CIA.

Ten minutes later they were walking toward a hangar under bright Parisian sunshine, seventy degrees, the tarmac warm beneath their shoes. A French mechanic in a bright orange jumpsuit met them at the door, spoke briefly to Grimaldi in a semblance of English and moved back toward a smallish office, leaving them alone.

"They'll have a tractor ready by the time we're squared away," Grimaldi said. "So far, so good."

The aircraft was an IAI Westwind 1124, Israeli manufacture, with twin Garrett AiResearch TFE 731-3 turbofan engines and a range of 2,700 miles. It seated ten, but they weren't expecting passengers. The storage space might come in handy somewhere down the line, and Bolan liked to be prepared for anything.

Preparedness was still the best insurance policy.

They went aboard to check the Westwind out. Grimaldi ran a sweep for bugs and homers, satisfied himself that they would not be tracked long-distance by potential enemies.

"We're cool," Grimaldi said when he was finished. "I'll feel better when we get some hardware, though."

"It's coming," Bolan told him. "What's our ETA for Rome?"

"I'd say an hour and a quarter once we're in the air."

It all came down to time, the element that no man could control. Each hour wasted gave his adversaries that much lead time, placing Bolan at a greater disadvantage. He would have to make it up somehow if he was going to succeed.

But first he had to reach the target zone.

They heard the tractor coming, saw it moments later. Square built, it was large enough to tow the Westwind from its hangar once the driver backed around and made his coupling. It felt strange proceeding at a snail's pace, creeping out of shadow into sunlight, but they got it done. Grimaldi took it over once the hangar was behind them and the tractor disengaged, twin turbofans winding up from a whisper to a hollow roar.

"We're cooking now," Grimaldi said, a bright smile on his face now that he found himself back in the driver's seat. "We're on our way."

Grimaldi chattered with the ATC, received his clearance, lined up to take his place for liftoff. Bolan sat beside his friend and waited while an Alitalia flight took off, immediately followed by a Swissair Fokker F100. Next up in the Westwind, they were cleared five minutes later, rocketing along the runway. Bolan felt acceleration press him back into his seat, the old, familiar roller-coaster feeling as they left the ground behind.

An hour and a quarter, give or take.

The enemy was waiting for him even now. Don Calo did not know that he was coming, but the soil of Italy and Sicily was steeped in the blood of those who took their enemies too lightly. That was never Bolan's failing, even when his opposition dressed in baggy suits and threatened adversaries with the evil eye.

Behind the old-world mannerisms there was muscle, all the hardware Calo and his fellow dons required to crush their enemies and grind them into dust. Radioactive dust if they fell back on their newest stock in trade.

But they were reckoning without the Executioner.

There was a new day coming on, and when the sun went down, some of the men who watched it rise would be among the dead. Those ranks were growing all the time, but there was room for more.

The moment he was back on solid ground, Mack Bolan would be working overtime to fill those vacancies.

They were an hour and a quarter short of total war.

The Executioner could hardly wait.

CHAPTER SIX

Traffic flowed along the Corso d'Italia to the Porta Pinciana, feeding the avenues of Villa Borghese. Bolan used his street map sparingly, navigating by instinct and his prior experience in Rome.

The ranking mafioso in the capital—identified as a disciple of the Star—was Don Carmelo Magno. He was fifty-two years old, a balding man who scowled from photographs as if the stench of death was permanently in his nostrils. Not unlikely, Bolan thought, considering the number of his brothers and civilians Don Carmelo had condemned to die for some infraction of the Mafia's sacred code.

Like most successful mafiosi, Don Carmelo Magno was a patron of the church. He paid lip service to the God of mercy, seldom missed a Sunday Mass, and even managed a confession once or twice a year. As far as absolution, Bolan wished him well. Forgiveness might be waiting for Don Magno in the next life, but he could expect none from the Executioner.

A daylight strike in Rome was risky to the max, but Bolan had the angles figured out as best he could. Forget about the variables; there was nothing he could do except prepare himself to meet the unexpected as it came.

He drove a Fiat four-door, hardware close at hand. The weapons were domestic: a Beretta Model 92 in armpit leather and a Model 12-S submachine gun underneath the driver's seat, both chambered in 9 mm parabellum. In the trunk, a Beretta SC-70 assault rifle and a Franchi SPAS 12 riot shotgun.

He drove past Don Carmelo's villa, not surprised to note it was a humble place. The old-line mafiosi often spent less money on themselves than flashy gangsters in the States, content to wield their power from a relatively modest home without conspicuous displays of wealth. It was enough for them—or some of them, at least—that lesser mortals recognized their wealth and power while the lire built up interest in a numbered bank account. A trip to Switzerland or Luxembourg to sit inside the vault, and they were happy for another year.

Carmelo Magno did not live in poverty, of course. His house and grounds were well kept, fairly stylish, manned by guards around the clock. His flower garden, which he tended personally, was renowned among his fellow dons. They didn't laugh at Magno's fondness for the earth, but rather spoke admiringly of his green thumb.

The garden was his weakness—one of several, possibly, but certainly the easiest for Bolan to exploit. He didn't plan to chat with Don Carmelo face-to-face, but he would need some room in which to work. The flower garden offered that and more.

He parked a block from Magno's walled estate and locked the Fiat, opened up the trunk. An O.D. duffel bag contained the SC-70 with folding stock, plus extra 30-round magazines and several 40 mm MECAR rifle grenades. The latter were useful in that they fit the Beretta's muzzle without a detachable launcher, and they were fired with normal rounds in place of special blanks. The 5.56 mm weapon was a killer, with a cyclic rate of fire around 650 rounds per minute on full automatic.

Bolan walked back from the Fiat to the neat apartment house adjoining Magno's property. Three stories tall, it overlooked his grounds and garden on the west, a hundred yards or so from where the capo spent most afternoons among his treasured roses. Bolan climbed a flight of outside stairs to reach the roof, rehearsing some Italian phrases in his mind to deal with any challenge from the tenants.

He made the rooftop unopposed and found his vantage point, extracted the Beretta from its bag and scanned Don Magno's garden through the sniper scope. In fifteen seconds Bolan had his target spotted. Rome's top mafioso, kneeling in the dirt with pruning shears in hand. A young man in vest and yellow shirt, his sleeves rolled up, stood watching from a corner of the garden, armed with a *lupara,* the classic Mafia double-barreled shotgun.

Bolan looked around for other guards, saw none in evidence and reckoned they would be inside the house. The sounds of battle would alert them, but he had no need to bring them out beforehand.

He was gunning for Don Magno, and he had the target in his sights.

He picked up one of the rifle grenades and slipped it over the Beretta's muzzle, snug around the built-in launcher. It added weight to the barrel, but that was all right. Less recoil when he squeezed the trigger to dispatch the high-explosive canister downrange.

Another moment while he found his mark again, with Don Magno still kneeling in the dirt as if in prayer. The MECAR round was set to blow on impact, and he fixed the cross hairs of his scope on a point several inches in front of his target, lining it up. A gentle stroke and the 40 mm projectile flew toward its target, an outsized insect with a deadly sting.

One moment, Don Carmelo Magno had a pale rose in his hand, examining the petals, then the world exploded in his face. The shock wave and a storm of shrapnel slammed him backward, flattening one bush before another stopped him short. The mafioso's face and chest were torn, blood streaked and smoking.

Bolan swung around to bring the sentry under fire, found Don Magno's soldier gaping at the crater where his boss had knelt a moment earlier. He tugged the shotgun off its shoulder sling and held it ready, searching for a target that he couldn't find.

Another squeeze, and Bolan put a 5.56 mm tumbler through the young man's forehead, dropped him in his tracks. The others would be coming, but he didn't wait for them. He retreated down the outside stairs and out of there, the duffel heavy on his shoulder, covering a multitude of sins.

As Bolan drove away, he watched his rearview mirror, checking for a tail. Found none and let himself relax.

It was a start.

THEY DROVE BOTH CARS from Rome to Naples, south along the coastal highway, through Latina, Terracina, Formia. Grimaldi understood the logic: two cars halved the chances of discovery and interception, let them carry twice the military hardware. Even so, he wished they could have been together on the drive instead of touching base at thirty-minute intervals by radio.

He dismissed the wish. Bolan knew what he was doing, always had. Grimaldi was a combat veteran in his own right, but he could not match the Executioner in terms of battlefield experience or expertise. Some soldiers were all guts and glory, charging down the cannon's throat, while others specialized in strategy and planning. Bolan was the rare example of a fighting man who mastered both domains, the mind and muscle. Brains and bullets, a perfect combination.

Sometimes, though, Grimaldi still worried. The odds were always changing, but they never seemed to be in Bolan's favor when he launched a new campaign. Some gigs were worse than others, granted, and the worst were those that called for infiltration of a district where the enemy was in control, had held the reins for years on end.

It felt like that to him in Italy, and it was only getting worse the closer he and Bolan came to Sicily, the birthplace of the Mafia. It was too late for an abortion, but the Star was young enough that maybe they could rub it out in infancy.

Or make a start, at least.

It didn't pay to think in terms of long-range victory when you were pinned down on the firing line. Big pictures made for pretty viewing, but a soldier had to keep his focus if he wanted to survive.

The strike in Rome had been a good first step, sent ripples through the Mafia from Trento and Milan to Catanzaro and Messina. Every mafioso in the country would be on alert from that point on, prepared to blast away at shadows. No association with the Star would be required; indeed, Grimaldi calculated that some mafiosi might have no idea the newer, international cartel existed.

Bolan meant to concentrate on members of the Star where possible, but he was not above removing "ordinary" mobsters when he had the chance. They didn't have enough hard data on the Star yet to prepare a comprehensive list of members and associations, much less eliminate potential contacts at a glance.

Hard times were coming for the syndicate in Italy, make no mistake.

Grimaldi felt no sympathy for them at all. Nor did he mind the dirty work. Most of his fighting was accomplished in the air, but he wasn't exactly helpless on the ground. A veteran of Southeast Asia and the Bolan wars, he was a born survivor... meaning that his adversaries generally did not survive.

It still remained to be seen if Italy would be a different story. Either way he meant to give the campaign everything he had.

It was the very least that he could do.

JULIANO BOCCIERI lit a fresh cigar and blew smoke toward the ceiling of his office, scowling at the man who faced him from across the spacious teakwood desk.

"You always bring bad news, Arturo."

Young Arturo Esquilino was uncertain whether he should laugh or frown, so he did neither, kept his face deadpan and nodded solemnly. "It's true, *padrone*, I realize. Accept my most sincere apology."

Don Boccieri never ceased to marvel at the way in which a normal man would willingly debase himself when he was summoned into close proximity with power. Those who lived within its aura were perpetually bowing, scraping, anything to hold their privileged position in another's shadow.

"Never mind," Boccieri told his young subordinate with an airy wave to change the topic. "These things happen. Please explain."

"We're still awaiting details," Esquilino said. "Police appear to have no suspects in the case. It is expected someone may attempt to question you, if not today, then certainly tomorrow or the next day."

"But of course."

Don Boccieri was neither surprised nor especially irritated at the prospect of another police interrogation. He was questioned frequently, perhaps a dozen times a year, when crimes or other strange events—like sudden disappearances among the rich and famous—had to be explained. Sometimes he knew the answer and refused to share it with detectives; other times, like now, he didn't have a clue and said so honestly. In neither case, he realized, would the police believe his words.

"The circumstances of the case—"

"A rocket or grenade, you said," Boccieri interrupted his subordinate.

"Yes, sir. That much is known. Police have found two cartridge casings on a roof adjacent to Don Magno's property. It must have been the sniper's nest."

"Who wanted old Carmelo dead?" asked Boccieri, almost speaking to himself.

There would be dozens, maybe hundreds on the list, he realized. Surviving relatives of murder victims. Merchants he had swindled, driven into bankruptcy. The families of children held for ransom. Public servants hounded out of office for their efforts at reform. Policemen steeped in decades of frustration as the Mafia resisted their best efforts to contain expanding crime.

Too many suspects.

Don Boccieri swiveled in his high-backed leather chair to face the windows, studying the bank and office block directly opposite, on Via Pisanetti. He had operated out of downtown Naples for the past twelve years while living in a villa on the coast. It had been years since he was frightened on his own account, and Don Magno's death was not the kind of news that made him quake in fear.

"Tell me, then, Arturo—"

Looking back, Boccieri could not say he actually saw the shot, but it would seem that way. The massive picture window shivered, cracked, then buckled inward, dropping like a sheet of fractured ice. Before Don Boccieri could react, he heard a loud, wet slapping sound and turned in time to watch Esquilino's face explode.

The younger man itched sideways off his chair, and there could be no question of surviving such a wound. His brains were steaming on the desk, and Boccieri took the opportunity to try to save himself.

He spun the chair around—a fragile shield, but better than nothing—and was lunging toward the floor when there was yet another shot. He heard the first one, like an echo much delayed, and then the second bullet hit him, ripping through his chair before it struck his shoulder blade and nearly ripped his right arm from its socket.

Don Juliano Boccieri struck the floor facedown. He smelled and tasted carpeting, lay motionless and felt his own blood soaking through the suit he wore. It was a miracle that he was even conscious, with the shock and pain. How long before he bled to death?

Boccieri tried to shout for help, but found that he could barely whisper. His bodyguards were already rushing in, pistols drawn, to find out what the matter was. The first man through the door was glancing down at Boccieri and his young lieutenant when a bullet struck him in the chest and slammed him back against the nearest wall.

A second gunman saw his comrade fall, attempted to retreat, find cover in the anteroom, but he didn't respond in time to save himself. A fourth shot drilled his face in profile, spewing blood, teeth and mutilated flesh before the man went down.

Boccieri's final bodyguard, Michele, leaped across the fallen bodies of his comrades, crouching on the threshold with an Uzi submachine gun in his hands. He couldn't see the target, but someone clearly had them spotted through the broken window and he turned his weapon there, unloading half a magazine in rapid fire.

Boccieri blessed the young man for his courage, vowed to make him wealthy when the smoke cleared. Felt the bitter tears of rage and pain well in his eyes as yet another rifle shot came out of nowhere, knocked Michele sprawling, his Uzi pumping useless rounds into the ceiling overhead.

So this, Don Boccieri thought, is how it feels to die.

And from the shadows slowly, painfully enveloping his brain, a small voice whispered, *Yes.*

IT IS TWO HUNDRED MILES from Naples to Taranto, over winding mountain roads. The drive gave Bolan time to put his thoughts in order, gauge what he had managed to accomplish in the past few hours since their plane touched down in Rome.

Two capos down so far, and that would have the others double-checking their security precautions, trying to determine what was going on. Gang wars were nothing new in Italy, but this had come from nowhere, in a climate of prevailing peace, where mafiosi were more or less united against official enemies. The added strain should soon produce some cracks in the facade that hid the Star from public view.

The target in Taranto was Don Vito Altamura, age sixty-three, a pioneer in the Turkish-Italian heroin trade. Although he was suspected of complicity in over forty homicides, his only time in jail had been a six-month stretch for smuggling penicillin in the 1950s. Altamura's payoffs and political connections had kept him out of court in the meantime while he pursued his varied enterprises.

It was time for that to change.

Intelligence from Leo Turrin linked Don Vito to the Star in drug and arms transactions, recently including a shipment of Kalashnikov assault rifles from Romania, intercepted en route to Somalia. He was also a longtime confederate of Don Luigi Calo, a neighbor from Calo's home village in Sicily who had moved to the mainland and set up shop on his own while maintaining links to his criminal roots.

Don Altamura's office was a third-floor walk-up in a smallish building, two blocks over from the central plaza in Taranto. Bolan parked a block east of the entrance, checked in with Grimaldi via radio and locked the car before walking back to the office building. Underneath his coat, the sixteen-inch Beretta submachine gun with its 32-round magazine rode on a leather swivel rig. Spare magazines filled up an inner pocket on the other side.

He breezed in through the lobby, moved directly to the stairs, taking them two at a time. Two secretaries passed him on the stairs, reminding him that it was almost closing time. The target's car was parked outside, confirming he was still upstairs.

On the third floor he checked the numbers printed on a wall directory, turned left and made his way along the corridor toward Altamura's office. A lookout was posted on the door, and you could figure on at least a couple more inside the waiting room. It would be difficult if not impossible to take them prisoner, and Bolan didn't even try.

He drew the right side of his open jacket back, exposing the Beretta SMG as he approached the shooter. Registered the shocked expression on his adversary's young-old face. The guy reached for his side arm on the left side of his belt, a cross-hand draw, but he was starting out behind the game with no hope of catching up.

The short Beretta rattled off four parabellum rounds and slammed the gunner back against the wall. A smear of crimson was left behind him as he slithered down into a seated posture, dead eyes glazing over. Bolan kept on going, hitting the outer door with a resounding kick and following through.

Three soldiers in the anteroom, all standing in response to the sounds of gunfire from the outer hallway. Bolan caught them reaching for their weapons, knew he could not drop them all at once and started on his left, the nearest gunner seeming quickest on the draw.

He hit the shooter with a rising burst that lifted him completely off his feet and pitched him over on his back. The second guy in line was almost there, his fingers wrapped around the fat grips of an automatic pistol. Bolan stitched him with a burst across the chest and kept on firing as he swiveled toward the final target, wasting several rounds by choice, preferring it to lifting off the trigger and sacrificing his advantage when a heartbeat could be critical.

The last man up had drawn his pistol, tried to find his target, triggering a hasty round that smacked into a wall directly opposite. Before he got it right, the Model 12 homed in and nailed him, parabellum shockers staggering the gunman, blowing him away. He went down firing, plaster dust cascading down around him as he fell.

In lieu of pausing to reload the SMG, Bolan drew his side arm, rushing Altamura's private office. One more flying kick and he went through the doorway in a diving shoulder roll, prepared for anything.

A shotgun blast tore through the air above him, shattering the doorjamb. Bolan came up firing at a stocky gunner on the far side of the room, three rounds from his Beretta ripping through the target's chest and abdomen. The impact dropped him to his knees, the second barrel of his stubby weapon blasting a ragged hole in a nearby filing cabinet as he collapsed.

Don Vito Altamura crouched behind his desk, nothing showing but his eyes, woolly brows and the shiny dome of his pink bald head. He stood on Bolan's order, not quite trembling, barely holding it together.

Bolan didn't know if he spoke English, and he didn't care. He hadn't traveled all this way for conversation. There was nothing useful he could learn from Vito at the moment, and he had no time to waste.

The fat old man was pulling money from his trouser pockets, tossing it across the desk, trying to buy his way out of trouble as he had so often in the past.

It was an easy twelve or thirteen feet between them, hardly any need to aim, but Bolan took his time and did it right the first time. Arm fully extended, he sighted down the slide, stroking the trigger once and placing a parabellum round between Don Vito's eyes. The shiny head snapped back, an abstract pattern painted on the wall in crimson.

Done.

He could have torched the office, but it would have meant destroying other businesses and putting blameless people out of work. It was just as useful to leave the bodies where they lay, another for the police and mafiosi to consider while he was in transit.

Bolan's task was almost finished on the mainland. His next stop, once he reunited with Grimaldi, would be Sicily. Luigi Calo waited for him, even if the old man didn't know it yet.

Their time was coming. Maybe they would even have a chance to talk.

He hoped so anyway.

The warrior made his way downstairs and walked back to his car.

CHAPTER SEVEN

Salvatore Lucania had driven through the afternoon to reach Cosenza, keeping one eye on the Alfa's rearview mirror all the way. He was concerned about a tail, the prospect of assassination on the lonely road, but it wasn't enough to make him miss the meeting.

He had come too far and risked too much for that.

Lucania still felt somewhat guilty for the step that he was taking, but he seemed to have no choice. For three years now he had pursued his struggle through official channels, in the courts and legislature, but the progress he had registered so far was insubstantial. Every time a capo went to prison, there were others standing by to take his place. While editorials were quick to hail the Mafia's demise, Lucania found the criminal society was far from dead. If anything, it was expanding, changing into something worse, more sinister than in the past.

Within the past twelve months, there had been three attempts upon Lucania's life. The first had been a time bomb planted underneath the chassis of his car. Ironically Lucania had worked late that afternoon. The dynamite exploded when he should have been a mile from home, but he was still inside his office, seven floors above the parking lot. Downstairs the blast had slaughtered three pedestrians, including a young mother and her child.

The second effort to eliminate him was a drive-by shooting, near the Coliseum in Rome. The gunman had been nervous, trigger-happy, and he started firing prematurely, wounding several passersby and missing Salvatore completely. No one had been killed in that assault, but it was due to luck and negligence, with no thanks to authorities who failed on both occasions to arrest the men responsible.

The third and most recent attack had almost been a comedy of errors. After bombs and guns had failed, Lucania's enemies resorted to a primitive technique. The killer waited for Lucania on the street outside his office and attacked him with a dagger. Lucania had seen him coming, raised his briefcase to deflect the thrust and in doing so, disarmed his adversary. That accomplished, he had slapped the young man's face and chased him three long blocks through traffic till the would-be killer met his ride and vanished up a side street, trailing curses in his wake.

It flattered Salvatore Lucania that his efforts to destroy the Mafia—and now the Star—had moved his chosen enemies to strike with deadly force. It proved that he was doing something right through his affiliation with Italy's large anti-Mafia party. As a private lawyer, he had forged alliances with several law-enforcement agencies and legislators, pushing hard for prosecutions and new laws to drive the Honored Society out of existence. Each new victory was qualified and balanced out with losses somewhere else, however, and it seemed to him that he would never see the struggle won.

And violence had been escalating recently, with the assassination of some leading figures in the fight against the syndicates. It was not the fear of death in itself but knowledge that he might be killed with work undone that moved Lucania to take the latest drastic step.

He had reached out for help to the Americans.

It was no easy task, this circumventing of the law, when he had served the courts for almost fifteen years. In all that time Lucania had never once accepted bribes or stepped outside the bounds of recognized procedure for a client or himself. He paid his taxes, watched his speed when he was driving, looked both ways before he crossed the street. In time, however, the corruption that surrounded him had made a mockery of everything that he believed, all that he held dear.

He started small, refusing to accept the mafiosi who approached him as potential clients, later screwing up the nerve to represent those clients who were brave enough to file a case against their local capo for extortion, usury, harassment—not much more than a show of resistance. The threats began to filter in at that point, most of them directed at his clients. Even brutal mobsters realized that lawyers take whichever side they were paid to champion, with little real conviction.

This time, though, they had misjudged their man.

Lucania had started filing claims against the Mafia for nothing, letting other segments of his practice bear the weight until they withered on the vine. An early widower, he had no wife or children to be threatened by his newfound enemies. In time his one-man fight against the families of crime put him in touch with allies from Rome to Palermo. Their loose affiliation grew into a regular organization of sorts, soliciting donations to support the fight, pressing weak-willed legislators to present new laws, compelling prosecutors—often for the first time since war—to do their jobs.

Even though he saw some progress, even though the foreign press ran eloquent obituaries for the Mafia, Lucania was not deceived. He spoke with victims, lawyers and investigators every day. They told him how the syndicate was going underground, regrouping, finding brand-new allies overseas.

And reemerging as the Star.

Lucania had sounded the alarm in Italy, for all the good it did him. Journalists were skeptical, dismissing him as paranoid, employing snide references to James Bond and Professor Moriarty. The police, when they took any action, moved against the enemies they recognized from long exposure. It was not for them to contemplate a new alliance that would pit their slim resources and marginal manpower against criminals from Japan, Thailand, Colombia, the Middle East.

When the violence had resumed, more furious than ever, Salvatore Lucania knew that it was time to try a different angle of attack. He needed help that he would never find in Italy, perhaps nowhere in all of Europe.

He asked around through covert channels, friends in government and law enforcement who might have something for him off the record. Names were mentioned, phone calls made, with no immediate result. The man who finally met with Lucania outside the Ministry of Finance was young and nondescript, a self-described diplomat. American. It took no great deductive powers to decide that he was working for the CIA or some similar agency with private agendas and dollars to burn.

Lucania was worried at the outset, almost feeling like a traitor as he spoke to the American. But he had tried his fellow Romans first and they had shunned him, made him feel that he was talking to a wall. If the authorities in Rome could not—or would not—move against the criminals who undermined society, then someone else would have to do the job.

At first Lucania wasn't sure what form the help from Washington would take. There was an interim while new investigations were completed, fresh leads followed, and he had begun to think that he had wasted one more meeting, spilled his hopes and fears to one more bureaucrat who would ''consider'' what he had to say but take no action to relieve the problem.

Then, two nights ago, the word had come via a phone call to Lucania's home at 1:00 a.m. A voice he didn't recognize summoned Lucania to Rome's Terminal Station. Dawn was still an hour off when he'd picked out his bench and sat down to await the contact. The stranger was a tall man, middle-aged, with thinning salt-and-pepper hair. He'd smoked incessantly and spoke around his cigarette, eyes shifting constantly around the terminal in search of spies.

The stranger had told Lucania that help was coming from the States, a man who would do everything within his power to relieve the situation. When Lucania had questioned the ability of any single man to make a difference in the fight, his contact cautioned him to wait and see.

That morning, as he sat for breakfast, there had been another call. The now-familiar voice directed him to meet his unknown savior in Cosenza, after nightfall. He was on the road and driving south before he heard the news from Rome about Carmelo Magno, murdered in his garden. When the next announcement spoke of Vito Altamura and his soldiers, killed in Naples, Salvatore Lucania understood the kind of help he had been sent from the United States.

Or had he known it all along?

From childhood he had loathed the tide of violence that engulfed his homeland. Murders, bombings, kidnappings, assaults. At first the thought of stooping to that level had disgusted him, but there was yet another side to the debate.

When all else failed, and evil triumphed in the face of helpless, hopeless men, there might be no alternative to bloodshed.

Guilt bore down upon him like a physical weight, threatening to break him down, but Salvatore Lucania was enough of a realist to shrug off the feeling. He had not agreed to anything as yet; his hands were clean. If someone else acted without his approval, beyond his control, it was not for Lucania to chastise himself.

He would cope with that dilemma later, if he did cooperate with the outsiders, shifting the issue from the realm of theory to reality. Meanwhile, he drew a guilty sense of satisfaction from the knowledge that at least two ranking leaders of the Mafia—both men also associated with the Star—had been removed from circulation permanently.

Between them, Magno and Altamura had killed hundreds, perhaps thousands of people. Some of those had been thieves and butchers like themselves, while many others had been innocent, caught up in debt or the pervasive blood feuds that were still a scourge in rural Italy and Sicily.

Rough justice, then. The biblical measure of an eye for an eye.

He saw the last sign for Cosenza, brought his mind back to the mundane mechanics of navigation and driving. Through the outer residential district, winding toward the center of the town on narrow streets that teemed with foot traffic, passing an older car here and there. He found a parking lot constructed with the tourist trade in mind and locked the Alfa Romeo, walking with a cool breeze in his face to reach the lighted square. He dawdled past shop windows, more alert to those around him than the merchandise on show.

The thought occurred to him that this could be a trap, another effort to remove him from the scene, but he dismissed the possibility. There was too much "coincidence" involved—the Yankee voice that called him out, the sudden deaths of Magno and Altamura—for his outing to be rigged against him.

Which was altogether different from pretending there would be no danger.

From this point forward, every step he took would be fraught with peril. If he went along or tried to disengage, his life would surely be at risk.

But then, that was nothing new.

He stood before a bakery, smelling bread and cakes inside, aware of someone gliding up beside him. Tall and dark, this man. He might have been a native, but he scuttled the resemblance when he spoke.

"Let's take a walk," said the American.

HE RECOGNIZED LUCANIA from photographs, both posed and candid. One of them at least was fairly recent. It portrayed the anti-Mafia crusader with the same small lines now visible around the mouth and eyes.

"Who are you?" asked Lucania.

"A friend," the Executioner replied. "You came to meet me. Shall we walk?"

"Yes, please."

They covered half a block before Lucania spoke again. "Are you alone?"

"Depends," said Bolan. He wasn't about to tip his hand, much less reveal Grimaldi's role in the campaign.

"Of course," Lucania replied. "Security."

"We've got a lot of opposition," Bolan said.

"But less than yesterday," Lucania came back. "I have concern about the recent news reports from Rome and Naples."

"Not to worry," Bolan told him. "It's contained."

That was an exaggeration maybe, but it was close. As they proceeded, things would start to bleed together, ripples spreading in the stagnant pond until they overlapped and jostled one another into chaos. Troops from Rome and Naples were unlikely to come south, but he couldn't entirely rule it out.

"I had not planned on so much...blood," Lucania explained.

Of course not. No one ever read the fine print going in. Regardless of the mayhem that preceded a request for help, it always came as a surprise when bodies started dropping on the other side. It made the former victims pause and think about the cost of fighting fire with fire.

Some couldn't take the heat; they broke and ran. Others found they liked retaliating, answering aggression with force. A few lost track of who and what they were, became no better than the predators they sought to regulate.

The Executioner was not recruiting front-line allies for his war against the Star. He needed information, hard intelligence that would direct him to primary targets. If Lucania could help him, fine. If not, then he would have to stand aside.

"You're in a war," said Bolan, "and the other side has been inflicting all the damage lately. Are you feeling sorry for them now?"

Lucania frowned and shook his head. "I have no pity for these men," he said, "but I had hoped it would somehow be possible to wipe them out without becoming as they are."

"You're not the same," said Bolan, "and you won't be when the smoke clears. Motives matter, Counselor."

"I hope so, for my soul's sake." Then, when they had covered half a block in silence, Lucania asked, "How may I assist you?"

"Information," Bolan said. "You've done more work on local targets than my other sources."

"Targets." Salvatore Lucania pronounced the word as if he didn't fully understand its meaning—or as if it left a bitter taste behind. No great surprise for Bolan in that regard, since he was talking to a noncombatant.

"Call it what you like," said Bolan. "We're agreed the Star has grown beyond the government's ability—or willingness—to cope through channels, yes?"

Reluctantly the lawyer nodded. "Yes. So it would seem."

"And you're aware of how the stakes have grown." No question mark this time.

"I am."

His tone of voice and the expression on his face confirmed that he was up to speed on the most recent threat. The thought of mafiosi peddling nukes did not sit well with Salvatore Lucania, but neither did the notion of compiling what amounted to a death list.

"You've been studying Luigi Calo," Bolan prodded.

"From a distance, yes. He is the central link between the Star and members of the Mafia in Sicily. At first the link came through his Asian drug connections, later via men in Eastern Europe. It would not be inappropriate to say that Calo *is* the Star, at least so far as Europe is concerned. His orders are unquestioned from the Riviera to the Bosporus."

"It's safe to say he'd know where any stolen nukes were going, then," said Bolan.

"Certainly, if the transaction was conducted in this hemisphere."

Which meant that Bolan had to speak with Don Luigi Calo, somewhere down the road, before he pulled the plug. It sounded easy when you put the thought in words, but getting there would be another story. Sicily was not a fortress, but it may as well have been. Once Bolan set foot on the island, he would for all intents and purposes find himself behind enemy lines. The Mafia had permeated every part of daily life in Sicily, compelling friend and enemy alike to serve the men they feared.

A challenge—that was the way to approach it. He had visited the Mafia's homeland before and come out alive, but the capos had been on their own in those days, without resort to arms and allies around the world.

"What I need," said Bolan, "is a look inside the operation. Names and addresses to start, along with rankings and relationships. If they have any special operations in the works, we have a chance for leverage. Whatever costs them money in the short run helps get their attention."

"I can check my files," Lucania said, "my sources on the island. Don Luigi and his men are seldom idle."

"Fair enough. I want variety, if possible. We'll hit them anywhere we can."

Lucania glanced up at Bolan. "We?"

"Figure of speech," Bolan answered, shrugging it off.

Lucania let it go. "I have associates in Sicily," he said. "They should be able to supply the information we require."

"Okay." He made a mental list and ran it down. "I'll need ID and points of contact for as many members of Luigi's family as your people can identify. Include locations for their offices and playtime hangouts, any groups or corporations fronting for the mob. Arms caches, contraband supplies. Political connections, if they're firm. No guesswork on the officeholders, though. I can't afford mistakes."

"I'll see what I can do," Lucania said.

"How soon can we expect results?"

"Much of the information you require is readily available. I should be able to retrieve it on the telephone. As for the front groups, some of those may take a little time, additional research in public records."

"See what you can do," said Bolan. "I don't want to keep Luigi waiting any longer than I have to."

"It is dangerous for you to leave without the necessary information," said Lucania.

Bolan frowned. He knew that standing still was also perilous, now that the battle had been joined. His enemies were in the dark so far, but he couldn't allow his edge to be reduced by lethargy. Don Calo would be thrown off balance by the news from Rome and Naples, but he hadn't managed to survive this long or rise to dominance within the Mafia by standing still and letting new events roll over him. His soldiers would be fanning out across the countryside already, seeking answers, looking for someone to punish.

The Executioner's best shot, he knew, was to remain in motion, keep on pushing. If he gave Don Calo time to scope out what was happening, seal off the island and redouble his defenses, it would only make his task more difficult—perhaps impossible.

To some degree he had already yielded the advantage of surprise by striking on the mainland, but he felt the move was necessary and correct. Don Calo's first reaction, based on long experience, would be suspicion of a war within the Mafia, potential causes complicated by involvement with the Star. It was enough to make Calo hesitate at least, and even fleeting hesitation worked to Bolan's advantage. Once he made the crossing at Messina, got things rolling on the island, it would be a whole new ball game.

Let Don Calo focus on the strikes in Rome and Naples, seeking danger on the mainland while it settled in his own backyard. The capo would awake tomorrow in a world of hurt and find himself confronted with the struggle of his life. He would use every trick at his disposal, every weapon in his arsenal, to save himself. The Executioner did not deceive himself into believing that the odds were on his side.

Not yet.

But odds were only numbers, Bolan realized, and numbers were manipulated all the time. The human element was something else, and Bolan was a master at performing the "impossible." He knew what he could do with minimal support...but he was not about to take a long-shot victory for granted, either.

Anything could happen in the next few hours.

And before he made the crossing, Bolan hoped to skew the odds by giving Don Luigi Calo something more to think about, more leads to take him in the wrong direction.

"Can you get me the intelligence I need by midnight?" Bolan asked.

Lucania thought about it, nodding. "Yes, I think so."

"Fair enough. Same time and place."

The lawyer frowned, making a decision of his own. "I want to come with you," he said, "to Sicily."

Bolan thought about it for a moment, weighing possible advantages against the risks involved, uncertain whether he could stop the man in any case.

"Okay," he said at last. "Why not?"

Another ally, then, and Bolan hoped Lucania's choice of causes didn't get him killed before his time.

CHAPTER EIGHT

Bolan's presence in Cosenza was an open invitation to surprise the local capo mafioso with a visit while he had the opportunity. Tomaso Abandando was a veteran smuggler of narcotics, cigarettes and weapons, in and out of Italy, for close to twenty years. His Mafia associations had prevented him from serving any time or even facing trial, a circumstance that made him cocky, nurturing a sense of personal invincibility.

But he was not invincible.

He had a debt to pay, and it was coming due. In blood.

The house was a midsize Mediterranean style one-story stucco, with faded Spanish tiles on the roof. There was a wall of sorts around the property, waist-high constructed out of native stone, but nothing that would stop the Executioner.

He made a drive-by, noting sentries on patrol. One man was betrayed by the glowing ember of his cigarette, another cast in silhouette against the lighter background of the house. Two out of how many?

It wasn't a great concern to him. He was here and he would go ahead unless he met some hopeless obstacle at the last minute.

Bolan was in blacksuit when he parked the car and left it, gliding through the shadows like a wraith. He went with silent weapons: the Beretta underneath his arm, the Model 12-S submachine gun fitted with a thick suppressor for the power punch. If worse came to worst, he was also carrying several V-40 minigrenades of Dutch manufacture, half the size of standard-issue U.S. frag grenades with no significant reduction in killing power.

He went in from the south, checked out the ancient-looking wall for any new security devices, finding none in place. He scrambled over, careful not to make a sound, and homed in on the house, alert for lookouts as he crossed the rocky ground.

And met one when the house was still a hundred yards away, a young man, his lower body mostly screened by a clump of bushes, heading toward the house. Bolan held the sleek Beretta kissing-close and stroked the trigger once, a parabellum shocker entering the sentry's skull behind his ear. He went down, poleaxed, no time for a sound or a last thought.

The Executioner moved on, reduced the gap to forty yards and met another lookout walking post around the house. His target was too far away to guarantee surprise. It took a steady hand and all his concentration for a head shot, forty feet and counting, but the soldier went down like a rag doll, stretched out on his face.

It wouldn't be long before another sentry found his body and shouted the alarm. No time to dawdle, with the house so close that he could smell fresh coffee brewing in the kitchen.

He circled eastward, found a door unlocked and slipped inside. A washroom, dark and still, light visible from the direction of the kitchen. Soldiers on the night shift would stop in from time to time for coffee or snacks to keep themselves alert. It figured that the sergeant of the guard would be there, standing by in case one of his sentries sounded the alarm.

In fact, he found two soldiers in the kitchen seated at the table, facing one another. They were playing cards, and Bolan made no effort to distinguish which of them was boss. It made no difference to his purpose.

He had the Model 12-S locked on target acquisition when they noticed him and turned to gape at the dark apparition in the doorway. Both men went for their guns as Bolan held the trigger down and tracked from left to right across the table, rattling off a dozen parabellum rounds.

The gunner on his left had reached his pistol, but he never cleared the holster, flopping over backward in a spray of crimson, dead before he hit the floor. His comrade made the draw but didn't have a chance to fire before the SMG rounds stitched a line of holes across his chest and pitched him sideways from his chair.

He had to make a decision where to head next, but there was no time for deliberation. He went with instinct, moving through the kitchen, through an empty living room, along a corridor that led to bedrooms on the west. No sound or light from any of the rooms in that wing, and he swiftly doubled back, perhaps two minutes wasted on the search. The east wing had a library and study that would serve as an office when the capo didn't feel like going into town.

Bolan found his quarry in the study, lounging in a wing-backed chair of Moroccan leather. He was sipping brandy, smoking a cigar, oblivious to death before it stepped across the threshold, calling him by name.

"Don Abandando."

Shock was written on the mafioso's face. He glanced in the direction of a desk across the room, presumably where he would have a weapon stashed for such emergencies. Too far away. Too late.

"Who are you?" he asked in Italian, taking Bolan for a native.

Bolan knew the language well enough from his protracted struggled with the Mafia. "A soldier," he replied. "I've come for you."

"Who sent you?"

"Does it matter?"

"I have money," Abandando told him. "I will double your advance."

"No sale."

The capo bolted then, a fairly decent effort for a man his size and weight, but he couldn't outrun the stream of bullets issuing from Bolan's submachine gun. Jerking, spinning, going down, Abandando gave a strangled cry and landed on his back, a final tremor rippling through his body as he fell.

All done.

If Bolan could make his way back to the car without encountering the other guards, so much the better, but he was prepared for anything. Reloading on the move, he backtracked through the silent house to exit from the same door that had been his entrance.

The night was young yet, and Lucania would need some time to tap his sources on the island. Bolan had the time to spare and targets waiting for attention close at hand.

Next up was a veteran pimp, extortionist and loan shark in Paola, twenty miles due north along the coastal highway. Bolan was lighting fires and hoping they would spread, become a raging conflagration that consumed his enemies.

But he would have to take it one step at a time.

ENRICO ROSSI was a happy man. At forty-one, he had accomplished more than anyone who knew him from his native Florence would have thought a sickly child could ever manage. From poverty and petty crime, he had grown up to field a stable of three hundred fifty prostitutes while managing extensive covert loans and operating a protection racket that included shipping, trucking firms and the majority of local fishermen. Enrico Rossi taxed the local peasants like a feudal warlord, in the honored Mafia tradition, and if he was not the richest mobster in the southern part of Italy, at least he was well satisfied with what he had achieved so far.

The news so far this Sunday had been troubling, but it had no personal effect on Rossi. What was it to him if capos met untimely deaths in Rome and Naples? There was no retirement plan from the Honored Society. Every member realized that he was in for life, and many met their endings prematurely, from a bomb, a shotgun blast, a knife thrust on a crowded sidewalk.

Rossi knew all this and took precautions to protect himself. His bodyguards were always on alert, well armed, prepared for any challenge. In the seven years that he had ruled Paola, only two men had been rash enough to make attempts on Rossi's life. Both men were dead, cut down in storms of gunfire, no complaint from the authorities. Both cases had been clear-cut self-defense and it had done no harm that Rossi had the local homicide detectives in his pocket, mollified by years of hefty bribes.

Tonight, when he stepped out onto his patio, Enrico Rossi felt no apprehension for himself. The night was pleasant, warm enough that he did not require a sweater, and his sentries were on post around the grounds. It was a perfect night for lounging in his deck chair with a glass of wine to help relax him all the more.

Don Calo would be calling soon. It was surprising that he hadn't called already, but Rossi knew he must have pressing matters on his mind, and Rossi had no immediate contribution to make. The war that had begun in Rome and Naples earlier that day had nothing to do with his work in Paola. Rossi had his share of enemies, but if they found the nerve to fight, they would be coming after him, not sniping capos in the larger cities of the north.

In short, he could relax . . . at least until the summons came, requiring that he field a team of soldiers to assist Don Calo in resolving the dispute. If called upon, Enrico Rossi would cooperate, of course. It was the rule, and he was not averse to helping out his brother mafiosi.

They would do the same for him, if it should be required.

The wine was vintage claret, served at room temperature. Rossi's third glass, and he had begun to feel the effects, a mild euphoria that told him he had nearly had enough. When he finished with this glass, he would consider turning in.

No woman for him on this Sunday night. When he had started pimping, he was like a young boy in a candy store, eyes bigger than his stomach—or, in this case, bigger than his pecker. Not that any of the whores complained, for what he paid them. Over time, though, Rossi found that quantity and quality were not synonymous. He liked to pick and choose now, singling out the most attractive of his women, limiting himself to one encounter each. A weekend, normally, say once a month, and they would never speak again.

Separating business from pleasure.

Rossi drained his wineglass, was about to rise and go inside the house when something most extraordinary happened. Halfway to his feet, hunched over like an old man with a walker, Rossi saw his knee explode.

It was the right one, and it took a heartbeat for the pain to register. At first he saw the blood and bone, the mutilated flesh, felt something like a hammer stroke that numbed him for an instant.

Then the pain.

The flagstone patio rushed up to meet him, struck his cheek with force enough to make his ears ring. He could barely hear the echo of the rifle shot, but even through the crimson haze of agony, he recognized a bullet wound.

He wanted to scream for his guards, but no sound issued from his shocked body.

Then Enrico heard them coming and struggled partly upright, his weight supported on his hands and the one remaining knee. His ruined leg bled scarlet on the flagstones, dragging awkwardly behind him.

Rossi heard his soldiers firing—automatic weapons, shotguns—strafing shadows in the night without a clear-cut target. Somewhere back there in the darkness, a determined sniper aimed his weapon, going for the kill.

And Rossi missed the second shot entirely, barely felt its impact as the bullet drilled his skull and mushroomed, plowing through his brain behind a shock wave of expanding tissue, fluid, blinding light.

Behind the light came darkness, instant and immediate.

The darkness of the grave.

Go EASY, thought Grimaldi, talking to himself. Last thing I need right now is any hassle with the cops.

The two-man squad car passed him westbound from the central square of Catanzaro, and he watched the taillights dwindle in his rearview mirror, disappearing on a left turn two blocks down.

He let himself relax a bit but held his focus. He couldn't afford to let his thoughts go traipsing through the twilight zone. Survival—much less the successful execution of his mission—called for concentration on the task at hand.

His target was Don Franco Giardini, fifty-one next week, best known for his infiltration and corruption of Italian labor unions. Nothing moved on Catanzaro's docks unless Don Giardini got his cut, a list of "token" payments adding up to better than a million dollars in the average month. When shippers tried to do without his services, a strike blew up from nowhere and their cargo languished on the waterfront. If local stevedores resisted paying dues, demanding the advances that were promised to them, they had accidents. A nasty fall. A forklift run amok. A fuel leak suddenly ignited by a spark.

On Sunday nights, Grimaldi knew from covert sources, Giardini liked to spend a few sweet hours with his teenage mistress in the plush apartment where he kept her like a living doll. Because he was a married man with three young children, Giardini made a vague nod toward discretion on his Sunday outings, traveling with only two men to protect him on his journey into town.

Grimaldi knew where the apartment was and found it on his first attempt. He drove past and saw Don Giardini's black Mercedes parked outside, the driver and his backup seated in the front. It was a sloppy way to cover anyone assuming the apartment building had at least one other entrance, and Grimaldi said a silent prayer of thanks for negligence.

He drove halfway around the block and parked in the alleyway out back of the apartments. Locked the car and left it, moving through the darkness toward his destination. Underneath his jacket on a swivel sling was the Model 12-S submachine gun with silencer attached.

The back door to the small apartment house was locked. Grimaldi picked it, thirty seconds flat, and let himself inside. No elevator, but the place was only four floors, top to bottom. Giardini's squeeze was on the second floor, a suite of rooms that faced the street.

The door to Giardini's home away from home was locked, of course. Grimaldi had a choice to make, depending on where Giardini and his woman were most likely to be killing time in the apartment. If they were already in the bedroom, he could pick the lock with little risk, slip in and catch the mafioso with his pants down—literally. On the flip side, though, if they were in the living room, odds were that they would hear him—either fiddling with the latch or coming through the door.

It was a judgment call, and Grimaldi had little choice if he was going to complete his mission. He could either pick the lock or kick the door in, go in shooting like a wild man and to hell with consequences.

He chose the picks, first listened at the door, heard distant music playing on a stereo. Romantic stuff, light classical. If nothing else, the background noise would help to cover his approach.

A moment later he was finished, one hand on the doorknob and the other on his submachine gun. Ready. As he cleared the threshold, tracking with the SMG, Grimaldi found himself alone inside the stylish living room. The stereo was playing on its own, its lilting melody not quite covering the voices emanating from the open bedroom door.

Grimaldi closed the outer door behind him, crossed the living room and took up station in the bedroom doorway. Giardini kept the lights on, liked to see what he was doing, and Grimaldi couldn't blame him when he glimpsed the girl in profile. If she wasn't working as a model, it was either someone's oversight or her deliberate choice. In either case, she showed distinct enthusiasm for her present line of work.

Grimaldi cleared his throat, almost regretfully. The woman heard him first, glanced to her right with hooded eyes, then vaulted from the saddle, letting out a frightened scream. Don Giardini was a trifle slower on the uptake, red faced and panting as he turned to face the enemy.

He saw Grimaldi, saw the gun and knew that it could only mean one thing. The guy was wilting as he struggled upright, babbling to Grimaldi in rapid-fire Italian, mingling threats and promises without distinction.

He was bound to make a move, and Grimaldi was ready when he lunged in the direction of his clothing, draped across a nearby chair. The Model 12-S spit a

short, staccato burst, and Giardini slithered off the
mattress, dragging sheets and blankets with him as he
took a nosedive to the floor.

His playmate was about to scream again, but when
Grimaldi swung his SMG around, she reconsidered in
a hurry. She was a survivor obviously, and Grimaldi
gave her credit for performing under fire.

"You may not want to be here when the cops show
up," he told her in Italian, backing out of there and
moving swiftly toward the exit.

She was on her own, whatever happened next. No
way for her to tip the goons downstairs and have them
cut him off. Unless he stumbled on the steps and broke
his neck, Grimaldi had it made.

And what of Bolan?

Would he make it through to midnight and their
rendezvous, before they set off on a new and even more
exacting phase of the campaign?

Grimaldi wouldn't bet against the soldier yet, but it
could still go either way.

THE DRIVE to Reggio was uneventful, Bolan watching
out for tails and finding none. He was on schedule so
far, but it would only take a minor obstacle to throw
him off—or worse.

The mark in Reggio, a small town at the very toe of
Italy's boot, was Don Giuseppe d'Agostino. Sixty-five
years old and five foot four, two hundred twenty
pounds, he was an evil dwarf, immersed in the narcotics trade and professional strikebreaking since the end
of World War II. He had acquired his reputation as a
bantamweight assassin in the days before accumulated
wealth and love of pasta combined to make him "a
man with a belly." In this case it was both the literal

truth and a fair approximation of the Mafia's cliché for respect.

As such things went, Don d'Agostino was a relatively minor cog in the syndicate machine, but Bolan had the time and he was willing to exert himself a bit in the pursuit of lesser villains while he waited for Lucania to corral the necessary battlefield intelligence for Sicily.

The capo had a smallish home outside of town, but he spent three or four nights every week in the penthouse of Reggio's four-star hotel. In fact, d'Agostino owned the hotel, reserving the grand presidential suite for his personal use. Sometimes he brought a mistress there. More often he preferred to be alone, drink wine and watch imported movies on the VCR.

It was reported that he favored gangster movies from America.

A night alone for Don d'Agostino was not precisely that. He had a team of bodyguards in place, three men downstairs and two outside his suite. The downstairs men were easy to avoid once Bolan came in through the back. D'Agostino had them staked out in the lobby where they had the elevator covered, but they didn't watch the alley or the service stairs.

That careless oversight would cost their boss his life.

Bolan took his time on the stairs, no hurry, with more risk in noise than delay. Nine floors meant eighteen flights, and he could feel it in his legs when he reached the penthouse level, peering through a tiny window in the metal door.

No gunners were visible from where he stood, but they were out there. Bolan knew the entrance to the penthouse would be some fifty feet to his left, directly opposite the elevator. Figure that the guards were there, watching out for anyone who turned up uninvited. The stairs, he theorized, were seldom used and more or less forgotten.

Bolan hoped so, anyway.

He eased the silent Model 12-S submachine gun out from underneath his jacket, flicked the safety off and held it ready as he tried the doorknob. It was open, as required by fire and safety codes. The door was heavy but it made no sound as Bolan eased it open, stepped into the corridor, faced left and saw his adversaries lounging outside d'Agostino's door.

Both men were slumped in metal folding chairs, not talking at the moment, one of them about to doze. His sidekick punched him in the shoulder, and the weary watchman muttered something that was almost certainly a curse. The Executioner was closing on them when the nearer of the sentries glanced in his direction, blinked and saw death coming.

He was quick, but the folding chair defeated him. He had it cocked back toward the wall, and when he tried to rise the sudden shift in weight produced a lurching, sagging movement that prevented him from hauling out his side arm.

Bolan shot the gunner in the chest, three rounds from thirty feet, and saw him topple over on the pale beige carpet. His companion was still blinking sleep from his eyes as he made out the danger, reacting with sluggish reflexes and no time to clear his head.

The second 3-round burst took off his face and slammed him back against the wall. That kind of noise would warn Don d'Agostino if he was still awake, and Bolan knew he had no time to waste.

A sprint to reach the penthouse door, and he went through it with a flying kick. The living room was empty, one lamp burning as a night-light. Bolan kept on going, toward the spacious bedroom, where he found his quarry sitting up in bed, white hair disordered from the pillow, squinting toward his unknown enemy with eyes like chips of flint.

The old man did not plead; in fact, he did not even speak. His lips curled in a sneer, and d'Agostino spit in Bolan's general direction, one last gesture of supreme contempt.

The Model 12-S stuttered, six rounds slamming d'Agostino backward, bouncing him onto the mattress. Crimson marked the sheets, the stains like blossoms opening before the sun. A smell of death and cordite lingered in the room.

And it was time to go.

He still had time and enemies to kill before the rendezvous with Salvatore Lucania, and he was on a roll. The war machine was moving, crushing everything before it, but he knew enough to realize that victory was never guaranteed.

He had to fight for every inch of ground along the way, and you could never move ahead by standing still.

CHAPTER NINE

Some men of power, looking backward, claim that they had recognized their destiny in childhood. Don Luigi Calo didn't make that claim. His early years were marked by poverty. The present boss of bosses, who had moved beyond the Mafia itself to lend a hand when men of vision from around the world first met to organize the Star, was one who had always looked for opportunities and squeezed them dry, but he wasn't a seer or psychic.

If he had been, Calo told himself, he would have seen his present trouble coming and could have taken steps to head it off.

Too late for that, but there was still a chance to cut his losses, minimize the future damage. He would have to keep his wits about him, use the tools at his disposal swiftly and decisively while there was time remaining.

How much time?

To answer that, Don Calo had to first identify his enemy. No easy task, but he would do his best.

And in the meantime he would take strong measures to defend himself.

The tide of battle had been moving southward, starting out in Rome and rolling down the long Italian boot, each new eruption claiming lives of men whom he had known for years—some of them friends, all businessmen of proved talent in their chosen fields. The thing now was to find out who was killing them and why.

The question had no simple answer. Calo's comrades all were members of the Mafia, most of them dealing with the Star in recent ventures, and as such were subject to the normal risks that came along with any life outside the law. Vendettas were a fact of life for mafiosi everywhere; Sicilians came up from the cradle watching blood feuds decimate their families and neighbors. In the past Don Calo had emerged victorious from many struggles to the death, but he would never take such a victory for granted.

He had runners out already, asking questions, seeking answers. Was there trouble in the families that Calo didn't know about? If so, how had it happened? Who was finally responsible? Were members of the Star involved? Was Don Calo's latest plan in jeopardy?

Unlike some members of the criminal fraternity, Luigi Calo didn't gloat on acts of violence. He was ruthless and efficient when the need arose, untroubled by a conscience, but he took no pleasure in remembering the slaughter of his enemies. The definition of success, for Don Calo, was an operation that returned a profit with the minimum of difficulty.

Still, experience had taught him that reward was normally commensurate with risk. His latest operation had potential for fantastic profits, and it stood to reason that whatever trouble should arise from its pursuit would also be unusual. At that, Don Calo had been gratified to note how smoothly everything had run so far. The lift had been accomplished right on schedule, the cargo safely transferred into neutral territory and delivery to the customer arranged for one week in the future.

It could still go up in smoke, though, if he let the current problem run away from him.

To date, the information from the field was sketchy. No one seemed to know who was responsible for the attacks or if in fact the killings were related. Calo, for his part, couldn't believe that half a dozen ranking mafiosi had been killed by sheer coincidence in one day's time. The odds against such a bizarre coincidence were astronomical, almost beyond belief.

He started with the obvious. Someone must be responsible for the attacks, and it was easier to see the killings as a series of connected incidents than as a flurry of unrelated flukes. With that in mind, he had to screen a list of his potential enemies to search for those responsible.

The list was not extensive. First he thought of jealous mafiosi who had chosen to reject affiliation with the Star. Their days were numbered in the present climate, and while Calo could not absolutely rule out an attack from certain quarters, he believed that they were more concerned with salvaging their own decrepit families at the moment.

Greedy foreign members of the Star might be another possibility, intent on stealing Calo's thunder and his customers, but most of them seemed dedicated to the common cause. They had been working long and hard to make the network function smoothly, and it would defeat their purpose—not to mention draining off their treasuries—to start a shooting war among their newfound friends.

Don Calo briefly considered the Ukranians, unwilling donors of his latest merchandise, and just as swiftly put them out of mind. They no doubt had the physical capacity to seek revenge, but tracing his associates to

Italy—much less effecting a reprisal on such unfamiliar ground—was far beyond their capability.

Another possibility, Don Calo thought, involved the would-be customers whose bids had not been high enough on this round to win the precious cargo for themselves. Some of them were described as terrorists in news reports and clearly had no qualms about resorting to the kind of violence lately witnessed on the mainland. Others represented lawful governments, but they were no less prone to using terrorism when it met their needs. Such tendencies aside, however, it made little sense for them to launch a shooting war against the Star when they could better spend their time collecting money for a future bid on new supplies.

What of the activists who pledged themselves to drive the Mafia from Italy? So far, they had confined themselves to lawsuits, legislation and the like. Some protest marches and petitions, nothing that would smack of violence—even when their spokesmen were eliminated by time-honored means. If they were suddenly inclined to change their tactics, they would first need more effective leadership.

None of the options seemed convincing, and Calo was compelled to face the prospect of a new, unknown opponent. It was disturbing that a stranger, and even more so if he didn't work alone, could operate with such impunity on Calo's native soil.

Still, they had not encroached on Sicily as yet, and that would be a very different game.

If anyone approached Don Calo on his private hunting ground, they would regret it while they lived.

And that, he told himself, would not be long.

IF MAINLAND ITALY is pictured as a giant boot, the village of Crotone lies near the arch, south of Sibar and east of Catanzaro. Fishing is the major legal industry, but smuggling holds an equal place in the economy, albeit more respected in some quarters since the income earned from contraband is tax-exempt. Hashish and opium have passed this way, along with military hardware, fugitives from justice, boys and women sold to harems in North Africa.

Demand for products varied, but the profit motive always ruled, and Don Pietro Maggiore took his share of each transaction off the top. He was a broker more than anything, but he wasn't afraid to kill in the defense of what had grown into a very lucrative concern.

Don Maggiore's villa faced the sea, a cliff-top home that offered him a panoramic view of his potential markets to the south. His wife and children lived a few miles inland in a second, larger home constructed with the profits from illicit business deals. Maggiore liked his privacy from time to time, while clinging to the public image of a family man.

The cliff-side house had two approaches—either from the highway, watched by bodyguards, or from the south, which meant a walk along the stony beach and climbing several hundred feet on trails that would have felt more comfortable to a mountain goat. Considering his options, Bolan chose the latter angle of attack and came in on the mafioso's blind side, taking full advantage of the night.

Don Maggiore's soldiers didn't watch the cliff, assuming no one in his right mind would attempt that approach. Crotone had been untouched by internecine combat during recent years, encouraging Maggiore and his men to drop their guard.

Tonight that laxity would work against them and to the Executioner's advantage.

Bolan watched his step along the narrow trail, leaning forward to balance himself on the climb. A slip from here would send him crashing to the rocks below—not dead, perhaps, but crippled, helpless when the tide came in at dawn.

But nothing happened, and he reached the top unnoticed, without incident. A quick check of the grounds showed no guards in evidence, and he was moving toward the house with the Beretta Model 12-S cocked and ready in his hands.

No opposition as he came in on the south side of the house. The nearest door was locked, and Bolan used the blade of his stiletto, slipped the latch and made his way inside. The door snicked shut behind him, and he started moving through the silent, darkened house.

He heard a shower running, tracked the sound through empty rooms and hallways, gliding toward the master bedroom and connecting bath. Lights burned in the bedroom, but no one was there to greet him. The sheets were turned back, waiting for Don Maggiore to retire.

Bolan passed the king-size bed and homed in on the bathroom, leading with the SMG. He nudged the door back with his toe, steam curling from the shower, condensation beaded on the mirror. Bolan saw his target dimly through a door of frosted glass. Maggiore must have felt the change as Bolan entered, something in the air, because he switched the shower off and slid the door back far enough to peer around the corner.

There was nothing to discuss, and Bolan saw him winding up to shout an SOS. The guards outside would have a hard time hearing him, but there was no point taking chances. Bolan squeezed the trigger, stitched a line of holes across the frosted door and slammed Pietro Maggiore back against the wall of dripping tile. Blood spouted, mingled with the suds and water swirling down the drain. A second burst collapsed the shower door, and Maggiore toppled forward, lunging from the stall like a demented stuntman trying one last gag.

Time was running as Bolan stood there, staring at the pallid corpse. Out front were an unknown number of guards, but maybe he wouldn't have to tangle with them. He would leave as he had come, invest a few more moments to avoid potentially disastrous confrontation.

He had done what he'd set out to do with Maggiore in Crotone, but he was not done yet.

THE MEETING had gone well enough. Salvatore Lucania was satisfied with the information he had received, and his sources were content to speak with him as long as their identities remained secure. In Sicily these days, a loose word was enough to get you killed . . . but then again, what else was new?

For one thing, it appeared that leaders of the Mafia were marked as targets for the same kind of violence they normally inflicted on others. It was poetic justice of a sort, but Lucania was still uneasy with his own role in the drama.

The American hadn't been idle—that was obvious. While Lucania was gathering the latest information on the Star in Sicily, five more capos had been killed in southern Italy, together with a number of their soldiers. There was no doubt whatsoever in his mind as to the man responsible—if not for the actual killings, at least for the overall plan.

In all his years of struggling against the Mafia, it had never once occurred to Lucania that he would follow this course, immersing himself in the violence of his enemies. Now he was surprised to find that the concept—while still a bit unnerving—no longer appalled him.

He had yet to pull a trigger himself. Lucania didn't know if he could bring himself to kill in self-defense, much less as an assassin, coldly and deliberately. The strange thing was that he no longer found the notion of associating with a killer absolutely horrifying.

People change, he knew, but this had the potential of a quantum shift.

He had driven by the house in Cosenza where Tomaso Abandando had been executed. The police were everywhere, lights flashing on their Lancia patrol cars, automatic weapons on display. Too late for Anbandando, but they had a job to do.

As if they really thought the killing would be solved.

It was a joke, of course. Convictions in gang-related murders were few and far between, invariably removing low-level triggermen from the streets while their masters went on as before. It made no difference in the end, since killers were—as the Americans would say—a dime a dozen.

Driving on, the blue lights fading in his rearview mirror, he considered the decision that would take him into Sicily within a few short hours, joining the American who called himself Belasko on a mission that could well result in death for one or both of them. He could as easily have turned around and driven back to

Rome, but how would he have faced himself tomorrow or the days after?

A wind of change was blowing through his native land, and it would without a doubt leave destruction in its wake. What followed was a question that couldn't be answered from the sidelines utilizing guesswork. Salvatore Lucania wanted—needed—to be present when the tide of history began to turn.

Perhaps it was a bit of self-indulgence, but he couldn't turn away, regardless of the cost.

He had a list of names, addresses, corporations and financial institutions, linked behind the scenes in a web of corruption that stretched beyond Sicily, beyond the Italian mainland, to the distant corners of the earth. How much could the American accomplish, on his own or otherwise, before his time ran out? Could Salvatore Lucania help in any concrete fashion or would he become an obstacle, a stumbling block?

The lawyer checked his watch against the dashboard clock, confirmed that he had ninety minutes left before his scheduled meeting with Belasko, after which they would be off to Sicily. He wondered fleetingly if either one of them would make it out alive.

Or if that was the crucial question in the last analysis.

A positive result was worth the sacrifice—worth *any* sacrifice. The Star had moved beyond mere criminal activity and government corruption into sponsorship for acts of terrorism that could ultimately threaten life on earth. The network's mercenary motive was irrelevant. The end result was all that mattered, and he couldn't think about the syndicate these days without imagining a giant mushroom cloud that blotted out the sun.

What was his life worth in comparison to that?

"I'VE GOT THE BACK," Grimaldi said, and thumbed the safety off his Model 12-S submachine gun.

"Give me five," said Bolan, double-checking the suppressor on his own buzzgun.

"Five's cool."

Grimaldi stepped out of the car and made his way across the street. The dark mouth of an alley swallowed him, and he was gone.

Lamezia Terme was Bolan's last stop prior to doubling back and meeting Salvatore Lucania at midnight. He was parked across the street from La Trattoria, a social club that doubled as headquarters for Don Giovanni Piliero, a middle-ranking capo with a stake in gambling and vice.

In other circumstances Bolan might have passed Piliero by, but he was looking for a final tag before he made the move to Sicily and faced the dragon in its den.

He crossed the street, pushed through the entrance, ready when the doorman moved to intercept him. Bolan let him see the submachine gun, giving him a choice. The soldier made his pick, went for his pistol, and the Model 12-S spit a silent 3-round burst into his chest at point-blank range. He went down kicking, and the way was clear.

There were a dozen soldiers in the club, most of them sipping wine and smoking as he entered. Don Piliero and his *consiglieri* had a table to themselves, back near the kitchen.

Bolan didn't need to check his watch. Grimaldi would be coming in the back at any moment, primed to back his play. The time was now, and it was do-or-die.

He switched the SMG's selector switch from 3-round bursts to automatic, went in firing from the hip. His nearest targets never saw him coming, swept away by parabellum manglers in a rush, their table going over with a brittle crash of glass.

Two down, and Bolan kept on tracking, held the trigger down. The other mafiosi recognized their danger and they were scrambling for the nearest cover, diving out of chairs, inverting tables, each man going for his weapon. On the far side of the tavern, Don Piliero was retreating toward the kitchen, looking for an exit through the back.

He ducked behind a nearby pillar, heard a pistol bullet smack into the wood, immediately followed by another. Every moment he delayed would give his adversaries time to organize and concentrate their fire.

Bolan palmed a V-40 mini grenade, yanked the pin and backhanded the frag bomb toward the middle of the spacious room. No aiming necessary, in the circumstances. When the blast came seconds later, Bolan made his move.

He broke out on the left, went low, the submachine gun seeking targets, spitting short precision bursts. He caught one mafioso reeling from the shock wave of the blast, blood streaming from his scalp, and dropped the guy before he could recover. Sweeping on, he found a second on his knees and drilled him, slammed him over on his back.

All hell broke loose inside the club, with the survivors pumping bullets randomly, few of them with any grasp of where their target was or what was happening. It made things easier for Bolan, but he had to keep his head down, knowing that a stray round through the head or heart was every bit as deadly as a well-aimed shot.

He rolled behind a capsized table, fed another magazine into his SMG. How many of the opposition down so far? It was a futile exercise in speculation while he still had bullets swarming overhead, and Bolan let it go.

Another frag grenade, the last one he had carried with him from the car. He pitched it overhand, in the direction of the bar, and ducked back under cover in a heartbeat. Counting down.

The blast stung Bolan's ears and rocked the table that was serving as his barricade. One of the mafiosi started screaming, pained and breathless. Bolan took the opportunity to break from cover, firing left and right.

The nearest gunner soaked up several rounds and went down in an awkward sprawl. The next in line was running for the cover of the bar when Bolan caught him with a burst between the shoulder blades and dropped him on his face.

He rose and started for the kitchen, met a soldier rising up from cover just in front of him. The young man had a shiny automatic in his hand, tried bringing it around to target acquisition, but he never had a chance. The Model 12-S stuttered, took the left side of his face off, spinning him away. Blood everywhere, the floor slick underneath his feet.

Away to Bolan's right, a pair of gunners rose and bolted toward the exit, running for their lives. He spun to cover them with the Beretta SMG and held the trigger down, expending half a magazine before he swept them off their feet, all tangled arms and legs as they went down together in a heap.

Was it too late for Piliero?

Bolan sprinted for the kitchen, burst through the swinging doors and stopped short with the muzzle of a submachine gun pointed at his face.

"That's close, man," Jack Grimaldi told him, lowering the gun.

Between them, stretched out on the floor, Don Giovanni Piliero wasn't going anywhere. The capo had a dazed expression on his face, eyes glassy, focused on a point somewhere beyond the ceiling, maybe miles above the earth.

What had he seen before the lights went out?

"They had a couple guys out back," Grimaldi said. "We're clear, though."

"Time to roll," said Bolan.

"Roger that."

They walked back through the tavern charnel house, examining the bodies only as potential threats, in case one of the gunners might still be alive. Relaxing slightly when they reached the street, they checked both ways for witnesses or passing cars, then jogged back to their waiting vehicle.

"I guess we made some waves tonight," Grimaldi said as he slid in behind the wheel.

"I'd say."

"You figure Don Luigi's got the welcome mat laid out?"

"I wouldn't be a bit surprised."

"Rough going, Sarge."

"With any luck he won't expect us quite this soon."

But luck was nothing they could count on, Bolan knew. A soldier made his own luck as he went along, and it would be a grave mistake to count on any favors dropping from the sky.

The only way to victory was straight ahead, and screw the risk.

"Let's keep that date," Bolan stated.

"Rolling," said Grimaldi as he put the car in gear.

CHAPTER TEN

Grimaldi parked behind a panel truck, switched off the compact's engine, set the brake. He locked the driver's door behind him and moved toward the stairwell that would take him to the ferry's upper deck. He bought his ticket at the cashier's booth and stuffed it in his pocket, moving past the snack bar to the outer deck, a place against the rail.

The ferry ride took twenty minutes once they pulled out from the dock. Grimaldi watched the cars and vans queued up to board, saw Salvatore Lucania's Alfa Romeo in line, creeping forward a yard at a time, following directions from the steward down below.

Bolan was driving across at Messina, but Grimaldi and Lucania had taken the ferry on his instructions, dividing their force to make it harder on their enemies. They would meet in Taormina, midway down the coast, and take the game from there. The target lay before them, waiting.

First, though, thought Grimaldi, they had to find out what that target was.

Luigi Calo held the key, and that made things more difficult to start with. It was no longer simply a matter of identification and elimination. They would have to grill Don Lucania if they could, and take the battle one step further. Sicily was a stop on the road, but it wasn't the end.

Not by a long shot.

They were nearly finished loading down below, the last few vehicles rolling on board and finding their places, engines switching off as soon as they were squared away. The loading ramp came up and locked in place, big diesels thumping as propellers churned the water into foam. The ferry started forward, lurching twice before it started making steady progress. Grimaldi felt the salt breeze in his face. It made a refreshing change, but he knew it was only a respite, a brief lull in the action.

When they landed on Sicily, they would be jumping from the frying pan into the fire. The trick, Grimaldi realized, would be to keep from getting burned.

He glanced around the deck, picked out a dozen-odd companions lined up at the rail. Ahead of them, due west, their island destination was a darker silhouette against the velvet night. Stars overhead, and pale lights winking from Catania on the coast.

Grimaldi focused on the lights, imagining the locals as they went about their business: working, drinking, stealing, making love. How many even had a clue that death was coming to their island? Would they care or were they so accustomed to the violence from generations past that it would make no difference to their daily lives?

Don Calo knew by now, of course—or he suspected anyway. A man in his position, boss of bosses in the Mafia and founding father of the Star, didn't last long unless he had a knack for smelling trouble in the wind, preparing traps to bag his enemies. Their mainland raids were all the warning he would need, but he could not know their schedule yet.

Not unless somebody gave him a clue....

The lawyer was a wild card, in Grimaldi's view. He had been working hand in hand with Interpol and DEA, but that didn't ensure that he was altogether straight. In Italy—much less in Sicily—a long tradition of subservience to mafiosi made it difficult to tell the players apart without a program . . . and even the programs were suspect when you thought about it long enough.

Grimaldi had no reason to suspect Lucania off the bat, but trust was a commodity in short supply. Grimaldi used it sparingly and never on a total stranger, even when the brass was sold on a particular approach.

The truth was that the brass was free and clear when bullets started flying. Grimaldi would be up there on the firing line—or close enough to see his best friend catching hell, in any case. Before he bet his life on someone else, he wanted time to check them out and see what they were made of.

Several minutes later, when Lucania came on deck, Grimaldi tracked him to a bench up near the prow. The pilot kept his distance, watching out to see if anyone was covering their contact, paying more attention to him than a stranger would to anybody else.

So far, it looked as though he was clear.

Grimaldi knew a little of the lawyer's history as it had been recorded in the Justice files, but it could still be bogus or mask for something else. The fact that he had lost his wife, apparently through violence, did not mean that he was straight. Bad guys had wives and children, too; some of them wandered into cross fires now and then.

For the moment Grimaldi was content to wait and see, but if the moment came when he felt Salvatore

Lucania was about to jeopardize their mission, much less his or Bolan's life, he would remove the threat.

By any means necessary.

IT WAS THE WAITING Marco Giuliani hated most of all. Despite the danger, he preferred the heat of combat to the phony war of watching, listening and spying, waiting for the other shoe to drop.

Don Calo was undoubtedly correct in his belief that the enemy—those responsible for the assassinations on the mainland—would be coming soon. And the sooner the better, for Giuliani's taste. He welcomed the chance to meet and dispose of the men who had slaughtered his friends and associates with such disrespect.

First, though, the enemy would have to be identified. For all their digging, all the questions they had asked so far, they still had no idea whom they were dealing with or what had prompted the attacks in Rome, in Naples and farther south.

Giuliani had a few ideas, but they were strictly negative. He was convinced that the attacks did not suggest a war within the Honored Society or the Star. There were always petty jealousies, of course, but he could think of nothing—no event, no argument—that would have sparked carnage on this scale.

Which meant that it was someone else, from the outside.

The night drive to Catania was a gamble in Giuliani's opinion, but he did as he was told, sent men to watch the land bridge at Messina and went on to check the ferry with another team.

The problem was that none of them had any clear idea whom they were looking for. How many gunmen were involved in the mainland attacks? Were they Italians or outsiders?

Always questions, begging answers.

Marco Giuliani was a man of action. When he faced a problem, Giuliani liked to grab it by the throat and squeeze until the problem was no more. It worked on animals when he was small, and later on with people when he started to assert himself around Palermo as a thug with promise. Don Luigi Calo had been younger then, already marked for greatness in the Mafia. Calo recognized a young man with potential and adopted Giuliani—first as an errand boy, later as a soldier and assassin, finally elevating him to the status of his second in command.

Giuliani had lost track of all the men—and women, too—whom he had destroyed on Don Calo's orders. Giuliani had not killed them all himself, of course. They had an army these days, standing by to carry out the capo's orders instantly, no questions asked. When there was killing to be done, the soldiers took their cue from Giuliani or from one of his lieutenants. On occasion—rarely, granted, but it happened—Giuliani called for an assassination on his own and justified the matter afterward, in private conversations with Don Calo.

Thus far, he had never been mistaken on a call, had never failed to make his case and justify the slayings ordered on his sown initiative. Don Calo trusted Giuliani with his business and his life, a special tribute in the grim Sicilian atmosphere, where treachery was commonplace.

For all their talk of honor and respect, it was a fact of life that mafiosi stabbed each other in the back repeatedly, almost predictably. Few capos died of old age or disease. Most were eliminated by subordinates, the very men they trusted to protect them, carry out their orders and defend their families. A truly loyal lieutenant, then, was worth his weight in uncut heroin.

Giuliani sat in the passenger seat of a black Mercedes Benz and watched the ferry from the mainland drawing closer, like a sluggish whale. The docking crew was standing by, some of them sipping coffee out of paper cups, some smoking cigarettes.

"What are we looking for?" the driver asked.

Giuliani thought about it for a moment, wondering how he could possibly respond without appearing ignorant. It seemed impossible, but he did his best.

"We're watching out for anything suspicious," he replied. "You know about the trouble on the mainland."

Nothing from the driver or the soldiers in the back. Of course they knew about the killings. Why else were they sitting out here in the middle of the night?

"Suspicious persons," Giuliani said, and desperately hoped he didn't sound ridiculous. "From the reports we have received, it seems that several men must be involved. Groups traveling together, then, or anyone you recognize from past experience."

The ferry was already within a hundred yards of docking, and Giuliani nodded to his soldiers. Instantly the three of them got out and started for the dock, where they would take positions on the sidelines, closely scrutinizing each and every vehicle that left the ferry. Giuliani personally thought it was a waste of time and knew his soldiers shared that view, but they would do as they were told.

It was a long shot anyway, this hope of spotting a familiar face or picking out an unknown adversary by the type of car he drove. If Giuliani was correct, their enemies would be too clever for a simple watchdog operation to detect them. They would find their way to Sicily by one means or another, make their presence known when they were ready. Only then, when fresh blood had been shed, would Giuliani and his soldiers have a chance to run them down.

He was looking forward to it now, another chance to prove himself, cement his role as Don Calo's heir. It would be tragic if the gunmen found his capo first, accelerating Giuliani's path to power.

Tragic, yes . . . but not entirely unexpected.

Something more for him to think about while he was waiting, watching.

And the prospect made him smile.

IT WAS PUSHING 2:00 a.m. when Bolan crossed the land bridge from Villa San Giovanni to Messina, taking his time and watching the mirror for any sign of a tail. He didn't have the highway to himself even at that hour. There were transport trucks and delivery vans abroad already, running back and forth between the island and the mainland, making ready for another day of business as usual.

For some, however, the routine was headed for a drastic change.

He half expected an official roadblock on the bridge, but there was nothing in the way of uniforms to slow him down. That didn't mean that he was in the clear, however. Bolan's greatest danger emanated not from the police, but rather from Luigi Calo's private army.

Spotting them would be more difficult, and Bolan knew that it could be a grave mistake to appear too inquisitive. He was supposed to be a normal traveler, perhaps on business or a holiday. With that in mind, he would appear suspicious—draw unwelcome notice to himself—if he appeared too interested in other vehicles or motorists.

He had to stay cool and forget about the military hardware he was carrying: the heavy gym bag on the floor behind his seat, more weapons in the Fiat's trunk. He had free access to his tools if an emergency arose, but he didn't anticipate an ambush on the open highway.

Don Calo's men would have to know whom they were looking for, and they were in the dark at this point, or so he hoped.

Lucania had given Bolan all the raw intelligence he needed for the blitz in Sicily, but that sword cut both ways. The information was derived from contacts, any one of whom might turn around and sell Lucania out—which meant, in turn, that Bolan and Grimaldi would be jeopardized.

It would have suited Bolan's purpose if the lawyer had returned to Rome, but he couldn't deny the possibility that Lucania might still be useful in the house ahead. His personal crusade against the Mafia had placed Lucania in touch with various officials and civilians who were dedicated to elimination of the criminal conspiracy that held their nation in a grip of fear.

In normal circumstances Bolan did his best to keep noncombatants at a distance from his war, but it wasn't always possible, especially when the bystanders had chosen to involve themselves by independent action. Crusaders had a way of drawing danger to themselves, like human lightning rods.

This time around, the Executioner decided, the phenomenon might help him in at least two different ways.

First up he had a source of information he could call on, through Lucania, if the need arose. And second Don Luigi Calo had a list of suspects waiting that would help distract him from the real source of his problems as the day wore on.

Beyond a certain point the jeopardy to noncombatants was their own concern, and even "Sergeant Mercy"—as he had been known in Southeast Asia—could not take responsibility for everyone who placed himself in harm's way. It was a burden he had tried to carry in the early campaigns of his private war, but it had grown too heavy over time, and Bolan came to realize that sometimes those who go in search of danger have to watch out for themselves.

Across the bridge he spied a Lancia sedan off to his left, a pair of hard-eyed men in casual dress lounging against the car. At a glance there was nothing peculiar about them, two friends engaged in conversation, maybe waiting for something . . . or someone in particular.

Bolan made a point of ignoring the soldiers as he passed, no sidelong glance to betray his interest before he rolled past them and into the outskirts of Messina. The city welcomed Bolan, swallowed him, and he could only hope the Fiat with its single passenger had looked mundane enough to throw the lookouts off their guard.

If not, would they be after him? Could they afford to leave their post unguarded, or would one of them be on the two-way radio already, beaming word ahead, a backup team prepared to intercept him?

Bolan watched his mirror, watched his speed, saw nothing that would justify a run for cover. Lacking evidence of hot pursuit, he would proceed to Taormina as planned, meet Grimaldi and Lucania on schedule. There was no good reason to expect the worst before a shot was fired in anger on the island, even though he knew the worst was surely coming somewhere down the road.

The last thing Bolan needed at the moment was to borrow trouble for himself when he had so much waiting in the wings.

It was still dark, but he could recognize the rocky landscape from his previous campaign in Sicily, the coastal highway leading southward from Messina toward his short-term destination. Driving put his mind at ease to some extent, gave Bolan time to think before the shooting started and he had to run on instinct all the way.

The quiet times were swiftly running out, he knew.

The only question left was whether he would survive to see the sun set on another day.

GRIMALDI HAD the lawyer covered when he walked into the restaurant and took a table by the window, where he had a clear view of the street. Lucania settled in and ordered breakfast, seeming not to pay attention to the traffic flowing past. In fact, Grimaldi knew the man was watching out for anyone who might turn out to be a threat.

Which, in the present circumstances, narrowed down the field to nearly everyone in town.

Another fifteen minutes slipped away before he saw the fiat coming, Bolan at the wheel. It pulled into the café's smallish parking lot, and after locking the driver's door behind him, Bolan moved toward the restaurant with easy strides.

Grimaldi left his car and crossed the street, pushed through the door a yard or so behind his oldest living friend. Lucania was waiting, tracking Bolan's progress toward the table, and he looked surprised when Grimaldi pulled up a chair to join them, settling in without an introduction.

"Who is this?" Lucania asked, concerned enough to scuttle the amenities.

"A friend," said Bolan. "He's been watching over you since you got on the ferry."

"Ah." The lawyer nodded, frowning. "A familiar face. I see that now."

"No tails?" The question was directed to Grimaldi.

"None that I could see."

"All right, then. Let's get started, shall we?"

"Yes," Lucania said. "We have no time to spare, with all that's happened."

"Fair enough," said Bolan. "We'll be splitting up from here." He nodded toward Grimaldi as he spoke. "You need to find a place where you can miss the line of fire and still be handy. Do your contacts know you're coming?"

"Yes," Lucania replied.

"And us?" the Executioner inquired.

"I told them nothing." If the lawyer was insulted, he concealed it well. "They think that I am visiting on party business. It is more or less correct."

"Will they be getting hinky when the fireworks start?" asked Bolan.

"Hinky?"

"Suspicious," Grimaldi explained.

Salvatore Lucania considered it and shook his head. "They are accustomed to such things," he said. "Not quite the same, perhaps, but still..."

He let it go at that, not asking where they planned to launch the first strike on Don Calo's island empire.

Not that Bolan would have told him had he posed the question. It had been Lucania's role to get them started and provide a list of targets. He had done so, but it didn't mean that he was automatically entitled to a full itinerary.

In fact, Grimaldi knew what was coming. They had discussed it on the mainland, parceling the targets out between them and selecting which would need two men for ample coverage.

Security.

The waitress brought their food, and there was little more to say as they dug in. Ten minutes later, sipping coffee over empty plates, Grimaldi knew that it was almost time to go.

Whatever lay ahead, he had to put his faith in Bolan...and himself. Grimaldi knew what he could do in battle, from experience. He felt more comfortable in an aircraft, granted, but he was no stranger to decisive confrontations on the ground. As for the Executioner...well, he had served with Bolan long enough to trust the man implicitly. If Bolan told him that the moon was made of sponge cake, then Grimaldi had a fair idea of what was on the menu for dessert.

Meanwhile his mind was focused on the main course, and no matter how he tried to slice it, it came up blood rare.

"I should be going," said Lucania.

"Seems right," the Executioner replied.

The lawyer rose, withdrew a wad of lire from his pocket, dropping several bills beside his plate. He put the rest away, fished in another pocket and withdrew a slip of paper.

"You can reach me at this number," he told Bolan, "night or day."

"Safe trip," said Bolan.

"And the same to you," Bolan replied. "Just now I think you need more help than I do."

"We'll get by," Grimaldi said. And wondered if it was the truth.

The lawyer left them, then, a short walk to the exit and out to his car. Grimaldi watched him go, more idle curiosity than anything. They would have been attacked by now if anyone had spotted them or figured out their mission on the island.

They still had time, but it was running short. Once battle had been joined, there would be no turning back, no margin for reflection on the course of action they had chosen for themselves.

"All ready?" Bolan asked him.

"Ready as I'll ever be."

"Okay, let's get it done."

Grimaldi followed him outside. They separated on the sidewalk, with Bolan heading for the parking lot while Grimaldi walked back across the street. There was no sign of Salvatore Lucania, and that was fine.

They had enough to think about without him.

They were off to get it done or die in the attempt.

CHAPTER ELEVEN

Don Calo's front man in Milazzo was Alfonse Mantova, forty-two, a pimp and triggerman with five years' prison time behind him on the mainland. He had kept his mouth shut in the joint and earned his just reward on getting out. The duty in Milazzo was supposed to be a sinecure—some smuggling runs from time to time, but little else that called for more than sipping wine and counting tax-free lire in the shade.

It had been nearly ten years since Mantova personally pulled the trigger on a man, and eighteen months since he had sent his soldiers out to kill. There was no danger in Milazzo these days, not with Don Calo firmly in control.

Until today.

The Executioner approached Milazzo from the east, with sunrise coming on. He drove the limit and a little more, no sign of traffic officers along the highway where he let the fiat's mill unwind. The dashboard clock reminded him that he was on a schedule, with Grimaldi counting on him to perform his tasks on time. There was a built-in margin of error, but Bolan wasn't anxious to test it.

Smooth running was the only way to go if he had any choice at all.

A mile outside Milazzo, Bolan took a side road off the highway, winding back through rocky foothills interspersed with olive groves. He took it slower here, aware that he was out of place and subject to the gaze of prying eyes.

Another mile, and Bolan started looking for a place to hide the car. The orchard offered several likely places, and he settled on a one-lane track that ran back from the access road in the direction of Mantova's rural home. He gave himself a thousand yards and parked the fiat under cover of some shade trees, ditched his slacks and jacket to reveal the skinsuit underneath. A quick trip to the trunk, and he was shrugging into combat webbing, lifting out the SC-70 with folding stock and slipping on a bandolier of extra magazines and MECAR rifle grenades.

He struck off overland, with pearly morning light to guide him, moving easily between the rows of olive trees. The ground was dry, and Bolan left a dust trail, but it wouldn't show unless the watcher had a bird's-eye view of Bolan's progress.

The orchard came within some fifty paces of a sprawling ranch-style house. He waited in the shadows, checking out Mantova's home. A curl of white smoke wafted from the chimney where he judged the kitchen ought to be. A cook preparing breakfast for the household, so that everything would be in readiness before Mantova got out of bed.

He made a walking circuit of the house and wound up where he started, settling in to wait. It might have sped things up for him to rush the house, but Bolan had a plan in mind that didn't involve the risk of being tagged by unseen snipers as he tried to cover open ground.

Another hour and a quarter passed before the front door opened and a pair of swarthy bodyguards emerged. They checked the yard halfheartedly, secure that no one in his right mind would attempt to nail Mantova at his home, and one of them turned back to nod a signal at the open door.

Alfonse Mantova was the next man out, with two more guns behind him. Bolan heard a car approaching, saw a BMW just emerging from the bar Mantova had converted into a garage.

And he was right on schedule, give or take.

The MECAR rifle grenade snapped into place while Mantova was climbing into the car, wedged in between his bodyguards. His driver closed the boss's door behind him, pitched a cigarette away and slid behind the steering wheel.

All set.

It was an easy shot from forty yards, no need to adjust his sights for elevation or wind. He held it steady on the tinted window, just above the left rear door, and stroked the trigger lightly with his index finger. Saw the sleek black shape of the grenade take off downrange and strike the target with a crack that blossomed into hungry flames.

He had a second MECAR ready by the time the shock wave of the first blast reached him, ruffling his hair. The BMW was still moving, even though the passengers were surely dead, the driver either gone or on his way. He could have let it go, but Bolan had a point to make.

The second blast derailed Mantova's limo, ripped the front wheels off and dropped its engine in the dirt. The BMW stopped dead in its tracks, flames spreading to the gas tank in a rush. He waited for the secondary blast, saw soldiers breaking from the house and faded back into the trees before they spotted him.

Let them think it was a bomb or simply puzzle over what the hell was going on. His job was done, and it didn't require a firefight with Mantova's hardforce once the boss had gone to his reward.

He heard the doomsday numbers running as he jogged back through the trees to reach his fiat. Moments later he was trailing dust in the direction of the highway and his next appointment with the Star.

Before Luigi Calo heard the news about his boy, Mantova would have company in hell.

GRIMALDI REACHED CATANIA before the sunrise, coming from the north along the coastal highway. It was good to be in motion once again, the infernal waiting behind him, even though he would have much preferred to fight at Bolan's side.

So far apart, and anything could happen in the next few hours. Both men moving in and out of danger, facing hostile guns on unfamiliar ground—at least where Jack Grimaldi was concerned. If his friend ran into trouble, found himself cut off, Grimaldi would not even know about it, much less have a chance to help him. By the time they missed the second scheduled contact, indicating an emergency, it would already be too late for one to help the other.

That was standard, though, and Grimaldi was not about to dwell on thoughts of death and failure. He had work to do, and time was slipping through his fingers.

Catania was the headquarters of Dario Siena, one of Calo's front men in the smuggling racket, moving cargo back and forth to Greece and northern Africa. A killer from his teens, Siena ran his pipelines smoothly and efficiently, enforcing discipline with pain and death. A first mistake, if not too costly or severe, might mean a beating, possibly a broken arm or leg. Strike two, and you were out.

As part of the intelligence received from Salvatore Lucania, Grimaldi knew Siena had a special shipment coming in at 4:30 a.m. The cargo, some eight hundred fifty pounds of uncut heroin refined by the Iranians, was large and rich enough to warrant Siena's personal attention at a time when he would normally be home in bed.

Grimaldi meant to be there, too.

He followed signs and common sense to reach the waterfront, checking names on the various warehouses against the one from Lucania's list. There, coming up, he had it: Genco Enterprises. There were several cars outside, and lights were visible through one small window.

It was all he had to see.

Grimaldi drove on past and parked his four-door rental in the shadow of another warehouse farther down. He chose his weapons, leading with the model 12-S SMG, and walked back through the early-morning darkness toward his target. By the time he got there, he was watching out for sentries, but Dario Siena's team was evidently more concerned with picking up their cargo than patrolling the vicinity for enemies.

He took advantage of their negligence and checked the building out, found an open door on the broad loading dock, made his way inside. He tracked the sound of voices past a vacant, smallish office, down a corridor to reach the warehouse proper.

Five men stood in a circle, talking. Two of them had shotguns tucked beneath their arms, the others empty-handed, though Grimaldi had no doubt there would be side arms underneath their jackets. Dario Siena had his back to the door as Grimaldi entered, but he showed his face in profile, speaking to the soldier on his left, and there was no room for mistakes.

Ten minutes, give or take, before the heroin was scheduled to arrive. That meant more guns, and Grimaldi was anxious to reduce the odds before Don Calo's ship came in. He raised the submachine gun, saw one of the soldiers gaping at him in surprise, about to warn the others as Grimaldi squeezed the trigger.

He had ditched the silencer for this engagement, and the short Beretta made a hellish racket in the confines of the warehouse. Spent brass rattled on the concrete floor around his feet, Grimaldi pumping bullets at his enemies before they had a clear chance to defend themselves.

The staring gunner took four rounds between his chin and solar plexus, pitching over backward in a boneless sprawl. The next in line was turning toward the sound of gunfire when a stream of parabellum manglers sheared his face off, spinning him away.

Siena swiveled to face the enemy, unarmed but shouting to his gunners for assistance, crouching as he tired to clear the line of fire. Grimaldi stitched a line of holes along his side, from hip to armpit, tracking on to catch the other shotgun-wielding soldier with his weapon on the rise.

Their guns went off together, the *lupara* prematurely, triggering a blast of shot into the floor, from when the pellets scattered, stinging his companions. Grimaldi was ready when the nearest gunner fell, his feet swept out from under him by buckshot, and a rising burst of parabellums met him halfway to the floor, ripped through him, tossed him over on his back.

And that left one, all thought of self-defense forgotten as the sole surviving gunner sprinted for the nearest exit. Fine. Grimaldi helped him get there with a burst between the shoulder blades that punched him forward, brought him down with adequate momentum for a facedown slide to nowhere.

Grimaldi reloaded, checking out the warehouse in a hasty search for hidden enemies, and came up empty. Glancing at his watch, he knew the heroin would be arriving at the docks outside in moments. If he stuck his head outside, the chances were that he could see its running lights.

When he had finished with the SMG, Grimaldi took a handful of incendiary sticks out of his pocket, looked them over briefly and returned them to their hiding place.

All set.

The deaths would put Don Calo on notice, but the loss of that much heroin would hit him where it counted—in the wallet.

Grimaldi was whistling softly as he walked out to the dock and leaned against the railing.

Any time now.

He could wait.

CAESARE GIGANTE drew on his cigar, rocked backward in his swivel chair and blew a plume of smoke in the direction of the ceiling fan. His eyes were on the telephone, not glaring, but regarding it with frank displeasure, as if he expected the instrument to rear back and strike at him across his desk.

It had been bad news all day Sunday, and his instinct told Gigante things were only getting worse. Don Calo had an order out to place his soldiers on alert, but what good would it do if they had no idea whom they were looking for?

Gigante had his own ideas about what form that vigilance should take. He had dispatched a team of soldiers to ask questions in Cefalu, watch for strangers, check out the hotels and so forth. For the rest of it, Gigante was concerned with looking out for number one. He had increased his private bodyguard from five men to a dozen armed with shotguns, automatic weapons, side arms. The police commander whom Gigante had been paying underneath the table for the past eight years was also on alert, prepared to move with all available force at the first sign of trouble.

Meanwhile, life went on—and that meant business must continue. Gigante was more concerned about his income at the moment than he was about potential threats against his life. There had been threats before, a few determined efforts to destroy him, but he still survived.

That didn't mean that he was indestructible by any means.

Gigante had killed enough men, ordered the deaths of enough others, to know that any man was vulnerable if he let his guard down. That was a mistake Gigante didn't plan to make. Not now, not ever.

He had come in early to the office, just as dawn was breaking, in the hope that it would reassure employees of a normal day in progress. They would see the extra troops, of course, and wonder, but Gigante didn't answer questions at the office, and his hired help didn't ask.

The telephone rang again, his direct line from Don Calo, and Gigante cursed softly, fluently, as he reached for the handset. After all that had been going on, he knew that it could only be bad news.

"Hello."

The low, familiar voice spoke swiftly, no emenities, delivering the latest bulletin from what had turned into a war zone. In Milazzo someone had eliminated Don Alfonse Mantova and a number of his soldiers. Bombs or rockets—something military. Not that it made any difference to the dead.

Gigante asked no questions, merely listened, acknowledged the message, assuring Don Calo that his men were on alert. That done, he cradled the receiver, slumped back in his chair and cursed again.

Mantova had not been a friend, but it was troubling that the violence had spread from mainland Italy to Sicily. Gigante had been hoping that the culprits would be found and neutralized before it went this far, resolve the matter once and for all. Now, with the enemy closer to home and still on a rampage, Gigante would have to take the threat more seriously.

Starting now.

He punched the button on his intercom and spoke a name, sat waiting for his second in command to enter, close the door behind him, cross the room and take a seat. Aldo Chiusi was a tall, thin man with nervous mannerisms, always shifting, twitching, glancing all around himself—except when it was time to kill. The close proximity of violent death was like a sedative to Aldo, calming him, investing him with nerves of steel. In almost twenty years of killing for the Mafia, he had not missed a shot or let a human target get away.

"I just got word that Don Mantova has been killed," Gigante said by way of introduction.

Chiusi gave a little shoulder twitch, blinked twice and brought his hands together in his lap. "At home?" he asked.

Gigante nodded. "The facts are still obscure. It makes no difference. We must be prepared."

Chiusi's fingers drummed his knees. He crossed his legs, uncrossed them, crossed them once again the other way around. "I've seen to everything," he said. "There is no word on strangers in Cefalu, but we will continue checking through the day."

"I want more guards around my home," Gigante said.

"Of course, *padrone.*"

Lanky Chiusi was still twitching when there came a loud crack from the window, and he turned in that direction. Caesare Gigante would have said that he knew all Chiusi's tics, but this was different. Lurching backward in his chair, Chiusi's face imploded, spewing blood. His body slithered to the floor, still twitching, but a glance assured Gigante that his first lieutenant was not nervous.

He was stone-cold dead.

Gigante swiveled toward the picture window, where a coin-sized hole was visible, a spiderweb of cracks surrounding it. As Caesare looked on, another hole appeared in the window, perhaps eighteen inches to the right of the first, and he felt the impact of a hammer stroke against his sternum. Impact drove him over backward, chair and all, his skull rebounding from the carpet.

As he died, Gigante knew exactly what had happened, but he couldn't grasp the raw mechanics of

how, why, and who had done this to bring him to the
end of everything he ever knew, felt, experienced.

ANOTHER FIFTY MILES west of Cefalu, Palermo was an
easy hour's drive along the northern coastal highway.
Bolan made good time, the sun behind him, chasing his
shadow toward the next target on his hit list.

Don Fabrizio Sulmona was a native of Palermo. He
had grown up on the streets and risen from pursuit of
petty thievery to serving as a runner, then a triggerman and soldier for the local Mafia. His rise had not
been meteoric, but he kept his wits about him, knew
when it would serve him best to quit one master and
adopt another in the interest of survival. At age forty-
seven, he was one of the top four Mafia capos in Sicily
and a recognized member of the Star.

Sulmona's public fronts were olive oil, which he
produced in two small factories, and operation of a
trucking firm created to transport his oil from factory
to market. On the side his trucks were known to carry
drugs and untaxed cigarettes, counterfeit currency,
arms and the occasional fugitive from justice. More
recently he had played host to visitors from Tokyo, Iran
and other nations when they came to meet Don Calo
and discuss their pending business in the world at large.

Sulmona's business office was located on the ground
floor of the Alto Pura factory, located in a southern
suburb of Palermo. Bolan checked his map when he
was still a mile outside the city, wound his way through
residential streets until he saw the factory ahead. No
problem parking, since the lot was barely half-full with
employees' vehicles.

He left his jacket on, concealing the Beretta SMG, and took a briefcase with him in his left hand. No one who observed him would have known that there was five pounds of explosive—C-4 plastic explosive—in the briefcase, with a battery and detonator wired up to a hidden trigger in the handle. One flick of the trigger, and a built-in timer started counting backward from the five-minute mark.

He entered the factory through the front door, veered left toward the office section, following the signs. Sulmona's receptionist was a bullet-headed bruiser with a pistol bulge beneath his tight, ill-fitting jacket. He met Bolan with a frown, rising from behind his desk, arrested by the submachine gun sliding out from under Bolan's cot.

He froze, considered reaching for his side arm and decided not to risk it. Bolan gestured with the SMG, directed the bruiser toward Sulmona's inner sanctum. The big man knocked twice, then opened the door without waiting for a summons. Bolan gave him a shove across the threshold and followed him inside.

Fabrizio Sulmona was standing with his back to the door as they entered, sorting through the top drawer of a wooden filing cabinet. His face darkened as he saw the stranger standing in his office, covering his bodyguard.

"What's this?" the capo asked.

"It's judgment day," said Bolan.

The bruiser chose that moment to attempt his break, pivoting to face Bolan, one hand reaching out for the Beretta SMG while the other slid into his jacket, seeking the pistol. Bolan let him grab the squat Beretta's silencer and tug it toward him, that much easier when three rounds ripped into the gunner's chest at point-blank range.

The bullets slammed him backward, draped his bulk across Sulmona's desk. Across the room the capo faced his unknown enemy, not begging for his life, but showing off defiance. Bolan didn't want to grill him, so simply shot him in the chest and watch him drop beside the filing cabinet in a crumpled heap.

He primed the briefcase, tucked it under Don Sulmona's desk and made tracks out of there. A few yards from the front door, mounted on the wall, he spied a fire alarm and yanked the lever downward, setting off a clamor that would send employees racing for the nearest exit.

It was clear and cool outside, a fresh breeze blowing in his face as Bolan walked back to the car. He slid behind the wheel, turned the ignition key and sat there waiting while the morning shift evacuated in a rush. They ran the drill as it had been rehearsed, not waiting for a glimpse of flame or whiff of smoke to send them on their way.

The blast, two minutes later, turned the northwest corner of the Alto Pura factory to smoking rubble, and chunks of masonry were hurled far and wide across the parking lot. He shifted into first gear, swung the Fiat out of line and aimed it toward the highway, checking out the rearview for another glimpse of hell.

The strike would not derail Don Calo's operation, nor was that Bolan's immediate goal. Before he got to that stage, he would put the fear of cleansing fire into his adversary's heart, wear down the capo's will to fight.

The battle was not over yet by any stretch. If anything, the worst was still ahead of Bolan, waiting for him at his next stop or the one after that.

He was prepared to play it out against increasing opposition as the day wore on. Whatever happened in the hours ahead, he would be giving it his best, no holding back.

The Executioner was rolling, and the only thing that would divert him from his chosen course was death.

CHAPTER TWELVE

"This isn't like you, Salvatore."

Anna Giacalone frowned as she spoke, staring hard at Lucania across the low-slung coffee table in her living room. The small apartment in Catania was perfectly secure, as far as either one of them could tell, but force of habit made them speak in muted tones.

"Don't be so sure," Lucania replied. "These animals took everything away from me except my life—a life which they made certain I could not enjoy."

If Lucania's words hurt the woman, she made a point of not letting it show. They had been friends and comrades in the anti-Mafia crusade for close to three years. She knew Lucania's moods and recognized his new ambivalence. The pain he felt was not a new sensation, but his latest means of coping with it was a change.

"But all the killing, Salvatore!"

"I know." He sipped his strong black coffee laced with whiskey, savoring its kick. "We have to think about our enemies, however."

"And become like them?"

"The choice was mine, and it is made. I have not asked the party's blessing, and my friends are not involved. Whatever comes of this, if anything goes wrong, the blame is mine alone."

"What of the others?" Anna asked.

Lucania shook his head. "I've said too much already. All I need this morning is a place to wait and rest."

"You will stay here, of course."

"If you are sure—"

"I won't hear otherwise. It's settled."

Trying to relax, he nodded. "As you wish."

It was a strange sensation to know that he was operating on the wrong side of the law, abetting murder. There could be no question of explaining to the court if he should be arrested. Never mind the cause or whether it was just. Lucania would be another convict, technically no better than the men he had been fighting all his adult life.

And how would he protect himself in prison?

He dismissed that particular concern. If things went that far, if the whole scheme fell apart, he knew that jail would be the least of his worries. Don Luigi Calo would destroy him, and that would be the end—of his ambitions, hopes and fears, his mourning and the long quest for a semblance of revenge.

Lucania had been living in death's shadow since the murder of his wife, and while he would not have described himself as feeling comfortable there, it was a simple face of life. Policemen knew the feeling, prison guards, fire fighters, pilots. Even so, it was a different thing, not only knowing that you *might* face death on any given day, but realizing that a group of ruthless men were actively conspiring to destroy you, taking certain concrete steps to put you in a grave.

The strain had not yet prevented Salvatore Lucania from going on about his business, but he wondered how much longer he could last. The present circumstances were a very different game, the first time he had been at risk from the police, as well as mafiosi and the Star.

And that might be the worst of it, Lucania decided. Knowing that he had become a criminal to fight against his enemies, surrendering the honor that had been his birthright and the banner of his cause.

"You look worn-out," said Anna.

"So appearances are not deceiving, after all."

She laughed at that, leaned forward, placed a soft hand over his. "Why don't you take a shower, make yourself at home. I haven't got a guest room, but..."

She left it hanging, open-ended, giving him the choice. Lucania could not deny a stirring in his loins, but it was too abrupt a change, despite the circumstances, to regard his friend as something more. A lover.

"I can sleep right here," he told her, reaching back to pat the cushions of the sofa.

"If you're sure."

Lucania smiled. "I will no doubt regret my choice tomorrow," he replied, "but at the moment I need rest."

She smiled. "Of course, I understand. You will not be disturbed tonight."

"I'm sorry, Anna."

"Don't be," she responded with an impish twinkle in her eye. "I made no guarantees about tomorrow."

He was smiling when she left to fetch his sheets and pillow, but he knew that Anna spoke the truth. There were no guarantees about tomorrow when it came to love—or life itself.

Lucania wished he had a weapon, then dismissed the notion as he had on previous occasions. He was not a warrior, if the truth be told, and he would not last fifteen minutes in the kind of war Belasko and his comrades took for granted.

He rose from the couch and went to take his shower. He could only hope it would relax him, help him sleep.

Maybe, he thought, it just might wash away the rancid smell of fear.

LUIGI CALO SCANNED the conference table, counting heads and ticking off the empty chairs. Two dead among the capos who would normally respond to any urgent summons, while several others had begged off, remaining close to home where they could supervise defensive measures in the field.

It was a crisis, granted, but Don Calo still had every confidence that he—with his associates—could save the day. There had been many other challenges before the present trouble, and the brotherhood of mafiosi had survived. French occupation, Mussolini and his fascists, sweeping prosecutions in the post-war years—the Mafia had weathered every storm, and Calo had faith that the Star would prove as durable if it was given half a chance.

"Thank you for coming," he began, a nod to the amenities before he settled down to business. "All of you know why we're here, I think."

No answer from the dozen men who faced him. None of them believed in wasting time on obvious remarks. There was a point when action had to take the place of words, and they had reached that point. If it was war—and so it seemed to be—these men were anxious to start shooting back.

"You have been asked to question all your local sources," Calo said, "in hopes we can identify our enemy. At this time I would ask if any of you have new information to report?''

Grim silence from the table, swarthy faces turned toward one another. Calo waited, shifting his gaze from one man to the next, making rounds and giving each of them a chance to speak.

''So, you have nothing, then?''

A hand went up, halfway down the table on his left. Genaro Magliocco waiting to be recognized.

''Speak freely, please,'' Don Calo said.

''Have we considered that the antimafiosi may be at the root of this unpleasantness?''

Magliocco had a gift for understatement that had marked him as a kind of diplomat among his brother pirates. Only he would think of Sunday's violence and the new assaults on Sicily as mere unpleasantness.

''I have considered it,'' Don Calo said, ''but our tenacious enemies among the antimafiosi fight a war of words. They pester us with litigation, agitate for prosecution and the like, but they have never taken action on this level. They are spineless pacifists.''

''Perhaps,'' Benito Andolini offered, ''they have had a change of heart.''

''Where is the evidence?'' Don Calo asked.

More silence from the group. Genaro Magliocco let another moment pass before he raised his hand again.

''Genaro?''

''I have cultivated an informant in the antimafiosi,'' Magliocco said. ''There is a chance that we may yet learn something useful. I expect a contact sometime in the next few hours.''

''Do your best,'' Calo said without much hope. ''We have no time to spare.''

''Of course, Don Calo. As you say.''

Renato Como didn't raise his hand before he spoke. "I am concerned about the impact of this business on our plans," he said. "Will it delay the schedule?"

"I anticipate no setbacks," Calo told him. "Everything has been arranged. The transfer is a relatively simple thing."

"The cargo is secure?" asked Como.

"Absolutely. I have no concern in that regard."

A few of his subordinates looked skeptical, but they kept any comments to themselves. They had enough trouble on their hands already without unnecessary confrontations in the family. There would be sufficient bloodshed when they finally identified their common foe.

But how much longer would it take? How many of the men now facing him would be alive when Calo knew enough to launch the counterstrike?

It didn't matter finally. Don Calo knew these men, some of them from his teens, and some of them were friends. But they were all expendable, himself included. No man was essential to the Star, and there would always be replacements waiting in the wings.

What mattered was the family, the task at hand. Of course, Don Calo meant to see that *he* survived at any cost, but that was simply common sense. His various subordinates would feel the same, and that self-interest helped ensure that they would fight with all their hearts and minds against the enemy.

In fact, their customer cared nothing for the recent violence going on in Italy, as long as Don Calo could deliver the selected merchandise on time and at the agreed-on price. So far, there had been no event of a sufficient magnitude to jeopardize delivery, and Calo reckoned the transaction would proceed on schedule.

From time to time, however, he was wrong.

"I would suggest," Don Calo said, "that each of you makes every effort to identify the man or men responsible for our discomfort. Present customers aside, it damages our reputation to be treated in this manner. We cannot afford to seem as weaklings in the public eye."

There was a murmur of assent around the table. These men knew the value of a fearsome reputation, and the speed with which voracious scavengers could strip a wounded predator of flesh and blood, of life itself. How often had they done the very same to others? Countless times.

"I shall look forward to dramatic progress in the next few hours," Calo said, as if his urging was enough to make it so. And almost as an afterthought he added, "dismissed . . . except for Don Genaro. Could you stay with me a moment longer, please?"

CALTANISSETTA IS the centerpiece of Sicily, though almost no one in the outside world is conscious that the town exists. By virtue of geography it is a crossroads for vehicular and railroad traffic, nearly equidistant from Palermo, Agrigento and Catania. The Mafia existed here, as everywhere in Sicily, but there were no outstanding targets in the neighborhood.

In short, the town was perfect for a breather and a chance for Bolan to touch base with Jack Grimaldi.

Bolan drove in from the north and parked his fiat in a lot two blocks beyond the central plaza. As he walked back to the tavern they had chosen from a guidebook, Bolan scanned the sidewalks left and right, checking faces, ready to move if any pair of eyes locked on to his or shifted away too quickly.

Nothing.

Grimaldi was waiting for him when he stepped into the tavern, seated at a booth in back, a subtle gesture with his hand enough to catch Bolan's attention. He sat down across the table from Grimaldi, briefly checking out the mirrored wall that let him watch the door that opened at his back.

The waitress took their orders for spaghetti, salad, coffee. Bolan spoke in generalities, about the weather and the countryside, until she brought their food and went away.

"So everything's all right?" asked Bolan.

"Getting by," Grimaldi said. "Yourself?"

"I'm keeping busy."

"Sounds that way, from what I'm hearing on the radio."

"We're not done yet."

"Luigi must be sweating," said Grimaldi.

"We can only hope," the Executioner replied. "He's used to heat, though, don't forget."

"I'd guess he's turning over rocks by now."

"No bet."

And there were lots of rocks in Sicily, thought Bolan. Hundreds of potential enemies for Calo to consider, even if they seemed unlikely at a glance.

"Too bad we can't just get it done."

"It won't be that much longer," Bolan promised.

Of course, he knew that anything could happen in the next few hours. Overconfidence was more than just a weakness; it was a disease that killed unwary soldiers in the hellgrounds.

"Salvatore come up with any intel on the cargo?" asked Grimaldi.

Bolan shook his head. "We haven't been in touch the past few hours."

"Why do you suppose the guy came over with us, Sarge?"

It was a question Bolan had already asked himself, and more than once. There was a list of possibilities that ranged from altruistic courage all the way to guilt and suicidal ideation. Probably the truth lay somewhere in between.

"I guess he's got his reasons," Bolan said.

"That business with his wife a few years back," Grimaldi said. "You think it pushed him over?"

"Doubtful. He's had time enough to blow it if the stress was working on him."

"I suppose. He's not exactly gung ho on the project anyway."

"He's not a soldier," Bolan said.

"What happens if they bag him?"

Bolan thought about it for a moment before answering. "Nothing. All he's got is a description and a phony name. The list he gave us puts him on the hook if he admits he passed it over. We're not taking any of the marks in order. I don't see a way for him to slow us down."

"Unless we have to stop and save his bacon," said Grimaldi.

Bolan had considered that, as well. It was a harsh choice but the only one available.

"He's on his own."

Grimaldi registered a mild surprise, then nodded understanding. Salvatore Lucania wasn't some innocent who'd stumbled into Bolan's war and gotten caught up in it by sheer coincidence. He had deliberately provoked the wrath of Don Luigi Calo and the others over time, and he had managed to survive this long while those around him bit the dust. Lucania had come to Sicily with both eyes open, knowing all the risks involved, and he wouldn't expect them to forsake their mission if he tripped and fell along the way.

"I'll bet he's wishing that he never made that call," Grimaldi stated.

"Could be," said Bolan, not believing it. "Or maybe he's just wishing that he made it sooner."

"Either way I hope he's got the nerve to see it through."

"You're headed for Vittoria from here?" asked Bolan, switching subjects.

"Right. You still on for Marsala?"

"That's the plan." The warrior checked his watch. "Okay. I show 1237 hours. We should regroup in Catania an hour after nightfall. Call it 2030 hours."

"Suits me fine," Grimaldi said, as if there was no question of a problem coming up within the next eight hours.

That was courage and determination, Bolan knew, not recklessness. Grimaldi didn't mind long odds, but he would never throw his life away without good cause.

If anything prevented him from keeping their appointment in Catania, the Executioner would know his friend had made the effort, given it everything he had.

He had one hand in his pocket when Grimaldi palmed a roll of lira notes and dropped a colorful assortment on the table. "My turn," he announced.

"I'll get it next time," Bolan said.

"Damn right you will," Grimaldi retorted. And smiled.

Before they separated on the sidewalk, Bolan shook his old friend's hand and cautioned, "Watch yourself out there."

"I got it covered, Sarge."

I hope so, Bolan thought as he retreated to his waiting car. I really do.

NO SIGN OF LIFE was showing from the small apartment when Anna Giacalone parked her compact car and locked it, walked across the street and climbed a flight of stairs to reach the numbered door. She knocked twice, paused before she rang the bell, then knocked again.

They had agreed upon the signal months ago, but she had only used it twice before. The meetings were infrequent, dangerous for all concerned if they should come to light.

But mostly they were dangerous for Anna.

She could only guess how Salvatore Lucania and her other friends within the party would react if they knew she was meeting with a capo of the Mafia.

It had been Anna's choice; there was no point denying that. We all have options, grim as they may be. No one had put a gun to Anna's head and forced her to cooperate with those whom she regarded as the enemy. Her baby brother was a different story, though. His taste for gambling had led him into trouble, prompted him to pay his debts with money stolen from the law firm where he was a junior partner. Fearing ultimate exposure and disgrace, he'd borrowed from the Mafia to square the books, but now he owed a sizable amount to Don Genaro Magliocco's loan sharks. He could pay or suffer, and when neither option was appealing, Anna's brother had turned to her for help.

From there the choice was simple. She could let him go, attempt to intercede with the police...or she could meet with Magliocco and attempt to cut a private deal to prevent the inevitable violence or disgrace to one she loved.

Don Magliocco had been understanding, even amiable. These things happened, but a debt was still a debt. It must be paid in one way or another. If she chose to help the family her brother's debt would be forgiven, and he would be barred from betting in the future, theoretically ensuring that he had no further trouble of the sort.

In return all Anna had to do was meet Don Magliocco on the sly when there were crucial matters to discuss. She would inform him of events within the party, bring him up to speed on what the antimafiosi were about and keep their little secret to herself.

The last part had been easy anyway. It shamed her every time she thought about her bargain with the devil, and would have killed herself before she told her trusting friends what she had done. In fact, the thought of suicide had preyed on Anna's mind of late, but she was either too strong willed or cowardly, depending on your point of view, to bring it off.

There still might be a way to purge herself of guilt and make things right, she thought. It simply had not yet surfaced in her conscious mind.

Don Magliocco answered the door himself, stood back and beckoned her inside. They were alone as far as she could tell, though Anna knew he must have bodyguards nearby.

He closed the door behind her, locked it, ushered Anna to the couch. He offered coffee, wine, a cocktail; she declined and sat down in the middle of the couch, compelling him to take a nearby chair.

"You are aware of what is happening around the island," Magliocco said, not asking her. A simple fact.

"I am."

"My friends are understandably concerned."

"So they should be."

"What can you tell me, little one?"

It was the moment she had dreaded from the start of their bizarre relationship. Till now she had been able to get by with office memos, statements on a pending lawsuit or a piece of litigation, this and that. To Anna's certain knowledge, she had never been responsible for anybody's getting killed or maimed.

This morning that might change.

"I don't believe the party is responsible for these attacks," she said.

"I also thought it seemed unlikely," Magliocco said. "But who, then, is to blame?"

"Outsiders, troubled by what they have heard about the Star."

Genaro Magliocco frowned. "It is one thing to recognize a problem, little one, but something else to strike specific targets. That requires direction, someone with the knowledge to ensure success."

"There is a man," she said at last. "He is affiliated with the party, but his actions in this matter are divorced from party policy."

"Of course." The capo was a reasonable man. He smiled to emphasize his understanding.

"He despises you for what was done to him. The murder of his wife."

"I killed his wife?' Don Magliocco spread his hands and looked bewildered, like a choirboy suddenly accused of rape.

"It happened on the mainland," Anna said. "In Rome."

"Ah, Rome. They can be savages."

"Just so you understand."

"Of course," Don Magliocco said. "If someone took my wife, I would no doubt react accordingly. Still, you must realize that this is bad for business. Everyone is suffering because of one man's grief. This cannot be."

"I've known this man for years," she said, delaying the inevitable moment.

"Yes, my little one. Perhaps if I could speak to him..."

She swallowed hard and said, "His name is Salvatore Lucania."

CHAPTER THIRTEEN

Marsala, on the western coast of Sicily, survives on fishing, shipping and some secondary agriculture. Olive oil and wine are staples of the local economy, but no one talks about the trade in narcotics, smuggled prostitutes and emigrants or other contraband. The capo of Marsala, charged with making certain the illegal traffic ran without a hitch, was forty-three-year-old Matteo "the Wolf" Tarantola.

In Bolan's view, Matteo Tarantola was less wolf than jackal, but the capo's character counted less at the moment than his personal defenses. Bolan didn't plan to lecture Tarantola or interrogate the capo. It would be enough for now to simply take him out.

Bolan's long-range weapon was a 7.62 mm Beretta Sniper, fitted with a six-power Zeiss Divan Z telescopic sight. The bolt-action piece featured a 5-round magazine, its forestock concealing a forward-pointing counterweight below the free-floating barrel to minimize barrel vibration on firing. The Beretta Sniper measures forty-six inches overall and weighs in close to sixteen pounds when fully loaded, with muzzle velocity on the 7.62 mm rounds of 2,838 feet per second.

Bolan's roost was a wooded ridge overlooking the winery where Don Tarantola passed his afternoons. There was a chance that he would scuttle his routine in view of all that had been happening around the island, but a phone call to the winery confirmed that Tarantola was expected shortly after 2:00 p.m.

The Executioner was waiting when a three-car caravan rolled into view, the point car with its hard-eyed gunners making a complete circuit of the parking lot before the sleek Mercedes limo and its tail car pulled in off the highway. Bolan lifted the Beretta Sniper to his shoulder, tracking with the telescopic sight until he had the cross hairs fixed directly on the Benz.

He saw the driver exit, walk about to open Don Tarantola's door. Marsala's capo was a short, square, balding man with heavy jowls and smudgy bags below his eyes. The suit was pricey, but it fit him like a garment bag.

The silk-purse syndrome, Bolan thought. No matter how you piled the lira on, a rat was still a rat inside the fancy cars and clothes.

Nine gunners, plus the driver, made eleven targets clustered in the parking lot. He thought about the order of attack, deciding it was riskier to let the don slide and hit the gunners first, in case his major target managed to escape. The soldiers posed a threat, but they were secondary to his mission of the moment. They could wait.

He fixed the rifle sights on Don Tarantola's pudgy face, took a deep breath and held it, his index finger taking up the trigger slack. The rifle bucked against his shoulder, Bolan holding steady on the eyepiece of the telescope and watching Tarantola as his face exploded, spewing crimson, shattered teeth and chips of bone.

The soldiers flanking Don Tarantola caught a splash of crimson as he toppled over backward. Both men stared at their fallen capo for an instant, stunned, before the echo of the gunshot reached their ears. Before they could react, the telescopic sight had framed its second target, and the Executioner was squeezing off.

The gunman staggered backward, one hand groping toward his chest, where blood was spurting from a tidy dime-size hole. A lung shot, Bolan estimated, and he put the soldier out of mind before his body hit the asphalt, swinging toward another target.

Number three was digging for a handgun underneath his coat when Bolan shot him in the forehead. The explosive impact snapped his head back, force enough to break his neck and put him down without a whimper to thrash briefly on the deck before his body came to rest.

Two rounds remaining, and he had eight targets left, all armed and staring toward the sound of gunfire, seeking his exact position. Bolan chose a soldier who had brought a stubby submachine gun out from underneath his jacket, probably a swivel rig. The first few rounds were high and wide, a dozen yards to Bolan's left, but he was trying and he could get lucky if he wasn't stopped at once.

The fourth round from his sniper rifle flew downrange and smacked into the gunner's throat. It stole his breath immediately, left him kneeling on the pavement, spitting crimson, with the SMG forgotten as he choked to death.

The seven gunners still on their feet were breaking ranks. Four scurried to the cars for cover, two more stood their ground and one took off in a mad dash for the winery. On impulse Bolan tracked the runner, no good reason other than the thought that he might bring back reinforcements. Squeezing off his fifth round at a range of some two hundred yards, his bullet going home between the sprinter's shoulder blades and dropping him like so much dirty laundry on the blacktop.

Bolan took eight seconds to reload, and Don Tarantola's six surviving bodyguards were busy in the meantime, four or five of them unloading on the ridge. Their rounds were coming closer now, and Bolan knew that he should disengage as soon as possible, before he found himself pinned down.

Five rounds, six targets. Math like that could get a soldier killed.

He chose his target, zeroed on the point car. Three men huddled in its shadow, popping up to fire at Bolan, dropping out of sight again. It could take hours to root them out of there if he kept trading shot for shot, but Bolan had a different plan in mind.

He sighed on the car itself, squeezed off and found his mark, a clean shot through the gas tank from one hundred fifty yards. It would require another shot to do the trick, but Bolan didn't mind. He worked the bolt and fired again, smiled grimly as the tiny spark became a fiery mushroom, swallowing the point car and the soldiers crouched behind hit. Two were flattened by the blast, their comrade staggering away and screaming, beating at the flames that ate into his flesh.

Next door, behind the Benz, two gunners came erect and gaped at their companions, stunned, uncertain whether they were threatened by the spreading lake of fire. He seized the opportunity and cut them down, a quick one-two with heat shots.

Easy.

That left one, but he was staying put behind the tail car, and he showed no inclination to pursue his unseen enemy. It did no harm to leave him where he was, and

Bolan started back in the direction of his waiting vehicle.

More targets waiting for him, down the road.

And he didn't intend to keep them waiting long.

THE HIGHWAY TO VITTORIA is one lane and a half at best and frequently in poor repair. Grimaldi was reminded of the roads in northern Africa, or parts of Eastern Europe where the Soviet collapse had meant an end to anything like normal maintenance. Despite the prevalence of cars in modern Sicily, he still passed donkey carts along the way, and it wasn't unusual to find the highway blocked by scrawny cattle or a flock of sheep. He made fair time in spite of everything, and used the travel time to plan his moves once he arrived.

Vittoria was the domain of Don Petrucchio Locarno, a notorious assassin who had built his reputation on the bleached bones of his enemies. Where many mafiosi came up through the ranks as money-makers, smuggling contraband or pimping, orchestrating major thefts and kidnappings, Locarno was a killer, plain and simple. From his first known slaying, at the tender age of twelve, he had dispatched an estimated eighty victims by himself, perhaps two hundred more by sending flunkies out to do the wet work.

The reward for his ferocity had been promotion through the ranks until he ran a territory of his own, two dozen soldiers under his command. Locarno did his share of loan-sharking and pimping these days, but his stock in trade was still assassination. Capos on the mainland had been known to hire his handpicked gunners for the kind of problem hits that needed special expertise, a veteran butcher's touch.

And it was time for him to die.

Grimaldi had no reason to believe it would be easy, but he meant to get it done. Petrucchio Locarno had been having things his way for years around Vittoria, and it was past time for the worm to turn.

Locarno had been twenty-one before he learned to read, and he was no great shakes at paperwork today, but he did business from a stylish office in the central business district of Vittoria. It stroked his ego and provided him with cover for the various illicit operations he conducted on behalf of Don Luigi Calo and himself.

Locarno didn't know it yet, but he had an appointment with disaster on this Monday afternoon. He might not be accustomed to donations at the office, but he was about to give his life.

At least that was Grimaldi's plan.

It still might go the other way, he realized, but he was game for anything. Grimaldi parked his car a block south of Locarno's office, checked the Model 12-S underneath his coat and locked the driver's door behind him and set out.

He could have called ahead, but Grimaldi preferred to run a risk of missing his intended target rather than alerting Don Locarno and maybe putting him to flight. This way, if he was forced to settle for a handful of the capo's soldiers, it would still impart a message to the family at large.

He encountered no opposition in the lobby of the office building, and Grimaldi waited for the elevator, rode it up alone to four. Emerging from the car, he saw two heavies heading toward him on an interception course, right hands inside their jackets.

There was no point trying to negotiate. Grimaldi raised the SMG and triggered two short bursts from twenty feet, the gunners twitching, jerking, going over backward with their weapons still undrawn. He stepped around them, moving toward Locarno's office, then through the outer door. He showed his Beretta SMG to the receptionist. She dropped the papers she was filing, made no protest as Grimaldi shooed her out the door, beyond the line of fire.

He walked directly to the inner doorway, turned the knob and pushed through with the Model 12-S leading. Don Petrucchio Locarno sat behind a desk that held a telephone and intercom, no indication that he ever tried his hand at paperwork. Three goons were standing over him, two on the left, one on the right, all of them staring at the new arrival on the scene.

The weapon told Grimaldi's adversaries everything they had to know about the situation, and they scattered to the corners of the room, Locarno dropping out of sight behind his desk. Two shooters on Grimaldi's left, and he was drawn in that direction automatically to cover the most pressing threat.

Two pistols showing as he faced the opposition, tracking with the SMG and milking short bursts at a range of something like a dozen feet. The taller of the gunman stopped four rounds and staggered backward, slammed against the wall and slithered down into an awkward seated posture, head slumped forward on his chest. The other got a shot off but missed Grimaldi by a yard in his excitement, and he never got a second chance.

Grimaldi nailed the second gunner with a 5-round burst that lifted him completely off his feet and spun him like a top. He fell across the other dead man's legs, made one attempt to rise on will alone and then collapsed.

As he swung back to face the gunman on his right, Grimaldi raked Locarno's desk with a short burst to keep the capo's head down, moving on to meet the shooter who was on his feet and lining up his shot. Grimaldi ducked and heard the bullet whisper past his face before he locked the Model 12-S into target acquisition, held the trigger down.

The gunman skittered through a jerky little dance before he lost his balance, went down on one knee, his automatic slamming two more shots into the floor. The last three bullets from Grimaldi's magazine drilled through the soldier's cheek, nose, forehead, and the dead man toppled over on his side, the pistol slipping from his fingers as he fell.

Instead of fumbling for another magazine, Lucania let the submachine gun drop and drew his side arm, circling around the desk to find Locarno on his knees. The capo seemed more furious than frightened, but he had no weapon handy, trusting in his soldiers to protect him here. Grimaldi let him see the automatic, waggling the muzzle up and down.

"Get on your feet," he ordered in Italian.

Grudgingly Locarno rose with muttered curses, finally standing upright to confront his nemesis.

"Who are you?" he demanded.

"I'm a bill collector," said Grimaldi. "You're way overdue."

"What means this, 'overdue'?"

"I'm calling in your tab."

"I pay you. Tell me what you want."

"You can't afford it, Petey."

Don Locarno made his move, then, seeing it was hopeless. With a snarl he launched himself across the six or seven feet that separated him from Jack Grimaldi, big hands reaching for Grimaldi's gun, perhaps his throat. Grimaldi shot him twice, the parabellum rounds exploding through Locarno's chest. They stopped him short and pitched him backward across across his desk.

And still, the capo would not give it up. He struggled upright, growling like a wounded animal, reached out for Grimaldi with blood-smeared hands. The last round drilled his forehead, just above the roman nose, and burst out from behind his left ear in a spray of blood and bone. The lifeless body toppled over backward, and the skull impacting on the desktop with a solid clunk.

Grimaldi tucked the pistol out of sight, removed the empty magazine from his Beretta SMG and snapped a fresh clip into the receiver. No one was waiting for him in the outer office, but he caught a couple of the secretaries from adjacent offices peering out into the hallway, drawn by sounds of gunfire. At the first glimpse of Grimaldi, they ducked back and out of sight.

Nobody tried to stop him as he walked back to the elevator, through the lobby, out and down the street. Locarno's neighbors would be on the telephone by now alerting the police, but Grimaldi had too much lead time. By the time they checked the office out and started looking for an unknown suspect on the streets, he would be out of town and on his way to yet another target.

Moving on.

The body count was piling up, but he had far to go.

The road ahead was paved with skulls and bones.

DON CALO LISTENED while Genaro Magliocco ran it down, absorbing every detail of his story, keeping his reactions to himself. It was a weakness to display excitement, anger, the emotions common to the herd. A leader had to hold himself in check if he was to command the full respect of his subordinates.

Finished talking, Magliocco raised a glass of whiskey to his lips, drained half of it in one long swallow. When he sat back in his chair, his face was open, waiting for his master to command.

"This woman," Calo said, "you trust her?"

"She has never lied to me before, *padrone*."

"You're sure of that?"

"I am. She would be dead if I suspected her of anything."

It was the kind of logic Calo understood. "I know this Salvatore Lucania," the boss of bosses said. "He's not an easy man to kill."

"We need to try more energetically, perhaps," said Magliocco.

"I agree."

But it was not enough to kill him, Calo realized. A lawyer like Lucania could not have raised such havoc by himself. It took a soldier, possibly an army, to inflict such damage on the Mafia's home ground.

"You have done well, Genaro," Don Calo said. "I will consider your report and take the necessary action."

Magliocco was dismissed. He did not argue, did not even speak. Instead, he drained his whiskey, rose and bowed to kiss Don Calo's signet ring before he left the study. Marco Giuliani waited in the outer hallway, moving in to take Magliocco's place without a special summons.

"You're familiar with this roman lawyer, Salvatore Lucania?" asked Calo.

"*Sì, padrone.* A driving force behind the antimafiosi on the mainland. He has friends in Sicily, as well, but he has been afraid to travel here for several years. We killed his wife by accident some time ago. A clumsy error. Those responsible were chastised."

"This much I recall. But he is on the island now if Magliocco's sources are correct."

"And you believe he is responsible for these attacks?" Don Calo's chief enforcer made no effort to conceal his skepticism.

"Not as the assassin, certainly. He lacks the skill and courage, or he would have sought revenge for the elimination of his wife. Even so, the man is not a total eunuch. He has friends in France, in Britain, the United States. It is within his power to direct these raids or to provide the necessary information to our enemies, at any rate."

"Why would he come to Sicily, *padrone?*"

"It makes no difference, for our purposes," Calo said. "It is enough to know that he is here, within our reach, and that he must be able to identify our enemies."

"I should retrieve him, then."

"As soon as possible," Don Calo urged. He paused and added solemnly, "Unharmed, of course."

"Of course, *padrone.* The lawyer does not travel armed, as I recall."

"It makes no difference," Calo said. "We need the information he possesses if we are to find and neutralize our enemies. He must be kept alive at any cost. You understand?"

"I do."

"As luck would have it, he is with us in Catania. You know a woman by the name of Anna Giacalone?"

"She is with the antimafiosi," Giuliani said. "A pamphleteer and general nuisance. We have not seen fit to punish her because her impact on the family is minimal."

"And did you know she works for Magliocco as a spy within the party?"

Giuliani blinked, his features taking on a vague expression of embarrassment. "No, sir."

"It came as news to me, as well," Don Calo said. "Genaro has some surprises for us yet."

"He should have let you know, *padrone*. The man bears watching."

"We'll concern ourselves with that another time. Right now it is enough to know the Giacalone woman has this man, Lucania, at her apartment in the city. You can doubtless find him there or somewhere close at hand."

"It shall be done, *padrone.*"

"Remember, Marco—dead men tell no tales, and this one is required to speak before we punish him."

"I understand."

"Go, then, and bring him back to me. The slaughterhouse, I think."

A smile and nod from Giuliani as he left the room and closed the door behind him, leaving Calo to his private reverie. They knew a great deal more about their enemies than they had known at this time yesterday, but it was not enough.

Don Calo was surprised at Salvatore Lucania's involvement in the mayhem. He recalled the lawyer, his performances in court, the way he had reacted with a show of public grief to the mistaken murder of his wife.

A real man, if he truly loved the woman, would have pledged himself to a vendetta, even if it cost his life. He would not—could not—rest until the men responsible for slaughtering his woman had themselves been laid to rest.

And now, with all these years behind him, Calo found that Lucania the coward had in fact been plotting his revenge in secret, waiting for the proper time to strike. It was a personal reaction he could understand, appreciate and deal with one-on-one, but he could not protect himself, his family, unless he learned the names of those responsible for the attacks.

And only Salvatore Lucania could tell him that.

Without him they would find themselves at what the Yankees called square one. His soldiers would be chasing shadows, hunting ghosts.

It made Don Calo look bad to his troops, his public. They expected more from him, if not omnipotence, at least a periodic demonstration of his power over lesser mortals.

It was time he gave them what they wanted, Calo thought, before he finally ran out of time.

The lawyer would assist him, willingly or otherwise. Lucania's choices would be obvious to anyone with eyes to see. A simple, relatively painless death if he cooperated or a screaming trip through hell if he refused.

Calo hoped the lawyer was a man of logic, common sense. That he would choose correctly when the time came.

It would all come out the same in either case, but forcible extraction of the answers took more time.

And time, if Calo judged his enemies correctly, was the one commodity in short supply.

CHAPTER FOURTEEN

Trapani lies twenty miles north of Marsala, yet another coastal town whose people owe their living, for the most part, to the sea. No town is all one thing, however, and Trapani has its share of minor industry, subsistence agriculture, local politics—and crime. The local violations ran toward vice and gambling, with the usual complement of smuggling on the side. It was enough to keep two dozen mafiosi working overtime... and bring the Executioner to town.

It was half-past three when Bolan rolled into Trapani, through the central marketplace that seemed to be a mandatory feature of Sicilian towns and out the other side. He had a target fixed in mind, but the direct approach was sometimes tantamount to suicide.

Trapani's man behind the scene was Santos Viareggio, a local boy made good—or bad, depending on your point of view. In terms of violence, Viareggio would probably have been considered moderate by old-world standards, linked reliably to only six or seven murders in his Mafia career. The fact that he preferred negotiation to assassination, though, wouldn't come close to winning him a free pass from the Executioner.

Trapani's capo had a place due north of town, a combination auto-body shop and metalworks where weapons were sometimes customized and stolen cars disguised for resale on the mainland. There were rumors that a few of Viareggio's persistent enemies had wound up in the furnace there, but local *carabinieri* were well paid to look the other way.

Adjacent to the factory was an auto junkyard, carelessly surrounded by a sagging chain-link fence. No obstacle for Bolan once he had satisfied himself that Viareggio didn't have guard dogs on patrol.

All auto graveyards look alike to some degree. The styles and models vary, but you have the same pervasive hues of rust and faded paint, the stacks of crumpled bodies, heaps of tires, untidy ranks of boxes filled with engine parts.

The smells of oil and gasoline and rot were overpowering as he wound his way through stacks of vehicles that had gone off to their reward through accidents, persistent breakdowns, the occasional abandonment along a rural highway. Some of them had probably been stolen, but police around Trapani had more pressing matters on their minds.

The Model 12-S submachine gun with its silencer attached was cocked and ready with a quick response to any challenge Bolan met along the way. Rats scuttled out of sight as Bolan passed, but they were not the scavengers he sought this afternoon.

He came up on the blind side of the metal shop, approaching from the rear. No sentries in the junkyard to observe his progress as he tried the door and found it open.

It was cool and dark inside a cluttered storeroom, spiders weaving in the corners, with a heavy smell of dust and grease. He picked up voices coming from the larger shop out front, tools clanking in a kind of punctuation. Bolan homed in on the sound, took care to keep from knocking over any of the auto parts and boxes stacked around him as he moved toward the connecting door.

Across the threshold two men worked on a compact car, with three others standing on the sidelines. From appearances, the deferential attitude adopted by his obvious subordinates, the short guy on the left was Viareggio. Five-four and stocky, iron gray hair cut short enough that the fluorescents overhead reflected off his scalp. Dark eyes behind a pair of wire-rimmed glasses that kept sliding down his nose, requiring him to push them back each ten or fifteen seconds, like a nervous tic.

Bolan wasn't sure about the two mechanics, but the three men standing off to his left were clearly Mafia. A step across the threshold put him in their line of sight, and they reacted instantly, Don Viareggio retreating while his soldiers stepped in front of him, both reaching for their side arms.

Bolan didn't hesitate. He stitched them with a burst that tracked from left to right and back again, both mafiosi going down before they had a chance to draw and fire. Behind them Viareggio had his hands raised, held in front of him as if he thought mere flesh and bone could stop the stream of bullets.

Bolan proved him wrong, another burst of parabellum shockers ripping through the outstretched hands, the face and chest behind them, and Viareggio was thrown backward into bruising contact with a nearby workbench.

By the time his target toppled forward, Bolan had already turned to cover the mechanics. Both men dropped their tools and shot their hands up toward the ceiling. Neither of them seemed to have a weapon, and he nodded toward the exit, watching as they scrambled out of sight.

And he was ready when their hasty exit brought another mafioso charging back inside to find out what was happening. He had a sawed-off shotgun, but he kept it pointed at the floor for safety's sake, too late to swing it up as Bolan hit him with a 4-round burst across the chest. Thrown backward, he had strength enough to squeeze both triggers on the short *lupara,* buckshot mangling his own feet in a final touch of overkill that added insult to injury.

Bolan waited a moment, half-expecting more gunners to surface, then left the chop shop as he had entered, through the storeroom, back across the rat-infested auto graveyard, and an easy climb over the old chain-link fence.

So many dead, and Bolan knew that he was nowhere near the end of his campaign. Beyond the battleground of Sicily, another war lay waiting for him, infinitely worse than what he had endured so far.

And if it got away from him, there would be more at stake than his life or Grimaldi's.

All the marbles, in fact.

IT SHOULD HAVE BEEN an easy life, thought Marco Giuliani, but he was uneasy with the guidelines Don Calo had imposed. The order to bring Salvatore Lucania back alive at any cost implied that Giuliani's soldiers were expendable. That came as no particular surprise, but it was one thing for a man to risk his life in battle and quite another to be told that he must sacrifice himself in the pursuit of someone who may not be harmed.

Still, there was logic in the order, knowing as he did that Salvatore Lucania was the only source who could identify their enemies. Once that was done, the lawyer would himself become expendable, a piece of surplus baggage they could throw away without a second thought.

As for the woman, Giuliani had received no orders either way. She was a member of the antimafiosi, but she also served Genaro Magliocco as a spy inside the party. It had not been Giuliani's place to ask how that arrangement came about, nor did he care. The woman held no interest for him, other than the possibility that she might somehow jeopardize his mission. Granted, she had told the family about this Salvatore Lucania's involvement with the enemy and thus put them on his trail. But she had once been friends with the attorney—might be still—and women were notorious for their erratic shifts of mood.

Giuliani planned to kill the woman if she gave him any problems. It would only take a word, a look, to set him off, and Magliocco could complain to Don Calo if he had the nerve. The one thing Giuliani hated worse than heights was an informer, never mind which side was being served. Once treason wormed its way into the mind and put down roots, trust was extinct. Betrayal soon became a habit, and the man—or woman—who would sell a friend this afternoon would turn around and sell the brotherhood tomorrow.

"Up ahead," the driver told him, pointing.

Giuliani knew where they were going, and he recognized the small apartment complex on his left from having driven by it in the past. The fleeting sense of déjà vu meant nothing to him, less than nothing. He was not a superstitious man, and he had work to do.

The easy way, he thought, would be to barge in on the lawyer, catch him in the woman's flat, subdue him. Take him out that way and show the guns to keep his neighbors from remembering what they had seen. Their only clear alternative—stake out the place and wait until the lawyer showed himself, then snatch him off the public street—was fraught with risks, from witnesses to chance encounters with police.

And if they missed him . . .

Giuliani cleared his mind of idle negativity and concentrated on the target. One way in that he could see, but there was probably another entrance on the western side or at the back. The trick would be to storm the woman's flat before Lucania had any chance to slip outside, much less locate an exit from the complex.

Giuliani checked his watch and frowned. The day was moving on, as all days must, but this one seemed to have a built-in deadline. If they didn't get a handle on their enemies, and soon, the family—The Star, the operation—would be seriously jeopardized. And Giuliani cherished no illusions that his charm and winning personality would save him if he failed.

The very least he could expect in that event would be a bullet, and it made no difference whether it was fired by one of Don Calo's soldiers or a faceless stranger.

Dead was dead, and Giuliani knew that when it came to killing, it was better to give than to receive.

"Who's that?" the driver asked him, focused on a suit and tie emerging from the wrought-iron gate that served the complex. Giuliani recognized his man immediately from the photograph faxed out of Rome. It was the same sharp profile, same short hair—same suit, he thought, or one of several that appeared to be identical.

"Goddamnit!"

"Now?" the driver asked him, slowing as he took his foot off the accelerator.

Giuliani glanced in both directions, checking traffic and pedestrians. There would be witnesses, of course, but they would have no choice.

He swallowed hard and nodded.

"Now!"

LUCANIA HAD FALLEN PREY to what Americans called "cabin fever," chafing at the boundaries of Anna Giacalone's little flat. The lawyer knew he should remain inside, watch out for being spotted on the streets, but he had seen enough of chintzy furniture, beige-painted walls, the mindless offerings on television.

Those whom the gods would destroy, they first make mad.

Who said that? It was something from a play or poem, harking back to school days. Never mind who wrote the words; it was enough to know that they were factual. Lucania had felt his concentration slipping in the small apartment, his imagination working overtime, until he had begun to think each sound, no matter how mundane, marked the approach of gunmen sent to kill him.

Better to enjoy a stroll around the block and thereby risk discovery, he told himself, than to remain indoors with curtains drawn and work himself into a minor nervous breakdown.

Anna kept a pistol by her bedside, and Lucania had swallowed his revulsion when he set his mind to going out alone. Picked up the gun, made certain it was loaded and secreted it inside his waistband on the left.

It was a gesture, nothing more. He would not need the gun, unless—

A squeal of tires behind him brought the lawyer's head around. He was in time to see a dark sedan swerve toward him, several men inside, hunched forward in their seats.

He bolted, fearing that they meant to jump the curb and run him down. The rush of panic gave him speed. Lucania surprised himself, a mad dash to the alley thirty yards in front of him, a sliding turn that took him off the sidewalk, sprinting through the passageway too narrow for the car to follow.

He heard the car screech to a halt behind him, slamming doors, and then the engine revved as it sped off again. Lucania glanced backward, terrified of stumbling in the littered alleyway, and saw two men pursuing him on foot. Instinctively he knew the car was on its way to head him off, a run around the block.

Would he be quick enough to reach the street ahead before the car got there? Could he outrun the mafiosi on his heels? Were they about to shoot him in the back and end the chase that way?

Lucania suddenly remembered the gun in his belt, an alien weight dragging his slacks down on the left, and he broke strike, reaching underneath his jacket for the pistol, turning to confront his enemies.

A jumble of chaotic thoughts intruded on his brain. Was there a bullet in the pistol's firing chamber? Was the safety on? Lucania fumbled with the semiautomatic weapon for a precious moment, thumbed the hammer back and jerked the trigger.

One shot gone before he thought to aim, and while it missed both men, at least it slowed them down. They cursed him, broke to right and left, both reaching for their hidden weapons.

It was now or never, Lucania realized, choosing the man on his left without thinking it through. He tried to aim, was sure he had it wrong and squeezed the trigger three more times in rapid fire. At least one bullet struck his target, slammed the mafioso backward, dropping him between two battered trash cans.

Now the other gunman had his pistol out and was firing. Salvatore Lucania heard bullets whistle past his face on either side. He found his target, braced the automatic in both hands and was about to fire when something struck him, low down on his side.

He staggered, gasping at the brutal pain, aware that if he lost his balance now he had no hope of getting out alive. The mafioso was about to fire another shot and finish him when Lucania unleashed two bullets of his own.

Another hit! The gunman clutched his stomach, shuddered, dropping to his knees. Not dead, but he was stunned at least. Lucania seized the moment, reeling away from his would-be assassin, heading toward the far end of the alleyway.

His cotton shirt was soaking through with blood now, and his legs felt heavy, almost wooden. Clinging to the pistol, he had no idea if it was empty or if he could still defend himself against the others. Were they close? Did he still have a chance? Was he already dying?

Lucania reached the open sidewalk, lurched out into daylight. Christ, the pain! He heard the car before he saw it, engine sounds, then brakes and rubber on the pavement.

In his present state it was hopeless to try outrunning them. He turned to face the enemy, saw two men bursting from the car and raised his pistol. One shot wasted as he hurried it, a distant crash of glass across the street. The nearest mafioso drew his pistol, but the other shouted at him, sounding furious.

"Alive! Don't shoot him!"

Lucania took advantage of the momentary confusion, sighting on the nearest mafioso, squeezing off two rounds before the pistol's slide locked open on an empty chamber. One round struck his target, knocked the gunman backward. As he slumped against the car, the mafioso's gun discharged.

It had to be a fluke, he thought; the bastard wasn't even aiming. Still, the bullet struck Lucania just left of center, drilled between his ribs and pierced his lung.

At once the lawyer felt that he was drowning, warm blood rising in his throat. He could no longer keep his balance, felt himself collapsing to the pavement.

Someone standing over him and bending down to twist the automatic from his grasp. Lucania let it go, no strength remaining to resist. The stranger slapped him twice and asked him something, shouting at him, but Lucania couldn't make out the words. A fit of coughing seized him, and he saw the mafioso jerk back from him to avoid the spray of blood.

And Salvatore Lucania could see the disappointment on his adversary's face.

It was almost enough to make him smile before he died.

BOLAN WAS FIVE MILES WEST of Caltagirone when he heard the news. He was driving with the radio on, using the music for background noise, when a female announcer's voice broke in with a special bulletin. A well-known member of the antimafiosi had been murdered in Catania, shot down while walking on the street.

He waited, feeling apprehension like a clenched fist in his stomach. When the woman's voice pronounced Lucania's name, Bolan cursed softly, slammed his open palm against the steering wheel...and kept on driving.

There was nothing else to do, in fact. Lucania was dead, and there was nothing to be done about it now. A hostage situation could be turned against the enemy by one means or another—through negotiation or strategic pressure—but the dead were hopelessly beyond his reach.

Revenge was something else, but it could wait.

He heard the broadcast out. Apparently Lucania hadn't gone down without a fight. Details were vague, but the police reported an exchange of gunfire, with at least two other men dead on the scene. It was assumed that both were mafiosi, and the broadcast finished with a recap of the prior attempts upon Lucania's life.

Another song came on, and Bolan switched it off. He concentrated on his driving for a moment, tried to put his thoughts in order. It would be a waste of time for him to break off his campaign and seek revenge for Lucania's assassination. They had talked about the risk beforehand, and he had no ready starting place. Lucania had been staying with "a friend," unnamed, and Bolan didn't have the capability of searching door-to-door around Catania until he found the right address.

What would it tell him even then?

The "friend" might have betrayed Lucania, but it was also possible that he—or she—was altogether innocent. In any case diversion from his course would only give the enemy more time to patch up his defenses and resist the Bolan juggernaut.

Grimaldi would be waiting for him in Catania, along with Don Luigi Calo and his private army. Bolan knew the best that he could do, in terms of getting even for Lucania's sacrifice, would be to forge ahead and stay the course.

Don Calo had a ton of payback coming, and the death of Salvatore Lucania was merely icing on the cake, one more example of a capo using terrorism to control his turf.

But this time there was more at stake than drugs and money, the routine that he had come to recognize in Mafia affairs. Don Calo had branched out beyond the normal, workday routine of classic mobsters, broadening his scope to infringe on international diplomacy and take advantage of nuclear proliferation.

From a big piranha in a little pond, Luigi Calo had evolved into a great white shark, a proven man-eater, with all the oceans of the world to hunt in. He could turn up anywhere—if not in person, then represented by associates who did his bidding for the Star.

In that scenario Mack Bolan was the fisherman, prepared to spend the time and energy required to reel the monster in.

This fishing expedition didn't call for bait, however. It was more akin to whaling in the old days, going up against a monster in its own environment with nothing but your nerve and a harpoon.

The weapons had improved, of course, and Calo couldn't disappear in Sicily the way a whale could dive and vanish in the sea. The boss of bosses was resourceful, granted, but he had the normal limitations of a human being, too.

He wasn't bulletproof, for instance. Neither could he make himself invisible. When push came to shove, he would bleed and die like any other man.

Bolan meant to test that hypothesis and soon, but first he had to rendezvous with Jack Grimaldi in Catania. Another fifty miles to go, but he was getting there. Grimaldi should be well ahead of him unless he had encountered problems on the way.

Luigi Calo, meanwhile, would be digging in and putting reinforcements on the job. The hit on Salvatore Lucania was a minor victory for Calo's side. From the description on the radio, it didn't sound as if the shooters had found time to grill the lawyer, but it made no lasting difference either way.

If Calo knew his adversaries came from the United States, so much the better. It would shake his confidence, without revealing any details of the plan, since Salvatore Lucania possessed no details to impart. He had an alias for Bolan, nothing for Grimaldi, possibly a contact with the DEA or Interpol.

The rest was silence.

And for Don Luigi Calo, boss of bosses, it would soon turn out to be the silence of the grave.

Catania was waiting for him, Calo's central base of operations, ripe and ready for a visit from the Executioner. The answers Bolan urgently required were waiting for him there. He merely had to seek them out, apply the necessary pressure. Keep it up until the first small cracks expanded into fissures, chasms, and the whole facade of Don Calo's evil empire shattered.

Bolan's war, the main event, was waiting for him on the other side, beyond the ruins of Luigi Calo's dream.

A nightmare in the making for the founding father of the Star.

CHAPTER FIFTEEN

There were some days, Don Luigi Calo thought, when everything went wrong. It made no difference how a man attempted to control events, the time and effort he invested in a master plan. Luck changed from time to time, just like the weather, and a man could no more dodge misfortune than he could escape the wind and rain.

Although, if a storm was coming, Don Calo stayed inside the house or took a raincoat and umbrella with him when he traveled. It was much the same with trouble in his business. When a conflict was inevitable, Calo went to ground, called out his troops, took steps to beat the opposition down.

It was a shame, he told himself, that Marco Giuliani could not follow simple orders. All he had to do was bring the lawyer in for questioning, an easy thing, but what a balls-up he had made! Two soldiers dead, a third who wouldn't live to see the sunrise, and the lawyer had been killed on top of everything. A pencil pusher dueling with his gunmen in the streets, of all the ridiculous things!

What challenge would confront him next?

He would be forced to punish Giuliani—that was obvious...but it would have to wait. Don Calo needed Giuliani fit for duty at the moment, standing ready for the next outbreak of violence.

It was coming; he could feel it. Calo still had no idea
of who his enemies might be, but they were out there
somewhere. Waiting for another opportunity to strike,
with no way of knowing when it would happen or
where.

At least, he thought, Catania was safe. No one who
knew Luigi Calo would be fool enough to move on him
directly in his own backyard. His fearsome reputation
was enough to make most adversaries wet their pants
and run away. The few with nerve enough to take him
on were also generally wise enough to nibble at the
fringes of his operation, stopping short of any personal collision.

Years of ruling like a feudal prince encouraged Calo
to believe he was untouchable. He had always managed to derail indictments, ferret out his enemies like
vermin and ruthlessly destroy them without a second
thought. The technique served him well and always
would, but now he was facing a different scenario.

It troubled him that he had no idea of who his latest
adversaries were or where they came from. Circumstances altered cases, and Don Calo liked to tailor his
response for a specific situation. In the past two days
there had been strikes throughout the mainland and all
over Sicily. For all he knew, he might be dealing with a
dozen trained assassins, maybe more.

But then, he was safe inside his villa, Marco Giuliani and a score of soldiers standing guard outside. Who
had a prayer of reaching him behind those guns and
walls?

The boss of bosses poured himself a brimming glass
of wine, drank half of it at once and topped it off again
before he walked back to his easy chair. The sun was
going down outside, but it would be a long night in

Catania. Two soldiers standing by the radio and telephone to let him know immediately when and where the next attack was made. If they were quick enough about it, there was still a chance that they could track their adversaries, head them off and finish them.

Meanwhile all Don Calo had to do was sit and wait inside his fortress. Life was good for those who managed to survive in style.

The wine was his own, a product of his vinyards near Trapani. He was not a connoisseur, but knew what he enjoyed. Good wine. Good food. A woman now and then...

The blast came out of nowhere, rocked his villa like a giant fist impacting on the roof above his head. Luigi Calo bolted from his chair, the wineglass tumbling from his hand, a splash like fresh blood on the Persian carpet.

Christ, not here!

He heard his soldiers shouting in the hall outside, paused long enough to rummage in the top drawer of his desk and find the Walther P-1 automatic pistol he kept hidden there. He pumped the slide to put a live round in the firing chamber, eased the hammer down to keep from squeezing off a round by accident and went to join his men.

If death had come for Don Luigi Calo, it would find him waiting, standing fast and fighting back until the last drop of his blood was spilled.

THE VILLA WAS a combination fortress and vacation home, the kind of hardsite where Don Calo could conceal himself from enemies or entertain a hundred of his closest friends. The walls were eight feet tall and topped with razor wire to keep trespassers out, and there were three men on the gate with shotguns very much in evidence.

The house couldn't be seen by a pedestrian or motorist outside the walls, but Bolan and Grimaldi had prepared themselves with aerial reconnaissance. They knew the layout of the grounds—Calo's villa, the detached six-car garage, three separate bungalows for servants, the Olympic swimming pool and tennis courts. And local sources informed them that the noncombatant household staff had been packed off for the duration.

It was now or never.

Bolan's watch read 9:15 p.m. when he approached the southern wall. Grimaldi, meanwhile, would be closing from the north, completing the two-man pincers movement that would fail or succeed according to their nerve and the advantage of surprise.

The outer wall was not a major problem. The razor wire could slow them down—or stop them dead, if it turned out to be electrified—but Bolan and Grimaldi came prepared. Each carried half a tubeless auto tire, cut through to form a rubber crescent that would shield their flesh from metal barbs and insulate against a lethal dose of electricity.

Besides the rubber "bridge," Bolan carried the Beretta SC-70 assault piece slung across his shoulder and the Model 92-F automatic underneath his arm. Spare magazines for both filled pouches at his waist and the bandolier across his chest. The last half-dozen ME-CAR rifle grenades completed his ensemble, leaving Bolan dressed to kill.

He scaled the wall and dropped the half tire into place, braced one hand on the rubber tread, then followed with a boot, pushed off. He landed in a crouch, concealed by shadows, ready with the SC-70 in case his entry was observed.

So far, no problem.

Bolan knew the grounds were overrun with sentries, but the guards couldn't be everywhere at once. It would require a dedicated force of fifty men to cover the perimeter without a gap. The house would need another fifteen, maybe twenty guns, and that still left the spacious grounds. Unless Don Calo had installed closed-circuit cameras and sensors following the last police inspection, eight months previously, Bolan knew there had to be weak spots in the defense.

He was betting his life on it—and Grimaldi's, as well.

The first guard Bolan met was standing with his back against a tree, a shotgun tucked beneath his arm, head bent to light a cigarette. The silencer-equipped Beretta pistol was within two inches of his skull when Bolan pulled the trigger and a parabellum mangler cured the gunman's nicotine addiction.

Number two was fifty yards beyond the first and facing toward the house when Bolan came up on his blind side with a double-edged stiletto in his fist. He clamped his free hand over the young mafioso's mouth and gave his head a sharp twist to the left, throat bared to the intruding blade. Warm blood splashed Bolan's wrist, and then the guy went limp, a dead weight in his arms.

Two down, and Bolan had a clear view of the house, which was dead ahead. He crouched beneath a tree that would have offered pleasant shade in daylight, eased the automatic rifle off his shoulder and fixed a high-explosive grenade to the muzzle. It was eighty yards or so, an easy shot, and all he had to do was wait for Grimaldi to reach his station.

Thirty seconds left and counting down.

He chose a corner of the house at random, focused on its lighted windows. Brought the rifle to his shoulder, sighting carefully. He couldn't hope to score a hit on Don Calo with the first shot, and did not want to take him out so soon, in fact. He simply had to get the party rolling so that he could take advantage of the chaos, trying to make his way inside.

Bolan checked his watch again. Grimaldi would be in position if he was coming.

He breathed calmly to pace himself, and his index finger curled around the rifle's trigger, taking up the slack.

THE AUTO TIRES WORKED fairly well, but Grimaldi still gouged his left hand on the razor wire before he cleared the wall. It pissed him off and made him all the more determined to be careful as he made his way across the ground with his Beretta Model 12-S submachine gun and the semiauto pistol slung beneath his arm. He had removed the buzzgun's silencer but left his side arm muted, just in case.

His foresight proved to be provident when he was thirty yards inside the wall. A young guy was coming toward him through the darkness, eyes downcast to watch his step, until he almost stumbled on Grimaldi. Lurching back a pace, he tried to bring his double-barreled shotgun up, but Grimaldi was quicker, slamming two hot rounds into his chest at point-blank range.

The gunner didn't have his finger on the trigger, and he dropped without a sound to warn his comrades.

Jack relieved him of the shotgun, for a little extra punch, and kept on moving. He didn't bother concealing the body. There would soon be death enough to go around.

The first shot was reserved for Bolan, but Grimaldi had to be in place when it went down. He didn't flatter himself into thinking he was indispensable by any means, but it would be a neater, cleaner hit with two men on the job.

Unless they encountered some disastrous twist of fate, they might come out of it alive.

He worked his way around the long garage until he had a clear view of the main house twenty yards away. Grimaldi's watch said he was early, maybe fifteen seconds, and he used the free time to spot sentries from his hiding place.

The nearest was a meaty thug whose belly almost hid the buckle of his belt. He wore his jacket open in the front, no weapon showing, so it had to be a pistol or a compact SMG. Across the lawn, much closer to the house, a younger gunman with a carbine cradled in his arms was walking beat.

Grimaldi spent another moment fleshing out his plan. He knelt and laid the submachine gun down beside him, double-checked the 12-gauge to make certain it was cocked and locked. The stubby barrels didn't give him much in terms of range, but it wouldn't take much to reach the big man guarding the garage.

There could be no mistake about the signal when Bolan made his move. A muffled pop of rifle fire, immediately followed by the crash of an explosion, smoke and flame erupting upstairs on the far side of the house.

The tubby shooter made a break in that direction, moving toward Grimaldi, unaware that death was waiting for him in the shadows. Grimaldi leaned out to greet him, didn't even have to aim with the *lupara* as he squeezed the trigger once and then again. A double charge of buckshot sent the fat man flying backward like a punctured helium balloon, blood spraying from his wounds in place of gas. He landed on his back, kicked once and then lay still.

Grimaldi dropped the empty shotgun, grabbed his SMG and pivoted to bring the second mafioso under fire. The young man had been posed to run around the south side of the house when Grimaldi blew up his partner, and he stopped dead on the spot, turned back and raised his carbine, searching for a target.

Grimaldi was not about to throw the game that easily, however. Aiming for the shooter's torso from a range of fifty feet, he triggered off a rising burst of six or seven parabellum rounds. The mafioso jittered through a jerky little dance before his legs gave way and dropped him on his face.

It was a short run to the house, and it looked wide open. Sounds of battle came from the north side of the villa, drawing soldiers off in that direction from the east and west. If he could cover twenty yards without a sniper dropping him, Grimaldi reckoned he could find a way inside and start to look for Don Calo.

While it looked simple enough to carry through, it was the kind of plan that started looking shaky if you stopped to think about it very long, and Grimaldi was not about to undermine his confidence with second thoughts. He didn't have the time to spare in any case.

Just sixty feet. No sweat.

He broke from cover, running for his life.

GIULIANI MET HIS CAPO coming down the hallway, coughing as the smoke began to spread downstairs. It smelled like cordite from the blast, and Giuliani did not think the house was burning yet. The outer walls were stone, more common in Sicilian homes than lumber, and it would be difficult for fire to spread, whatever happened next.

Still, they had trouble on their hands. One bomb or rocket had already struck the house, and Giuliani heard the sound of automatic weapons now, unloading on the grounds.

"What is it?" Don Calo asked. And then, as if he knew the answer for himself, he quickly added, "How could they get inside?"

Giuliani was stuck on that one. "Come with me, *padrone,*" he said in place of answering. The heavy automatic in his hand seemed puny in the present circumstances, but he knew where there were more guns and a relatively safe place they could hide. Let Don Calo's soldiers do their job and stop the raiders cold.

In countries where the weather runs to hurricanes and cyclones, many dwellings are equipped with special rooms designed to help the occupants survive a storm. In Sicily, where mafiosi were more likely to be felled by paid assassins than a whim of nature, the precautions ran toward bombproof rooms and armor-plated cars.

Don Calo's war room was located in the center of the house, ground floor. It had no windows, and the only door was fitted out with double bolts inside. Two shotguns and a rifle occupied a gun rack on the wall, and there were also gas masks, plus a fire extinguisher. The room was twelve by fifteen feet, not much for jogging, but Calo never really thought that he would have to use it, much less spend a great amount of time locked up inside.

But he was wrong.

The door could only be locked from the inside, a hedge against anyone's being trapped against his will. Don Calo hesitated on the threshold, glancing back at Giuliani, blocking his way. The capo's face was solemn as he spoke.

"The soldiers need you, Marco."

Giuliani stiffened, tried to think of some reply that would not make him seem a coward. All that he could think of was a simple *"Sì, padrone,"*

"I'll wait here for you, then," Don Calo said, and closed the door in his lieutenant's face.

Inside, Giuliani heard the double bolts slide home. With no choice left, Don Calo's second in command retraced his steps to reach the parlor, found three soldiers waiting for him there, confused expressions on their faces. Waiting for a leader.

"This way," Giuliani ordered, leading by example, glancing back across his shoulder to make sure they followed him. He reached the door and pulled it open, stepped outside.

There was a dead man lying on the porch, Arturo something, leaking crimson from a shattered skull. Taking two steps around the pool of blood, Giuliani waved the others forward.

"Hurry!"

Scattered firing echoed from the yard, but it was fading now. He couldn't tell if that meant victory or failure, but he saw no soldiers racing back to boast of wiping out the enemy. Perhaps they were engaged in mopping up, and yet his instinct told him it wasn't over.

He cleared the steps and moved around another fallen soldier, snapping at his gunmen to keep up. More bodies were scattered on the lawn in front of him, and they were all familiar faces—those that still *had* faces anyway. The troops detailed to guard Don Calo had been something less than skilled at covering themselves.

Away to Giuliani's left, a tall man was approaching them across the lawn. Tall, dressed in black, his face and hands smudged dark against the night. An automatic weapon aimed in their direction.

"Scatter!" Giuliani shouted, suiting words to action as he broke off toward his left.

His soldiers did their best, but they were sluggish. The stranger fired from sixty feet away, a single shot, and Giuliani never saw the missile coming. He could hear it, though, the crash of the explosion flinging him head over heels.

He landed on his back with crushing force, ribs knifing deep into one lung. His eyes swam out of focus, coming back again by slow degrees to find the stranger standing over him.

"Don Calo."

It was not a question, in the normal sense, and Giuliani never thought the stranger had mistaken him for the Sicilian boss of bosses. Stubbornly the soldier shook his head.

Another shot rang out, and Marco Giuliani screamed as white heat blossomed in his knee, raced up his leg to set the lower portion of his body burning.

"Don Calo." In the same, unnerving tone.

Despite himself, his years of dedication to the family, he pointed toward the house. "Inside," he said, "beyond the kitchen. In a special room."

He had a fleeting moment to reflect on how a rat must feel, then the next shot drilled a hole between his eyes.

GRIMALDI HAD the special room staked out when Bolan got there, crouching off to one side of the door. A dead man lay before the threshold, facedown on the floor.

"This joker's heart was set on getting in," Grimaldi told him, nodding toward the corpse. "He didn't make it."

"Someone did," said Bolan.

"Yeah, I figured. Don Calo?"

"So I'm told."

"That's metal," said Grimaldi, reaching out to tap an index finger on the painted surface of the door. "You want to try grenades?"

"C-4," the Executioner replied. He opened up a pouch on his right hip and palmed a four-inch square that looked like clay and smelled like marzipan. The timer-detonator came out of a different pocket, and he fixed the charge beside the doorknob while Grimaldi watched his back, prepared to deal with any soldiers they had missed on the way in.

"All set," he said, retreating out of range in one direction while Grimaldi took off in the other.

Twenty seconds later the door went down, a thunderclap that filled the corridor with smoke and swirling dust. Grimaldi was a step behind him at the threshold, Bolan ducking through behind his SC-70.

Luigi Calo had been standing when the blast went off, and it had thrown him back against the wall with force enough to split his scalp. Blood streaked his face like war paint, dribbling from his chin and soaking through the green silk shirt. A shotgun lay beside him, close enough to reach, but Calo made no move to pick it up before Grimaldi kicked the gun away.

Bolan knelt beside the boss of bosses, used the muzzle of the SC-70 to lift his chin. The capo tried to focus on his face, but he was having trouble with it, blinking like a man emerging from a coal mine into brilliant sunlight.

"Can you hear me?"

Don Calo thought about it for a moment, then he nodded dully. Bolan thought his head would have lolled forward without the rifle wedged beneath his chin.

"I hear," he said at last.

"It's your call, how we go from here," said Bolan. "What I need is your connection for the cargo from Ukraine. Location, names, delivery schedule. Make it easy on yourself."

It was a long shot at the very best. Don Calo had not lived this long or risen to his present rank by spilling secrets to a stranger—even when a gun was pointed at his head. The circumstances here were different, though. Calo had to know that if his enemies had tracked him to his inner sanctum, then his troops were dead, his empire crumbling around him.

"Names?" he said after another pause.

"To start."

"I never meet the customer," Calo told his nemesis. "It is a matter of security."

"You had to make the contact somehow," Bolan said.

Calo thought about it, weighed his options, maybe thinking there was still a chance that he could walk away.

"We use a broker. A professional."

"The name."

The eyes blinked twice, Calo working out that he was not in any great position to negotiate. Besides, he may have calculated, it would not be quite the same if he betrayed a lowly foreigner.

"I only know him as Hajik Mahoud. We found him in Algiers."

It would be pushing, Bolan realized, to ask the capo for a number or address. Too many cutouts in the trade, and he couldn't expect the top man on the totem pole to keep such details in his head.

"He has the shipment now?"

"Is on the way."

"And you don't know who's buying?" Bolan pressed.

"What difference does it make?"

Not much, the warrior thought. Just life and death.

"We're finished here," he told Grimaldi, rising from his crouch.

"I'll do it if you want," Grimaldi said.

"No problem," Bolan said, and shot Don Calo once between the eyes.

"Algiers?" Grimaldi asked him as they reached the porch.

"Algiers."

CHAPTER SIXTEEN

They left the cars and military hardware in Palermo for a pickup by Brognola's local contact in the CIA, and paid a young Sicilian helicopter pilot seven million lire for a lift to Rome. The IAI Westwind 1124 was waiting where they left it, no apparent evidence of tampering, and Jack Grimaldi had them airborne ninety minutes after their arrival at the airport.

It is six hundred fifty miles from Rome to Algiers as the buzzard flies, across the Tyrrhenian sea, the rocky spine of Sardinia, and three hundred fifty miles of the blue Mediterranean. They had filed a flight plan for Algiers, and Grimaldi expected no red tape beyond the usual customs snarl to hamper their arrival. The only reception committee Grimaldi expected was being arranged by Hal Brognola, via Stony Man.

He hadn't asked while they were on the ground. Too much to do in preparation for their takeoff, but the wind was at their back now, with Sardinia behind them and a brand-new battleground ahead. New players, allies, adversaries—but the same old stakes.

He didn't have to ask whose life was riding on the line, but Grimaldi was curious to find out who was on their side.

"So who's this guy we're looking for?" he asked.

"Brognola's guy? Ahmed Ben Salah," Bolan said. "He does some free-lance work for Langley off and on. Spots terrorist arrivals, weapons shipments, this and that."

"Hal thinks he'll have a handle on Hajik Mahoud?"

"He ought to if the guy's a major weapons broker operating from Algiers. It's worth a shot at least."

Grimaldi didn't want to say it, but the words kept coming anyway. "You know, Calo may have just been pissing in your ear. The sumbitch has been lying since he learned to talk. It's second nature."

Bolan nodded, frowning to himself. "It's still a shot," he said. "Without it we got...what?"

Grimaldi didn't have to think about the question. They had nothing, dammit. Figure there were four pounds of stolen uranium somewhere in the world, held by persons unknown. Where did the hunter start without a lead? Antarctica, perhaps, or Timbuktu?

It was hopeless and sometimes, in a hopeless situation, even total bullshit was a bonus if it got you started. No one got to bat unless he found the ballpark, and you had to start the action somewhere.

"Could be this guy will have a handle on the cargo even if Calo wasn't playing straight."

"We live in hope," said Bolan.

Grimaldi had to smile at that, the smile expanding into outright laughter. Everything the two of them had been through, all that Bolan had endured in the years before they met, and still the guy was being absolutely honest.

After all of it, the blood and savagery, he lived in hope.

Of what, Grimaldi sometimes asked himself...but then again, deep down he knew.

The big guy lived in hope that he would see a day when predators were kept outside the fences and the law began to work again—not just for those accused of heinous crimes, but for society at large. He lived—and risked his life—against the hope that there would come a time when peace and safety were the norm instead of just a fleeting intermission in the global carnage.

He was dreaming, sure, but that was part of it. A burned-out cynic has excuses right and left for sitting on his ass and watching as the world goes by. Things never change unless it's for the worse. The bad guys always win, and good guys don't just finish last—they wash out in the middle of the game. Corruption is the rule, and rules don't change.

A dreamer, though, knows better. Change is constant, and the end result is never preordained. The clash of good and evil is a contest; it can still go either way. Each man and woman has potential—to excel, break all the records, go for broke.

And sometimes, every now and then, the good guys win.

"Me, too," Grimaldi said when he was finished chuckling to himself. "I live in hope. It couldn't hurt."

But that was wrong, Grimaldi realized almost before he spoke.

Not only could it *hurt* to live in hope if you went at it wrong, but Jack Grimaldi reckoned it could get you killed.

ALGIERS IS LIKE a time machine, an open door between the old world and the new. On one hand, you can see the space age here in the financial district, where computers do the talking, beam their messages by satellite and handle cash transactions with the banks of Switzerland, the Caymans Islands, Liechtenstein and the Bahamas. On the other hand, there is old Algiers—the ancient Kasbah district, where anything, including slaves, can be obtained by those with ready cash and the appropriate connections. Women veiled themselves, men carried daggers in their belts and first-time visitors could be forgiven for suspecting that the goods displayed in open market stalls had recently arrived by caravan.

In many cases it had done exactly that.

Algeria, in most respects, is still considered primitive. Three times the size of Texas, with a population slightly less than California's, the country is divided into trackless desert—eighty-five percent, or everything below the rugged Atlas Mountains—and the fertile Tell, a coastal strip with moderate climate and adequate rainfall that varies between fifty and one hundred miles in depth. An estimated ninety percent of Algeria's population resides in the Tell, supporting themselves through agriculture, light industry and oil production. The per-capita income peaks around twenty-one hundred dollars per year.

The desert nation has a troubled history. Ruled by French colonial authorities from 1830 until 1962, Algeria was considered an "integral part" of France, its loss so traumatic for some Frenchmen that embittered veterans of the foreign legion schemed to murder President Charles de Gaulle in revenge for his "treasonous" grant of independents.

Three years of infighting between Arab nationalist factions followed the breakup with France, and violence was endemic by the mid-1960s, when the new government began inviting terrorists from all around the world to live and train in special camps set up for their convenience.

Religious conflict was another problem, and the government canceled elections in January 1992, when Islamic fundamentalists were expected to carry the field. All nonreligious activities were banned in Algeria's ten thousand mosques—a move that didn't save the president from being killed by Muslim triggermen that June.

The rule of thumb around Algeria was much the same as any other Third World nation. Money talked and it could ask for anything it wanted: guns, explosives, drugs, safe passage—even human lives.

And information.

They walked through customs with a minimal delay. The standard questions at passport control, no trouble with the luggage. When it came to contraband, most Europeans and Americans who visited Algiers were buyers rather than suppliers. They were more inclined to travel light, show up with nearly empty bags and stock up on hashish or opium before they left.

They had two rental cars on standby, and a rendezvous that called for Ahmed Ben Salah to meet them in the Kasbah shortly after noon. A certain tavern—El Shebaz—was specified. If Bolan missed the meet, their contact was supposed to try again at 6:00 p.m. and then again at midnight. After that he would assume the worst and sever all connections to the project.

Inside each car was a Browning BDA-9S, the double-action autoloader, with a pair of extra magazines. The other weapons would be purchased through their contact, if and when they found him.

Bolan and Grimaldi drove in tandem to the heart of new Algiers, left one car in a subterranean garage and took the other to the outskirts of the Kasbah district. They were forced to walk from there through narrow, teeming streets that smelled of spices, incense, sweat and dung. The street signs were in Arabic, where they existed, but the warriors knew where they were going . . . more or less.

The cooking smells reminded Bolan that he hadn't eaten since a hasty breakfast at the airport back in Rome. His stomach growled but it would have to wait.

The streets were crowded, but their stature and complexion set the two Americans apart. The natives stared—some frankly hostile, others simply curious— but Bolan concentrated on his mission. Difficult to say if they were being followed in the crush, but there was no good reason to believe they were expected in Algiers by anyone except their rightful contact. Don Calo was in no position to alert his broker that the Executioner was coming. They had left no useful tracks in Sicily, and anyone who traced them from the final clash would have to be clairvoyant.

That did not suggest that they were safe by any stretch. Algeria was hostile territory, rife with hatred of America, and while tourism was officially encouraged by the government, those same officials sponsored training camps for terrorists at war with the United States and Britain, France and Israel. If they fell into trouble here, despite the possibility of marginal assistance from the CIA, they would be on their own. But then, there was nothing new in that.

Their contact would be well aware of the potential risk, and Bolan counted on the man to watch his back, take every possible precaution to avoid exposure. After all, while Bolan and Grimaldi could be classed as visitors, their would-be ally was a native. He had nowhere else to go, and it was certain death for him to foul his nest.

Self-interest made for good security in Bolan's prior experience. A man who stood to profit nicely from a deal—or lose his life, if it fell through—was strongly motivated to succeed. More to the point, he knew the local player and could often match them move for move.

It was the way he stayed in business, how he stayed alive.

"Looks like the place," Grimaldi said.

The El Shebaz tavern was small by Western standards, its interior twenty feet by thirty, with a pall of smoke that hovered near the ceiling like a bank of clouds. Dim lights and haunting music—heavy-metal rock had yet to gain a foothold in the Kasbah—with a belly dancer jiggling on a small stage at the far end of the room. The small, round wooden tables had been jammed together with economy in mind, to hell with comfort, but the place was less than half-full when they entered on the stroke of noon.

"You have a clue what this guy looks like?" asked Grimaldi.

Bolan shook his head and answered, "He'll find us."

"I hope so, man. If anything goes wrong in here, we're on the menu, wait and see."

AHMED BEN SALAH SAW the two Americans walk into El Shebaz. He didn't follow them at once, but rather stood across the street and waited, making sure they weren't followed. Only when he satisfied himself that it was safe would he approach them for the rendezvous.

He was accustomed to such meetings after nearly three years of cooperating with the CIA. Ahmed Ben Salah didn't know these men, had not been told what they expected of him, but he knew there would be danger. That was standard in the business he had chosen for himself. It was the risk that let him charge outrageous prices for his services, as long as he was able to deliver on command.

They didn't look like spies, these white men—more like soldiers—but he knew that looks were frequently deceiving. Who would have suspected that twenty-five-year-old Ahmed Ben Salah was a full-time smuggler and a part-time secret agent working for America?

The latter pastime sprang from his idealism, yet another quirk that was not obvious to prying eyes. A native of Algiers, he had grown up despising terrorists of all persuasions. One of them had killed his parents years before—an "accident," the parent group decreed—and Ahmed Ben Salah was left to run the streets at seven, living hand to mouth before finding his calling as a thief and trickster, picking pockets, looting market stalls and milking tourists for gratuities.

The shift to smuggling came with age as he acquired experience and liquid assets. On occasion he had sacrificed a handsome profit by refusing to do business with the rabid Palestinians and their associates, but he got by. These days he sold more information than imported contraband, and most of that to the Americans.

What would it be this time?

Another moment, and he crossed the street to enter El Shebaz. The bartender, a friend and sometime business associate, saw him coming and nodded toward a table in the back where the Americans were seated, bottles of imported beer in front of them.

Ahmed Ben Salah started across the room, winding his way between tables, smiling at the dancer when they made eye contact. They had done some business in the past, as well, and might again. She was a tigress in bed, but he had little time these days for entertainment.

And Americans had spotted him, were watching him as he approached. Without preamble he pulled out a chair and sat down, facing them, a broad smile on his face.

"Ahmed Ben Salah, at your service," he announced. "How may I serve you?"

"WE NEED INFORMATION and equipment," Bolan told the young man after he had ordered wine and tipped the waitress with a dashing smile.

"Equipment?"

"Weapons."

"Ah."

"Is that a problem?" asked Grimaldi.

"Not if you have money."

"Time's important," Bolan said.

"Of course, I understand. What is it you require?"

"Two rifles. Can you get the AK-47?"

"Certainly," said Ahmed Ben Salah. "What else?"

"A pair of Uzi submachine guns," Bolan said. "An RSP-7, with rockets. Hand grenades, let's say a dozen—fragmentation and incendiary."

"You are planning on a war?"

"I wouldn't be surprised."

"For what you seek, with ammunition for the guns, I will require 150,000 dinars."

Bolan did the math, came up with something in the neighborhood of 6,500 dollars, depending on the day's exchange rate. "That's agreeable," he said.

Their contact's smile grew broader, brighter, letting Bolan know he had a fair commission riding on the deal. "The standard terms call for half payment in advance, half on delivery."

"No problem," Bolan said. He palmed a wad of bills and started counting, passed seventy-five thousand dinars to his contact under the table.

Ahmed Ben Salah did not insult him by counting the money. Folding it up in his hand, he tucked it into a pocket. "I can have the weapons for you in an hour's time."

"Sounds fair."

"As for the information you require..."

He left it hanging, waited for the Executioner to speak. Bolan studied his face for a moment, reading the young man, looking for something to trust. He found it in the eyes, a warmth that Ahmed Ben Salah could never quite conceal.

"We're looking for another man who deals in weapons on a major scale," he said at last. "The name's Hajik Mahoud. You know him?"

Ahmed Ben Salah sat back and sipped his wine before he spoke. "I know the name," he said. "We have not met."

"I'm told that he does business from Algiers."

"That is correct. His clients are primarily political."

"You mean they're terrorists," said Bolan.

The young man nodded. "As you say."

"Can you direct us to him?"

"Possibly."

"The price?"

Ahmed Ben Salah thought about it for another moment, then he shook his head. "I take my profit on the goods," he said. "Hajik Mahoud shall be my gift to you."

"We're interested in a specific cargo," Bolan said, "and his intended customers."

"I don't keep track of Hajik's business dealings as a rule."

"But you could ask around?"

"Indeed." Another smile. "For that, I may require more money."

"Understood."

"This cargo... it would help if I had more details."

"Uranium," said Bolan. "Weapons grade. A theft from the Ukraine, transshipped through Italy or Greece. I'm told Hajik Mahoud is dealing for the buyer."

"It would not be out of character," said Ahmed Ben Salah. "Of course, without enquiries I cannot confirm the story."

"How much time?"

The Arab shrugged. "It's difficult to say."

"Could you have something for us by the time we take delivery on the guns?"

"It's possible."

The man seemed confident, and Bolan made the choice to let him run with it awhile. An hour or two would make no concrete difference to their mission in Algiers. Beyond that, Bolan reckoned he would have to put some wheels in motion on his own.

"You've come a long way," Ben Salah said, "to hunt the—how you say it?—needle in a straw stack."

"Haystack," Bolan said, correcting him. "You think our chances are that slim?"

Their contact shrugged expressively. "Unfortunately in Algiers there are many terrorists. They all want better, large weapons. Any one of them would slit his mother's throat for access to a nuclear device."

"That doesn't narrow down the field much," said Grimaldi, sounding glum.

"Let's talk to this Hajik Mahoud before we start to worry," Bolan told him.

Ahmed Ben Salah was watching them with interest, glancing back and forth from one face to the other. "When you find this man, Hajik Mahoud," he said, "what will you do to him?"

"We need to have a conversation," Bolan said. "If he can tell us what we need to know, he ought to be all right."

It was a lie, of course, but he saw no good reason to begin by frightening their contact with the prospect of a shooting war around Algiers. He might refuse to help them if he knew what Bolan had in mind.

"Such men are known for secrecy," Ahmed replied. "Their customers require discretion, and they punish those who break the faith. It will not be an easy thing to make him talk."

"Let's take it one step at a time," said Bolan. "First we have to find him."

"Yes."

"How many weapons brokers are there in Algiers?" Grimaldi asked.

Ahmed Ben Salah smiled and spread his hands. "Who knows? Our government invites all manner of fanatics to regard the country as their home away from home. They all need weapons for their training or their missions. There is money to be made in meeting the demand.''

"You know the business well?" asked Bolan.

"I have friends who make their living in the trade," said Ahmed Ben Salah. "I do not deal in arms myself . . . except for special friends, you understand."

"Must be our lucky day," Grimaldi commented.

"Perhaps," the Arab countered, "but I would not—how you say it?—count the chickens yet. Algiers has many secrets and she guards them jealously. More men have vanished in the Kasbah than in your Bermuda Triangle. As for the desert . . ."

Ben Salah frowned and shook his head, as if he reckoned there was no more to be said. The message came through loud and clear.

"We've got a job to do," said Bolan.

"This I understand," Ahmed Ben Salah replied. "What *you* must understand is that the men you seek are much the same. They have a job to do, as well. They deal in death and they are skilled professionals. Perhaps you are the same, I do not know. The difference, my friend, is that they know the country. You do not."

"I don't suppose you ever hire out as a guide?" Grimaldi asked.

"It would depend upon the journey. I avoid those where there seems to be no prospect of returning home again."

"He's got a point," Grimaldi said to Bolan almost ruefully.

"Too late," said Bolan, smiling back at his partner. "You bought your ticket."

"Don't remind me."

"Is there something else?" their contact asked.

"Not off the top," Bolan answered. "If I think of something, we'll be back in touch. Meanwhile..."

"The items you require, of course. One hour from the time I leave you, meet me on the waterfront." He mentioned an address, described the warehouse in detail.

"No problem," Bolan said.

"I'll see you then," Ahmed Ben Salah concluded. "If you have any further questions at that time..."

"We'll let you know."

He sat and watched the Arab leave, registered the Arab's parting nod to the bartender before he stepped into the street.

"You trust him?" asked Grimaldi.

"I'll consider it. Let's wait and see how he does on the hardware."

"And the rest of it?"

"We'll get there," Bolan told him. "One way or another."

And regardless of the route, he knew they would be wading in through blood.

CHAPTER SEVENTEEN

The pickup went without a hitch, and Bolan finished paying off Ahmed Ben Salah when the hardware had been parceled out between his rental and Grimaldi's. For an extra twenty thousand dinars—something under nine hundred dollars—Ben Salah rattled off a short list of addresses where, his contacts said, there was a good chance of encountering Hajik Mahoud. The bonus was a glossy photograph of three men huddled on a crowded sidewalk, deep in conversation. Ben Salah pointed out the middle of the three as Bolan's man. In parting, Bolan also got a contact number where a message could be left for their Arab contact in emergencies, to fix another meeting.

Two of the addresses were clearly business oriented, one of them a shop in the bazaar, the other for a downtown office, both in the name of Najik Exports. That left one, a nightclub on the outskirts of the Kasbah, and the Executioner was betting that Hajik Mahoud would not be killing time in either shop or office after sundown.

As for home, the information had been unavailable, but they could always try to shake it out of Mahoud's personal acquaintances if they should miss him at the club.

"More dancing girls," Grimaldi said when they were back together, standing in the dark outside the club. "I love it."

"Anything to make you happy," Bolan told him, smiling. "Just don't let the entertainment distract you, guy. Stay hard."

"I'm hard already, sarge."

"But you can still walk, right?"

"I'll do my best."

"Okay. You want to take the back?"

"Sounds good."

"Five minutes."

"That's affirmative."

Grimaldi crossed the street and vanished down an alley on the west side of the tavern. Bolan waited, watching patrons come and go. Each time the door swung open, light and music spilled into the street, like fleeting glimpses of another universe where everything was fun and games.

Beneath his jacket, Bolan wore the Browning automatic in a shoulder rig, left side, the Uzi on a swivel to his right. He hoped it wouldn't come to that, full-auto firing in a crowded nightclub, but he had no way of knowing if Hajik Mahoud was covered, whether he had two or twenty guards to watch his back.

The last thing Bolan wanted was a public firefight, more especially since he would have to grill Mahoud for names before he took the broker down. Hajik Mahoud was not his target in Algiers, but rather a convenient stepping stone to help advance the Executioner's campaign. Without him they would have to find another angle of attack, and that could waste all kinds of time... assuming that they ever got it right.

He checked his watch again and slowly crossed the street. A doorman looked him up and down suspiciously, and palmed fifty dinars for the cover charge. Across the smoky threshold, Bolan stepped immediately to the left side of the doorway, covering his back while he took time to let his eyes adjust and sweep the room.

They had a crowd tonight, all male. The waitresses were dressed in harem outfits, while the dancers had dispensed with clothing, save for vails that hid the lower portion of their faces. The peculiar costumes were surprisingly erotic—stemming from the hint of mystery, he thought—but Bolan followed his advice to Grimaldi and concentrated on the customers.

He found Hajik Mahoud relaxing in a booth against the far wall on his right. The broker appeared to be alone, though it was possible he might have bodyguards positioned elsewhere in the room. In that case, Bolan knew that he would have to take his chances, risk a cross fire in the club if he was going to confront his man.

If they waited for Mahoud to leave, they faced a risk of losing him outside in the narrow, winding streets that he would surely know by heart, from childhood.

Grimaldi should be in place by now, though Bolan couldn't see him at the moment. It would have to do.

He left his place against the wall and started walking slowly toward the booth.

HAJIK MAHOUD ENJOYED his nights out on the town. By day—and sometimes nights, as well—he was immersed in business, selling death for profit to the world at large. He didn't give a second thought to those who bought his weapons, much less to the victims they would maim or murder with the tools he supplied.

Why should he?

It was strictly business, after all, and if there had not been a market for such military hardware, he would be reduced to selling something else. Young women, for example. Stolen artwork or narcotics. He had dealt in all these things and more since he was old enough to call himself a man. At present weapons were the hottest-selling item in Algiers, not only to the terrorists in residence, but to a list of wealthy clients in the Middle East at large.

His latest contacts were the best by far. Mahoud could take no credit for the merchandise they offered, but he had been quick to close the deal once it became available. It meant a vast improvement on his own commission, over the percentage earned on rifles and machine guns and grenades. Demand so far outran supply that he could quote a price without expecting endless arguments, negotiations, carping over pennies.

As always, when the deal was made, he wiped his mind clear of the consequences. He didn't care when or where the bombs went off, as long as *he* was safe from lethal fallout. Anyone who faulted him for making money off the suffering of others was a hypocrite, consumed with envy for the golden opportunity he had found.

He sipped his drink and watched the dancers, wondering if he should make an offer on the tall one for the night. Mahoud was friendly with the manager—they had done business once or twice, though not for weapons—and he knew the man would intercede on his behalf. It was pleasurable to deliberate on the idea.

A stranger slid into the booth beside him, startling Hajik Mahoud. He didn't introduce himself, but drew the right side of his sport coat back to show the submachine gun hanging in a leather sling and said, "We need to talk."

American, that much was obvious from his appearance and his accent. Mahoud thought about his options, wondered if he should pretend he spoke no English, maybe signal for the manager to come and take the man away. Or should he simply flash the signal that would bring his watchdogs with their guns, strategically positioned in the corners of the room.

If all the stranger wanted was to kill him, he would not be sitting down. Still, there was something in his face that sent a chill down Mahoud's spine.

"I beg your pardon?" Keep it formal. Act surprised, all injured innocence.

"Let's step outside."

The chill turned into something more like panic, and Hajik Mahoud knew he would never see the sun rise if he left the nightclub with this man. Whatever the American was looking for, no matter what he had in mind, the end result would be Mahoud's demise.

The broker raised his right hand from the table, clenched the fingers tight into a fist and then released them. Nothing that would put the stranger on alert, but it was all the watchers needed. Mahoud didn't glance around the room to see if they were moving, since that surely would have given them away.

"That strikes me as a dangerous idea," he said at last.

"It wasn't a suggestion," the American replied. "You're coming with me one way or another.

"And if I refuse?"

"It's not an option."

Mahoud forced a smile. How long before his soldiers reached the booth?

As if in answer to the silent question, shots exploded from his right, in the direction of the toilets. He spun in that direction, saw Tabriz, one of his men, unloading with his Skorpion at someone near the exit.

The crowded room exploded into chaos. Mahoud was about to bolt for cover when the tall American reached out and caught him by the collar, slammed his face into the tabletop and dragged him to the floor.

GRIMALDI CAME IN through the back, no doorman to delay him. They had latched the door, but it was child's play to unlock it with a penknife. Fifteen seconds put him in a dingy corridor, the reek of urine emanating from an open doorway to his left. Ahead of him a beaded curtain partly screened his vision of the nightclub proper. Raucous music, a peculiar blend of East and West, pulsed through the narrow hallway. For a moment Grimaldi imagined that he had been swallowed by a dragon with a noisy heart condition.

A glance inside the smelly restroom showed no one in there. He went down the corridor and out, the strung beads rattling at his back. Grimaldi faded to his right and put his back against the wall, eyes sweeping back and forth across the smoky room. It wasn't SRO, but they were getting there, with almost every table filled. The dancers knew their business, and the patrons were appreciative, applauding, tossing coins and folded currency up toward the stage.

He made the sweep and found Hajik Mahoud off to his left, all by his lonesome in a booth that could have seated four or five. Bolan glided toward him through the crush, maneuvering around the tables, homing in. He slid into the booth and said something to the broker, and Mahoud went rigid, glancing down at Bolan's side.

Brief conversation passed between them, then Mahoud did something with his hand—a nervous twitch, perhaps, but Grimaldi had his doubts on that score.

A man stood up, ten feet or so to Jack Grimaldi's right, and started moving toward the booth where Bolan and Hajik Mahoud were seated. At the same time, here and there around the club, Grimaldi spotted half a dozen others on their feet, all turning toward the broker and his uninvited guest.

Grimaldi fell in step behind the nearest gunner, keeping pace. He withdrew the Browning automatic from its shoulder rig and raised his voice to make it audible above the music.

"Yo, there! Ali Baba!"

Curious, perhaps, the gunner looked back toward Grimaldi, saw the pistol in his hand—and made his move. His left arm shot out toward the nearest table, swept it clean of bottles, glasses and the small oil lamp that was an omnipresent decoration in the club. Grimaldi ducked below the flying glass and knew what had to follow, rolling to his left and putting several bodies between himself and his assailant.

The shooter whipped a Skorpion machine pistol out from under his jacket, firing wild before he had a clear fix on his target. Somewhere overhead a cry of pain told Grimaldi the guy had scored on some bystander, drawing blood.

The room exploded. Someone stumbled over him and wrenched his ankle painfully. He kicked back, came up looking for a target as the gunman fired another burst. Behind Grimaldi screams and thrashing as another body hit the floor.

Grimaldi found his mark, lined up the shot and squeezed off two quick rounds from fifteen feet. His bullets drilled the gunman squarely in the chest and slammed him backward, blasting with Skorpion as he went down.

Grimaldi scrambled to his feet, almost went down again as an excited patron slammed into him from the left, but he maintained his balance with an effort, hobbling on the injured ankle.

He glanced back at the booth, but Mahoud and Bolan were out of sight now, maybe on the floor. Grimaldi started looking for another target, bulling through the crowd in the direction of second-nearest gunman he had seen. Around him gunfire sputtered with a sound like fireworks, voices shouting curses, questions, women screaming from the stage.

He spied another gunman in the middle of the weird, chaotic crowd scene, glancing back and forth from Mahoud's booth to the location where his friend had just gone down. Which way to go? Where was his master?

Grimaldi was moving by the time the guy made up his mind, a rough collision course, the Browning held in front of him. He kept his head down, moving in a kind of duck walk, fending off the frightened customers who ran in all directions, threatening to knock him down and trample him.

The shooter was coming up, and Grimaldi was almost close enough to touch him when he reached up with the Browning, from the shooter's right-hand side, and pumped two shots into his rib cage. No risk of an innocent civilian wandering into the line of fire. The guy went down, a twisted scowl of pain etched on his face, and Grimaldi reached out to twist the semiauto pistol from his twitching fingers.

Even as he determined to get a fix on the others, he wondered where Bolan was and whether he had the broker with him.

Armed and dangerous, Grimaldi kept on moving, seeking friends and enemies.

AFIF MATALKA CLUTCHED his MP-5K submachine gun, searching desperately for targets as the crush of frightened men and women swirled around him. He could still hear shooting, but the source was difficult to fix in those surroundings. Hajik Mahoud had dropped from sight, together with the stranger in his private booth, and it was anybody's guess where they had gone.

Not far, Matalka was reasonably sure of that. It might be possible for them to slip past in the crowd, but there had not been time for them to reach an exit. Matalka had placed himself between the master's booth and the front door, a logical position if he wanted to prevent the enemy's escaping.

All he needed now was to find his target....

Sudden movement on his left, and he turned back in that direction, tracking with his SMG. He caught a glimpse of flying fists, a snarling face, and fired into the mass of swirling bodies. Three men fell, at least a dozen other scattered for their lives, but there were no apparent weapons in the group.

Matalka barked a curse and turned back toward the booth where his employer had been sitting when the whole mess started. Who had started firing over by the toilets? Actually it made little difference. The fight was on, and he had seen a couple of his comrades fall, cut down by gunmen whom Matalka could not see.

At least it seemed reasonable to assume that the enemy could not see him. The thought was comforting to some degree, but it would do him no good if he was shot down by a stranger creeping up behind him.

There! A glimpse of color in between the thrashing, running bodies. Had it been Hajik's red tie...or something else?

He had his submachine gun braced, prepared to fire, when someone struck him from the left flank, drove him to his hands and knees. Matalka kicked backward with his left leg, desperate to maintain his balance. If he fell, he might be trampled in the crush.

A wild-eyed Arab loomed above him, shouting curses, brandishing a chair above his head. Matalka did not know the man from Adam, and there was no time to reason with him in the circumstances. Firing wild, a short burst from the floor, Matalka shot him in the chest and slammed him over backward, screaming as he fell.

Some insane pretender from the crowd, but he was nothing now. Matalka's concern was still the same. More crucial, now that he had been distracted from his focus on the master and his enemies. He struggled to his feet, lashed out to strike a man who almost knocked him down again and faced in the direction that his master would be, or should be, coming from.

And suddenly Mahoud was there, a dazed expression on his face, the stranger pulling him along as if he were a child. Afif Matalka saw his chance and raised the submachine gun, sighting quickly on his adversary.

He held himself back from being hasty and running the risk of injuring his master. In the heartbeat that was left before he fired, Afif Matalka used his thumb to

switch the weapon's fire selector switch from automatic mode to 3-round bursts. Control was everything
in the given circumstances.

He squeezed the trigger, then bit his tongue to keep
from screaming as an old man lurched across his line
of fire and took the bullets low down, in his groin. His
inadvertent target went down, kicking, spraying blood
and sobbing in his agony.

The stranger saw him now! He squeezed off another burst, too late, as Mahoud and his captor shifted
to the right. Matalka's bullets punched holes in a table
that had overturned in the confusion.

One of the nude dancers suddenly appeared before
him, saw Matalka's gun and shrieked in fright. He was
about to shoot her, clear the field of fire by any means
available, when she gave out another squeal and bolted
toward the exit.

In her place he saw the stranger standing tall, a pistol aimed directly at Matalka. Hajik Mahoud was
down on hands and knees beside the tall man, the expression of a trapped rat on his narrow face.

Matalka saw death there, in the stranger's eyes, and
tried to save it, squeezing off another burst before he
had a chance to aim. He missed, his bullets gouging
divots from the wooden floor, and then he saw a bright
flash from the muzzle of his adversary's weapon.

It felt as if a giant fist had slammed into Matalka's
chest, propelled him backward, downward, sprawling
on the floor. The submachine gun skittered from his
grasp and spun away. Warm liquid soaking through his
shirt and jacket, oozing underneath his arm.

The light was fading, but he still had time to see the
stranger looming over him, his free hand clutching at
Hajik Mahoud. The master stared down at Matalka

with an expression of contempt before the stranger yanked him out of there, and they were gone.

And there was only darkness, smothering Matalka like a heavy blanket, blocking out the light, the air, his life.

OUTSIDE, the street was teeming with escapees from the club. He tucked the pistol out of sight, against his captive's ribs, and drove Hajik Mahoud ahead of him across the street.

The car was waiting. Bolan shoved his hostage into it, backseat, and scrambled in behind him. Moments later, still no uniforms in sight, Grimaldi shouldered through the crowd and slid behind the steering wheel. He gunned the engine, then took them out of there.

"Let's not waste time pretending that you don't speak English," Bolan said.

"Of course I speak," Hajik Mahoud replied.

"That makes it easy, then. I need some information."

"Then you kill me, yes?" A vague note of defiance in the broker's voice, behind the fear.

"Depends on you," said Bolan. "Maybe we can cut a deal."

"What is it you require?"

"You have a shipment coming in or here already," Bolan said. "From the Ukraine. Uranium. That ring a bell?"

Mahoud blinked twice, apparently surprised, as if he were expecting something else. "Uranium."

"That's it. You want to make believe you don't know what I'm saying?"

Bolan raised the Browning, thumbed the hammer back for emphasis.

"There was a shipment," said Hajik Mahoud. "It has already been delivered to the buyer."

Bolan felt a knot of tension twisting in his stomach. Up in front Grimaldi cursed and slapped an open palm against the steering wheel.

"I'll need some information on the customer," said Bolan.

"And for this," Hajik Mahoud inquired, "you let me live?"

"Sounds fair," said Bolan, lying through his teeth.

The broker thought about it for another moment, then he forced a crooked smile. "They call themselves the Scourge of Allah," said Mahoud. "Their leader is a man named Hafez al-Zuabi."

"This group hangs out in Algiers?"

"Hangs out?" The weapons broker looked confused.

"Where is their headquarters? The base of operations."

"Ah. They have men in Algiers, of course, but their headquarters, as you say, is somewhere in the desert to the south. Beyond the mountains."

"That's a little vague."

"My business is to sell them weapons," Mahoud told him, "not to follow them around. The less I know about these men, the better for myself."

That made sense, of course. The terrorists would give up no more information than they absolutely had to, and they would be naturally suspicious of a prying stranger—even one who sold them guns and bombs. As for Hajik Mahoud, he knew these people well enough to recognize their paranoia, understand that some of them would rather kill him on a whim than take the chance that he would sell them out.

What else could Mahoud tell him? There were many questions, off the top of Bolan's head, but instinct told him they would either fall outside the broker's range of knowledge or be met with fluent lies. Could he believe the information that Hajik Mahoud had given up so far? Did Bolan have a choice?

"Pull over, Jack."

Grimaldi curbed the rental, kept the motor idling as Bolan reached across his captive, opening the starboard door.

"Okay. Get out."

"You let me go?"

There was no question of releasing him, of course. The first thing that Hajik Mahoud would do, once he had put some ground between himself and his abductors, would be to alert his customers to danger in the wind. The warning would be phrased to clear himself of obvious suspicion, but the end result would be to make the job of tracking down Hafez al-Zuabi and the Scourge of Allah much more difficult—perhaps impossible.

"You're free," said Bolan, knowing he would have to live with it.

The broker scrambled clear, didn't look back as he began to run along the sidewalk. Bolan stepped out of the car and braced the browning in a firm two-handed grip. He squeezed off two quick shots at twenty feet, a double punch between the runner's shoulder blades, and saw his man go down. No need to check and see if he was still alive. The boneless sprawl told Bolan everything he had to know.

And he was back inside the car a moment later, settling in.

"Let's roll."

CHAPTER EIGHTEEN

The leads came back from Ahmed Ben Salah in thirty minutes flat, from Bolan's query to the call back. He had names and street addresses in Algiers to start—a good half-dozen marks—and he was putting feelers out for a location on the Scourge of Allah's desert campsite.

They would take it one step at a time, with all deliberate speed. There was a constant sense of urgency behind his quest, but Bolan could not let himself be driven to distraction by the prospect of disaster. Even with the nuclear material in hand, his enemies would need some time and expertise to put a bomb together, even more time to select a target and deliver. Knowing they had someone on their case—as they were bound to know, within the next few hours—had to work against them, rattle concentration and divert their energy from one cause to another.

With their focus on survival they would have less time to plot against the innocent and put their schemes in motion.

Bolan started from the top of Ben Salah's hit list, an apartment just outside the Kasbah, where Hafez al-Zuabi's soldiers were alleged to congregate. He made the drive-by on his own, Grimaldi off to hit the second target on the list and alternate with Bolan's marks from there.

The small apartment house was square, three stories, stucco painted beige, as if to match the color of the desert sands. A kind of open tunnel ran between apartments on the ground floor, with a metal staircase serving those above. There was no fire escape, and since Ahmed Ben Salah said his targets occupied at least one third-floor room, it meant that Bolan had to take them from the front, with nothing but his nerves and hardware to sustain him.

Walking up the stairs, the Uzi in his hand, he knew that it was possible there could be enemies behind him and below, prepared to cut off his escape at the first sound of trouble. Bolan reckoned he would have to cope with that eventuality when it arose and do the best with what he had.

On the third floor he stood and listened. Two doors faced him on either side, dead silence on the left, a sound of voices backed by music from the first door on his right. If Ben Salah had his facts straight, this was Bolan's target. If he had it wrong—well, then, the tenants were about to get a rude surprise, but broken locks aside, they would be none the worse for wear.

He braced himself, reared back and hit the flimsy door with a resounding kick beside the job. Charged through and caught three young men seated at a table, drinking wine and playing cards. Two were wearing pistols, with a trio of Kalashnikovs lined up against the wall on Bolan's left.

He let his Uzi do the talking, held the trigger down and tracked from left to right across the table. Number one was gaping at him, trying to make sense of the intrusion, when a stream of parabellum slugs ripped through his chest and slammed him backward, chair and all.

The other two were slightly quicker off the mark, one grabbing for the pistol in his belt, the other lunging from his chair to try to reach the nearest AK-47. Bolan hit the runner first, a 3-round burst that tripped him, pitched him face forward into the stacked rifles.

That left one, and Bolan met him with a burst of parabellum manglers as the young man leaped up from his chair, the pistol in his hand. He triggered two wild shots before he fell, heels drumming briefly on the wooden floor.

Bolan was retreating from the small apartment when a door directly opposite swung open and a young man barged into the hallway, brandishing a pistol. Bolan met him with a rising burst that punched him backward, out of sight.

He took a moment to survey the second flat, found no one else to challenge him and hit the staircase running. Doors slammed shut ahead of him, the neighbors wise enough to know they shouldn't borrow trouble.

See no evil, reap no evil.

Bolan slowed down when he reached the street, walked calmly to his waiting car, the Uzi hidden underneath his jacket. No one tried to stop him or record the license number of his rental as he pulled away.

Algiers was long accustomed to the sound of guns, and there was worse to come before the Executioner moved on to seek his adversaries in the desert to the south.

JAMAL AKBAR WAS PROUD to serve the Scourge of Allah. Barely nineteen years of age, he was a man in all the ways that mattered, from his active sex life to the five men he had executed on command from Hafez al-

Zuabi. Two of them were Jews; the other had been traitors to the cause of Arab unity, espousing peace in Palestine when only war could ever balance out the scales of justice.

So it was that he was spending Tuesday night on guard when he would much prefer to find himself a woman in the Kasbah and make love until the sun rose. Every soldier has a duty to perform, and this was his.

The warehouse was an old, decrepit structure on the waterfront. In any Western nation it would certainly have been condemned, but this was not the West. In olden times, before Akbar was born, slaves had been auctioned here—young women for the harems to the south, others bound for European brothels—but the trade in human flesh had been officially "suppressed"...which simply meant that it was driven underground, away from prying eyes.

These days the ancient warehouse served as a repository for the kind of contraband that didn't walk and talk. Narcotics, stolen goods and weapons were the norm, some marked for sale and export, other items— the military hardware, mostly—earmarked for the war against the Jews. Hafez al-Zuabi owned the warehouse now, although the legal paperwork would not reveal his name.

The Scourge of Allah owned this property, and it had served the movement well so far.

Tonight Jamal Akbar was guarding rifles, ammunition and grenades. A shipment from Iraq on credit. Baghdad was less interested in payment than results, the more spectacular the better. Anything to nettle Tel Aviv and cause more grief for the United States.

Akbar was idling on the seaward loading dock, legs dangling, with a rifle braced across his knees, when an explosion rocked the warehouse at his back. He scrambled to his feet, nearly lost his balance as the shock wave hit him, but he managed to stay upright, facing toward the warehouse and the town beyond.

Bright flames were visible from where he stood, and smoke was pouring from the roof, blotting out the sky. The heat washed over him and brought tears to his eyes.

Filled with fear and confusion, he had no clue what was going on. There was another guard on duty, watching out along the street. Where had he gone? Akbar began to run in that direction, circling the east side of the warehouse, calling to his comrade in a voice that sounded breathless, strained. He swallowed hard and tried again, but he knew it would be difficult for anyone to hear him through the roaring of the flames.

It was a moment later when he saw the other guard…or what was left of him. Akbar would not have recognized the ruins of the face, but those were blue jeans smoldering on twisted legs, and he could always spot Italian shoes. The dead man clutched an AK-47 in his right hand, but his left arm had been torn off at the shoulder, flung away somewhere beyond his line of sight or maybe swallowed by the flames.

Jamal Akbar was trembling, clinging to his rifle, when a tall, dark man stepped out of nowhere, backlit by the fire, a submachine gun braced against his hip. He did not speak or gesture, but rather stood and waited for Akbar to make his move.

There was only one choice open in the circumstances. Sobbing at the sudden rush of fear, Akbar brought up his rifle, probing for a target, wondering if he had flicked the safety off. Before he had a chance to check it, blue fire erupted from the submachine guns' muzzle, and he felt the bullets slapping into him like power kicks and punches from a martial artist, shattering one kneecap, pummeling his rib cage, dropping him like so much dirty laundry on the pavement.

It was cold despite the fire close by and Akbar knew that meant that he was dying. He had seen men shiver as their life ran out through open wounds.

So much for glory and his war against the Zionists. Somebody else would have to carry on without him. At least he had the satisfaction of a soldier slain in Allah's service. No one could deny him that, the automatic ticket into Paradise.

He just had time for one last scary thought. What if he was wrong?

GRIMALDI'S FIRST STOP was a brothel in the Kasbah, where Hafez al-Zuabi's men were said to congregate. From what he heard and saw during his first two minutes on the premises, Grimaldi had to give them credit. For a band of Muslim warriors in the midst of a crusade, the Scourge of Allah's troops knew how to party.

He was greeted in the main room by a stylish pimp who started out in French, then switched to English when it didn't fly. Grimaldi made his pick at random from the six or seven girls who were not occupied with other clients, handed over several hundred dinars to the pimp and trailed his pick upstairs. Along the way he spotted three apparent gunmen, and two more were visible through the partly open doors of rooms they passed upstairs.

Say half a dozen he was sure of, and there could be others tucked away somewhere beyond his line of sight. It would require some fancy footwork, but it was not hopeless.

Yet.

Inside the tiny bedroom, he got down to business. Raising a warning finger to his lips, he showed his silent Uzi to the hooker. She recoiled, on the verge of screaming, but Grimaldi closed the gap in two long strides and hit her with a solid left that left her draped across the bed, unconscious.

His knuckles ached, but that was nothing. If he blew it, in the next few moments Grimaldi knew he was looking at a world of hurt—not that the pain would last too long once everybody started shooting at him.

He had to get it right the first time, and no mistakes.

He left the hooker snoozing, slipped out of the bedroom, turning to his left along the indoor balcony. If anyone was watching from below, they gave no sign. The moment that he started shooting, Grimaldi knew it was anybody's game, so he would have to get the most bang for his buck and do it right while there was time.

The next door on his left was cracked an inch or two, enough for him to peer inside and see a man of thirty-something laboring atop a woman half his age. There was an automatic on the nightstand, easily within his reach, but Grimaldi didn't intend to give him any room for play.

He breezed in through the door and kicked it shut behind him, not quite hard enough to slam. The panting Arab glanced up, gaped at death incarnate, opening his mouth to curse or scream. A 3-round burst of parabellum shockers silenced him forever, snapped his head back at a crazy angle, rolled him off the girl.

There was no way Grimaldi could keep the scream from bursting out of her unless he shot her where she lay. Instead, he chose to keep the ball in play, moved on to hit the next room down, and by the time she started wailing, he was on the threshold, staring over gunsights at a young man with his pants around his knees.

Grimaldi waited long enough to glimpse the side arm hanging in a shoulder rig beneath his arm, and then the Uzi stuttered, gouging bloody vents across his chest. Another female voice wailed the alarm, and this time, when he came back to the landing, there were angry shouts and curses from below.

Grimaldi peered across the railing, saw his three intended targets on their feet with weapons in their hands. Clearly they hadn't come expecting trouble, but they all packed handguns, and the boldest of them pegged a shot as soon as Grimaldi showed his face.

Grimaldi ducked back, felt a bullet sizzle past his ear. The last door on his left came open simultaneously, and a gunman with a drooping mustache stepped out in his underwear, prepared to fight or die.

He died, a short burst from the Uzi almost disemboweling him before he toppled over backward, sprawling on the threadbare carpet. Crimson streaked the grimy walls and soaked into the rug beneath him, spreading sluggishly.

Which still left three downstairs.

He had grenades, but that meant wasting everyone downstairs—or, at the very least, endangering the working girls—so he refrained from taking what would be the "easy" route to beat his enemies. He checked the Uzi's magazine, replaced it with a fresh one to prevent himself from running empty when he needed it the most and started edging toward the stairs.

One of his adversaries had begun the climb to meet him, moving in a crouch, the shiny automatic pistol probing out ahead of him. Grimaldi started firing when he glimpsed the gunner's head and shoulders, spending half a dozen rounds to knock him backward, tumbling down the staircase in a twisted knot of arms and legs. Before that one reached the bottom, the surviving enemies were cutting loose with everything they had, slugs ripping through the banister and wall above his head.

Grimaldi kept on going toward the stairs, using the distraction of the moment to advance his own position. When he reached the staircase, there was nothing for it but a rush against the odds. He bolted from a crawl into a crouch and found his targets, standing several yards apart, still firing at the spot where he had been short moments earlier. The shift appeared to take them by surprise, as if they didn't realize their enemy could move.

He started down the staircase, firing from the hip and targeting the closer of his adversaries first. The gunner tried to save himself, broke to his left, kept firing with his automatic, but the slide locked open on an empty chamber after three more shots. The wild-eyed Palestinian was frantic, grappling with the empty magazine and reaching for a new one in his pocket, but the guy was out of time.

A slashing burst of parabellum rounds ripped through the gunner's chest and stomach, spinning him around and stitching more holes in a zigzag pattern down his spine before he fell across a low-slung coffee table, crushing it beneath his weight. A couple of the house girls screamed anew and bolted from the sight, but Grimaldi didn't allow himself to be distracted, homing on his sole surviving enemy.

And number six was full of fight, regardless of the carnage all around him. He was packing two guns, blue-steel autoloaders, keeping up a steady stream of fire. Grimaldi held the Uzi's trigger down and let it rip as he continued down the stairs. A bullet smacked the wall behind him, then another and another, but he kept on firing, finally scoring hits when he was two or three steps from the bottom of the stairs. His target staggered, going over backward, and rebounded from a heavily upholstered sofa on his way to impact with the floor. The dying man rolled over on his face and lay, unmoving, crimson blotches soaking through his pastel cotton shirt.

Grimaldi spent another moment checking out the battlefield, reloading, then he turned and started for the door. The greasy pimp was huddled near the exit, covering his head with diamond-spangled hands. Grimaldi swallowed the temptation to eliminate him, shouldered through the door and tucked his Uzi out of sight beneath his jacket as he reached the sidewalk.

The job was done.

He started back in the direction of his car, already thinking of the next mark on his hit list, wondering if Bolan was all right.

No sweat, he told himself.

In any given confrontation, those who needed special sympathy would be the big guy's enemies.

THE BIG GUY, at that very moment, was approaching the next Algiers target, an office building near the heart of town. By local standards it was a high rise, seven stories, with a forest of antennae sprouting from the roof. His destination lay on four, the middle floor, and from the lights that Bolan spotted on his drive-by, he was confident of finding someone home to take his message.

Most terrorists conspire to show the world a mask of innocence, complete with dedication to philanthropy and human rights. Many groups support a political party designed to promote their general aims in more moderate terms, talking sweet reason while the rank and file collected weapons, planned their aids on schools and churches, embassies, department stores and private homes.

Hafez al-Zuabi's cover in Algiers for the Scourge of Allah was the Palestinian Deliverance Party, pledged— on paper—to the reclamation of occupied territory from Israel and establishment of a separate Palestinian homeland. To that end the party circulated petitions, collected "relief" funds earmarked for homeless Palestinian refugees and published a monthly newsletter detailing the real or imagined sins of the Zionist government.

The party's actual activities included planting bombs, assassinating its critics and engaging in other terrorist acts supposedly in the name of "peace."

There would be no peace for the Scourge of Allah in Algiers tonight, however. Not if Bolan had his way.

A number of the offices were open later than they would have been in Western countries, and he took advantage of the lag time, parked downstairs and locked the rental car. The folding-stock Kalashnikov was heavy on its swivel rig beneath his overcoat, but Bolan didn't mind. The extra punch would serve him well upstairs.

A uniform was snoozing in the lobby, slumped behind an imitation marble counter. Bolan passed him by and caught the elevator, rode it up to four and stepped out into bright fluorescent lights. The corridor was empty, no guards visible, but telephones and typewriters were audible behind a number of the doors.

He turned left from the elevator, ticking off the numbered doors until he came to 418. The door swung open at his touch, and Bolan stepped through into the reception area, his AK-47 sliding out from under cover as he crossed the threshold.

There was no one at the cluttered secretary's desk when he came in, but muffled voices led him down a narrow hall with office cubicles on either side. The first one on his left was empty, but he turned in to the right and found two young men huddled over papers on a desk. He cleared his throat and watched them jump, surprised by his appearance. Bolan could not understand their words, but there was no mistaking the excited tone as one man ripped a desk drawer open, shoved his hand inside, while his companion bolted for a filing cabinet in the corner.

Close enough.

The AK-47 stuttered, dropped the nearest gunman with a short burst through his side that penetrated vital organs. Tracking on, he caught the second shooter rummaging inside the top drawer of the cabinet, his back exposed as the Executioner unleashed another short precision burst. He stitched a line of holes along the soldier's spine and left him sagging where he stood, one arm still trapped inside the drawer.

There was a babble of excited voices farther down the hall. He left the office cubicle and found two young men gaping at him. One of them had an automatic pistol aimed somewhere between his knees and feet; the other Arab was unarmed.

Before the gunner had a chance to aim and fire, another burst from the Kalashnikov reached out to slap him down. He stumbled backward, slumped against the wall, then left crimson smears behind him as he slithered to the floor.

His frightened sidekick bolted, shouting the alarm in case someone had missed the sound of gunfire. Bolan shot him from the hip, a stream of bullets ripping through him, lifting him and dropping him again, facedown.

How many left?

The Executioner kept moving, sweeping with the AK-47, wishing he could understand the shouts that issued back and forth between at least three soldiers ahead, and on his left and right. Bolan triggered three rounds into the partition on his left, the general direction of a high-pitched voice, and braced himself to see what happened next.

A heartbeat later one of Bolan's targets burst into the open, jabbering excitedly and pumping wild rounds from a revolver. Bolan heard the second round zip past him, close enough to scorch his ear. He answered with a burst that ripped his enemy from hip to shoulder, a diagonal that spun him like a dervish, arms and legs extended in a windmill pattern as he hit the floor.

The last two waited for him in an office on the right, unloading stray rounds through the open doorway. Bolan palmed a frag grenade, released the safety pin and tossed it through left-handed, completing the movement by sliding into a crouch.

One of his intended targets spotted the grenade and burst from cover, running for his life. It didn't help, as Bolan tracked him with the AK-47, dropped him with a quick burst on the run. The sole survivor held his ground and took the full brunt of the blast four seconds later, jagged bits of shrapnel zinging through the flimsy walls.

Bolan rose and stepped across the smoky threshold, saw enough to know that it was finished and retreated through the reception room and out. He waited for the elevator, noting witnesses who poked their heads out of adjoining offices, but no one tried to stop him. In the lobby, jarred away perhaps by the concussion of the hand grenade, the drowsy guard called out a question. Bolan breezed past him with a grunted monosyllable to reach the sidewalk.

He was ready to roll on.

The battle had been joined, and he was not about to let off on the pressure now. The Scourge of Allah had begun to feel the kind of heat it had been dishing out for years, but it wasn't enough. Not while Hafez al-Zuabi still had nuclear material in hand, with plans to set the world on fire.

The Executioner was on a mission to extinguish those unholy flames before they caught and spread. He meant to douse that fire by any means available.

Even if it cost his life.

CHAPTER NINETEEN

Hafez al-Zuabi growled into the telephone, "How many dead so far?"

Ali Jabir was miles away and sounded it. "Nineteen that I am certain of. There may be more."

The Scourge of Allah's founding father slammed his fist against the army-surplus desk and growled a bitter curse. "You have no information on the men responsible?"

"Not yet. I hope to learn the answers soon."

"Do more than hope, Ali." There was a warning in al-Zuabi's tone. "We can't afford this kind of interruption at the moment. Do you understand?"

"Yes, sir."

"Where are you looking?"

"Everywhere. We have compiled a list of known informers in the city, and we plan to question all of them."

"Israeli agents?"

"If they can be found," his first lieutenant said. "The man described by Rani and his women at the brothel did not have the look about him."

"So you still think all Jews look alike?"

"No, sir. I meant to say—"

"Check the Israelis first, then go to work on the informers if you have enough men left."

"I have enough, don't worry."

Was there suppressed anger in his understudy's voice? It was of no consequence to him, and actually anger could be a useful motivator. If Ali should take offense, perhaps he would be more aggressive in his search for those behind the recent series of attacks.

"You have enough, then do your job," al-Zuabi replied. "I want no more embarrassment, no damage to our plans. Understand, Ali?"

"Yes, sir."

He hung up without a parting comment, left Jabir to listen to the dial tone buzzing in his ear. The lazy bastard should have started hauling suspects in by now, instead of waiting for approval from his master.

Dammit! How could this thing happen now, of all times, when their destiny was hanging by a thread?

This coup would be the pinnacle of his achievement as a revolutionary pledged to endless war against the Zionists, if only he could pull it off. The raw material was in his hands already, but he needed time to make his dream—a nightmare for the enemy—a reality.

The day would come, Hafez al-Zuabi told himself, when he would see a mushroom rise above the smoking ruins of Jerusalem or Tel Aviv, but there was still no end of work to do before that vision could become reality. He had technicians under contract, ready to begin construction on the nuclear device, but they required some time and space in which to work. From there he would confront the transport problem, choose the perfect soldiers for the job. A man or men who valued revolution and the triumph of his people over life itself.

He didn't grieve for those who had been killed around Algiers. He would miss them in the same way that he missed a tool that turned up missing in a time of need, but there was no emotional attachment to his troops. The men and women who enlisted with the Scourge of Allah knew what they were asking for. They came prepared for death—or worse if the Israeli's captured them alive—and they were ready to present themselves as willing sacrifices for the cause.

What troubled him tonight was the apparent ease with which his unknown enemies were able to invade Algiers and strike at will, demolishing his trusted cadres in the city that had sheltered them for more than two years. The army and police would be involved, of course—jarred out of their deliberate apathy and forced to launch what passed for an investigation. They would not embarrass him, Hafez al-Zuabi thought, but it was still an inconvenience. It would slow him down, make things more difficult in terms of implementing his master plan.

He meant to remedy that situation soon. The sooner the better, in fact. He would take it as a challenge, rise to the occasion . . . but he would not risk himself. Not yet.

The Scourge of Allah needed his direction, guidance, inspiration. There might come a time at some point in the future when al-Zuabi could afford to man the front lines on his own, but for the moment he would use the willing soldiers who embraced his cause. How many generals grabbed a rifle and went out into the trenches with their men to face an overwhelming enemy?

Hafez al-Zuabi's courage was unquestioned by the loyalists who served him, and it would remain so. They would do his bidding, give their lives if necessary to advance the scheme he had conceived for total victory.

How could the Zionists maintain their hold on Israel if there was no Israel? Would they rally to the flag when it was flying in the dirty breeze above a giant graveyard with irradiated bodies rotting in the desert sun?

No man alive could keep him from his destiny.

He dared the enemy to try.

GRIMALDI MADE THE CALL to Ahmed Ben Salah and left a message. Some guy on the other end came back with broken English, telling him it would be twenty minutes, give or take, before his man could take the call. Grimaldi did not care for killing time on hostile ground, but he appeared to have no choice, and he resolved to make the best of it.

That meant avoiding garbled conversation with the natives, mainly keeping out of sight, since it was past the time when tourist shops shut down and foreigners went back to their hotels or found a bar in which to pass the time. Grimaldi wasn't drinking, and he didn't want to make himself more visible than absolutely necessary.

The police would be reacting to their early hits by now, but he had no idea what that meant to him in concrete terms. To what extent were the authorities in league with terrorists their government made welcome in Algiers? Would the police take extra steps to guard their violent guests and ferret out the enemy?

It was another wrinkle in the plan, but they had been expecting problems from the outset. Nothing came easy when you were operating behind enemy lines, but he had grown accustomed to the special challenge in his years with Bolan. Stepping out with Sergeant Thunder, there was one thing you could always expect.

The unexpected.

Grimaldi found a place to park where he could stretch his legs and stay within sight of his rental car. He dawdled past shop windows, checking out the jewelry and clothing on display, a shop with books he couldn't read, a walk-in movie theater with Bruce Lee posters on the wall outside.

Never say die.

Foot traffic had begun to thin, but there were still enough pedestrians around to help him take it easy when a red-and-yellow squad car passed him, eastbound, both cops eyeballing the action on the street.

Were they on notice to watch out for any foreigners they saw? Had the survivors from the brothel broadcast his description? Was the Scourge of Allah working on retaliation even now?

Grimaldi checked his watch again—four minutes left, if Ben Salah was on time—and started walking slowly back in the direction of his car. He had a public phone booth spotted near the parking lot, but it was occupied as he approached, and he was forced to wait three minutes longer while a young man with a pockmarked face wound up his business on the line. When it was clear, Grimaldi stepped into the booth and closed the door behind him, dropped his coin and dialed the contact number one more time.

The same guy answered him in Arabic and listened while Grimaldi spoke to him in English, dropping Ahmed Ben Salah's name.

"Wait, pliz."

He waited, listening to laughter and discordant music in the background. Tavern noises. Thirty seconds more, and Ahmed Ben Salah came on the line.

"Hello?"

"I'm calling back," Grimaldi said. It would be Ben Salah's job to recognize his voice.

"Of course."

"We're waiting on coordinates for that vacation spot," Grimaldi said. He had no reason to believe the line was monitored, but the precaution came from force of habit. Better safe than sorry.

Better safe than dead.

"I may have something," he contact said, "but I cannot discuss it now."

So maybe the precautions weren't a waste of time, Grimaldi thought. "You want a meeting?"

"I believe that's best."

"Say when and where. I'll set it up."

Ben Salah named another nightclub, Le Jardin, on the outer fringes of the Kasbah, and told Grimaldi he could be there in approximately half an hour.

"That's affirmative," Grimaldi told him. "Thirty minutes."

Hanging up, he knew it would be too much to expect Ahmed Ben Salah to show up on the dot, but so far there had been no major hitch in their communication. Checking both ways through the full-length windows of the phone booth, Grimaldi reached into a pocket of his sport coat and withdrew an object resembling a compact calculator. Next he cracked the door an inch or tow, tapped out the pay phone's number for an LED display and pressed the blue transmitter button with this thumb.

Wherever Bolan was—within a range of twelve to fifteen miles, depending on the weather—he would feel the pager on his belt begin to vibrate. Nothing in the way of beeping sounds that would betray him at a crucial moment. When he got a chance, the number would be on display, and he would make the call.

It took the best part of five minutes, Grimaldi in place and feigning conversation while he held the button down. It was incongruous, the sudden ringing while he still had the receiver in his hand, but he released the button instantly and spoke.

"It's me," Mack Bolan said.

"We've got a meet," Grimaldi told him, and repeated the location.

"Time?"

"I make it twenty-four."

"I'll see you there."

And that was all. His comrade broke the link, and Jack Grimaldi could picture Bolan, already moving toward his vehicle, prepared to roll.

He left the phone booth, walked back to his car and slid behind the wheel. It started at his touch, and Grimaldi was moving, little traffic in the neighborhood to slow him down.

Another step in the direction of a climax to their mission.

And the final step, Grimaldi knew, would hinge on what their contact had to say.

AHMED BEN SALAH spent a moment frowning at the telephone before he turned back to the bar. A glass of wine was waiting for him, and he drained it in a single swallow, set the glass back down and left some coins beside it on the bar. He looked around the tavern, tried to see if anyone was paying more attention to him than they should, but he caught no one staring. It was not unusual for people to receive a phone call at the tavern in a city where the private ownership of telephones was for the most part still restricted to a wealthy ruling class.

He left the tavern, spent a moment on the street outside. Ahmed Ben Salah had a car, but it wasn't with him this evening. As a rule, he didn't drive unless he had long distances to travel or a piece of merchandise to transport that would be conspicuous if traveling by foot or on the bus. The meeting place that he had chosen, Le Jardin, was twenty minutes north on foot, and he reckoned he would be there well before the two Americans.

So far, his transitory allies had enjoyed a busy evening in Algiers. From his delivery of weapons to the present time, he was aware of four attacks directed at the Scourge of Allah, better than a dozen of Hafez al-Zuabi's soldiers killed. The city was recoiling, stunned by the ferocity of violence that had come to pass.

Of course, Algeria was not immune to crime. Drug runners fought their battles here from time to time, but they were normally discreet. A body floating in the surf or cast off in a Kasbah alleyway, perhaps a home invasion with the tenants killed. Political aggressors saw the nation as a sanctuary and a training ground, bent over backward to cooperate with the authorities . . . or pay them off to look the other way. Their paramilitary exercises were conducted in the desert, miles beyond the Tell.

The recent string of incidents would change all that. In theory it could spark a crisis in the government. If nothing else, the military and police had been provoked into unprecedented action, scouring the streets for suspects, pressing their informants for a lead.

Ahmed Ben Salah didn't work with local officers. There was no money in it, and he chose not to jeopardize himself by fraternizing with the very men who served his enemies. It would have been both a risk and a betrayal of his principles.

If the police came knocking on his door, Ben Salah would play the fool and tell them nothing. He had no connection with the Scourge of Allah, did no business with politicals if he could help it, and that fact was known to the authorities. His denials, if it went that far, would have the ring of truth.

There was another risk, of course, which he had deliberately postponed considering. Hafez al-Zuabi's men—the soldiers who survived—would be intent on finding out the names of those responsible for their misfortune. They were not constrained by law, as the police were, theoretically. When it came down to asking questions, they could cast a wider net, use harsher methods. They might also work on different lines, approach the problem with a new perspective.

Ben Salah did not serve the Scourge of Allah, but the revolutionaries knew his name, at least some measure of the business he conducted on his own. How long before they started grilling members of the Kasbah underworld at random, seeking any leads—however tenuous—that might identify the enemy?

Ben Salah had traveled half a dozen blocks, through darkness, when he got his answer in a scuffling sound of footsteps from an alley he had passed by seconds earlier. He turned to face the sound, alert to danger, wishing that he had the pistol from his flat. It did him no good in the nightstand by his bed, and it was too late now for him to run back home.

Two scruffy-looking men burst from the alley shadows. They were young, both Arabs, nothing in their dress that would identify a tribe or a political affiliation. From the grim expressions on their faces, Ben Salah did not have to ask about their state of mind.

His stomach did a slow roll as the taller of the two men spoke to him, addressing him by his name. They knew him! It was not a random mugging, then, but something worse.

"Who are you?" he demanded.

"Friends," the spokesman said. "We need to talk."

"With pleasure, at another time. I have some pressing business at the moment."

"There will be no better time."

They both drew pistols, and he heard a car approaching from behind him. Running dark, thought Ben Salah, or they would be bathed in light by now. Instead of driving past, it stopped a few yards back and sat with the motor idling. He heard doors opening, more footsteps coming up behind him on the sidewalk.

"Are these weapons necessary?"

"That's for you to say," the seeming leader of his captors answered. "We prefer that you should be alive to answer questions, but the choice is yours."

"What questions?"

"All in time. Will you get in the car?"

He saw no way around it, no way out.

"Of course."

His mind was racing off in search of answers, but his heart already knew exactly what was happening. His first glimpse of the driver nailed it down. The name escaped him, but he recognized the face, all right. A minor gunman for the Scourge of Allah, known in certain quarters of the city for his taste in teenage boys.

They had him, then, and he could guess at what would follow. Questions, and his own lies in response.

Would they be satisfactory? Would Hafez al-Zuabi's men use torture as a means of verifying what he said? How long could he last, protect his recent allies, once the pain began?

And afterward what reason was there to expect that he would be allowed to live?

In his heart he knew the answer to that one. No reason. None at all.

THEY WAITED half an hour past their deadline at the nightclub, hoping Ahmed Ben Salah had been delayed by business or traffic—anything rather than their common enemy. At last, when it was obvious that Ben Salah wasn't coming, they bailed out and regrouped on the street to organize a backup plan.

"You think somebody bagged him?" asked Grimaldi.

"Possible," said Bolan. "We can try to check it out."

"His place?"

"It's worth a shot."

Ahmed Ben Salah didn't know it, but the Executioner possessed more information on him than the Arab had supposed. He knew where Ben Salah lived, for starters, and a fair bit of his background. He had marked the club where their contact took his phone calls, knew exactly where it was, how far from Le Jardin and how long it should take Ben Salah to walk or drive the distance.

They could always trace his path, but what did Bolan hope to learn? Unless their man was dead and lying in the gutter, they would still have no idea of what had happened to him, who had picked him off in transit.

"I'll follow you," Grimaldi said to Bolan as they walked back to their waiting cars.

He led the way, Grimaldi's headlights in his rearview mirror. Seven minutes, winding through the narrow streets, before they passed the old apartment house and started looking for a place to park. Grimaldi had to drive around the block, leave his compact on a side street and walk back.

"He's on the second floor," said Bolan as they went in through a kind of lobby, homing on the stairs.

Their jackets were unbuttoned, side arms close at hand. If Ben Salah had been burned, his cover blown, an ambush could be waiting for them here, but it was still a chance that Bolan felt he had to take. Regardless of the risk, he had fo know.

The door to Ahmed Ben Salah's apartment was ajar perhaps an inch, as if the raiders had no interest in concealing their design. The Browning in his hand, Mack Bolan nudged it farther open with a foot and edged his way inside, Grimaldi on his heels.

The place was trashed, for certain. Someone—several someones—had gone through the flat like a tornado. Furniture was toppled, cushions slashed, drawers spilled and the kitchen cupboards swept clean. The TV's picture tube was smashed, a table lamp protruding from the glass-and-plastic cave. It was a combination search and object lesson, rubbing Ben Salah's nose in the destruction of his private property.

But there was no sign of Ben Salah.

Same thing in the bedroom, the gutted mattress sagging on the floor. Drawers spilled and splintered. Shattered pieces of a radio alarm clock crunching underfoot. The closet door stood open, clothes ripped out and shredded, strewn about the room like rags. A storm of feathers from the ruptured pillows lay like frosting on a large, untidy cake.

Grimaldi checked the bathroom, found the cabinets emptied, toiletries and other items flung into the shower stall. The toilet tank had been uncapped, its lid removed and dropped into the bowl of the commode to protrude like a monolith from murky water.

"If I had to guess," Grimaldi said, "I'd say he took the dump before he dropped that in there. Otherwise—"

"I get the drift," said Bolan.

"Still no Ahmed, though."

"He wasn't here," said Bolan. "This was incidental."

"Searching, though. These guys were after something."

"Right."

It hardly mattered what the raiders had been seeking, since Ahmed Ben Salah had nothing in the way of documents or evidence that pointed back to Bolan and Grimaldi. They had introduced themselves with pseudonyms, and while their contact could certainly describe them, it would not prevent the war machine from rolling on.

It would be easy to dismiss Ben Salah as a casualty of war and let it go at that, but Bolan had dual motives for pursuing it. First he hated giving anything away to mortal enemies, and that included someone he had barely met. A second reason was that Ahmed Ben Salah professed to know where Bolan could locate the Scourge of Allah's training camp, perhaps the site of their experiment in building homemade nukes.

Without that pointer, he was flying blind. It could be days or weeks before he bagged a member of the group who had the necessary information, squeezed it out of him in anything approximating a coherent format. In the meantime, Hafez al-Zuabi would be fortifying his defenses, maybe even fleeing out of range.

Bolan needed a distraction, something that would keep the terrorists off balance and guessing, confident of nothing but the fact that they had grabbed a tiger by the tail.

The trick now would be letting go before that tiger turned the tables and devoured them alive.

"You've got a plan" Grimaldi said, not asking. "I can smell it."

"What's it smell like?" Bolan asked him.

"Trouble."

He was right on that score, Bolan granted. There was trouble coming to Algiers that would eclipse the early raids and make them seem like minor disagreements. Maybe he could rescue Ahmed Ben Salah and maybe not. In any case the Scourge of Allah was about to take a beating.

Bolan frowned, imagining that he could smell the backup plan, as well.

It smelled like death.

CHAPTER TWENTY

The trick, thought Bolan, would be not so much in finding Ahmed Ben Salah, but finding him alive. His disappearance was a hopeful sign in that regard, since someone who desired his death would probably have killed him on the street and left him there. Kidnapping indicated that the snatch team had another purpose—probably interrogation—that required a living subject.

How long Ahmed Ben Salah would stay alive in custody, however, could be anybody's guess.

Assuming that they were grilling him for answers, the question was whether it was part of a more general sweep around Algiers, or if the enemy had information linking Ben Salah more specifically to Bolan's war.

In either case, there was only one way Bolan knew of extricating hostages that always got results. Sometimes, admittedly, the outcome was bad news for all concerned, but it was still a vast improvement over groveling and pleading with the savages.

Two phone calls, and the CIA kicked in a name that Ahmed Ben Salah was not aware of. Hassan Igli Abbas was not an actual member of the government, but he was known throughout the halls of power as a man who got things done. His influence around Algiers was legendary, but except for a few people in the know, he managed to conceal the fact of his alliance with the terrorists who used his homeland as a combination training ground and health resort. Of late, smart money said that members of the Scourge of Allah were his special friends.

The power broker had a penthouse flat downtown, five minutes from the waterfront, where he could sit in comfort with his latest concubine and scan the waters of the Mediterranean in air-conditioned comfort. Years had passed since Abbas held a normal job of any kind, and when he was not on the party circuit or confined to smoky meeting rooms, he was predictably at home.

Tonight was no exception.

Bolan knew Abbas had bodyguards, and that was fine. The more the merrier. It would cement his first impression, when he took the big man's soldiers down.

He rode the elevator up to nine, got off a floor below the penthouse, switching to the service stairs. Instead of staking out a gunman on the stairs alone, Abbas was careless. He allowed his watchdogs to hang out around the door of his palatial suite and guard the elevator, with the nearby staircase covered as an afterthought.

Bolan cracked the access door and peered along the hallway toward the penthouse entrance. Three goons on duty, dressed in shiny suits, one of them lounging in a chair kicked back against the wall, the others on their feet. His Uzi had a silencer attached, and Bolan had a firm hand on the pistol grip as he eased through the door, stepped out into the hall.

He wanted it as close as possible, point-blank if he could swing it. Moving down the corridor with easy strides, he had the gunners covered going in, but several seconds passed before the seated watcher saw him coming. An alarm in Arabic, and all of them were scrambling for weapons, with Bolan less than thirty feet away.

He started with the two men on their feet, a sweeping burst from left to right that blew them both away with parabellum manglers. Neither of them cleared his weapon from the hidden shoulder rigs they wore, and Bolan watched them fall together, twitching from the impact of his bullets, writhing briefly on the floor.

And that left one.

The seated gunner tried to rise but lost his balance, toppling over backward with sufficient force to slam his head against the wall. That ruined his attempt to draw, and Bolan finished it with a precision burst that opened up his chest. A slow roll over to his left, a boneless sprawl, and Bolan's target crumpled to the floor.

He stepped around the corpses, stood before the penthouse door, the Uzi braced against his hip. Reaching out to try the knob, he was amazed to feel it turn. A hedge, he guessed, against the shooters waking up their master when they wanted access to the kitchen or the toilet.

Nice of them to smooth the way for him.

It was solid luxury inside, befitting the status and bankroll of Hassan Igli Abbas. The oil paintings on the walls must have been expensive, since he couldn't make out what the hell they represented. Heavy crystal on the coffee table. Polished, built-in gear throughout the kitchen.

Bolan found his target in the bathroom, following the shower noises, and barged in to catch the power broker in his birthday suit, hair dripping, towel in hand.

"You want to live?" he asked Hassan Igli Abbas by way of introduction.

"Who...who are you?" The man was startled but coping fairly well, all things considered. Abbas tried to see beyond the threshold, obviously looking for his bodyguards.

"They're dead," said Bolan. "You can join them if you want, or you can do yourself a favor."

"Favor?"

"Take a message back to Hafez al-Zuabi for me. Fair enough."

"I do not wish to die."

"Smart boy. So, here's the message. Do you need a pen and paper?"

"No." There was a tremor in the Arab's voice, but he stood fast. "I will remember."

"Fair enough. The Scourge of Allah has a friend of mine. They snatched him off the street. I want him back, okay? Unharmed. His name is Ahmed Ben Salah. Until such time as he's released to me, it's open season on the Scourge. Nobody's safe. Got that?"

"I have it."

"I was you, I'd make the call right now, first thing, before I bothered calling the police about those boys out front. I'll check in with you for an answer. Sixty minutes, right? If there's a double cross, I'm going to assume it came from you. It could get messy."

"I will do as you command."

"I hope so, guy. For your sake."

Bolan left him standing there and rode the elevator down, a bit surprised when no one tried to intercept him in the lobby. Would Abbas try to spare himself embarrassment, spirit the bodies of his watchmen away before they were noticed?

It made no difference either way, as long as the kingmaker did what he was told.

Meanwhile, the Executioner had other work to do around Algiers.

HIS CHAIR WAS BOLTED to the floor, and Ahmed Ben Salah felt as if his body had been welded to the chair. In fact, he was secured with twists of silver duct tape at the ankles, knees, wrists and elbows, with a final loop around his waist. Stark naked, with the air cool on his skin. Improbably his mind was focused at the moment on the way that tape would feel when it was ripped away.

The incongruities of the human mind, Ben Salah thought. What was there in the present situation to make him think that he would be alive by then to feel it?

Seated just in front of him in a normal chair, no duct tape, was Ali Jabir, the second in command of Hafez al-Zuabi's Scourge of Allah. It was bad news, meeting him this way, and worse yet when a couple of his soldiers carried a hand-crank generator, jumper cables, heavy rubber gloves.

The worst was yet to come.

"You must be curious about the reason for my invitation," said Ali Jabir. His smile was tight and twisted, like a puckered scar.

Ben Salah kept silent, staring at his captor.

"You are known for the diversity of your activities," Ali Jabir remarked, "including certain projects sanctioned in advance by the authorities."

"It is a lie."

"I think not, but the question must be raised. We have a problem, my comrades and I. There is a possibility that you can help us solve it."

"It would help if I knew who you were," said Ben Salah. When in doubt, play ignorant.

Jabir's odd smile took on the aspect of a grimace. "Names are unimportant here. It is enough for you to know I represent the Scourge of Allah."

"You are not Hafez al-Zuabi."

"No. I am his eyes, his good right hand."

"If you have eyes, then you must realize I have no interest in your army or your problems."

"And you call yourself an Arab? You should be ashamed." Ali Jabir stood up, his hands deep in his pockets. "Same or not, I am required to ask you certain questions."

"And am I required to be humiliated in the process?" Ben Salah challenged.

"The removal of your clothing was a matter of convenience. Should we be required to use persuasion—" Ali paused and nodded toward the generator at his feet "—it will be easier this way."

"I'll tell you what I can," said Ahmed Ben Salah, "but it will be of little help."

"Let me judge that," Ali Jabir replied. "First question—what is your connection to the CIA?"

Ahmed Ben Salah laughed out loud and hoped that it didn't sound forced. "America? The CIA? You must have lost your mind!"

"Let's find out, shall we?"

Ali Jabir nodded, snapped his fingers, and the younger of his goons slipped on a pair of rubber gloves, picked up the jumper cables with their vicious alligator clips. His partner knelt beside the generator, one hand resting on the handle of his crank.

"A touch, no more," Ali Jabir instructed.

Ahmed Ben Salah tried to cringe away, but there was no place he could hide. He closed his eyes, the next best thing, and started trembling when he felt cold metal press against the soft head of his penis. Still no pain, until the second alligator clip brushed his nipple, closed the circuit, and his body lurched against its bonds, his every nerve exploding, crackling with a bolt of white-hot agony.

A heartbeat later it was over, and he slumped back in the chair. Sweat beaded on his face and torso, leaving tracks across his livid skin. He eyes swam out of focus for a moment, then came back.

"Just a small taste," said Ali Jabir, "to help you understand the fate of liars."

"You have no authority to do this," Ben Salah answered weakly.

"I don't need authority," his captor said. "I have the means."

"You have the wrong man," Ben Salah told him, knowing it was lame.

Before Ali Jabir could answer, yet another of his goons appeared—from a door behind him, Ben Salah thought—and spent a moment muttering in his leader's ear. At first the terrorist commander's face was bland, then curious. By slow degrees it darkened, and the odd smile disappeared entirely. There was flint in Ali Jabir's eyes as he dismissed the soldier with a nod.

"It seems that someone is concerned about your health," he said. "A stranger in Algiers. American. We need to talk about this, Ahmed."

"I have no idea—"

"Enough of lies!" Ali Jabir interrupted. "No one can help you here. Before we finish, you will tell me what I need to know, I promise you. In fact, you may suggest some topics of your own, to ease the pain."

"I don't know anything," said Ben Salah woodenly.

And then, a moment later he began to scream.

HAFEZ AL-ZUABI SAT and waited for the call that would relieve his mind. An answer to the riddle of his late misfortune, which had mushroomed in a few short hours to endanger everything he had worked for all these years.

The weapon was within his grasp, and nothing must distract him now. It did not matter if the recent forays had been launched from Washington or Tel Aviv, as far as Hafez al-Zuabi was concerned. The motive was irrelevant, with all the world against him, and he only cared for the identity of his assailants so that they could be efficiently destroyed.

They at least had a source who could help them, if Ali Jabir was not too energetic with his questioning. He had a tendency to lose control in stressful situations—something he would have to work on when he had the time to spare. Just now, though, some restraint was needed.

Afterward . . . well, that would take care of itself.

And now the enemy was conscious of their strategy. Hassan Abbas was crying for protection in Algiers. His anonymous assailant threatened dire reprisals if the source—this worm in human form—was not released at once. Hafez al-Zuabi was not worried for himself, but neither did he plan on sacrificing his entire Algiers continent if he had a choice.

Assuming that he *had* a choice.

He thought of going north to take command himself, but that would be a foolish risk, with things in total disarray. He had to trust Ali Jabir, let him extract the necessary information from their source and use it to the best advantage.

The Romanian technicians needed time to finish the device. Once that was done, selection of the target would begin. The possibilities were limited this time around. The Zionists were Hafez al-Zuabi's mortal enemies from childhood. He could not resist the sitting target that was Israel, but elimination of the stolen Jewish homeland would not end his war. The Jews had numerous supporters in the West, contributors to the humiliation of his people spanning close to half a century.

From Downing Street to Pennsylvania Avenue, Hafez al-Zuabi's enemies were legion. All were equally responsible for the displacement of the Palestinians, and all of them would pay. If he could do it once, unleash hellfire on earth, it could be done repeatedly. He had the source for more uranium, a pair of willing hands to build the bombs and willing soldiers who would sacrifice themselves upon command to see it done.

But first he had to manage the initial strike—and that would be more difficult, if not impossible, with jackals snapping at his heels.

The terrorist leader resisted the temptation to pick up his telephone and call Ali Jabir, find out if they had any useful information yet with which to track and terminate their enemies.

Outside, his men were running exercises in the dark, a standard preparation for the day when they were into

Syria or Jordan, booked for raids across the border into Israel. If his master plan succeeded, the guerrilla raids would cease, become a bittersweet, heroic memory.

But there would be an end to Hafez al-Zuabi's war.

The struggled had begun in 1948, ten years before his birth, when the United Nations manufactured Israel out of Arab territory. The redress of that great insult would not end the killing, though. Not while his people lived in poverty, manipulated by the Western powers and their boundless appetite for oil.

Hafez al-Zuabi did not want to rule the world, but he had ancient scores to settle—with America, with France, with Britain, with a host of Arab traitors in the Middle East. The spineless idiots who wept and moaned for peace at any price, when logic said they should have massed their forces, pushed the Jews into the sea.

Hafez al-Zuabi was prepared to deal with traitors, cowards, scum who valued profit over the security of Arab brothers. He would not forget, and it was not within his nature to forgive.

In that respect the present challenge might be beneficial. It would sharpen his responses, challenge his commandoes to the utmost. They would have to prove themselves, and when the great day came, when Israel lay in smoking ruins at their feet, they would be ready for the next phase of Hafez al-Zuabi's endless war.

He hoped that it would not take long.

So many men to kill, so little time.

THE WARNING to Hassan Igli Abbas had only been a starting point for Bolan in his blitz against the Scourge of Allah. Even if Hafez al-Zuabi took him seriously—

and there was no reason to expect he would—the terrorists would not give in without a fight. Indeed, his very challenge might encourage al-Zuabi's soldiers to increase the heat on Ahmed Ben Salah, to try to find out who and where his sponsors were.

It would be Bolan's task to hit them hard and fast, prevent them from coordinating any countermoves.

His first stop, after dropping by the penthouse, was a small plant on the outskirts of Algiers, where artisans spent six days every week producing "native handicrafts" for disposition in the tourist trade. Behind the scenes, according to the CIA, the factory was also used for modifying weapons and constructing bombs for use outside Algeria.

The place was dark when Bolan got there, but he didn't take for granted that it was deserted. Nighttime brought the Scourge of Allah's gremlins out to work their evil magic under cover of shadows.

Bolan parked outside the ten-foot chain-link fence and cut himself an entrance on the south perimeter. He was in a blacksuit, dressed to kill, the silent Uzi slung across one shoulder and a heavy canvas satchel on the other. C-4 plastic charges in the bag, with timers fixed in place. His side arm was the Browning automatic in an armpit rig, with a stiletto in his belt.

No lookouts were evident as he approached the plant, but he could see a faint light showing at the rear. He moved in that direction cautiously but picking up his speed. It might turn out to be a janitor at work, but Bolan was not banking on it.

Then he made his sighting. Two men crossing open ground, a heavy crate between them. They disappeared through a door that swiftly closed, cut off the spill of yellow light. Bolan was hard on their heels, ready for anything when he tried the door and felt it open at his touch.

And now he had the gremlins spotted, two men hunched above a workbench to his left, another pair across the room, unloading automatic weapons from the crate that he had watched them carry. New Kalashnikovs, the AK-74s, still packed in Cosmoline and waiting to be cleaned before they went to war.

The gremlins carried pistols, and he saw two submachine guns close at hand. Despite protection for authorities around Algiers, they knew the risks involved with trafficking in weapons, and they clearly took no chances.

Neither would Bolan.

Warning them before he opened fire would be a waste of time, a costly affectation lifted from a Gary Cooper Western. Bolan had a job to do, and anything that slowed him down or gave his enemies an edge was out the window.

Bolan shot the two men with the rifles first, a tracking burst that dropped them both and scattered weapons on the floor. Across the room the two bomb-builders came awake to danger, spinning off in different directions from the bench and groping for their side arms, still not sure exactly what was happening, no time to take it in.

He took the gunner on his left and stitched a burst of six or seven rounds across his chest. Explosive impact slammed the human target backward, bounced him off a corner of the waist-high workbench and he toppled to the floor from there.

Before the dead man hit concrete, his sole surviving comrade was already coming under fire. The Arab had his pistol drawn, squeezed off a hasty shot with no attempt to aim and lost it somewhere in the rafters overhead. He was about to try another when the Uzi found him, spun him like a rag doll in a cyclone, shirt and jacket rippling with the impact of a dozen slugs.

Four up, dour down, and Bolan took a moment at the bench, examining the late technicians' handiwork. It would have been a killer, several pounds of Semtex packed in nails, prepared for detonation by remote control. He knew the kind of havoc the explosion could have wreaked in a department store or shopping mall, a bank or office building.

Not this time.

He spent the next two minutes fixing charges in the workshop, setting timers. Moving on, retreating toward the exit and his vehicle, he left the last two parcels at strategic corners of the larger plant and set the timers counting backward, down to doomsday.

Outside he stowed his weapons, slid behind the rental's steering wheel and twisted the ignition key. He was in motion when the charges started going off like giant fireworks, lighting up the night and sending shock waves through the darkness.

Hafez al-Zuabi's factory was out of business. He would have to build his bombs and clean his weapons somewhere else in future... if he had the time. Before he started shopping for a new location, though, the terrorist would have to deal with Bolan, one-on-one.

It was a new day coming in Algiers.

The Executioner could not reverse a policy of coddling terrorists that dated from the 1960s, but he could inflict sufficient damage on one group of militants to illustrate that blind subservience to violence was a critical mistake.

Above all else he had to block Hafez al-Zuabi's march toward nuclear annihilation of his chosen enemies. The campaign would amount to nothing if he chased al-Zuabi's soldiers endlessly but let the central players slip away and work their lethal mischief unopposed.

The night was still young from the Executioner's perspective. He had yet to score a fatal blow against his adversary, but the time was coming, if he did not drop his guard.

Another strike or two, and he would touch base with Hassan Abbas, find out if he was gaining any ground toward the release of Ahmed Ben Salah.

Beyond that he had time and men to kill.

CHAPTER TWENTY-ONE

The Scourge of Allah's motor pool was housed in what appeared to be a semipublic parking lot, west Algiers. Surrounded by a chain-link fence with razor wire on top, the lot was always full, so far as casual arrivals were concerned. Signs on the gate declared, in Arabic and French, that spaces were reserved for staffers of the ComTec Company and the Scherazade department store. It would have taken several hours of homework to find out that neither firm existed in Algiers.

In fact, the trucks and cars—plus half a dozen motorbikes—were constantly on call to members of the Scourge. When Hafez al-Zuabi's soldiers need transportation in the city, this was where they started. Vehicles were changed at frequent intervals, the damaged ones or those identified by the authorities replaced through purchase, theft, whatever seemed appropriate and easy at the time.

Tonight—this morning, Grimaldi corrected, noting that the time was after midnight—there were thirteen cars, one van, one flatbed truck and four new-looking motorcycles in the lot, lined up with space enough between them that a chosen vehicle could be retrieved without a total rearrangement of the layout. In the bogus cashier's booth, a solitary watchman stood guard over Hafez al-Zuabi's rolling stock.

The sentry's heart was clearly elsewhere, even with the recent news of violence directed at his comrades in

Algiers. He smoked, thumbed through the pages of a magazine and placed a phone call as the hour struck.

Reporting in, Grimaldi thought. It was the same with watchmen everywhere, repeated check-ins through the night at periodic intervals to reassure employers of their vigilance. No sleeping on the job for Hafez al-Zuabi's men.

In Grimaldi's experience such calls were typically required at sixty-minute intervals, sometimes less frequently, but he had never seen a watchman forced to call in more than once per hour. If his guess was accurate, and no surprise inspections lay in store, he now had ample time to do his job.

But first he had to get inside the wire.

He went for the direct approach, a canvas gym bag slung across one shoulder, with the Browning automatic in his fist, held out of sight against his thigh. He put a bit of stagger in his walk, enough to make himself look tipsy to a casual observer, kept his head down to disguise the fact that he was obviously not a native. Closing on the guard shack, he was conscious of the sentry watching him, still not tremendously concerned, but more alert than he had been a moment earlier. There had to be a gun inside the booth, though it was presently concealed from view.

At twenty feet Grimaldi knew it would be now or never. He appeared to stumble over something, wound up in a fighting crouch and swung the Browning into target acquisition with a firm two-handed grip. The silencer reduced velocity, but he was close enough that nothing mattered. Two rounds through the flimsy glass, his human target slumping off his stool and sprawling halfway out the open door.

The sliding gate was locked, but Grimaldi retrieved the dead man's key ring, tried three keys before he got it right. Inside the lot, he closed the gate behind him, left the padlock off and went to work.

He didn't have enough C-4 to goop each vehicle in turn, but it was not required. With some creative thinking, he affixed his charges to the truck and van, plus five strategically positioned cars. The detonators were remote control, keyed in to the transmitter on his belt.

Before he wrapped it up, Grimaldi wheeled the motorcycles out of line and repositioned each in turn beside a vehicle that he had wired for doomsday. There was no point leaving anything undamaged if he had the time and opportunity to do it right.

Grimaldi's car was stashed two blocks away. He paused when he was halfway there and palmed the detonator, turning back to face the parking lot. He pressed the single button with his thumb and flinched a little, even though he was expecting it, when fire and thunder tore the night apart.

The charges had been spaced so that one blast would take out several vehicles, spread flaming gasoline around the lot and touch off fuel tanks in a string of secondary detonations. Fifteen seconds after he'd thumbed down the button on his detonator, every vehicle inside the chain-link fence was trashed and burning.

Perfect.

There was no replacing that mess overnight, and Hafez al-Zuabi's team was running out of time.

Grimaldi walked back to his car and wheeled out toward the next mark on his list.

AHMED BEN SALAH was unconscious when they came
for him again. The first slap failed to rouse him, but his
captors kept it up until the stinging blows cut through
the crimson haze inside his skull and brought him back
to something like awareness.

There was pain in every fiber of his being, from the
superficial contact burns and bruises to the deeper ache
that settled in his bones and muscles, product of the
tremors and convulsions he had suffered as electric
current rocked his body.

Now they meant to start again. It was uncertain how
much more he could endure—but what choice did he
have? Escape was not an option, and his bonds like-
wise prevented him from attempting suicide. He was
entirely at the mercy of Ali Jabir, who stood before him
now, arms folded, glaring down at him as if Ben Salah
were something he had stepped in by mistake.

"Your friends are causing us some difficulty," said
Ali Jabir. "You must be pleased."

In fact, the news meant little to Ahmed Ben Salah.
He was still trussed up and helpless, like a laboratory
specimen, but there was abstract satisfaction in the
thought that he would be avenged.

Not much, but it was something.

He made no response to the announcement from Ali
Jabir. His captor waited for a moment, then bent forward, staring into Ben Salah's bleary eyes.

"You don't have anything to say? No words of triumph? Nothing?"

"No." It came out sounding like a croak.

"So you have learned humility, at least. It is a serious mistake to let yourself believe that anyone can help
you."

Ben Salah held his tongue. There was no point in wasting breath when he was obviously running out of time.

"It is a minor inconvenience," said Ali Jabir, still frowning, "but I have decided to remove you from Algiers. A more secure location has been found outside the city."

Ahmed Ben Salah did not like the sound of that. It as could easily mean death as relocation to another holding cell. There had been little he could tell them, even when the pain became unbearable, and he could not imagine why the bastards wanted him alive, no reason whatsoever unless....

New hope enlivened Ahmed Ben Salah. If his abductors wanted him alive, perhaps they were prepared to trade, release him in exchange for some assurances of peace from the Americans. But would the men who had already killed so many soldiers of the Scourge desist on his behalf? Why should they? What was he to them?

Of course, there *was* a piece of vital information they still needed, one that he had not been able to deliver. If Ali Jabir should set him free...

The terrorist produced an automatic pistol from inside his jacket, thumbed the hammer back and aimed the muzzle at his hostage's chest. A nod, and someone reached around from the left, a long knife glinting under the fluorescent lights. The silver duct tape parted easily, his right arm first, and then the cool blade pressed against his ribs. The right leg next, and then the process was repeated on his left. He was about to stand, or try to, when the man behind him grabbed the strip of tape encircling his chest and ripped it free.

The cry of pain was automatic, irresistible. It brought a mocking smile to Ali Jabir's thin lips.

"Your clothes are on the floor, behind the chair," said his captor. "You will dress yourself without delay. It would be very foolish to attempt resistance."

Not that Ben Salah had the strength to fight in any case.

He rose on trembling legs and did as he was told, came close to falling over twice while he was grappling with his trousers. Every contact between fabric and his burns reminded him of the recent torture session, made him wonder how long it would be until they tied him down again and started over.

He would keep one eye open for a chance to run, of course, but in the meantime he would hope for rescue.

Even knowing that the odds were all against him, it was still the only hope he had.

THE WAREHOUSE WENT UP like a tinderbox. One thermite bomb and sixty seconds later, it was totally engulfed in flames. The smoke that issued from beneath its sagging eaves was heady stuff, a product of the hashish stored within.

It was the classic export of the Middle East and northern Africa, retailed in Europe and the States for cash that kept the wheels of terror turning on a global scale. How many Palestinian guerrillas, Muslim fundamentalists and others had financed their "holy wars" by dealing drugs? Hafez al-Zuabi was the latest in a long, dishonorable tradition, but he would not be taking this crop to market.

Bolan's rental car was parked upwind, where he could breathe without debilitating side effects. The fire brigade would be arriving soon, and it was time for him to go.

He had a call to make before he scratched another target from his list.

Hassan Igli Abbas was waiting by the telephone, or so it seemed. He answered midway through the first ring, sounding tense and nearly breathless from anticipation.

"Yes?"

"I'm waiting for an answer," Bolan said, not troubling to identify himself.

The Arab clearly recognized his voice. "You have created major difficulties in Algiers tonight," he said. "Our mutual acquaintance has been...inconvenienced."

"He can stop it any time," said Bolan. "What's the word?"

"His spokesman wishes no more trouble in the city. He agrees to give you what you want if you will leave his friends in peace."

"I don't suppose he has a meeting place in mind?"

"He left the choice to me...if you approve."

"I'm listening."

Hassan Igli Abbas was silent for a moment, and when he spoke again, his voice was cautious, as if waiting for the Executioner to cut him off.

"Eleven miles due west, along the coast, there is a fishing village called Ghardaj. Your friend will be there in one hour's time. Look for him on the waterfront, a boat called *Rajaleen*. It is agreeable?"

"I'll be there," Bolan answered. "Pass the word."

He smelled the trap immediately, knew the Scourge of Allah had not earned its reputation by retreating from a fight. Ahmed Ben Salah was the bait, alive or dead, and Bolan was the prey.

He lingered in the public phone booth, used his pager to alert Grimaldi, tapping out the number where he could be reached. Six minutes later, when the phone rang, he was waiting.

"Sarge?"

"We've got our meet."

"You think it's straight?"

"Don't bet your savings."

"So?"

"We'll talk about it on the way. Where can I meet you?"

Grimaldi responded with coordinates, a major intersection on the west side of the city. "We can leave from there, okay?"

"Suits me. I'm on my way."

He dropped the handset back into its cradle, left the open booth and walked back to his car.

One hour, give or take, and this phase of the game would be behind him. Victory was by no means assured, but Bolan thought he had at least an even chance . . . assuming Ahmed Ben Salah was still alive.

Of course, the game might be for nothing. If his contact had been killed outright, then Bolan would be wasting precious time exposing himself and Grimaldi to needless danger. When the smoke cleared, if the two of them were still alive, they would be forced to start from scratch.

Still, there was only one way to be sure.

He had to keep his date with Hafez al-Zuabi's gunmen in Ghardaj and see which way it played.

At the moment it was the only game in town.

ABOUT FOUR HUNDRED SOULS lived in the fishing village, but none of them was in evidence when Bolan and
Grimaldi reached the waterfront at 2:15 a.m. They had
both cars, and Grimaldi left his a few blocks from the
water, settled in the shotgun seat of Bolan's as they
eased down toward the pier.

The *Rajaleen* was not immediately visible by name.
They counted half a dozen boats docked at the waterfront, but only one of them was showing lights as Bolan set his parking brake and switched the engine off.
He made it forty yards.

"We'll walk from here."

"Seems right," Grimaldi said. "You want the seaward side?"

"Okay."

They both took Uzis, minus silencers, with extra
magazines. Two frag grenades apiece, in case it went to
hell, and they were ready. Bolan got out on the driver's side and waited for Grimaldi, saw his partner on
his way before he crossed the narrow street and started
walking westward, water lapping softly on his right.

The *Rajaleen* was waiting for him, third ship down
in line, but Bolan's first concern was for the dark sedan immediately opposite. At least two men were
waiting in the car, black silhouettes that would not be
asleep no matter how relaxed they seemed from thirty
yards away.

Grimaldi had them spotted, too. It wasn't the most
expert ambush Bolan had observed, but then he had no
reason to believe the gunmen were alone. His eyes
caught furtive movement on the *Rajaleen*'s rear deck,
below the pilothouse, and that meant they were being
set up for a cross fire.

Where was Ahmed Ben Salah?

The only way to answer that was by proceeding on his present course. He switched the submachine gun's safety off and kept on walking with the weapon braced against his leg.

It crossed his mind that Ahmed Ben Salah might not be present at the meet, but there was only one way to be sure. He had to see it through.

The shooting started when he had reduced the gap to twenty yards, but the initial burst of fire came neither from the car nor from the *Rajaleen*. Instead, a gunner opened up on Bolan from the second boat in line, an automatic weapon tracking him as he threw himself down on the pavement.

It took perhaps five seconds for the shit to hit the fan. Both gunners bailed out of the dark sedan and started firing at Grimaldi, two or three more blasting from the *Rajaleen*. Across the road a sniper opened up at rooftop level, angling toward the street.

Instead of leading with the Uzi, Bolan palmed a frag grenade, released the safety pin and lobbed it toward the second fishing boat in line. The steel egg bounced once on the cabin roof and dropped into the well of the companionway. The gunner crouching there had time to recognize his peril, take a long stride toward the rail and then a smoky thunderclap went off behind him, pitching him into the water on the starboard side.

Bolan came up firing toward the *Rajaleen,* a probing burst to keep the gunners down. He heard Grimaldi cut loose on the far side of the street and glanced in that direction, saw one of the shooters buckle, going down. Grimaldi broke for cover, bullets snapping at his heels, and Bolan left him to it, pivoting to find the sniper on the rooftop opposite.

The guy was on his feet, an automatic rifle braced against his shoulder, going for the bull's-eye. Bolan smoked him with a rising burst from thirty yards, the Uzi bucking, spewing brass into the gutter. On the roof his target did a spasmodic dance and dropped the rifle, pitching forward, plunging after it. The shooter landed on his head and folded like a cheap accordion, rolled over once and didn't move again.

The rear deck of the *Rajaleen* was spitting fire and bullets, but he dared not use the second frag grenade in case the blast took Ahmed with the others. Bolan swung around to bring them under fire, aimed high to keep their heads down while he worked in closer, for the kill.

Across the street Grimaldi targeted the second gunner from the dark sedan and dropped him, squirming, on the sidewalk. Turning toward the *Rajaleen,* he broke across the street on a diagonal, unloading short bursts from his Uzi on the run.

It did the trick, distracting Bolan's adversaries long enough for him to make his move. It was a simple rush, no way around it, and he went in firing from the hip. One of the shooters bolted upright, answering his fire, and Bolan stitched a line of holes across his chest, kept charging as the guy went over backward, pumping bullets toward the stars.

And that left two.

It was the shooters in a cross fire now as Jack Grimaldi raced across the street to join the party. Halfway there his magazine ran out, and in the momentary lull, their enemies saw hope.

One of the soldiers bolted upright, aiming at Grimaldi, squeezing off a long burst that went high and wide. Grimaldi hit the deck, and Bolan raked his would-be killer with a figure-eight that slammed him over sideways, toward the port-side railing.

One gun left, and Bolan saw him turn back toward the cabin of the *Rajaleen*, his submachine gun spitting fire. Toward Ahmed Ben Salah! The guy was scrubbing it, prepared to take the hostage with him if he couldn't carry out his mission.

Bolan hammered toward the *Rajaleen*, knees pumping, holding down the Uzi's trigger. He had ten or fifteen rounds remaining in the magazine, and the demented gunner soaked them up in nothing flat. The stream of bullets held him upright for perhaps a second and a half, then Bolan's gun was empty and his target folded, struck his forehead on the railing as he fell. Too late to feel it, dead before he hit the deck, facedown.

The Browning autoloader filled his hand as Bolan sprang across the rail, sidestepped the corpses, searching out his contact. Ahmed Ben Salah was sprawled out on the cabin floor, hands bound behind his back, blood oozing from a thigh wound and another at his groin.

Grimaldi got there seconds later, bringing up the rear. He was in time to find his comrade fastening a tourniquet around the Arab's wounded leg.

"How bad?" the pilot asked.

"It's bad enough."

"We'd better get him out of here. They're bound to have a cop around here somewhere."

"Wait!" the Arab blurted out. "I have to tell you something."

"When we get you stabilized," said Bolan.

"Not time," Ben Salah gasped. "I found Hafez al-Zuabi's base camp. I must tell you."

"Where?" asked Bolan.

"In the desert to the south. Beyond the mountains."

Bolan frowned. "That's it?"

Ahmed Ben Salah shook his head. "Beyond the Grand Erg Occidental, north of Timimoun. I have coordinates."

"I'm listening," said Bolan.

"Two degrees east, twenty-nine degrees north. In the foothills."

"No problem," said Ben Salah. "I can find it."

"Let's move," Bolan said.

He got one of the Arab's arms across his shoulders, left the other to Grimaldi, hoisting the informant up between them. It was awkward, lifting him across the railing, but they made it to the dock and back to Bolan's car before lights stared showing in the houses farther down.

The nearest hospital was in Algiers, but they would have to double back in any case to fetch the Westwind. Driving south would be a waste of time and leave them too exposed for Bolan's taste.

He dropped Grimaldi at the second car, saw headlights in his rearview as he motored out of Ghardaj, eastbound toward Algiers. The moonlight on the sea was striking, and it would have been romantic under other circumstances, but his mind was focused solely on the task at hand.

The cargo he was looking for might not be stashed at Hafez al-Zuabi's base camp, but it was the only hope remaining, short of psychic flashes, and he had to take the chance. If all else failed, the Executioner would have to ask the terrorist leader himself, and find out what the Scourge of Allah's founding father had to say.

Whichever way it went, it would not count on a protracted interview.

Hafez al-Zuabi didn't know it yet, but he was racing toward extinction at the speed of light. Mack Bolan meant to help him get there, in another day or so.

But first he had to find a certain nasty package and defuse it.

Before it blew up in his face.

CHAPTER TWENTY-TWO

Coordinates were one thing; getting into range for a surprise attack was something else. The fix received from Ahmed Ben Salah enabled Bolan and Grimaldi to obtain a set of aerial reconnaissance photos, bounced via satellite from Stony Man Far, in the Blue Ridge Mountains of Virginia. They had the layout of the compound, took a guess at which specific buildings served what functions, but the problem of an adequate approach remained.

They were unable to secure a helicopter in their present setting, and obtaining military aircraft on short notice, with the risk of violating "friendly" airspace, was impossible. The Pentagon and CIA would be delighted if their mission was successful, but the big guns were required to stay at home.

That left the Westwind, excellent for transport, useless for attack. The desert north and west of Timimoun was mostly flat, hard baked, and it would serve them as a giant landing strip, but Bolan and Grimaldi would be hoofing in from there. The pilot had rejected all suggestions that he stay behind and guard the plane while Bolan did the dirty work, outnumbered twenty-five or thirty guns to one.

A long day, killing and making ready for the trip, the midnight battle that would follow. Checking out equipment, loading guns and sharpening stilettos, gassing up the plane and checking out the engines just in case. Time dawdled, dragged its feet, and they were more than ready when the sun went down.

They flew southwest from Algiers, starting after nightfall, with four hundred miles to cover on the first leg of their journey. Fifty minutes from the time they took off, skimming the peaks of the Atlas Mountains and the less dramatic hillocks of the Grand Erg Occidental. Touchdown was a pilot's dream, Grimaldi switching off the engines for a classic dead-stick landing, but the dream was fleeting.

Once they hit the ground on foot, it would become a waking nightmare.

They were dressed in desert camouflage fatigues and armed identically. Each man had an AK-47 and a Browning semiautomatic pistol, with a complement of frag grenades. Besides the basic load, Mack Bolan packed a loaded RPG-7 rocket launcher, Grimaldi toting three spare rockets in a sling across his back.

They were a mile northwest of the intended target, far enough that lookouts at the compound would have missed their landing. Grimaldi had doused their running lights ten minutes from Algiers, and while the Westwind's engines might be audible, the Scourge of Allah's troops would have no reason to suspect a landing in the neighborhood. Another aircraft bound to Mauritania, perhaps, or Mali.

So they hoped, at least, to keep the critical advantage of surprise.

The moonlight helped, together with the gently rolling foothills that should cover their approach. With no real obstacles, they made good time and found themselves within sight of the camp by 10:30 p.m. That gave them ninety minutes for an on-site recon, using glasses from a distance, later circling the perimeter on foot, in opposite directions, nothing left to chance.

They had their marks fixed in advance, before they left Algiers, but it was good to know that nothing had been changed around the compound since the firefight in Ghardaj. If Hafez al-Zuabi was concerned that Ahmed Ben Salah would betray his whereabouts, the camp displayed no such anxiety. Lights burning in a number of the tents and huts, but nothing on the wire, since floodlights in the open desert made the camp an easy target from the air, for photographs or bombs.

The Executioner was on his station by 11:52 and, while he reckoned Grimaldi was also ready to proceed, he let the last eight minutes go. No point in starting early, now that they were on the scene. Still nearly seven hours left before the sun came up again and turned the vast Sahara into the world's largest hot plate. By that time Bolan and Grimaldi would be gone... one way or another.

Bolan took the RPG and sighed on the prefab structure that was obviously, from its bristling antennae, the communications hut. The Scourge of Allah had no reinforcements in the area, but Bolan didn't trust the group's relationship with the Algerian authorities. He did not wish to risk last-minute intervention by the army, for example, which would doom his mission at the very least and place him in the grim position of provoking what could only be a major incident between Algeria and the United States.

If he could silence Hafez al-Zuabi with the first shot of the battle, he would come out points ahead, and that is what he meant to do.

At midnight, on the dot.

THE TECHNICIANS had refused to work around the clock, insisting that fatigue would breed mistakes. Hafez al-Zuabi had considered forcing them at gunpoint, but he reasoned it was better to accept delays, wind up with an acceptable end product, than to rush and risk humiliating failure that would set him back five years.

Another week, they told him, maybe two. Some parts were missing, had been ordered from a dealer in the onetime Eastern Bloc. When the parts arrived and assembly was completed, they could move on to the final planning stage.

So close and yet so far away.

Hafez al-Zuabi had never been a patient man, as indicated by his choice of a profession, and it grated on his nerves to wait another day for his revenge to be dealt out against the Zionists. Still, every passing day, with its anticipation, stood to make his final retribution that much sweeter.

He had trouble sleeping these days. The disruption in Algiers was part of it—Ali Jabir among the casualties—but there was also a desire to see the battle joined. It had been too long since he had fielded troops against the enemy. Perhaps he should arrange a demonstration within the next few days while he was waiting for the specialists to finish off his masterpiece.

Yes, that would help. Another raid across the border possibly, against the kibbutzim. Teach the Israelis they could never live in peace or stolen land.

But first there were other matters to be settled—

His thoughts were abruptly cut off as the shock of an explosion nearly swept him off his camp chair. He bolted to the entrance of his tent and yanked the flap back, leaning out into the darkness. It was bright as day now, with the leaping flames that had enveloped his communications hut. As he stood watching, yet another rocket hurtled from the outer shadows, riding on a tail of fire, and detonated with a crash inside the mess tent.

They had found him somehow! The Israelis, or someone else?

He started shouting orders to his men, a general alarm. They had rehearsed for situations such as this, al-Zuabi believing in his heart that the Algerians would always stand between his little army and the enemies outside. It was beyond his comprehension, how this thing could happen here and now, but he would not go down without a fight.

He went back to fetch his weapons, buckled on his pistol belt, picked up the AKM assault rifle and stalked out of the tent, into the firelit night.

He had to find out what was happening, how many men were in the raiding party. There were thirty-two soldiers in camp, the hard core of his fighting force, and while he trusted them to handle any problem that arose, they needed targets if they were to stage an effective defense.

The sounds of automatic fire were audible throughout the camp, at least a dozen weapons lighting up the night with muzzle-flashes, tracer rounds. The camp looked like a light show or a fireworks celebration, taking on an almost festive air, except for the ungodly screams of stricken men.

One of his soldiers staggered past, bleeding from a ragged scalp wound with his rifle trailing in the dust behind him. He looked dazed, disoriented, more robot than man. The terrorist leader reached out to grasp the soldier's arm and shake him, find out what was happening. His shouted questions seemed to fall upon deaf ears, the soldier blinking back at him with vacant eyes. A stinging slap did nothing more than smear his palm with blood.

He turned away and went in search of someone who could still communicate, the sounds of gunfire drawing him along. Another blast behind him rocked al-Zuabi and almost knocked him down, the hot breath scorching him. He turned and saw his own tent going up in flames. If he had been a moment later, hesitated briefly while collecting his equipment, he would be a smoking cinder now.

A sudden panic gripped him, and he spun to face the tent where his technicians slept. Unscathed, so far, but what if something happened to them and his dream went up in smoke? He had to reach them, take them out of there before a wild shot or a hurtling rocket ruined everything.

Retrieve the precious cargo and equipment, load it on a vehicle and flee. His soldiers would be left to deal with the attacking enemy, and he could always come back when the smoke cleared, see what he could find out from the bodies.

But the most important thing was to protect the embryonic weapon and technicians who would make his dream of vengeance come to life. Without them he would have to start again from scratch.

Assuming that he got the chance.

So he would have to save himself, as well. Above all else, the war could not go on without Hafez al-Zuabi. In a very special way he was the cause that drew his soldiers from the hinterlands to stand against the common enemy.

He set off running, shoulders hunched against the bullet that could come from anywhere and strike him down. There was as much risk from his own men at the moment as from unseen enemies.

It was impossible that the Romanians could sleep through all this racket. They were bound to be awake and doubtless terrified. If only they stayed put until he reached them and could lead them out to safety. Otherwise, if they slipped out ahead of him, they would be killed or simply lost, and Hafez al-Zuabi would have nothing.

His mouth tightened into a grim line. Allah help me! Give me strength to smite my enemies!

GRIMALDI WAITED for the rocket, lying prone and sighting down the barrel of his AK-47, picking out initial targets. There were sentries on patrol, no fence to pen them in or keep the base secure, but there had never been a need for one out here in the middle of godforsaken nowhere.

He made the range approximately fifty yards, no major challenge even in the semi-darkness. When the rockets started coming in, though, he would have all kinds of light.

Too much, perhaps, when it was time for him to make his move and rush the camp. His enemies weren't blind, and they would have no trouble spotting him, his desert camo standing out in contrast to their khaki, *kaffiyehs* and canvas shoes.

Whatever, he would have to do it when the time was—

There, it had begun!

The first of Bolan's rockets sizzled in and shattered the communications hut. Grimaldi watched his chosen target stop short, swivel toward the rising fireball, gaping in surprise. The Arab would have run in that direction, tried to help, but Grimaldi was not about to let him have that chance. A 3-round burst from the Kalashnikov went in on target, punched neat holes along the sentry's spine and pitched him over on his face.

A quick glance, left and right, showed no one homing on his muzzle-flash. Grimaldi scrambled to his feet and rushed the compound, keeping low. His destination was a line of tents adjacent to the camp's latrine. The low-rent district, he supposed, for those who didn't mind the odors wafting over them around the clock. Grimaldi caught a whiff and wiped it out by breathing through his mouth.

The soldiers in the tens were scrambling, day-shift workers from the looks of it, awakened rudely by the sounds of gunfire and explosions. They were strictly out of uniform as they came spilling from the tents, each Arab with a weapon, none immediately clear on targets. No fewer than a dozen gunmen, every one of them a tried and proved killer.

Grimaldi was waiting for them with a frag grenade, an easy lob from thirty feet that dropped the egg into their midst. None of them saw it coming, though one or two may have become conscious of the danger by the time it detonated, spewing shrapnel in a killing radius of fifty feet.

Two-thirds of them were dead or wounded when Grimaldi started mopping up, his AK-47 spitting short precision bursts. He took the standing gunners first, the greatest threat by far, and wasted three of them before the other two recovered their composure well enough to mark a target. Still too late, as Grimaldi moved in to point-blank range and dropped them with the last rounds in his magazine.

Reloading where he stood, he didn't bother with the soldiers torn by shrapnel. Four or five of them were clearly dead, the others either dying or disabled, none of them a threat to Grimaldi or Bolan in their present situation. Turning from the slaughter pen, he made a quick check on the tents, confirmed that all of them were empty, then proceeded on his way.

A top priority was pinning down the nuclear material, wherever it might be, and he was carrying a compact Geiger counter on his belt, a plastic earpiece barely whispering now as it picked up the normal background radiation found in almost every situation.

He had to move on, keep looking. Finding their objective was vital, and this close to success, they had to ensure that the evening didn't spirit the dangerous substance away to start the threat anew someplace else.

If they had any sense at all, the U235 would be secure inside a lead container, cutting off the bulk of radiation, but the holding shed or ten would still be "hot" beyond the normal reading for the camp at large.

Bolan rattled past his face, reminding Grimaldi that he could lose it in a hurry if he didn't concentrate. He swiveled toward the source of gunfire, spied a shooter lining up another burst with trembling hands. Grimaldi's aim was better, and his nerve was stainless steel. The hot rounds from his AK-47 scored a bull's-eye, drilling through the Arab's chest with force enough to lift him off his feet before he fell.

The mess tent was a roiling mass of flame, a Quonset on Grimaldi's left reduced to smoking rubble. No more rockets coming in, but he had not been counting the explosions, and he had no way of knowing whether Bolan still had ammo left remaining for the RPG. He knew his partner would be moving in to closer quarters soon to make it personal.

Grimaldi passed two corpses, checked the one face that remained and verified that it was not Hafez al-Zuabi. Running down the Scourge of Allah's leader was the number-two priority, after nailing down the embryonic A-bomb. Missing either goal would mean at least a partial failure, and Grimaldi was unprepared to settle for anything short of success.

He moved on, listening to automatic-weapons fire and muted static, following the scent of death.

It smelled like home.

THE FINAL ROCKET GONE, Mack Bolan dropped the RPG, scooped up his rifle and charged toward the camp. In front of him the compound was in disarray, defenders running here and there without direction, seeking cover or targets, some unloading bursts of automatic fire at random intervals, endangering their comrades.

It was all he could have hoped for, and he had to take advantage of the chaos swiftly before his enemies recovered their composure.

He had nailed a Quonset hut, a barracks, but the other two remained unscathed. He was unable to divine their function from a distance, and he couldn't risk obscuring the stolen nuclear material with heaps of rubble. Any doubt about the disposition of the U235 would leave his mission incomplete.

One of the sentries blundered into Bolan's path, glanced up in time to see death coming. He was carrying a submachine gun, trying desperately to bring it up and into line, but there was no time left. A burst from Bolan's AK-47 socked him in the chest and pitched him backward to the ground.

It was a free-for-all inside the camp as discipline unraveled. Drifting smoke and aimless gunfire, angry shouts and cries of pain transformed the desert compound into something out of Dante, a preview of Hell on Earth.

And that was old, familiar territory for the Executioner.

He listened to the whisper of his earpiece, waiting for the Geiger counter to alert him to the location of his prize. There was at least a chance, he knew, that Hafez al-Zuabi would have stashed the cargo elsewhere, left it in the hands of specialists, but he was acting on his knowledge of the man—the terrorist's built-in paranoia and suspicion—to presume that al-Zuabi would maintain his treasure close at hand.

More furtive movement on his right, two gunners barging through the pall of smoke, apparently surprised to find their enemy before them in the flesh. They broke in opposite directions, bracketing their target from a range of thirty feet. It was a good move, seemingly rehearsed, but they were not quite fast enough to pull it off.

The gunner on his right was slightly closer, possibly a greater threat, and Bolan took him first, a rising figure-eight that cut the Arab's legs from under him first, then tore into his abdomen and skull.

Immediately spinning to his left, he triggered off another burst and saw the gunman stagger, one leg folding under him, his automatic rifle spitting bullets at an angle toward the midnight sky. A second burst ripped into Bolan's target and nailed him down.

How many cartridges remaining in the AK-47's magazine? He took a chance and let it go, turned to his right, proceeding toward the nearest standing Quonset hut. It was some kind of storage building, Bolan calculated as he observed two Arabs dashing in and emerging moments later, draped with bandoliers of ammunition.

Worth a look in any case. He ran in that direction, hearing bullets whisper past him in the semidarkness, weaving like a broken-field runner on his way to the goal line. Bolan flattened himself against the south wall of the Quonset, peered around to check the open door, found no one waiting for him.

Three strides took him to the threshold and across, into warm darkness on the inside of the hut. Nothing but reflected firelight illuminated the stacks of wooden crates around him, rifles lined up in a standing rack against the nearest wall. The Geiger counter registered no more than standard background radiation emanating from the chase of arms.

He palmed a frag grenade and yanked the safety pin, pitched it underhand toward the center of the Quonset, where the stack of crates was highest. Bolan had no way of knowing whether there was ammunition in the stash, but he would take the chance and keep his fingers crossed.

He sprinted from the hut, kept moving, shoulders hunched against the coming blast. It was initially contained, with shrapnel spattering the walls, and then the blast caught something else inside the Quonset, setting off a chain of secondary detonations, ripping through the hut as if a giant can opener was gouging at the corrugated steel.

The shock wave raced up from behind him, pushed him like a straight-arm thrust between the shoulder blades and knocked him down. He went down on all fours, maintained his grip on the Kalashnikov and scrambled to his feet again in seconds flat. Shrugging off the brush with sudden death, he raced toward the next hut, fifty yards away.

Besides the last remaining Quonset, there were two square wooden structures he had not been able to identify with any certainty. He had to check them all unless Grimaldi got there first, and at the same time he would have to watch out for Hafez al-Zuabi, do his best to keep the Scourge of Allah's founding father from escaping in the midst of chaos.

Bullets started raising puffs of dust around his feet, and Bolan veered off course, responding with a short burst from his AK-47 in the general direction of his latest adversary. Muzzle-flashes guided him, picked out a kneeling gunner twenty-five or thirty feet away, and Bolan slid into a prone position, sighting down the barrel of his rifle even as he squeezed the trigger.

Half a dozen rounds snapped off within a heartbeat, homing on the target, and the angry rounds stopped rippling overhead. He waited briefly, met no further challenge from that quarter and was off again, legs pumping as he covered ground.

One of the flat-topped prefab structures, its windows darkened, the door ajar, was just ahead of him. Was this the one? Bolan didn't know if he would find what he was seeking there, or be faced with gunman crouching in the dark, prepared to cut him down.

There was only one way to find out.

He reached the open doorway, hit a fighting crouch and made his way inside.

CHAPTER TWENTY-THREE

It should have been a simple thing for Hafez al-Zuabi to collect the necessary men, no more than half a dozen soldiers from his total force, and bear his precious cargo to a point of safety. Even so, in the confusion it was all that he could manage, standing in the open and exposed to hostile fire, shouting for his men to rally around.

At last he had five soldiers he could trust and sent two of them off in search of the Romanian technicians, pledged to bring them back no matter what. He led the other three across the compound, jogging toward the last remaining Quonset hut. They had no special gear for handling the uranium, but it was safely boxed in lead, secure as far as he could tell.

And if his soldiers ran a slight risk of contamination, it was no more than the danger that would greet them on a border raid or any other mission that Hafez al-Zuabi might ordain. They had enlisted with the Scourge of Allah looking for a chance to sacrifice themselves, for honor's sake and for their people. He was simply giving them the opportunity they craved.

They reached the Quonset, found its walls already pocked with bullet holes. The door was closed and fastened with a hasp, no lock in place, and Hafez al-Zuabi quickly let himself inside. The darkness sheltered him, but he couldn't remain for long. There was no safety here, and he would only find it when he took himself and his masterpiece away.

"The crate!" he snapped. "Two of you grab it. Quickly!"

It was relatively light: two kilos of uranium, some twenty-five pounds with the crate and layers of led installed for insulation. The handles were rope, stapled to each end of the crate, and two of the soldiers lifted it easily, holding the box slung between them.

There was more—the mechanism, its construction still in progress—but more hands would be needed for the work of hauling it away. Hafez al-Zuabi moved back to the doorway, peering out into the night. Across the compound, coming toward him, he could see his runners, prodding the Romanians in front of them. The weapon builders both had wild-eyed looks about them, cringing at the sounds of battle, scuffling their feet and glancing fearfully around in search of enemies.

Hafez al-Zuabi stepped back inside the hut, allowing them across the threshold, covering their entry with his AKM. The two Romanians were babbling in fright. He couldn't understand what they were saying, and he cut them off with a decisive motion of the rifle. They stood silent, watching him until he spoke.

"The mechanism! Warp it up in oilcloth right now and bring it with us. Nothing must be left behind."

They hesitated, glancing from his hard eyes to the automatic rifle in his hands, and moved reluctantly to carry out his orders. The device was relatively small, no larger than a common suitcase in its present state, and they had no great difficult wrapping it or carrying the bundle back to where he stood.

"We must not stay here," said Hafez al-Zuabi. "We shall carry the device away until this difficulty is resolved, then bring it back again. The work must not be interrupted."

"How can we escape?" The older of the two Romanians could barely speak, such was his fear.

"The vehicles have not been damaged," he replied. "But we must hurry!"

He turned and took another look outside. A bullet struck the metal wall six inches from his face, but Hafez al-Zuabi didn't flinch. He scanned the open ground for enemies, saw none and reckoned that the shot had been a stray.

The sounds and smell of battle summoned memories of younger days, when he had crossed the border into Israel as a young guerrilla, serving Arafat before the great betrayal and his sniveling talk of peace. These days, though, Hafez al-Zuabi was the field commander, others did his bidding and it had been years since he was called upon to kill a man himself.

You never lost the edge, though, once it had been drilled into your brain and written on your heart in blood. A man did not forget such things, not while he lived.

The motor pool was on their right, some eighty yards away, with open ground and no protection. It came down to speed this time, a race against the odds, against the unseen enemy. If they were intercepted on the way, then they would have to fight. If not...

"Stay close to me," he snapped. "Defend yourself as necessary. Come!"

He led the way outside, glanced back to reassure himself that they were following and struck off toward the compound motor pool.

THE FLAT-TOPPED structure seemed to be another storage area, this time for uniforms and such, no weaponry in evidence. A glance told Bolan he was in the wrong place for the items he was seeking, but he reached inside a pocket, drew out an incendiary stick and primed it, then pitched it toward the back wall of the hut. Before it sparked and sizzled, spreading flames among the stock of goods, the Executioner was back outside and moving on.

A fair percentage of the firing was now concentrated on the east side of the compound, where he reckoned Grimaldi must have encountered opposition. Bolan flipped a mental coin, decided it would only slow him down if he went off to help the pilot. As it was, Grimaldi was providing a diversion for his own search of the camp.

A terrorist charging through the veil of smoke almost ran into Bolan, cursing as he staggered back, recoiling. He was armed, and Bolan shot him in the chest without a second thought, no hesitation when the choice came down to do-or-die. His bullets knocked the young man sprawling, facedown in the dust.

Move on.

The stench of burning filled his nostrils, made his blue eyes water, but it wasn't thick enough to slow him down. It worked against his enemies, in fact, providing cover, keeping them from singling out a target on the move.

When they were hardly ten minutes into the attack, he knew that they were running out of time. Hafez al-Zuabi was a trained guerrilla warrior, skilled at hit-and-run techniques and eluding enemies who sought to run him down and kill him. Even now he would be bending all his energy toward getting out.

He needed transportation, Bolan realized, and that would take him to the motor pool, a line of vehicles parked under camo netting at the far end of the camp. The jeeps and flatbed trucks were still undamaged, Bolan having used his rockets elsewhere, and he had to run a gauntlet of the compound just to reach them now.

Weapons chattered all around him as he started moving toward his destination, bullets snapping high and low. The gunners didn't have a fix on Bolan yet. Some of them clearly did not even see him but were firing wildly, aimlessly, in hopes of getting lucky or to keep their courage up. He answered them with short bursts from his AK-47, some rounds finding human targets, others wasted on the night.

When he was almost to the burned-out mess tent, three guerrillas broke from cover, moving out to block his path. They must have seen him coming, recognized their nemesis by his uncommon uniform and stature. Somehow they had kept from dropping him on the approach, but they were bent on making up for that misfortune now.

The gunners fanned out in his path and opened up with automatic weapons. Bolan jogged hard left and threw himself into a flying shoulder roll, a swarm of bullets cutting through the night where he had stood a heartbeat earlier. He came up firing with the AK-47, fighting for his life.

The left-hand gunner first, since he was closest, blasting with an Uzi submachine gun braced against his hip. He was correcting for the target's sudden movement, when a rising burst from the Kalashnikov ripped through his arms and kept on going, opening his chest, his throat, his face. The sagging straw man fell apart in front of Bolan's eyes, but there was no time for him to observe the transformation, busy as he was with the remaining two.

The middle gunner of the trio had an AKM assault piece, pivoting to follow Bolan as the Executioner spun out of line. At fifteen feet their firepower was equal, so the end result came down to speed and reflexes. Bolan had experience behind him, a whole lifetime on the firing line, against a youth's impetuous desire for glory.

It made all the difference in the world.

The bullets ripped through Bolan's target, slammed him off his feet and nailed him to the ground. The young man kept on firing, lifeless index finger clenched around his rifle's trigger until the weapon kicked free of his grasp and spun away.

As Bolan turned to face the last man in the trio, squeezing off, he felt the AK-47's hammer come down on an empty chamber. The magazine was empty!

Bolan didn't even have to think about it. Instinct took control, and when he threw the rifle at his adversary, aiming for the young man's face, he was already reaching for his side arm in its shoulder sling.

It was enough to get him killed, that lapse, but somehow Bolan pulled it off. The flying AK-47 struck his target in the chest and spoiled the shooter's aim enough to let him make the draw. He swung the Browning out and into line, no need to cock the double-action autoloader prior to firing. Three rounds hammered into Bolan's target, stunned him with their crushing impact. When he toppled forward, dead, there was a dazed expression on his face.

Bolan retrieved his rifle, muttering a curse, and ditched the empty magazine. He replaced it with a fresh one, taking time to clear the action, chambering a live round, freeing it of any dust it might have picked up when it fell.

One careless slip, but he had managed to survive. He would not count on getting lucky twice.

From now on he would have to make his own luck—and make sure his enemies had luck, as well.

All bad.

FOR SEVERAL MOMENTS Grimaldi thought his own luck had run out. The sentries had him spotted, swarmed him with a dozen soldiers or more and tried to pin him down.

It almost worked.

Converging streams of fire, complete with tracers, laced the air above his head and rippled through the canvas of the large tent on his left. He crabbed in that direction, drew his blade and slit the canvas high enough to let him wriggle through.

The tent would not protect him from a bullet, but at least it masked his movement from the troops outside. He crept across the dirt floor on his belly, hearing bullets rattle overhead, until a voice cried out in Arabic and suddenly the hostile fire fell off.

Grimaldi took a breath and looked around, saw long crates stacked up in the middle of the tent with smaller wooden boxes on each side. He couldn't read the labels, but he used the K-bar fighting knife to crack one of the smaller crates and smiled when he found three fat rockets packed in straw. The larger crates looked right, and he wasn't surprised when he broke into one and found the RPG-7 launchers waiting for him.

Bingo!

It was obvious his enemies were holding back in fear of damaging their heavy weapons, maybe setting off a catastrophic blast. Grimaldi took advantage of the lull to grab two empty launching tubes and set them down beside the smaller stack of ammo crates. He loaded both with easy, practiced movements, quickly opening a second crate of rockets to have backup rounds on hand.

He didn't know how well the hasty plan would work or how long he could hold the opposition off, but it was worth a try. In fact, he didn't really have a choice.

Grimaldi was about to shift his weapons closer to the entrance, give himself an open field of fire, when a young gunman barged into the tent, the automatic rifle looking shaky in his hands. He was the sacrifice, selected by his fellows, sent—perhaps at gunpoint—to investigate, find out if the invader was dead or wounded, ready for the coup de grace.

Grimaldi met him with a short burst from his AK-47, blew him backward through the open tent flap, out into the smoky darkness. Moving quickly, then, and half-expecting some return fire, he began to haul his new-found weapons into their position on the firing line.

He shouldered the first launcher, chosen at random, and peered through the sights at the wedge of night visible outside the tent. Saw gunmen shifting back and forth, trying to find a vantage point. He aimed low to keep the rocket from caroming off across the compound. Then he checked behind him to make sure the back-blast from the launcher would not set the nearest stack of ammo crates on fire.

He squeezed the trigger, dropped the smoking tube before the rocket found its mark and detonated on the ground outside. He had the second RPG braced on his shoulder in a heartbeat, shifting farther to the right, another angle of attack, and swiftly fired the second round.

Reloading, Grimaldi heard angry, frightened voices raised outside. A couple of the Arabs started firing back with automatic weapons, but their comrades quickly silenced them, afraid of what the end result might be. Grimaldi took advantage of his momentary freedom from attack, edged closer to the entrance of the tent and fixed his sights on a group of four soldiers perhaps a dozen yards away.

They saw the rocket coming when he fired, but there was nothing they could do to save themselves. A ball of fire enveloped three of his selected targets, while the shock wave of the blast pitched number four beyond his line of sight, a tumbling sack of broken bones.

How many left? Grimaldi wasn't counting, and he had no way of knowing whether reinforcements had arrived. It stood to reason that the shooting would attract more soldiers, and the longer he delayed his exit from the tent, the worse off he would be.

Grimaldi saw his chance and took it, sent his next round from the RPG directly through the north wall of the tent. It sliced the canvas like a red-hot blade through butter, and he dropped the launching tube at once, scooped up his AK-47, sprinting in the opposite direction. Opening a new flap with the K-bar, Grimaldi burst through as echoes from the blast rocked the camp. Circling to his left, he closed in on the wounded Palestinians while they were still disoriented, reeling from the blast.

He went in firing from the hip and caught his adversaries with their guard down, nailing two before the others recognized their latest danger. Too late for the others to regroup and meet the attack as he raked them with slugs, bodies sprawling beside those mowed down by the RPG blast.

He reloaded in haste, discarding the spent magazine where he stood, eyes sweeping the field for new targets. Where was Bolan? Had he found Hafez al-Zuabi? The uranium? Was Bolan even still alive?

Grimaldi couldn't tell from where he stood, and at the moment there was nothing he could do but forge ahead, continue with his mission. If he spotted Bolan in the process, then so much the better. And if not...

He left the dead and dying where they lay, moved on in search of adversaries and a very special friend. Grimaldi knew he might find death instead, but there had been no mystery about the risks involved when he signed on.

Whatever happened, he was ready. Riding on to the end of the line.

BOLAN REACHED the final Quonset hut and crouched against the southern wall, checked left and right before he slipped around the corner, edging toward the open door. His earpiece had begun to crackle louder by the time he reached the threshold, sounding off an octave higher as he stepped inside the hut.

He had been briefed on the equipment in advance and knew the louder signal did not mean he was in danger of contamination at the present level. All the same he understood that at last he was close to the object of his quest.

Bolan used a penlight, searching hastily around what seemed to be a workshop. Scattered tools, a drill press, waist-high wooden benches, spools of insulated wire and heavy tape. He moved around the wooden crates and cardboard boxes piled up in the center of the room, but spotted nothing marked with radiation warnings, nothing that appeared to be a case designed for hauling hazardous material.

The Geiger counter kept on buzzing, but the tone told Bolan he had missed the prize. Someone had gotten there ahead of him and carried the uranium away.

The questions was, how long ago?

The reading was ambiguous, and Bolan didn't have the fine-tuned expertise to say with any certainty if it had been removed the day before or moments prior to his arrival. In the former case, his cause was hopeless, but if he was running on Hafez al-Zuabi's heels he still might have a chance.

Outside he listened to the signal from the Geiger counter fading. The machine wasn't a bloodhound, couldn't tell him which way the uranium had gone once it was carried from the Quonset hut. In terms of answers, Bolan was no better off than he had been five minutes earlier.

Until he saw the group of runners headed for the motor pool.

Eight men, by Bolan's count, a pair of gunmen leading. Next in line, two held a squarish crate between them, rifles tucked beneath their arms. The next two were not dressed in khaki like the others, but they shared an awkward burden wrapped in some dark cloth or plastic. Bringing up the rear were two more riflemen who glanced back periodically, as if to see if they were being followed.

Logic told him he was looking at the makings of Hafez al-Zuabi's bomb. He plucked the compact walkie-talkie from his belt and hailed Grimaldi.

"Flyboy, can you read me?"

From somewhere in the camp Grimaldi replied, "Affirmative."

"Our cargo's headed for the motor pool. Eight guns so far."

"I copy, Striker. On my way."

Bolan clipped the radio back on his belt and set off in pursuit of the escaping transport party. Up ahead his quarry had already reached the motor pool, and Bolan saw them piling into vehicles. The cargo went aboard a flatbed truck with canvas stretched across the back, three gunners riding with the crates, while two more piled into the cab. Three others scrambled for a jeep and got the motor running, pulling out behind the truck as it began to roll away.

He fired a long burst after the retreating vehicles, heard yet another weapon blasting from his flank, and turned to see Grimaldi firing after the retreating vehicles. The soldiers in the jeep were answering with automatic weapons, but they took no time to aim and make it count.

Bolan reached the motor pool before his quarry cleared the compound. He couldn't be sure Hafez al-Zuabi was among the runners, but he had to take the gamble. Taking out the Scourge of Allah's leader would mean nothing if he let the deadly cargo get away. Al-Zuabi's heir apparent—or some other resident extremist—could pick up where this team had left off and try to set the Middle East on fire.

He chose a jeep and slid behind the wheel. It was the standard military version, with an automatic starter, no ignition key, and Bolan had it running in a heartbeat. Glancing back, he saw the .50-caliber machine gun mounted on the deck behind him, with a box of belted ammunition snug in place. Grimaldi climbed across the shotgun seat as Bolan reached down to release the parking brake, took up his place behind the heavy-barreled .50-caliber.

"Let's do it," said Grimaldi.

Bolan stood on the accelerator, running through the gears, and set off in pursuit of the escaping vehicles. The fuel gauge showed a tank three-quarters full, but he didn't intend the chase to last that long. If he couldn't catch up with his intended quarry, force them to a halt and finish it within a few miles of the camp, he feared that it would be a hopeless case.

"Hang on!"

A handful of survivors from the compound were approaching at a run, their weapons spitting fire, and Grimaldi responded with a long burst from the machine gun, dropping one and scattering the others, forcing them to run for cover. Spent brass rattled on the desk around his feet.

His main advantage, thought Bolan, was the truck, its greater weight and slower speed. They were outnumbered and outgunned, but that would take care of itself.

A wild round whispered past him, drilled the windshield, but he kept on driving. Never mind the handful of survivors in the camp. If they gave chase, he and Grimaldi would confront them as they came.

His focus had to be ahead of him, on dwindling taillights and the tire tracks leading off across the open desert.

Bolan's destiny, the outcome of his mission, lay within his grasp, and he couldn't allow it to escape him now.

Whatever happened in the next few miles and moments, he was holding on. The road to hell or victory lay open to the south, unfurling in his headlights. Even victory did not exclude the possibility of Bolan's death.

He was prepared for anything right now.

In fact, the Executioner would not have had it any other way.

CHAPTER TWENTY-FOUR

Hafez al-Zuabi had no destination fixed in mind when he drove south, the compound dwindling in his rear-view mirror, smoke and flames receding by the moment. Mali lay somewhere ahead of him, as did Maritania, though both were several hundred miles away. Hafez was hoping that he wouldn't have to drive that far. A few miles out, he could perhaps find a sanctuary in the desert, wait until the signal from his soldiers told him it was safe to turn around and go back to the camp.

And then he saw the headlights in his mirror.

Not the jeep his soldiers occupied. That vehicle was close behind him, keeping pace. His life insurance. There were other headlights, though, some miles behind and racing to catch up.

His enemies.

He bit off a curse, turned toward his driver, snapped a warning. He hoped that his gunmen in the jeep behind him had noticed the pursuers. They stood between him and the enemy. It was their job to intercept the opposition, and he saw no way for his pursuers to avoid them, short of going airborne.

Still, he didn't let himself relax. Pursuit meant danger, to himself and to his sacred mission. He must deal with these, his enemies, and forcefully, before they ruined everything.

Hafez al-Zuabi understood instinctively that he would have no second chance to get it right.

The land was flat here, almost featureless between his compound and the border, save for gently rolling dunes and unpredictable arroyos cut by flash floods on the rare occasions when it rained, say once or twice a year. A headlong plunge into a gully would be sheer disaster, no way to proceed on foot with the uranium and bomb components. Still, he wouldn't ask his driver to slow down.

Not yet, while there were enemies behind them, drawing closer by the moment.

Hafez al-Zuabi held the AKM across his knees, the safety off, a live round in the chamber. He was ready to defend himself, entirely capable of killing, but he counted on his soldiers to protect him, standing as the first line of defense.

How many gunmen in the chase car? As he sat there, Hafez al-Zuabi still had no idea of who his adversaries were, how many had attacked his camp or whether they would overrun his soldiers. The frustration grated on his nerves, but there was nothing he could do about it at the moment. Short of stopping where he was and mounting a defense on open ground, his best hope lay in flight.

The vast Sahara had protected him for years, but it seemed hostile now. A place where anything could happen and no sanctuary was available. Hafez al-Zuabi wished that he could radio for help from the Algerian authorities, but they had struck a bargain in the early days. The army and police would tip him off to any danger they saw brewing in the early stages, but they would not mount a permanent defense around his camp.

In terms of private jeopardy from day to day, al-Zuabi was on his own.

He had accepted it then, as he did now. He would place his fate in Allah's hands and trust his god to stand behind a warrior fighting in the holy cause. His own death, when it came, would be the ticket into Paradise, his just reward for putting everything he had into the struggle.

Closer behind, the headlights glowed like a pair of hungry eyes. He leaned across to check the truck's speedometer and found the needle hovering at forty-five. It was about the best he could expect on open ground, no pavement underneath the knobby tires. The trailing jeep could easily have passed them, but it hung back, drifting slightly to avoid the flatbed's dust cloud, hanging in as Hafez al-Zuabi's buffer layer.

His eyes were on the rearview when a ragged muzzle-flash erupted from the second jeep in line. Still well behind his soldiers, they were firing, feeling out the range. Red tracers hurtled through the night.

If there was any doubt about his soldiers recognizing opposition on their tail, that doubt had vanished right away. He could not see his men, the headlights blinding him to anything behind them, but he knew these soldiers, had participated in their training and he trusted them to sacrifice their lives, if necessary, in defense of his.

Hafez al-Zuabi needed time, and they could buy it for him. Once the battle had been joined, he would command his driver to switch off their lights, run dark for several hundred yards at least and try to gain some ground that way.

With a rush of satisfaction, Hafez al-Zuabi saw his bodyguards swing out of line, the jeep reversing its direction, taillights showing in his mirror. A showdown in the desert, with Allah's help, his enemies would be destroyed.

If not, then he would simply have to do the job himself.

THE WEAPON WAS an FN heavy-barreled version of the classic Browning M-2 .50-caliber machine gun, manufactured with sustained-fire capabilities in mind. No weapon encountered by foot soldiers had more stopping power, but the heavy weapon also had its drawbacks. Chief among them was a cyclic rate of fire that ranged between 450 and 550 rounds per minute, operating with a belt that typically held fewer than 250 rounds. That would supply about thirty seconds of sustained fire at an average cyclic rate before Grimaldi had to reload.

And there were no spare ammunition boxes in the jeep.

Grimaldi used the heavy machine gun sparingly, unable to resist a parting burst before they left the camp, then holding off until the taillights of their enemies were easily within his range. Even then, he restrained himself from hosing down the moonlit countryside and wasting precious bullets, rather milking short bursts from the .50-caliber weapon, firing for effect.

His first rounds missed the jeep, but they were close enough, with tracers in the mix, to catch the hostile driver's full attention. Would he run for it? Peel off or turn and fight?

The answer was not long in coming. Hafez al-Zuabi had his soldiers trained, and they were obviously dedicated to the cause. In seconds flat the jeep swung out of line and made a hot one-eighty on the open flats, dust flaring from the rear tires as it swung around to face the charging enemy.

Grimaldi thought back to his first glimpse of the other jeep, in profile as it sped out of the camp, its passengers unloading with their their SMGs and rifles. In his mind's eye, he saw no machine gun mounted on the vehicle!

It wasn't much, but he would take what he could get. The FN's range was double that of a Kalashnikov, quadruple that of any standard submachine gun. With the extra reach at least they had a fighting chance against the larger hostile force.

He started firing when the enemy was still two hundred yards away, short bursts aimed well above the headlights that would sting his eyes as they drew closer. Six or seven rounds per burst, fine-tuning it, with thunder ringing in his ears. He barely felt the rough ground passing underneath their tires, so focused was he on the target racing toward him at an estimated fifty miles per hour.

And the target was returning fire.

Not tracers from their small arms, but he saw the muzzle-flashes clearly, wondered if the guns were AKMs or AK-47s. Either way a hit would bring him down—or pitch him from the speeding jeep—and that would be the end of Grimaldi, perhaps of his companion, too. It was a crazy, modern variation on medieval jousting, with contenders charging toward each other on a near-collision course. Instead of ten-or twelve-foot lances, though, these modern nights had weapons that could reach out over several hundred yards to score a kill.

Grimaldi tried to guess how many rounds were left inside his ammo box, gave up and concentrated on his target, holding down the paddle trigger with his thumbs. He focused on the driver, knowing that the gunners in the jeep were helpless, stranded, if he put their charger out of action. All it took was one clean shot and—

There!

He didn't see the bullets hit, but there was no mistaking when the headlights swerved across their path, tires spewing plumes of sand. At first Grimaldi thought the jeep would roll, but it stayed upright, rapidly decelerating till the engine stalled and died.

The gunners in the back were still unloading with their automatic weapons, trying for a hit to pay him back, but Bolan swung their jeep wide of the obstacle and held the pedal down. Grimaldi stood his ground as best he could, rotating the big gun on its pivot mount to keep the stranded gunners covered as he passed. In parting, he could not resist a final burst that raked the jeep from end to end and dropped one gunner squirming on the sand.

So much for Hafez al-Zuabi's rear guard.

Up ahead the flatbed truck had doused its lights, the driver running dark. It hardly mattered in the desert moonlight, but the fleeing terrorists would grab at any edge in their attempt to slip away.

Good luck, Grimaldi thought, not meaning it.

He gripped the .50-caliber's spade grips, remaining upright on the rear deck of the jeep as Bolan poured the speed on, straining to catch up. When he had closed the gap to something under sixty yards, Grimaldi took a chance and fired a short burst toward the covered flatbed, tracers looping through the bright cone of their headlight beams like fireflies.

Never mind the U235 right now. It stood to reason that the bomb was still unfinished, safe from detonation, and Grimaldi didn't plan to handle the uranium himself. He did hope to disable any gunmen in the truck if he could manage it, and make the last phase of their mission that much easier.

Was Hafez al-Zuabi riding with the others? Would they come up empty on the Scourge of Allah's leader and be forced to start from scratch tomorrow?

But Grimaldi felt the Arab's presence in his gut the way a veteran hunter sometimes feels his prey nearby.

The hunt was winding down, and they were getting closer to the kill.

The only question now was, who would die?

HAFEZ AL-ZUABI HEARD the first round strike somewhere behind him, tracers whipping past him on the left. He checked the mirror, slammed his fist against the dashboard in anger as he saw the enemy was drawing even closer. There was nothing to prevent them overtaking him now that his rear guard had been swept away.

"More speed!" he shouted at the driver. "Hurry!"

Bearing down, his driver urged anther three or four miles per hour from the laboring engine. He started to swerve, left to right, in an effort to fake out the gunmen behind him, leaving broad sidewinder tracks in the dust.

The terrorist leader glanced through the window on his left, into the rear bed of the truck, and saw the cargo shifting crazily from side to side. The two Romanians were hanging on with difficulty, staggering like players in a slapstick comedy, while al-Zuabi's one surviving soldier kept up a defensive fire as best he could. The soldier's automatic rifle was no match for the machine gun wielded by their enemies, but he was doing all he could.

More bullets struck the flat bed, one exploding through Hafez al-Zuabi's mirror, ripping most of it away. That blinded him to what his enemies might do next, unless he chose to lean out through the open window and expose himself to sudden death. He wasn't ready for that yet.

"Faster!"

No verbal response from the driver, but his knuckles whitened as he gripped the steering wheel. He didn't lift his foot from the accelerator, but Hafez al-Zuabi understood that there was nothing left. This vehicle, in these conditions, had achieved top speed.

How long before the engine overheated or a lucky bullet struck one of the tires? Al-Zuabi did all he could to brace himself. There were no seat belts in the truck, of course—a useless bit of frippery where soldiers were concerned—but he could brace himself against the floor and dashboard if they crashed, try not to be ejected from the wreckage if they rolled. He kept a firm grip on his AKM assault piece, knowing he would need it when the truck was forced to stop.

And if they managed to defeat their enemies... what then? He did not relish being stranded in the middle of the desert, with the weapon half-completed, too much for him to carry on his own. Four men remaining who could help him with his burden, if they all survived the final shoot-out, but it still looked bad.

He wondered how far they had run from the camp. It would be a grueling hike, especially in daylight, but he still had hopes of help and reinforcements from the camp. A number of his men were still alive back there, and they had vehicles in working order. They would recognize their duty when they finished mopping up around the compound. Always sure of his men before, he knew they would come to rescue him, then a vicious uncertainty assailed him. Having survived their willingness to die, maybe they would not be as eager to put it to the test again so soon.

Brooding doubt made Hafez al-Zuabi scowl. Before the mood could smother him, however, he had more important matters to consider. Like short-term survival, with his unknown adversaries breathing down his neck.

And at the moment they were breathing fire.

Another burst of tracers swarmed around the truck. He heard a cry of pain above the engine sounds and wild roar, the staccato sound of dueling automatic weapons. Peering through the window on his left, he saw one of the gray Romanians now writhing in the truck bed, clutching at his abdomen with blood-slick fingers.

"Look for cover!" he commanded the driver.

"Where?" the harried man asked him, an incredulous expression on his face.

"You're driving!" snapped Hafez al-Zuabi. "Do it!"

They would find a place to make their stand and fight it out, if such a place existed in the godforsaken wasteland. One bright spot—his enemies were chasing Hafez al-Zuabi in a stolen jeep, one of his own, and that meant they would have no extra ammunition for the .50-caliber machine gun. At the present rate of fire, he reckoned they would soon run dry, be forced to fall back on their small arms. Four men, maximum, inside the jeep, and that would mean a nearly equal contest.

He had a chance in spite of everything that had gone wrong so far!

Hafez al-Zuabi scanned the dark horizon, searching for a rocky outcrop, anything that could provide the necessary cover for a stand. The land was flat, though, nothing in the way of shelter that would recommend itself, and he tried to guess how long could they keep up the present pace before the initiative was taken from their hands.

Without the headlights, Hafez al-Zuabi and his driver never saw the gully up ahead. It looked more like a shadow on the desert floor until the truck nosed over, front wheels spinning uselessly in empty air, and they dropped ten feet to a jarring impact with the ground.

Hafez al-Zuabi hurtled forward, taken absolutely by surprise, and slammed into the dashboard. He heard metal crumpling, hood and fenders, while the weight of crates and bodies slammed into the cab behind him. It was difficult to breathe, the air was forced from his lungs and he smelled motor oil, plus something else.

The fuel line? Was it rupture? Would the diesel fuel catch fire?

He turned around with difficulty, sandwiched in the space below the dashboard, reaching for the inner handle on his door. The driver stepped on Hafez al-Zuabi, scrambling to escape on his side of the cab, and pain knifed through the Arab leader's ribs.

It seemed to take forever, but the door came open, spilling him face foremost to the ground. Against all odds he had retained his firm grip on the AKM. If nothing else, at least he could defend himself.

And he would have to soon.

Above him, rapidly approaching from the north, Hafez al-Zuabi heard his adversaries closing for the kill.

IT FELT LIKE MAGIC, something from a movie, when the desert opened up and swallowed Hafez al-Zuabi's' truck. A cloud of dist erupted from the gully where the truck had disappeared, and Bolan took his foot off the accelerator, slowing into the approach.

His headlights showed him that the truck had not completely vanished. He could see the tailgate and a bit of canvas still protruding from the open gully. Overhead Grimaldi fired a final burst into the truck before the belt ran out.

"I'm empty," he told Bolan.

"Never mind."

The .50-caliber weapon would be no use to them from this point on, the flatbed having fallen out of range. He stepped down from the jeep and took the AK-47 with him, while Grimaldi jumped clear on the other side. They moved in cautiously, aware that they had started out with five men in the truck, presumably all armed. So far, they couldn't tell if any of the five had been eliminated by Grimaldi's fire or rendered helpless by the crash.

As if in answer to the thought, a squirming figure reached above the tailgate, struggled into view and blinked at the advancing enemy. One hand dropped out of sight and came back with an automatic pistol, sighting hastily on Bolan, less than forty feet away.

Both AK-47s opened up at once. Converging streams of fire ripped through the gunner's head and shoulders, blew him backward, down and out of sight, inside the truck bed. That was one, at least, they could be sure of as they closed the gap, advancing on the wreckage.

Bolan's Geiger counter started hissing at him, and he pulled the earpiece out. It was too much distraction at the moment, and he knew where he was going, where the cargo lay. The trick was getting close enough to finish it without a lucky shot from one of the defenders hitting home.

He risked a glance into the gully, pitch dark at the bottom, where the moonlight couldn't reach. What now? Should they stand back and wrap it up with hand grenades, not knowing whether Hafez al-Zuabi was alive or even in the truck?

"I'm going in," he told Grimaldi. "Cover me."

"You're covered," his partner replied.

Rather than climb down beside the truck, Bolan moved off forty yards and scrambled down the steep side of the gully, sliding the last few feet and ending in a crouch, his AK-47 pointed toward the truck. He paused for a moment while the loose earth dribbled down behind him, waiting for the silence that would let him pick up sounds of movement from his enemies.

And there was someone coming toward him now. Soft footsteps, sneaking, but the sand and gravel made it nearly impossible to move in silence.

Bolan waited, tracking on the sound, his eyes adjusting to the murk. A slouching figure stepped into his field of vision, hesitated, cocked a weapon Bolan couldn't see.

He fired a burst from twenty feet and watched the silhouette lurch backward, going down. He waited, half-expecting some return fire, edging forward when it did not come. The dead man lay across his path, blood soaking through a khaki shirt, and Bolan stepped across him, concentrating on the truck.

Two dead, at least, and that left three to deal with, in the worst scenario. He reached the cab, smelled leaking fuel and held the AK-47 ready as he stepped up on the running board to peer inside the cab.

Hafez al-Zuabi was not in the cab, but rather waiting somewhere on the other side. He fired on instinct, maybe glimpsing Bolan's shadow as he rose above the driver's windowsill, a muzzle-flash like lightning in the darkness of the gully.

Bolan vaulted backward, landed on his rump and spun around to aim beneath the undercarriage of the truck. He heard boots scuffling on the sandy earth and fired in that direction, squeezing off a short burst at the unseen enemy.

A shout of pain or anger came back in response, and Bolan's adversary crouched to fire back through the same gap, in between the flatbed's chassis and the north wall of the gully. Bolan dodged away, heard bullets slapping into sand, the loud, metallic clang of ricochets.

And sparks.

The dripping fuel caught fire, flames licking underneath the truck, along its ruptured fuel line. Spreading, lighting up the gulch on either side.

He saw Hafez al-Zuabi now and recognized him in the firelight, crouching, looking for a target. Overhead Grimaldi started firing down into the gully, missed his man, but it was still enough to make Hafez al-Zuabi duck and cover, flattening himself against the gully's northern wall.

It was the break that Bolan needed, squeezing off with the Kalashnikov, a dozen rounds from maybe fifteen feet away. Hafez al-Zuabi staggered briefly, going down, his AKM discarded as he fell.

The flatbed's canvas hood was already burning around the edges. Bolan knew that he had moments left, or maybe seconds, till the fuel tank detonated, spreading flames along the gorge. He took a chance and rushed the truck instead of turning back. One leg up on the running board, he braced his left foot against the driver's window frame. From there he climbed across the cab and reached the canvas, grabbing for the metal struts that held the tarp in place.

Grimaldi had a hand out, reaching for him, dragging Bolan clear. They stumbled backward from the gully, sprawling as the truck exploded in a ball of fire, the chassis buckling, sliding out of sight into the gorge.

He thought about the U235 in its container. Was it ruptured? Scattered far and wide? Were they exposed?

He replaced the earpiece of the Geiger counter. It whispered to him, nothing radical, once they had stepped back several paces from the gully. Even so, the smoke felt dirty to him, a contaminant. He couldn't wait to get away.

"We finished?" asked Grimaldi.

"Finished," Bolan told him. "Let it burn."

The day was hot and muggy in Algiers, but there was air-conditioning in Ahmed Ben Salah's hospital room. The wounded man sat up in bed, a stack of pillows underneath his wounded leg, and smiled despite the bruises on his face.

"It's finished, then?" he asked as Bolan and Grimaldi stood beside his bed.

"For now," said Bolan. "Mopping up the Scourge is someone else's job. They're still around."

"Of course. And others like them. It's a long, old story in my country."

"Policies can change," Grimaldi said. "It has to start somewhere."

"Agreed," said Ahmed Ben Salah. "There is a movement to withdraw the so-called welcome mat from terrorists. It will take time."

"I put a word in with the Company," said Bolan. "You should have a bonus coming pretty soon."

"It will be spent to drive the killers from my homeland. Someday we will live in peace."

"I hope so," Bolan told him, but his skepticism lingered. There was more than racial and religious animosity involved. How many generations had been raised on hate and violence in the Middle East, in Northern Ireland, in the Balkan states, in Africa, in South America?

Where would it end? How could it end, except in blood?

He had no answers, only brooding questions, and no time to linger on, discussing it. They had a flight to catch, connecting through from Paris to the States and back to Stony Man.

Where, Bolan had no doubt, another crisis would be waiting for him. Maybe not today, but soon.

The endless war would continue. The names and faces changed, objectives were revised, but motives, provocations and responses were the same. Men suffered, bled and died, regardless of the label on their cause. One soldier could not bring the killing to an end, but he could do his part. Take up the burden where he found it and move on.

Tomorrow was a new day, right, but it still bore a strong resemblance to yesterday and all the days before.

The Executioner was moving on, no end in sight. Today he had the upper hand.

And tomorrow, Bolan knew, would have to take care of itself.

**Don't miss out on the action in these titles featuring
THE EXECUTIONER®, ABLE TEAM® and PHOENIX FORCE®!**

SuperBolan

#61438	AMBUSH	$4.99 U.S.	☐
		$5.50 CAN.	☐
#61439	BLOOD STRIKE	$4.99 U.S.	☐
		$5.50 CAN.	☐
#61440	KILLPOINT	$4.99 U.S.	☐
		$5.50 CAN.	☐
#61441	VENDETTA	$4.99 U.S.	☐
		$5.50 CAN.	☐

Stony Man™

#61896	BLIND EAGLE	$4.99 U.S.	☐
		$5.50 CAN.	☐
#61897	WARHEAD	$4.99 U.S.	☐
		$5.50 CAN.	☐
#61898	DEADLY AGENT	$4.99 U.S.	☐
		$5.50 CAN.	☐
#61899	BLOOD DEBT	$4.99 U.S.	☐
		$5.50 CAN.	☐

(limited quantities available on certain titles)

TOTAL AMOUNT	$
POSTAGE & HANDLING	$
($1.00 for one book, 50¢ for each additional)	
APPLICABLE TAXES*	$_____
TOTAL PAYABLE	$_____
(check or money order—please do not send cash)	

To order, complete this form and send it, along with a check or money order for
the total above, payable to Gold Eagle Books, to: **In the U.S.:** 3010 Walden Avenue,
P.O. Box 9077, Buffalo, NY 14269-9077; **In Canada:** P.O. Box 636, Fort Erie, Ontario,
L2A 5X3.

Name:_____

Address:_____ City:_____

State/Prov.:_____ Zip/Postal Code: _____

*New York residents remit applicable sales taxes.
Canadian residents remit applicable GST and provincial taxes.

GEBACK11A

A perilous quest in a hostile land

JAMES AXLER

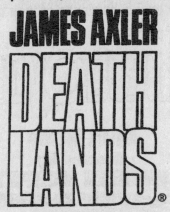

DEATH LANDS®

Emerald Fire

In EMERALD FIRE, Ryan Cawdor and his band of warrior survivalists emerge from a gateway into an abandoned U.S. military complex, now a native shrine to the white gods of preblast days. Here the group is given royal treatment, only to discover that privilege has a blood price.

In the Deathlands, you're always too far from home....

**Remo and Chiun come face-to-face with the
most deadly challenge of their career**

THE Destroyer

Last Rites
Created by
WARREN MURPHY
and RICHARD SAPIR

The Sinanju Rite of Attainment sounds like a back-to-school
nightmare for Remo Williams. But as the disciple of the last
Korean Master, he can't exactly play hooky. Join Remo in
LAST RITES as Remo's warrior skills are tested to the limit!

Don't miss the 100th edition of one of the biggest and
longest-running action adventure series!

SURE TO BECOME A COLLECTOR'S ITEM!

Look for it in August, wherever Gold Eagle books are sold.

In September, don't miss
the exciting conclusion to

D. A. HODGMAN

STAKEOUT SQUAD

THE COLOR
OF BLOOD

The law is the first target in a tide of killings engulfing Miami
in the not-to-be-missed conclusion of this urban police
action series. Stakeout Squad becomes shock troops in a
desperate attempt to pull Miami back from hell, but here
even force of arms may not be enough to halt the hate and
bloodshed....

Don't miss THE COLOR OF BLOOD, the final installment of
STAKEOUT SQUAD!

Look for it in September, wherever Gold Eagle books are sold.